學生摘星
英語寫作

The Elements of
Effective Writing

Marcus Hung

商務印書館

責任編輯： 黃家麗
裝幀設計： 趙穎珊
排　　版： 高向明
印　　務： 龍寶祺

學生摘星英語寫作 The Elements of Effective Writing

作　　者： Marcus Hung
出　　版： 商務印書館 (香港) 有限公司
　　　　　 香港筲箕灣耀興道 3 號東匯廣場 8 樓
　　　　　 http://www.commercialpress.com.hk
發　　行： 香港聯合書刊物流有限公司
　　　　　 香港新界荃灣德士古道 220-248 號荃灣工業中心 16 樓
印　　刷： 寶華數碼印刷有限公司
　　　　　 香港柴灣吉勝街勝景工業大廈 4 樓 A 室
版　　次： 2024 年 10 月第 1 版第 2 次印刷
　　　　　 © 2024 商務印書館 (香港) 有限公司
　　　　　 ISBN 978 962 07 0639 4
　　　　　 Printed in Hong Kong

怎樣使用本書 How to Use the Book

本書可供中學生自學，也是家長指導就讀小學的孩子的輔助教材，以提高升上心儀中學的機會。

本書有三大章節和五個附錄，分別給不同年級的學生使用。

» 小一、小二學生要學習寫簡單句子，小三更要寫一篇 30 字的英文作文，小四要寫 60 字，小五 80 字，小六 100 字。一般程度的小學生都需要家長輔導。在這種情況下，家長首先要掌握一定的寫作技巧才可指導孩子，所以家長必須仔細閱讀本書，尤其是第一章「寫作原則」裏的作文和第二章「選詞」介紹的例句，可以輔導孩子寫作，提高應試技巧。

» 中一學生開始可以自學，但總會覺得不知英文怎樣表達，常常執筆忘字，因為這年級的學生英文詞彙有限，雖然可以查字典或用電腦翻譯完成功課，但容易導致中式英語 (Chinglish)，更會因長期依賴電腦做功課，考試時不懂落筆。這年級的學生特別要練好英文基本功，例如生字、短語、句型等，寫作時便事半功倍。本書附錄一：範文字彙一覽；附錄二：範文短語一覽；附錄三：寫作必記句型和附錄四：寫作百搭公式，都包含本書出現過的詞彙、短語、寫作公式和寫作技巧，方便學習。

» 中二學生開始要精研寫作步驟和技巧，本書第一章「寫作原則」指導學生寫作原理分三部份：寫作大綱、組織結構和語言應用，也有文章範例詳細解釋，認真參考這一章，學習怎樣寫段落：首段、正文段和結尾段，也學習怎樣寫主題句、支持句和結論句。

» 中三學生已操練英文寫作一段時間，但仍然用詞錯誤，包括拼寫錯誤，用了無意義的字詞，甚至用中式英語來寫作，所以在這學年必須閱讀和研究第二章「選詞」，以達到選擇正確字詞的學習目標，本章也提供基本句子結構；在這個階段，要更認真參考範文的句型和寫作公式，以提高寫作能力。

» 中四學生要強化運用英文的能力，在此學期，要強化英文寫作的四個層次：詞彙、句型、段落和篇章。香港中學文憑考試（HKDSE）英國語言科沒有英文語法的個別考試，但在寫作方面就要求語法要達到一定水平才可及格，所以要多運用已學懂的語法來練習寫作技巧，在這過程中，更要重溫本書第一二章和附錄裏必記的句型和寫作百搭公式。在平日的寫作練習裏，要認識自己常犯的錯誤，做改正練習，以避免重複錯處，養成不良習慣。

» 中五學生該準備翌年的中學文憑試，所以要學習不同的寫作體裁。本書第四章「文體範例」列出 18 種文體，包括專題文章、博客、日記、社論、電郵、私人信函、投訴信、報告、故事等。每種文體都介紹寫作目的、佈局結構和寫作要點。在這年度，一定要多看，多讀，多寫，盡量運用從本書學會的詞彙、短語及句型表情達意，更要學會和在限定時間內解題、組織和套用寫作公式。

» 中六學生要參加考試了，要重溫本書每個章節，用已學會的知識練習寫作技巧，邏輯要清晰，書寫要整潔，要符合考試時間的時限。要學會有話可說，換言之要懂得思考，發揮想像力，不要墨守成規，除了格式和佈局結構外，每個話題可以變化無窮，沒有對或錯，平時要積累作文素材及時事常識，要多寫多改。切記「羅馬非一日建成的」，正所謂「熟能生巧」，重要的是多操練英文能力。

» 最後，每位讀者，若從購買本書第一天開始，直至中學文憑考試前一天為止，每日都抽時間閱讀本書，可以是一小段、一小部分、半篇或整篇範文、或者只是幾個詞彙或句子公式，都可以有助累積知識。朗誦範文的學習目標是藉朗讀來提高語感，如果還是用中文思考句子怎樣寫，再將它翻譯成英語，英文水平和寫作能力便難以提升，所以必須訓練自己用英文思考，久而久之，文章便不難「妙筆生花」了。

Marcus Hung（洪秉鉞）

目錄 Contents

範文目錄 Sample Writing of Different Text Types

自我測試 Self Test

以下是英文寫作常識和典型錯誤，讓你測試自己的寫作水平。答案在附錄。

1. 寫作大綱要列出你的想法、意見和所有相關話題，具體來說，就是用「5W1H」的思維來撰寫寫作計劃。甚麼是「5W1H」？

2. 以下不是一個良好段落的寫作方法，請圈出它的問題。

My mother is a very busy person. My toy car is broken. Every day, I have a lot of home-work to do. My home does not have an air-conditioner. I live in the New Territories. My name is Alice Wong. A mouse is a little creature.

3. 以下段落缺少了甚麼？請舉例改正。

The first reason is that the school summer holidays are long. I can visit my grandparents who are living in the US. The second reason is that I was born in July. My parents always give me lucky money on my birthday. Finally, I like summer because I like swimming.

4. 首段通常有三個要素，即是「開場白」、「主旨」和「文章佈局」。以下是一篇議論文的首段，在空白位置，應該是「開場白」。從下面「a,b,c,d」選出此文章最好的「開場白」：

_____ . This story brings out the issue of this question that being celebrities, they have problems as well as benefits. I am of the opinion that the problems are generally greater than the benefits. In this essay, I shall explain my reasons.

答案：

a. Princess Dianna and her boyfriend, who were in an attempt to escape the press photographers trying to steal pictures of the famous couple, were killed in a car crash in 1997.

b. There were many problems to being celebrities.

c. There are many reasons that being celebrities, they have more problems than benefits.

d. I would like to tell you a story about a car crash incident in 1997.

5. 以下句子有錯漏嗎？

On arriving in Hong Kong, his friend met him at the airport.

6. 圈出以下句子的語法錯誤：

She couldn't decide between the University of Hong Kong, the Chinese University of Hong Kong or the Hong Kong University of Science and Technology.

7. 請按照精簡原則修改以下句子。

The letter was sent by someone who did not provide his or her name.

8. 請根據文意，將下列選項填入適當空格中：

A. As a result　**B.** And　**C.** Moreover

Fortunately, Hong Kong eventually refined its pandemic control policy and implemented anti-Covid measures. The Hong Kong Hospital Authority set aside beds in public hospitals for Covid-19 patients and introduced new oral anti-Covid drugs. _____, the government bought a large number of Covid-19 vaccines and encouraged people to get vaccinated. _____, Hong Kong did not suffer significant hardship in recent months, _____ the confirmed case figures have reduced substantially.

9. 找出以下句子的錯處：

Without having student's union, we would have more time with after-school activities.

10. 找出以下句子的錯處：

2021 was also the best and worse years for a lot of people.

寫作原則 Writing Principle

　　寫作技巧要由小學開始訓練，初期要學會怎樣寫好一個句子，然後學會寫簡單的文章，到了中學階段，便要深入了解英文寫作的原則，提高寫作能力。

　　以下是一篇小三學生的文章，題目是 My Best Friend and I（我和我最好的朋友）：

My best friend is Larry. He is thin. He likes going cycling and reading books. I knew him in primary 4, Larry's favourite food is hamburgers, potato chips, hot dogs and pizza. My best friend have big eyes and small ears, I have small eyes and big ears, We are the same age but I am different. I like him. I want to be his good friend forever.

　　他能夠寫出簡單的句子，但用詞有些不當，裏面有中式英語，語法和標點符號也有錯誤。在小學階段，我們便要改正他的錯處，讓他能適當運用字詞，使英語更地道，我們除了教導他怎樣寫好簡單句（simple sentence）之外，還要開始教導他認識較複雜的句子，如複合句（compound sentence），複雜句（complex sentence），複合 - 複雜句（compound-complex sentence）。

　　下面是改良版本，注意這小三學生需要學習的地方：

改良文章	小學生需要學習的地方
My best friend is Larry. He is <u>slim</u> and <u>enjoys</u> cycling and reading books. I <u>met</u> him in Primary 4, and <u>I learned that</u> his favourite <u>foods are</u> hamburgers, potato chips, hot dogs, and pizza. Larry <u>has</u> large eyes and small ears, <u>while</u> I have small eyes and big ears. <u>Although</u> we are the same age, <u>we are different from each other.</u> I like him <u>very much</u>, <u>and I hope to be</u> his good friend forever.	1. 比 thin 更常用的是 slim 2. 用 enjoys 代替 likes，英文更自然 3. knew 是中式英語，英文說 met; want 和 I am different 也是中式英語 4. 用錯語法，應該是複數名詞（food），也需要第三人稱單數（has） 5. 懂得用修飾語（I like him very much） 6. 學習複合句（compound sentence）例如 and 和複雜句（complex sentence）例如 although, while, that 從句

英文的寫作原則分為三部份，即**寫作大綱、組織結構和語言應用**。

⭐ 寫作大綱 Writing Plan

考官在作文試卷上會提出一些問題，你第一件事就是去理解這些問題，即是解題。例如：題目是 How Does Climate Affect Our Life（氣候如何影響我們的生活）。動筆寫作之前，要先思考你想說甚麼和要表達的中心思想又是甚麼，這樣定出文章架構，想出一個寫作大綱，即是內容。經過腦震盪，以下是這篇小四學生文章的內容：

1. Air pollution – change climate – global warming
2. Fog, rain, gale, storm, cold, earthquake, tsunami – affect life
3. How – agricultural products, transport, health
4. Conclusion – government, ordinary people, protect environment

文章內容	文章結構
Climate plays a significant role in our daily lives. Air pollution caused by human activities has led to changes in the climate, including global warming. Natural phenomena such as fog, rain, gales, storms, cold weather, earthquakes, and tsunamis can also have a significant impact on our lives.	**首段**：說明氣候變化由空氣污染和自然現象引起，因而影響我們
These weather patterns affect various aspects of our lives, including agriculture, transportation, and health. Changes in the climate can lead to decreased crop yields, disrupted transportation routes, and increased health risks due to extreme weather events.	**正文段**：描述這些天氣轉變方式怎樣影響着我們生活的各方面
It is essential that both the government and ordinary people take steps to protect the environment and mitigate the effects of climate change. This can include reducing carbon emissions, investing in clean energy, and practising sustainable living habits. By taking action, we can help ensure a healthier, more sustainable future for generations to come.	**尾段**：指出政府和普通民眾都必須採取措施保護環境

參考譯文

氣候在我們日常生活中起着重要作用。人類活動造成的空氣污染導致氣候變化,包括全球變暖。霧、雨、大風、風暴、寒冷天氣、地震和海嘯等自然現像,也會對我們的生活產生重大影響。

這些天氣模式影響着我們生活的各方面,包括農業、交通和健康。氣候變化可能導致農作物減產、運輸路線中斷以及極端天氣事件導致的健康風險增加。

政府和普通民眾都必須採取措施保護環境,並且減輕氣候變化的影響。這可以包括減少碳排放、投資潔淨能源以及養成可持續的生活習慣。通過採取行動,我們可以幫助確保子孫後代擁有一個更健康、更可持續的未來。

通常寫作大綱是用 5W1H(Who, What, When, Where, Why, How)來思考,然後填寫細節,最後用英文寫作公式撰寫句子和段落層次,這樣才可完成一篇正確無誤的文章。

以下是一條小五的作文題目:Write a Presentation on 'The Importance of Healthy Habits'(介紹健康習慣的重要性)。我們用 5W1H 來思考,寫出一個寫作大綱,例如:

What are healthy habits?

Why must we keep healthy habits?

What are healthy habits in relation to daily living habits:

When will you sleep and get up?

How often do you exercise?

What will you do before you eat or go home?

What are healthy habits in relation to eating habits?

What is healthy food?

How much water do you drink each day?

根據寫作大綱撰寫以下文章:

A Presentation on 'The Importance of Healthy Habits'

Hello everyone! Today, let's talk about the importance of healthy habits. Healthy habits are things we do every day to take care of our bodies and minds. They help us stay strong, happy, and healthy.

Why must we keep healthy habits?

We must keep healthy habits because they help us stay strong, happy, and healthy. When we have healthy habits, we are less likely to get sick, have more energy, and feel good about ourselves.

What are healthy habits in relation to daily living habits?

Healthy habits in relation to daily living habits include:

» - Sleeping and getting up at regular times to help our bodies rest and recharge.

» - Exercising regularly, for example, playing sports, running, or dancing, to keep our bodies strong and healthy.

» - Washing our hands before we eat or go home to keep germs away.

What are healthy habits in relation to eating habits?

Healthy habits in relation to eating habits include:

» - Eating healthy food like fruits, vegetables, whole grains, lean proteins, and healthy fats to give our bodies the nutrients they need to stay healthy.

» - Drinking enough water every day to keep our bodies hydrated.

Conclusion

In conclusion, healthy habits are essential for staying strong, happy, and healthy. By sleeping and waking at regular times, exercising, washing our hands, eating healthy food, and drinking enough water, we can take care of our bodies and minds. Let's all try to develop and maintain healthy habits every day!

Thank you!

大家好！今天，讓我們來談談健康習慣的重要性。健康的習慣是我們每天為照顧身心而做的事情。它們幫助我們保持強壯、快樂和健康。

為甚麼我們必須保持健康的習慣？

我們必須保持健康的習慣，因為它們可以幫助我們保持強壯、快樂和健康。當我們養成健康的習慣時，我們就不太可能生病，精力充沛，自我感覺良好。

與日常生活習慣相關的健康習慣有哪些？

與日常生活習慣相關的健康習慣包括：

» 定時睡覺和起床，幫助我們的身體休息和充電。

» 定期鍛煉，例如運動、跑步或跳舞，以保持身體強壯和健康。

» 在我們吃飯或回家之前洗手，以防止細菌滋生。

甚麼是與飲食習慣相關的健康習慣？

與飲食習慣相關的健康習慣包括：

» 吃水果、蔬菜、全麥、瘦肉蛋白和健康脂肪等健康食品，為我們的身體提供保持健康所需的營養。

» 每天喝足夠的水以保持身體水份。

結論

總之，健康的習慣對於保持強壯、快樂和健康至關重要。通過定時睡覺和起床、鍛煉、洗手、吃健康的食物和喝足夠的水，我們可以照顧好自己的身心。讓我們每天努力養成和保持健康的習慣！

　　寫作大綱可歸納為三件事：**目的**、思路和對象。

1　目的（Objective）

　　首先，您應該問自己：「老師出這條題目，目的究竟是甚麼？」例如題目要求可能是「寫人」、「寫物」、「寫景」或「記事」，也可能是「議論」、「故事」，更有可能是寫一封正式信件如「邀請函」、「申請信」，又或是作一篇「評論」、「報告」等。你首要的寫作技巧就是要完整地回答他的問題，而你的答案試卷亦要符合他心中所指定的目的。

以下是一條小六作文題目：Write a Play Script about a Fairy Tale（寫童話話劇劇本）。當思考這題目時，需要認清這題目的目的：其一是話劇劇本，所以在格式上，要符合話劇劇本的形式，例如：話劇名稱、場景編號、舞臺佈景、主角人物、對話和舞臺指示等。再其次的目的是童話故事，所以是一個虛構的故事。

Title: Stone Soup   話劇名稱

Characters: 主角人物

> - John: A traveller

> - Sarah: Another traveller

> - Villagers: A group of poor villagers

> - Fairy: A magical fairy

Setting: A poor village   舞台佈景

John and Sarah, two hungry travellers, walk into a poor village.   舞台指示

John: (*rubbing his stomach*) I'm so hungry. Do you have any food or money left?

Sarah: (*shaking her head*) No, I don't. We spent it all on our last meal.

They ask the villagers for food, but everyone is poor and cannot spare any.   舞台指示

Villager 1: Sorry, we don't have any food to spare. We're all struggling to make ends meet.

Villager 2: If we had money, we would have bought some meat, but we can't afford it.

John: (*sighs*) Looks like we're going to bed hungry tonight.

John gets an idea and approaches the villagers.   舞台指示

John: Do you have a pot and some water?

Villager 3: Yes, we do. But what are you going to do with it?

John: (*smiling*) We're going to make stone soup.

Villagers: (*puzzled*) Stone soup?

Sarah: Yes, it's a special soup that we make with just water and a stone.

The villagers watch as John and Sarah prepare the soup. They put the stone in the pot and add water. They start stirring the pot. 舞台指示

Sarah: (*smiling*) This soup is going to be delicious.

Villager 4: (*smirking*) I doubt that. It doesn't even have any smell.

Suddenly, a magical fairy appears. 舞台指示

Fairy: (*amused*) What are you two doing?

John: We're making stone soup.

Fairy: (*curious*) Stone soup? Tell me more.

John and Sarah explain their situation to the fairy. 舞台指示

Fairy: (*smiling*) I see. Let me help you out.

The fairy waves her wand, and a piece of beef appears in the pot. 舞台指示

John and Sarah: (*surprised*) Wow!

The soup is ready, and John and Sarah distribute the soup to the villagers. 舞台指示

John: (*handing out soup*) Here you go. Enjoy.

Villagers: (*surprised*) Mmm, this soup is delicious.

Villager 5: (*smiling*) We haven't had soup with meat for a very long time.

Villager 6: (*grateful*) Thank you so much for sharing your soup with us.

John and Sarah smile at each other, happy to have helped the villagers. 舞台指示

Sarah: (*whispering*) Who would have thought that stone soup would turn out to be so tasty?

John: (*smiling*) And who would have thought that a fairy would come to our aid?

參考譯文

劇名：石頭湯

人物：

» 約翰：一個旅客
» 莎拉：另一個旅客
» 村民：一羣貧窮的村民
» 仙女：一個有魔法的仙女

背景：一個貧窮的村莊

約翰和莎拉，兩個飢餓的旅行者，走進了一個貧窮的村莊。

約翰：(*揉着肚子*)，我好餓。你有剩餘食物或錢嗎？

莎拉：(*搖頭*) 不，我不知道。我們把所有錢都花了在最後一頓飯上。

他們向村民討飯吃，但大家都很窮，一點也不能省。

村民 1：對不起，我們沒有多餘的食物了。我們都在努力維持生計。

村民 2：我們要是有錢就買點肉吃，可是我們買不起。

約翰：(*歎氣*) 看來我們今晚要餓着肚子睡覺了。

約翰有了主意並接近村民。

約翰：你有鍋和水嗎？

村民 3：是的，我們有。但是你打算用它做甚麼？

約翰：(*微笑*) 我們要做石頭湯。

村民：(*不解*) 石頭湯？

莎拉：是的，這是一種我們只用水和石頭做的特殊湯。

村民們看着約翰和莎拉準備湯。他們將石頭放入鍋中並加水。他們開始攪拌鍋。

莎拉：(*微笑*) 這湯會很好吃的。

村民 4：(*傻笑*) 我懷疑。它甚至沒有任何氣味。

突然，一位有魔法的仙女出現了。

仙女：(*被逗樂了*) 你們兩個在做甚麼？

約翰：我們在做石頭湯。

仙女：(*好奇*) 石湯？告訴我更多。

約翰和莎拉向仙女解釋他們的情況。

仙女：(*微笑*) 我明白了。讓我來幫你。

仙女揮動她的魔杖，一塊牛肉出現在鍋裏。

約翰和莎拉：(*驚訝*) 哇！

湯做好了，約翰和莎拉把湯分發給了村民。

約翰：(*遞湯*) 給你。享受啦。

村民：(*驚訝*) 嗯，這湯很好喝。

村民 5：(*笑*) 好久沒吃肉湯了。

村民 6：(*感激*) 非常感謝您與我們分享您的湯。

約翰和莎拉相視一笑，很高興幫助了村民。

莎拉：(*小聲説*) 誰會想到石頭湯會變得如此美味？

約翰：(*微笑*) 誰會想到仙女會來幫助我們呢？

　　以下兩篇範文，都是寫一個有特殊成就的人物。但兩者寫作目的不同，你的寫作大綱要清楚説明各自特定寫作目的。

範文一：體育明星 —— 張家朗

A Sport Star–Cheung Ka Long, Edgar

這篇文章介紹張家朗，一位體育明星，主題是描述他的成就、背景和他的言行品性。目的要突出他對我們的鼓勵及他不屈不撓的精神。

原文	寫作大綱
A Sport Star–Cheung Ka Long, Edgar	姓名
Cheung Ka Long, Edgar made us proud at Tokyo Olympics 2020, not only ending Hong Kong's 25-year wait for a gold medal, following Lee Lai San's windsurfing gold in Atlanta in 1996, but also marking our city's first Olympic glory in fencing history.	開場白注重介紹他的成就
Edgar comes from an athletic family, having inherited talent from his parents, who both played in the National Basketball League in China and Hong Kong. Edgar's father originally hoped to develop him into a basketball star when he was young, but soon discovered his passion for fencing after taking him to a class. Thanks to his hard work and the support of his family, Edgar was able to participate in big competitions and won a good few sports trophies at a very young age.	正文段（一）：他的背景和成長的過程
Since winning Hong Kong's first Olympic champion in the fencing competition, Edgar has become a household name in Hong Kong overnight. Despite his fame and high social status, Edgar remained humble. He said, 'I'm not the best. I don't consider myself superior compared to other people. I still have to work hard.' He recalled that a long time ago, he did go through a period of lows and self-doubt, but he never gave up. In fact, those failures allowed him to mature and ultimately succeed.	正文段（二）：介紹他的言行、品性。中心思想突出他對我們的鼓勵和他不屈不撓的精神
His personal motto, 'Don't lose your way—never forget who you are' is now well-known.	尾段用他的座右銘來總結這篇文章的目的

參考譯文

體育明星 —— 張家朗

張家朗在 2020 年的東京奧運會讓我們感到自豪,這不僅結束了香港繼 1996 年李麗珊在亞特蘭大奧運會奪得風帆金牌後 25 年的金牌等待,還標誌着我們城市在劍擊歷史上的第一個奧運殊榮。

張家朗來自一個運動世家,從父母那裏繼承了天賦,他們都在中國和香港打過全國籃球聯賽。張家朗的父親在他年輕時原本希望將他培養成籃球明星,但在帶他上一節課後很快發現了張家朗對劍擊的熱情。由於他的辛勤工作和家人的支持,張家朗能夠參加大型比賽,在很小的時候就獲得了好幾個運動獎盃。

自從在花劍比賽中獲得香港首項奧運冠軍後,張家朗一夜之間在香港家傳戶曉。儘管成名並獲得了很高的社會地位,張家朗仍然保持謙虛。他説,「我不是最好的。與其他人相比,我不認為自己優越。我還得努力。」他回憶説,很久以前,他確實經歷過一段低谷和自我懷疑的時期,但他從未放棄。事實上,那些失敗讓他成熟起來,最終取得了成功。

他的個人座右銘「無忘初心 —— 永遠不要忘記自己是誰」現在廣為人知了。

範文二：名人 —— 李小龍

A Celebrity–Bruce Lee

這篇文章同樣介紹一位人物，但他已過世，所以寫作大綱與上一篇不同，這篇突出世人對他的懷念。文章注重描述他成名的經過、社會地位和貢獻。

原文	寫作大綱
A Celebrity–Bruce Lee	名人的姓名
Bruce Lee (1940-1973) was an actor and martial arts master. Lee is known for his martial arts and his Hong Kong film breakout Hollywood. He was named one of the 100 most influential people of the 20th century by *Time* magazine. Sadly, he died of a 'drug allergy' at the age of 32. In 2013, he was posthumously awarded the Asian Film Festival's most prestigious Founder's Award.	開場白注重介紹他的社會地位
Lee's father is a famous Cantonese opera star, so he has the opportunity to be a child actor in many Hong Kong movies. At the age of 18, he moved to the United States to study drama and Asian and Western philosophy at the University of Washington in Seattle.	正文段（一）：説出他的背景和學歷
It was during this time that Lee began teaching martial arts and became revered for his kung fu attitude. In American television productions, he was required to fight in typical American style with fists and boxing. But Lee declined because he, as a professional martial arts master, prefers to fight in his professional style, which is speed and quick movements. Later, he created a new style of Chinese Kung Fu known as 'Jet Kune Do' (or the Way of Intercepting Fist) .	正文段（二）：他在武術上的成就
In the early 1970s, Lee returned to Hong Kong and began acting and directing roles in martial arts films such as 'Big Boss', 'Fist of Fury', and 'Way of the Dragon'. They both broke the box office records he set. This makes Hong Kong films best-selling worldwide and well-known internationally.	正文段（三）：他在香港電影事業上的貢獻
In order to respect this great man, a theme park named after him was built in Jun'an County, Guangdong Province, and Hong Kong also plans to retain Lee's residence in Hong Kong.	尾段：人們怎樣懷念他

名人 —— 李小龍

李小龍（1940—1973）是一位演員和武術大師。李以武術和他的香港電影突破荷李活而聞名。他被《時代》雜誌評為 20 世紀 100 位最具影響力的人物之一。悲痛的是，他死於「藥物過敏」，享年 32 歲。2013 年，他被追授了亞洲電影節聲望最高的創始人獎。

李的父親是著名的粵劇明星，因此他有機會在香港許多電影中當童星。18 歲那年，他移居美國，在西雅圖華盛頓大學學習戲劇以及亞洲和西方哲學。

正是在這段時間裏，李開始教授武術，並因其功夫態度而備受推崇。在美國電視節目製作中，他被要求用典型的美國風格以拳頭及拳擊進行搏鬥。但是李拒絕了，因為他作為專業的武術大師更喜歡以自己的專業風格進行搏鬥，即速度及快速動作。後來，他創造了一種新的中國功夫風格，稱為「截拳道」（即「截擊拳道」）。

在 1970 年代初，李回到香港，開始在武術電影中演出和導演角色，例如《唐山大兄》、《精武門》和《猛龍過江》。他們都打破了他創下的票房紀錄。這使香港電影在世界範圍內暢銷，並在國際上廣為人知。

為了尊重這位偉人，在廣東省均安縣建造了一個以他命名的主題公園，香港也計劃保留李在香港的住所。

2　思路（Ideas）

　　思路是寫作大綱最重要的一環，利用你的思考能力去思考題目，包括你的想法、意見和所有相關話題。具體來說，就是用 5W1H 來提供細節，例如：你要寫一篇評論，目的是介紹一間餐廳，要寫的細節可能包括：

» 餐廳名稱（What is its name? XX 茶餐廳、XX 酒樓？）

» 餐廳類別（What kind of restaurant is it? 中式酒樓、泰式餐廳？）

» 餐廳位置（Where is it located? 在中環、大埔。怎樣到？）

» 餐廳顧客（Who are its customers? 高收入、平民化？）

» 餐廳裝潢（How was it decorated? 高級裝修、普通裝修、設計、飾物等？）

» 餐廳食物（What kinds of food does it provide? 菜式、特色、招牌菜等？）

» 侍應生的服務態度（How is the service? 友善、惡劣？）

» 價錢（What is the price? 平、貴、合理？）

» 營業時間（When is it opened and closed? 供應早餐、午餐、晚餐、宵夜或 24 小時

營業？）

» 為甚麼你會推薦它？（Why do you recommend it? 甚麼原因促使你推薦它？）

下面兩篇文章，是評論體制，用來示範寫作大綱的思路過程：

範文三：典型的香港茶餐廳

A Typical Hong Kong Tea Restaurant

原文	寫作大綱
Good Taste Cha Chaan Teng **A Typical Hong Kong Tea Restaurant**	茶餐廳名稱 典型香港茶餐廳
Good Taste Restaurant has been in Hong Kong for more than 50 years. It is located in Wan Chai. We can easily get there by MTR, and its customers are mainly ordinary people with low and middle income.	餐廳的歷史及位置 餐廳的顧客對象
The decor of this restaurant did not impress me. The interior is plain. The white brick walls, tiled floors and wooden four seat booths purely make it feel like a restaurant.	裝潢
The laminated menu offers a wide selection of food, both Chinese and Western. I went for the signature dishes, pineapple oil and Yeung Chou fried rice. The pineapple oil is so tender and juicy; it's one of the best pineapple oils I've found. The Yeung Chou fried rice was so delicious that I ate the whole plate and it made me so full that I just wanted to sleep.	食物種類和質素
Of course, all these are inexpensive. I only spent $70 to buy these two kinds of food and a cup of lemon tea. What's more, its business hours are from 6:30 am to 12:30 pm.	價格 餐廳營業時間
I really recommend you to visit this restaurant not only because the food is delicious but also cheap.	為甚麼推薦

好味茶餐廳

典型的香港茶餐廳

好味茶餐廳已經在香港開業五十多年。它位於灣仔，我們可以乘港鐵很容易到達那裏，它的顧客對象主要是中低收入的普通羣眾。

這家餐廳的裝潢並沒有給我留下深刻印象。內部很樸素，白色的磚牆、瓷磚地板和木製四位卡座純粹使它感覺像一間餐廳。

層壓式的菜單提供豐富的食物選擇，包括中餐和西餐。我去買了招牌菜、菠蘿油和揚州炒飯。菠蘿油是如此柔嫩多汁，這是我發現的最好的菠蘿油之一。揚州炒飯是如此美味，以至我把整碟都吃完了，這讓我太飽了，於是我只想睡覺。

當然，這一切都不昂貴。我只花了七十元去買這兩種食物和一杯檸檬茶。更重要的是，它的營業時間是早上六時半到晚上十二時半。

我真的建議您去光顧這家餐廳，因為是價廉物美。

A Thai Restaurant

原文	寫作大綱
Café de Tastes **A Thai restaurant**	餐廳名稱 餐廳類別

Café de Tastes is a Thai restaurant located in Wan Chai North. It is located near the Hong Kong Convention and Exhibition Centre. So, it can be reached via MTR East Rail Line. Since it claims to be one of the best Thai restaurants in Hong Kong, our family of three went to see if it was true. It has a beautiful view, overlooking Victoria Harbour on three sides.

餐廳位置

餐廳類別

景色優美

The restaurant is spacious enough to accommodate hundreds of guests. We were very impressed with the decor of the restaurant; it looked like a refined and exotic paradise. It is decorated with Thai ornaments and wooden sculptures. There are some paintings on the walls, showing the talents of some Thai artists. The restaurant's service is outstanding. We are welcomed by a group of efficient staff dressed in traditional Thai costume. They are very attentive and always have a friendly smile.

餐廳裝潢

服務態度

Regarding the food, they are delicious and of the highest quality. The waitress recommended several mouth-watering dishes, including Tom Yum Goong (Tom Yum soup with seafood) , Gai Pad Prik Pow (fried chicken with Thai chili sauce) , Khaophat (fried rice) and Khao tom mat (glutinous rice and banana) . They are all prepared in the traditional Thai style, so they have a wonderful and rich flavour.

食物種類和質素

Now comes the crunch — and the prices are surprisingly reasonable. The bill we had to pay was less than $300 per person. For a restaurant that serves good Thai food, it's good value. There are not many places in Hong Kong where you can find this type of Thai food cooked at such a high quality.

價錢

Is Café de Tastes a good Thai restaurant? I totally agree with this restaurant. The prices are affordable and you can rest assured that the staff will provide you with friendly and attentive service. As for the food, you will easily find dishes that satisfy and suit your taste. Therefore, I sincerely recommend it to you. Remember it opens from 12 noon to 10 pm.

推薦的原因

營業時間

參考譯文

好味餐廳

泰式菜館

好味餐廳是一間位於灣仔北的泰式餐廳。它位於香港會議展覽中心附近。所以，它可以通過港鐵東鐵線到達。由於它號稱是香港最好的泰國餐廳之一，我們一家三口就去看看它是不是真的。它景色很美，可以三面眺望維多利亞港。

該餐廳很寬敞，足以容納數百位客人。餐廳裝潢給我們留下了深刻印象，它看起來像一個精緻而有異國情調的天堂。它以泰國裝飾品和木製雕塑作為裝飾。牆上掛有一些畫作，展示一些泰國藝術家的才華。該餐廳的服務是出色的。一羣穿着傳統泰國服裝的高效率員工歡迎我們。他們非常細心，總帶着友善的微笑。

關於食物，它們美味且質量最高。女侍應推薦了幾種令人垂涎的菜餚，包括 Tom Yum Goong（海鮮湯）、Gai Pad Prik Pow（泰式辣椒醬炸雞）、Khaophat（炒飯）和 Khao tom mat（糯米和香蕉）。它們都是用傳統泰式風格製作的，因此具備美妙而濃郁的風味。

現在到了關鍵時刻，價錢令人驚訝地合理。我們要付的賬單每人不到 300 元。對於一家提供優質泰國美食的餐廳而言，這是物有所值的。在香港沒有很多地方可以找到如此高品質的泰國美食。

好味餐廳是一家不錯的泰式餐廳嗎？我完全同意。價格實惠，你可以放心，員工會為您提供友善周到的服務。至於食物，你會很容易找到滿足和適合你口味的菜餚。因此，我真誠向您推薦這餐廳。記住它的開業時間為中午 12 時到晚上 10 時。

3　讀者（Reader）

所謂讀者，就是閱讀你文章的人。作為一個學生，閱讀你文章的讀者是你的老師、給你打分的評卷員，也就是我說的「讀者」了。你的文章必須有吸引力，讓他們有興趣看下去。

當然，每篇文章都有其真正不同類型的讀者。寫作之前，你應該問自己：「誰是我的讀者：朋友、親人、刊物編輯、機構管理人或校長？」這樣你才能正確針對他們的需要，並用適當的語氣寫你的文章。你的文章才能和他們達到溝通的目的。換句話說，你寫文章應考慮語氣、風格、語言以及體裁等。例如：一封寫給校長的信，你不會用 Hi Principal（嗨校長）來稱呼他。

一篇好文章要有真情實感，才能打動你的「讀者」，首先要打動自己，才能打動你的老師。寫作時要有「代入感」，把自己當作文章中的主人公，想像你生活中正在發生將要寫的事情，

代入其中。只有這樣，才能從實際出發，添加情感表達，進而形成一篇有血有肉的文章。

　　所以，在你的寫作大綱中，要添加對讀者的感情，對每類讀者都有不同的寫法。以下例子是兒子寫給父親的信。你要設身處地想像你與父親相隔兩地，而你又不能回來與他過節，現在應該怎樣安慰他呢？又要使他放心你在外地的生活，這就是你寫作大綱要注意的要點了。

　　以下是一篇基礎版本的初中文章，英語語法的運用十分正確，並沒有錯誤句子。但是看下去，你有親切感嗎？對父親的關懷夠嗎？

原文	評注
Dear Father, The Father's Day is coming and I would like to say 'Happy Father's Day' to you. To support our family, you have to work very hard. Sometimes, you are so busy that you can't even get home to have a meal. I feel very grateful for what you have done. I am very sorry that I can't spend that day with you at home. Please don't worry about me, for I will take care of myself at school. By the way, I am doing very well in my study. Anyway, I hope you will have a wonderful Father's Day. Your son, Jack Chan	1. 可用通俗一些的稱呼 2. 對父親說話不要太生疏，不要用太公式化的句子 3. 多一些關懷的語氣 4. 要有結尾敬語，如 love, warmly 等等

　　請看下面的改良版本，注意它的語氣、格式、語言以及體裁與上一篇基礎版本的差別：

範文五：父親節 —— 給爸爸的信

Father's Day – A Letter to Father

改良版本	寫作大綱
Dear Dad,	稱呼
I hope this letter finds you well. I just wanted to take a moment to wish you a very Happy Father's Day!	直接問候
I know how hard you work to support our family and raise me. Even when you are too busy to join us for dinner, I always keep your dedication in mind and feel incredibly grateful for everything you have done for me.	對父親的感謝，發自內心
I am sorry that I cannot be there with you on this special day as I have an upcoming exam to prepare for. However, rest assured that I am studying hard and have adapted well to my new environment. I have made many friends and am taking good care of myself at school.	感到歉意，不能回來和他過節，說明原因。多一些說話讓父親對自己現在的生活狀況感到安心
I wanted to remind you of taking care of yourself as well. Please make sure to get plenty of sleep and exercise. Your well-being is just as important to me as it is to you.	對父親的一些關懷
Once again, Happy Father's Day! I love you very much.	要離開的話語
Warmly, Jack	結尾敬語 簽名

親愛的爸爸：

我希望這封信能使我知道您安好。我只想花點時間祝您父親節快樂！

我知道您為了養家糊口養我有多辛苦。即使您太忙無法與我們共進晚餐，我也始終牢記您的奉獻精神，並對您為我所做的一切感到無比感激。

很抱歉在這個特殊的日子裏我不能和您在一起，因為我要準備考試。不過，請放心，我正在努力學習，並且已經適應了新環境。我交了很多朋友，在學校也能照顧好自己。

我想提醒您也要照顧好自己。請確保充足的睡眠和鍛煉。您的安康對我和您一樣重要。

再次祝父親節快樂！我非常愛您。

親切的，

傑克

★ 組織結構 Structure

　　組織結構就是將寫作大綱構思成一個框架，然後圍繞着這個框架，用文字將它寫成句子，然後又將句子（sentence）使它成為段落（paragraph），每個段落只可包含一個主旨。

　　良好的組織能使你的思路在邏輯上編排合理又清晰縝密。每個段落都只能有一個話題，而各個段落之間要連貫一致，使文章能達成一致。

★ 怎樣寫段落（Paragraph）

　　段落寫法應考慮兩個級別 —— 句子級別和段落級別。

　　句子有三級：主題句（topic sentence）、支持句（supporting sentence）和結論句（concluding sentence）。主題句最重要，它表達這個段落的話題，其次是支持句，它提供詳細信息使讀者明白主題句的話題內容，最後是結論句，它總結話題要點和將本段與下一段作連結。

　　段落有三個級別，首段（introduction）、正文段（body）、和結尾段（conclusion）。將三個段落級別整合起來就是一篇完整文章了。

　　好的段落只討論一個小話題，如果一個段落同時討論多個話題，則會混淆不清，讀者將很難理解究竟該段落的中心話題是甚麼。試比較下列例子：

例子	原文	譯文
一	My mother is a very busy person. She works twelve hours a day. She went to work early in the morning and came back very late at night. Sometimes, she even has to work on Sundays and public holidays. She has no time for play or leisure activities.	我母親是個大忙人。她每天工作十二個小時。她一大清早上班,晚上很晚才回來。有時,她甚至要在星期日和公眾假期工作。她沒有時間遊玩或進行休閒活動。
二	My mother is a very busy person. My toy car is broken. Every day, I have a lot of homework to do. There is no air conditioning in my house. I live in the New Territories. My name is Wong Mei Fun. Mice are small animals.	我母親是一個非常忙碌的人。我的玩具車壞了。每天,我都有很多功課要做。我家沒有冷氣。我住在新界。我叫黃美芬。老鼠是小動物。

例一,是一個好的段落,表達的內容是單一的,只討論一個話題、一個中心思想,清楚告訴讀者作者想要談的話題:就是他「母親」。

例二,讀者會覺得很茫然,它表達多個中心思維,讀者會無法理解這個段落的話題,究竟作者想說甚麼,好像是他想到甚麼就說甚麼,內容雜亂,不合邏輯。

每個好段落必須包含**主題句**、**支持句**和**結論句**。主題句通常是段落的第一句,它總領段落的中心思想,說出主題,也是此段落的目的。如果這個段落不是首段,它還有一個作用,就是承接上一個段落,開闢另一個新的小主題。

試看下面有主題句和沒有主題句的例子,亦即是好段落與壞段落的分別:

例子	原文	譯文
一	**Hong Kong athletes are our glory.** This year at the Tokyo Olympics, fencing champion Edgar Cheung Ka Long won our first gold medal in fencing in 25 years. Siobhan Bernadette Haughey made history by winning silver medals in the women's 200 m and 100 m freestyle finals. The strong women's table tennis team, karate star Grace Lau Mo Sheung and famous cyclist Sarah Lee Wai Sze each won a bronze medal.	香港運動員是我們的榮耀。今年在東京奧運會上，花劍冠軍張家朗在劍擊比賽中獲得了我們 25 年來的第一個金牌。何詩蓓在女子 200 米和 100 米自由式游泳決賽中獲得了銀牌，創造了歷史。強大的女子乒乓球團隊，空手道明星劉慕裳和大名鼎鼎的單車手李慧詩都各奪得一面銅牌。
二	This year at the Tokyo Olympics, fencing champion Edgar Cheung Ka Long won our first gold medal in fencing in 25 years. Siobhan Bernadette Haughey made history by winning silver medals in the women's 200 m and 100 m freestyle finals. The strong women's table tennis team, karate star Grace Lau Mo Sheung and famous cyclist Sarah Lee Wai Sze each won a bronze medal.	今年在東京奧運會上，花劍冠軍張家朗在劍擊比賽中獲得了我們 25 年來的第一個金牌。何詩蓓在女子 200 米和 100 米自由式游泳決賽中獲得了銀牌，創造了歷史。強大的女子乒乓球團隊，空手道明星劉慕裳和大名鼎鼎的單車手李慧詩都各奪得一面銅牌。

「例一」的首句：香港運動員是我們的榮耀，就是主題句。它讓讀者可以明確知道這段落想表達我們的運動員是我們的榮耀。「例二」沒有了這主題句，雖然內容與例一完全相同，一模一樣，但它沒有說清楚作者要表達甚麼。

跟隨着主題句是支持句和結論句。主題句說出本段的中心思想，支持句提供詳細及可發展的信息，而最後的結論句提示正文的內容。

以下例子介紹段落的寫作公式：

★ 怎樣寫首段（Introduction）

「首段」又稱為「引言段」，目的是提供一個良好的開端，開頭好的文章會使評分老師留下好印象，是得分的秘訣，所以，首段是學生寫作重中之重，技巧就是有效地將主題句、支持句和結論句結合起來。「主題句」是開場白。「支持句」提供細節、論點，介紹文章主旨。「結論句」提供閱讀路線，文章結構，帶領讀者怎樣閱讀這篇文章。

以下兩個例子都展示出良好首段的寫法。主題句的開場白，沒有交代太多細節，最重要的目的就是要吸引讀者的注意力，使他們有興趣看下去。支持句提供詳細細節，包括背景、訊息、主旨等。結論句要用與主題句不同的表達方法，說出文章佈局。

例一

句子級別	原文	寫作公式
主題句	My hometown Hong Kong is a small but cosmopolitan city.	開場白介紹香港是國際城市。
支持句	It belongs to China. The official name is the Hong Kong Special Administrative Region of the People's Republic of China.	提供細節，說出香港是中華人民共和國的特別行政區
結論句	Although the majority of the city's population is Chinese, Hong Kong is a place where Eastern and Western cultures coexist. It is a favourite destination for overseas and mainland tourists.	閱讀路線，香港是中西文化匯聚的地方和旅遊勝地

例二

句子級別	原文	寫作公式
主題句	There is no doubt that going to a foreign country to learn a different language and culture can be a frustrating and sometimes painful experience.	開場白直接説出海外留學的苦處。
支持句	Although studying abroad has its drawbacks, the benefits far outweigh the difficulties.	主旨清楚説出文章作者的觀點：好處多過壞處
結論句	In fact, those who study abroad gain experience that those who stay at home do not.	閲讀路線「提示」文章內容和論點

★ 怎樣寫正文段（Body）

以下介紹正文的寫法為兩段式，適合中學生使用。

正文段必須支持首段，它可能包含資訊、例子、想法和看法等。好的正文段，邏輯必須縝密，與首段連貫引伸，承上啓下，圍繞着主題展開。

兩段式的正文，每段只可有一個話題，即是主旨，兩段要分開表達不同主旨，不要試圖在一段中表達過多東西。整體而言，正文的寫法較容易犯錯，它的毛病往往是與首尾兩段不一致，或者一段中有多過一個中心思想，又或者不斷重複一個中心思想，並沒有不同的實例。所以，我建議學生在寫作大綱的思路上，要清楚思考正文每段的主旨，用舉例、數據和實例支持它，而緊守「一個段落只包含一個主旨」的原則。

寫正文段之前，要確定每段的主旨或中心思想，思路更要考慮到它們的順序。

正文段的寫作公式也必須包括主題句、支持句和結論句。試看以下例子：

正文	原文	寫作公式
第一段	Hong Kong is a multicultural city with both western and oriental cultures influenced by Britain and China. Historically, it was administered by the British after the First and Second Opium Wars in the 1880s, and returned to China in 1997. As a special administrative region, Hong Kong implements a different governance and economic system from mainland China in accordance with the principle of "one country, two systems".	首句是這段的主題句，其後為支持句和結論句。主題句帶出的中心思想是香港中西文化匯聚。支持句提供詳細訊息解釋香港中西文化的歷史由來。結論句以一國兩制來作總結
第二段	Hong Kong is known as one of the world's most significant financial and commercial centres, and operates a <u>free-market economy</u>. Hong Kong's economy is dominated by services, including banking, financial services and tourism. Hong Kong's economic strengths include a sound banking system, almost no public debt, an independent legal system, ample <u>foreign exchange reserves</u>, strict anti-corruption laws and low and simple taxes. In addition, the rulc of law and freedom of speech in Hong Kong are better protected than in the Mainland. As a popular tourist attraction, Hong Kong provides tourists with a wealth of leisure and entertainment facilities.	首句是這段的主題句，用來説明此段的中心思想：香港是金融和商業中心，沿用自由市場經濟制度。其後的支持句描述香港的金融、經濟體系並與內地的分別。結論句介紹香港的旅遊服務業，也帶出結尾段的閱讀路線

正文	原文	寫作公式
第一段	Critics argue that there are many good reasons against studying abroad. For instance, most students lack life experience when they first go abroad. Living away from home, they may feel helpless. They will be discouraged by lack of sufficient knowledge and understanding of foreign customs and ways of life. They may also experience pain from loneliness and homesickness, or worse, they may be overwhelmed by it.	首句是正文第一段的主題句。主題是：海外留學的壞處。支持句更詳細解釋其壞處。最後結論句作一小結
第二段	Proponents claim that studying abroad has many advantages. Firstly, it can broaden students' horizons. They have the opportunity to experience a completely different culture. Secondly, students can receive different education, for example, different teaching methods, and they will find that communication in western countries is completely open and direct. Thirdly, studying abroad can improve students' foreign language ability, because they have to talk with native speakers every day. The above advantages have been guided to their growth in self-improvement and self-understanding.	首句是正文第二段的主題句。主題是：海外留學的好處。支持句詳細解釋其好處。最後結論句作一小結

★ 怎樣寫結尾段 (Conclusion)

　　文章最後的段落為結尾段。不同體裁的文章有不同結尾段。一封書信與一篇專題文章的結尾段大不相同。但總括來說，它們都來自正文部分的「緊縮」。所以，你不應在其上添加任何新信息。一個好結尾通常包含一個總結句，總結你的思路、論點或評價，目的是要使讀者有共鳴及行動。

例五

原文	寫作公式
Hong Kong is considered as a wonderful and unique destination for travellers, with surprises around every corner. It will dazzle them with its culture, skyscrapers, nightlife, food, theme parks and scale. With the implementation of the 'Northern Metropolis Development Strategy' by the government, Hong Kong will be further enhanced and continue to prosper. So, please come and visit my hometown.	承接正文段，結尾段總結香港是一個旅遊景點。**主題句**說出香港遊客必到的地方。**支持句**簡單總結細節。**結論句**提出香港前景和歡迎到訪。

例六

以下是一篇專題文章的結尾段，它是正文部分的「緊縮」。它並沒有添加任何新信息。總結作者的想法：人工智能的好處大於害處。

原文	寫作公式
In my opinion, although studying abroad has its disadvantages, the advantages are obvious. It can broaden people's horizon. Young people can become more independent and able to gain opportunities for personal growth and development. Therefore, my conclusion is that the benefits of studying abroad for young people outweigh the disadvantages.	結尾段是正文段的「緊縮」，不能添加任何新信息。此段的**主題句**重複作者的立場，其後的**支持句**和**結論句**也如此。就是總結作者的想法：留學的好處大於害處。

將上述例子整合為範文如下：

範文六：我的家：香港

My Hometown: Hong Kong

原文	寫作大綱
My hometown Hong Kong is a small but cosmopolitan city. It belongs to China. The official name is the Hong Kong Special Administrative Region of the People's Republic of China. Although the majority of the city's population is Chinese, Hong Kong is a place where Eastern and Western cultures coexist. It is a favourite destination for overseas and mainland tourists.	香港是一個國際城市；海外和內地旅客喜愛旅遊的城市
Hong Kong is a multicultural city with both western and oriental cultures. Historically, it was administered by the British after the First and Second Opium Wars in the 1880s, and returned to China in 1997. As a special administrative region, Hong Kong implements a system in accordance with the principle of 'one country, two systems'.	香港的文化、歷史和回歸後的情況
Hong Kong is one of the world's most important financial and commercial centres and operates a free market economy. Hong Kong's economy is dominated by services, including banking, financial services and tourism. Hong Kong's economic strengths include a sound banking system, almost no public debt, an independent legal system, ample foreign exchange reserves, strict anti-corruption laws and low and simple taxes. As a popular tourist destination, Hong Kong provides tourists with a wealth of leisure and entertainment facilities.	香港作為金融中心推行市場經濟，以服務業為主導。最後介紹香港為旅遊景點
Hong Kong is considered as a wonderful and unique destination for travellers, with surprises around every corner. It will dazzle them with its culture, skyscrapers, nightlife, food, theme parks and scale. With the implementation of the "Northern Metropolis Development Strategy" by the government, Hong Kong will be further enhanced and continue to prosper. So, please come and visit my hometown.	總結香港為旅遊勝地。迎合北部都會區發展策略，歡迎來訪

參考譯文

我的家香港是一個細小但國際化的城市。它屬於中國，正式名稱為中華人民共和國香港特別行政區。儘管這城市大部分都是中國人，但香港是東西方文化共存的地方。它是海外和內地旅客最喜歡旅遊的城市。

香港是一個多元文化的城市，具有西方和東方文化。從歷史上看，在 1880 年代第一次和第二次鴉片戰爭後，它由英國管轄，1997 年回歸中國。香港作為特別行政區，按照「一國兩制」的原則施政。

香港是世界上最重要的金融和商業中心之一，並推行自由市場經濟。香港的經濟以服務業為主導，包括銀行、金融服務和旅遊業。香港的經濟實力包括健全的銀行體系，幾乎沒有公共債務，獨立的法律體系，充足的外匯儲備，嚴格的反貪污法案和低廉而簡單的稅收。香港作為深受遊客歡迎的旅遊勝地，為遊客提供了豐富的休閒娛樂設施。

香港被認為是旅客的一個美妙而獨特的目的地，每個角落都有驚喜。它的文化、摩天大樓、夜生活、美食、主題公園和規模會讓他們眼花繚亂。隨着政府實施「北部都會區發展策略」，香港將進一步提升，繼續繁榮發展。所以，請來參觀我的家。

範文七：出國留學的優點和缺點

Advantages and Disadvantages of Studying Abroad

原文	寫作大綱
There is no doubt that going to a foreign country to learn a different language and culture can be a frustrating and sometimes painful experience. Although studying abroad has its drawbacks, the benefits far outweigh the difficulties. In fact, those who study abroad gain experience that those who stay at home do not.	留學生有其苦處，但益處卻遠遠超過了困難。
Critics argue that there are many good reasons against studying abroad. For instance, most students lack life experience when they first go abroad. Living away from home, they may feel helpless. They will be discouraged by lack of sufficient knowledge and understanding of foreign customs and ways of life. They may also experience pain from loneliness and homesickness, or worse, they may be overwhelmed by it.	反對海外留學：學生遠離家庭，會感到無助、孤單、思鄉，也可能承受不起這些困苦
Proponents claim that studying abroad has many advantages. Firstly, it can broaden students' horizons. They have the opportunity to experience a completely different culture. Secondly, students can receive different education, for example, different teaching methods, and they will find that communication in western countries is completely open and direct. Thirdly, studying abroad can improve students' foreign language ability, because they have to talk with native speakers every day. The above advantages have been guided to their growth in self-improvement and self-understanding.	支持海外留學：擴潤視野、不同教育制度、外語能力
In my opinion, although studying abroad has its disadvantages, the advantages are obvious. It can broaden people's horizon. Young people can become more independent and able to gain opportunities for personal growth and development. Therefore, my conclusion is that the benefits of studying abroad for young people outweigh the disadvantages.	益處大於壞處

毫無疑問，去外國學習不同語言和文化，可能會令人沮喪，有時甚至是痛苦的經歷。儘管海外留學有其弊端，但益處卻遠遠超過了困難。實際上，出國留學的人經驗發展所得，而那些留在自己家的人不會有。

批評者認為，有很多充份的理由反對出國留學。例如，大多數學生初次出國時都缺乏生活經驗。住在遠離家的地方，他們可能會感到無助。他們又會因對外國的習俗和生活方式缺乏足夠的知識和了解而情諸低落。他們亦會因為孤獨和思鄉而體驗到苦痛，更壞的是，他們可能因此而崩潰。

支持者聲稱出國留學有很多優勢。首先，它可以擴大學生的視野。他們有機會體驗完全不同的文化。其次，學生可以接受不同的教育，例如，不同的教學方法，他們會發現西方國家的溝通是完全開放和直接的。第三，出國留學可以提高學生的外語能力，因為他們每天必須與說母語的人交談。以上的優點都指引着他們在自我完善和自我體會方面的成長。

我認為出國留學雖然有其弊端，但優勢卻是顯而易見的。它可以拓寬人們的視野。年輕人可以變得更加獨立，並能夠獲得個人成長和發展的機會。因此，我的結論是，出國留學對年青人來說益處大於壞處。

★ 英語應用：原文 vs 改良版

英語寫作考試目的是測試學生的英語表達能力，看他們能否運用學過的英語知識和技巧進行思想交流，當然最重要的是英語語法的準確性。以下是一篇小六學生的作文：購物商場歷險記（Adventure in the Shopping Mall），含有很多語法錯處，請注意它的改正方式：

學生原文	語法錯處
One day, little Bob went to a shopping mall with his *parent. It was very crowded. Bob saw a toy *on a shop window. He liked it *so very much *that he quickly walked into the shop. After *looks at the toy for some time, he turned around and *found *where his parents were missing. Bob was scared and *begun to cry. A woman saw him crying and *telling him to wait outside a shop. Five minutes later, Bob saw *parents. *Mum said, "How nice to see you again! Dad and I were *terrible worried." Bob promised her that this would never happen again.	*parent → parents（父母要複數） *on → in（在櫥窗內要用 in） *he liked it so very much → he liked very much（so 放錯位置） *that → so（不能用 that，要用連詞 so） *looks → looking（介詞後面要動名詞） *found → realized（中式英語） *where → that（錯誤關係代詞） *begun → began（要用過去式） *telling → told（saw 的平行結構） *a → the（特指的店鋪要用 the） *parents → his parents（parents 前面需要特指限定詞） *Mum → His mum（mum 前面需要特指限定詞） *terrible → terribly（要用副詞修飾形容詞 worried）

以下是這故事的改良版本：

購物商場歷險記

Adventure in the Shopping Mall

Bob went to a crowded shopping mall with his parents. He saw a toy in a shop window that he really liked, so he quickly went into the shop to take a closer look. But when he turned around, he realized that his parents were missing. This made Bob scared and he began to cry. Luckily, a kind woman noticed him and told him to wait outside the shop. After five minutes, Bob saw his parents again. They were very worried, but relieved to see him. Bob promised his mum that he would never wander off like that again.

參考譯文

巴布和他父母去了一個擁擠的商場。他在一家商店的櫥窗裏看到一件自己很喜歡的玩具，就趕緊進店仔細看了看。但當他轉身時，他發現他父母不見了。這讓巴布很害怕，他開始哭泣。幸運的是，一位好心的女士注意到他，讓他在店外等候。五分鐘後，巴布再次見到他父母。他們很擔心，但看到他就鬆了口氣。巴布向他媽媽保證，他再也不會像這次一樣四處閒逛了。

在高中學生的情況來說，一篇文章得高分與否也取決於英語的應用，如果詞不達意，語法錯誤，不但讀者對話題混淆不清，評卷老師也可能要花額外時間去理解文章的內容，因而影響分數。在英語應用評分方面，評卷老師通常會用下列因素作為評分標準：

1. 能掌握簡單、複合及複雜句子
2. 能準確運用各類句子結構
3. 能準確運用語法，如人稱代詞、時態、單雙數等
4. 以適當語調和適當詞彙來表達文章的含義
5. 準確使用標點符號和拼寫準則

下面是一篇香港中六學生的演辭，在內容及組織方面都可得到高分，但在英語的應用就有很多錯誤及需要改進的地方。

學生原文（含錯誤）	本書作者評論
Good morning everyone.	第一段是連續句子（run-on sentence），混淆不清，應改為兩句
Although I am using English for this speech, it is easy to understand and I hope that you can pay your attention to me.	語法錯誤：原文含有介詞缺失、動詞形式不正確等語法錯誤。
We feel very grateful to all of our teachers. Thank you for teaching us in this 6 years. Miss Chan T K, thank you for your patient to teach us even though we always make a mistake. Thank you Mr Ho L M, always answer all of our questions and help us to solve them. All of you are not only our teachers, but also like our friends.	標點錯誤：原文含有多處標點錯誤，如漏掉逗號、句號等。人名等專有名詞要大寫。
Apart from you Ms Smith. You are our mummy. Smith mummy treat us like her children, do everything she can to help us and take care of us. I can remember that when we were in F4, almost all of us complain about our Smith mummy. Since we couldn't follow Smith mummy's speaking speed. On the other hand, we couldn't adapt the English lessons without any Chinese. However, Ms Smith noticed that and she therefore try to slow down, make sure all of us can follow and understand what she talked about. It is no doubt that the idea is work. It pushed us to the higher level in English. Thank you so much. We are always your babies, Smith mummy.	歧義（ambiguity）：原文含有一些歧義的短語，可以用不同的方式解釋。
Thank you!	非正式用語：原文含有一些非正式用語，可能不適用於正式演講。

中學畢業禮演辭
Secondary School Graduation Speech

Good morning, everyone.

Although I am delivering this speech in English, I hope that you can understand me easily.

First of all, we are very grateful to all of our teachers for teaching us over the past six years. Miss Chan TK, thank you for your patience in teaching us despite our mistakes. And Mr. Ho LM, thank you for always answering our questions and helping us to solve problems. All of you are not only our teachers but also our friends.

I want to give a special thanks to Ms. Smith, who we affectionately call 'Smith mummy'. She treats us like her own children and does everything she can to help and take care of us. I remember when we were in Form 4, many of us struggled to keep up with Ms. Smith's speaking speed and found it difficult to adapt to English lessons without any Chinese. However, Ms. Smith noticed this and made an effort to slow down and ensure that all of us could follow and understand what she was talking about. This approach undoubtedly worked and helped us to improve our English skills significantly. Thank you so much, Smith mummy. We will always be your babies.

Thank you!

參考譯文

大家，早安。

雖然我是用英文演講，但我希望你能輕鬆地理解我的意思。

首先，非常感謝所有老師過去六年的教導。陳老師，感謝您在我們犯錯時耐心教導我們。還有何老師，感謝您總是回答並幫助我們解決問題。你們不僅是我們的老師，也是我們的朋友。

我要特別感謝史密斯老師，我們親切地稱她為「史密斯媽媽」。她對待我們就像對待自己的孩子一樣，竭盡所能幫助和照顧我們。記得我們上中四的時候，很多人都跟不上史密斯老師的語速，在沒有中文的情況下很難適應英語課。然而，史密斯老師注意到這一點，並努力放慢速度以確保所有人都能聽懂及理解她在說甚麼。這種方法無疑奏效了，幫助我們顯著提高了英語技能。非常感謝，史密斯媽媽。我們永遠是你的寶貝。

謝謝你！

　　總括來說，現在將中小學寫作需要注意的英語應用規則介紹如下：

類別	語法規則	模糊或錯誤寫法	正確寫法
逗號運用	由兩部分組成的獨立句子，如果後面那個部分是由連詞如 for、and、nor、but、or、yet 及 so 等引導，則連詞前需要一個逗號。	I like him very much and I hope to be his good friend forever.	I like him very much, **and** I hope to be his good friend forever.
連詞運用	包含兩個獨立從句，個別從句可能含有完整或不完整思想，撰寫時要用連詞、副詞或連接詞將之隔開。	Larry has big eyes and small ears. I have small eyes and big ears.	Larry has big eyes and small ears, **while** I have small eyes and big ears.
錯位修飾	位於句首的分詞短語必須與句子主語相關，否則就是「錯位修飾語」	With the spread of the COVID-19 pandemic, this trend grows further as people are forced to stay at home.	With the spread of the COVID-19 pandemic, **people** have been forced to stay at home, **and** the trend of online shopping has further expanded.
選擇語態	在一般情況下，主動語態比被動語態更生動簡潔。	Your application for refund of your purchase dated May 30, 20XX is referred.	**We** refer to your application for refund of your purchase dated May 30, 20XX.
減少使用 **not**	最好以肯定形式來表達否定的意思。	I am afraid that I do not agree with them on this.	I respectfully **disagree** with them on this viewpoint.
簡潔原則	消除含有重複意義的單詞或短語	More specifically, it facilitates face-to-face interaction between students and their teachers.	**Specifically**, it facilitates face-to-face interaction between students and their teachers.

類別	語法規則	模糊或錯誤寫法	正確寫法
平行結構原則	平行結構就是用相同形式表達相似思想內涵，換言之，不同語項要保持高度的一致性	The play was written in beautiful Shakespearean English with touching poetry and consists of several dramatic techniques that shifted from hope to despair and from comedy to tragedy.	The play was written in beautiful Shakespearean English, **containing** touching poetry and **employing** several dramatic techniques that shifted from hope to despair and from comedy to tragedy.
位置的重要性	關係緊密的詞語安排在一起，修飾語要放在正確位置上。	This vandalism is not only to clean up and maintain costly, but it also poses a safety risk to our students, staff, and teachers.	This vandalism is not only **costly** to clean up and maintain, but it also poses a safety risk to our students, staff, and teachers.
避免混濁不清	重點是講清楚，切勿求簡損意	Special thanks to Ms Smith. You are our mummy.	I want to give a special thanks to Ms. Smith, who **we affectionately call 'Smith mummy'.**
強調原則	如果作者想突顯某一個成份，則將最需要強調的成份，放在句尾。	You said that it was your responsibility to decline any remuneration for this film.	You declined any remuneration for this film and said that **it was your responsibility to do so.**

選詞 Word Choice

寫作該選擇正確字詞來表情達意。本章將中小學生的易混淆字詞列表如下：

易混淆字詞	註釋	例句	譯文
a / an 和 one（一）	a / an 表示「一」，但僅表示泛指，不可與其他數詞對比。	I need a screwdriver to do this job properly.	我需要一把螺絲批才能好好完成這項工作。
	one 表示「一」，可與其他數詞對比，如二、三、四等。	It was one coffee I ordered, not two.	我叫了一杯咖啡，而不是兩杯。
about 和 on / over（關於）	about 用於一般關注性。	There's an article about tourism in today's newspaper.	今天報章刊登了一篇旅遊業的文章。
	on 用於具體信息。	Have you read this article on the newspaper?	你在報章上看過這篇文章嗎？
	over 用於爭論、關注及爭執之後。	Let's agree to differ. Let's not have an argument over it.	讓我們求同存異，不要對此爭論。
absent（缺席）和 away（離開）	absent 是形容詞，表示「不在場」。	How many students were absent from your class today?	今天你班裏有多少個學生缺席？
	away 是副詞，表示「離開」。	I'm going on holiday and I'll be away for a week.	我要去度假，所以要離開一個星期。
accept（接受）和 except（把……除外）	accept 表示「接受」。	Please accept this gift.	請接受這份禮物。
	except 表示「把……除外」。	We visited every tourist attraction except the Peak.	我們參觀了除山頂以外的所有旅遊景點。
accomplish（完成）和 perform（執行）	accomplish 表示「做成功」。	Marcus accomplished a great deal while he was the Manager of the Bills Department.	馬克斯擔任出入口部經理期間，取得了許多成就。
	perform 表示「完成一項工作、任務或事業」。	Soldiers must perform their duties loyally.	士兵必須忠心履行職責。

易混淆字詞	註釋	例句	譯文
across（橫過）和 cross（渡過）/ through（穿過）	across 是介詞，表示「橫過，穿過」，指動作是在物體表面從一邊移到另一邊。	He walked across the bridge.	他走過橋。
	cross 是動詞，表示「橫過，渡過」。	You must be careful while crossing the street.	橫過馬路你要小心。
	through 是介詞，表示「穿過」，指動作是在特定空間移從一頭到另一頭。	The sunlight is coming in through the windows.	陽光從窗外射進來。
accurate（精確）和 exact（準確）	accurate 主要用於描述沒有錯誤的內容。	These figures can't be accurate, surely.	這些數字肯定不準確。
	exact 表示「正確且盡可能詳細」。	I cannot give you the exact date of my arrival yet.	我還不能給你確實的到達日期。
achieve（獲得）和 attain（達到）/ get（取得）	achieve 表示通過努力而獲得成功。	With these new policies the government hopes to achieve political stability.	通過這些新政策，政府希望實現政治穩定。
	attain 表示「達到、獲得」，是比較莊重的用詞，含較強的抱負和渴望意味。	He attained the position of General Manager at the age of 28.	他 28 歲時出任總經理一職。
	get 指以各種方式取得各種東西。	How long does it take to get a visa?	簽證需要多長時間？
adverse 和 averse（反對的）	adverse 作為形容詞，可以用作定語。	Do you think the judge will deliver an adverse opinion?	你認為法官會發表對你不利的意見嗎？
	averse 作為形容詞，只可用作表語，常與 to 短語配搭。	Is he averse to eating meat?	他厭惡吃肉嗎？
adore（非常喜愛）和 like / enjoy / love（喜愛）	adore 表達非常強烈的感覺。	She adores her grandchildren and is always buying them presents.	她很寵愛她的孫兒女，並一直買禮物給他們。
	like / enjoy / love 表達一般的感覺。	I like / enjoy / love meeting new people.	我喜歡結識新朋友。

易混淆字詞	註釋	例句	譯文
advantage（優點）和 merit（長處）/ worth（價值）/ benefit（益處）/ profit（好處）	advantage 表示有利條件，指「使你比其他人處於更好位置的事物」。	A healthier lifestyle is just one of the advantages of living in the country.	健康的生活方式只是生活在該國優勢之一。
	merit 表示「良好品質；長處」，強調實際價值。	Although the film has its merits, it also has a serious flaw.	儘管這部電影有其優點，但它也有嚴重缺陷。
	worth 着重人或物本質中的優點或價值。	Her worth was not understood while she was alive.	在世時她的價值不被了解。
	benefit 指個人或社會所獲得的對身體、智力、道德及精神等方面的益處。	Television provides many benefits.	電視提供許多好處。
	profit 表示「從一些行動中獲得的好處」。	I read for profit and pleasure.	我讀書是為了獲益和樂趣。
advice 和 advise（忠告）	advice 是名詞	He refused to take my advice.	他拒絕接受我的忠告。
	advise 是動詞	My teacher advised me to study computer science at the university.	我老師建議我在大學修讀電腦科學。
affect（影響）和 effect（引發）（動詞）	affect 指受不良影響，通常由表示「事物」的名詞作賓語。	This problem has also affected the automobile industry.	這個問題也影響了汽車工業。
	effect 着重結果。通常以表示「變化」的名詞作賓語。	We hope this medicine can effect an improvement in his health.	我們希望這種藥可以改善他的健康。
affect（外表情感）/ effect（效果）和 result（結果）（名詞）	affect 表示「某人外表的心理狀態」。	His affect was one of cheerful indifference.	他外表是一種愉快的冷漠。
	effect 表示「某物造成的影響，可用於時尚、音樂、繪畫和其他藝術的隨意描述中」。	The director has used practical visual effects and gritty fighting scenes with an aim to create a stunning, but very believable film.	導演使用了實用的視覺效果和強勁的打鬥場面，目的是創作出令人驚歎但令人信服的電影。
	result 表示「從先前的情況或行動發展而來的情況或行動」。	The anti-smoking campaign has produced excellent result.	禁煙運動取得了優異成績。

易混淆字詞	註釋	例句	譯文
aggravate（使惡化）和 irritate（刺激）	aggravate 表示「使變得更糟；加劇」。	Do not aggravate the situation; it's bad enough as it is.	不要使形勢更惡化，現在已經夠壞啦。
	irritate 表示「打擾；煩惱」。	The way she puts on that accent really irritates me.	她擺出這種語氣的方式確實惹起了我的惱火。
allude（暗指）和 elude（逃避）	allude 表示「間接提及」。	Who do you allude to?	你指誰說的？
	elude 表示「逃脫」，通常是通過迅速或明智的行動。	The robber managed to elude the police for two years.	那搶匪成功躲避了警察兩年。
almost（差不多）和 approximately（大約）/ roughly（粗略地）	almost 表示「幾乎；差一點就」。	I like almost all of them.	我幾乎全部都喜歡。
	approximately 表示「幾乎但不完全準確或正確」。	She left at approximately 9pm.	她大約晚上 9 點離開。
	roughly 表示「幾乎，或多或少，但不完全是」。	They were roughly 200 people there.	他們在那裏大約有 200 人。
alone（獨自）和 lonely 寂寞的	alone 表示「周圍沒有其他人」。	I've thought about getting married, but I prefer living alone.	我曾考慮過結婚，但我更喜歡一個人住。
	lonely 表示「難過，因為自己孤獨一人而覺得沒有人關心」。	I was very lonely at first but then I made some friends.	起初我很寂寞，但後來結識了一些朋友。
along（沿着）和 through（穿過）	along 表示「（移動）在諸如道路或河流之類的旁邊」。它強調「與長度成一直線」。	There are trees all along the river banks.	沿着河流兩岸都是樹木。
	through 表示「從一邊到另一邊」。它指的是「從開始到結束」。	All through the journey she kept complaining.	整個旅程中她一直抱怨。
already（已經）和 all ready（準備好了）	already 表示「目前為止；之前」。	You're not leaving already, are you?	您還沒有離開，是嗎？
	all ready 表示「準備好出發；準備好的」。	Are you all ready?	你都準備好了嗎？

易混淆字詞	註釋	例句	譯文
alter（改變）和 exchange（交換）/ change（改變）/ replace（更換）/ substitute（用……代替）/ supplant（取代）	alter 表示「變得與眾不同及有所作為」。	Prices did not **alter** significantly during 2020.	2020 年價格沒有明顯變化。
	exchange 表示「做某事並得到回報；物換物」。	The two brothers often **exchange** blows.	兩兄弟經常拳來腳往。
	change 表示「變得不同」。	Peter hasn't **changed**. He looks exactly the same as he did at school.	彼得沒有改變。他看起來和在學校時完全一樣。
	replace 表示「頂替，指填補那些陳舊破爛或遺失的東西」。	I **replaced** the cup I had broken.	我因摔破杯子而換了另一個。
	substitute 表示「代替，用某物代替另一個，常與 for 連用」。	Don't **substitute** milk *for* cream!	不要用牛奶代替奶油！
	supplant 表示「代替某人或某物，尤其是指以不正當的手段來取代之」。	The Prime Minister plotted to **supplant** the President.	總理密謀取代總統。
alternate（輪流）和 alternative（兩者擇一）	alternate 表示「（兩種事物），首先是一種，然後是另一種」。	I have to work on **alternate** Saturday.	每隔一個星期六我必須去工作。
	alternative 表示「在兩事之間作出選擇」。它的意思是「可以代替通常的一種或你計劃使用的一種」。	We decided to make **alternative** arrangements in case the hotel was fully booked.	我們決定另作安排，以防酒店預訂滿座。
altogether（徹底）和 all together（一起）	altogether 表示「完全，絕對」。	Would the job change her life **altogether**?	這份工作會徹底改變她的生活嗎？
	all together 表示「同時，在一起」。	We found the boys **all together** in the playground.	我們發現男孩子們都在操場上。
ambition（抱負）和 aim（目標）	ambition 表示「您想做或很長一段時間很重要的事情」。	Parco's **ambition** is to become a surgery in a hospital.	帕高的志向是成為醫院的外科醫生。
	aim 表示「做某事時希望達到的目標」。	The **aim** of the book is to help students develop their writing skills.	這本書的目的是幫助學生提高寫作技巧。

易混淆字詞	註釋	例句	譯文
among（在多數之中）和 between（在兩數之間）	**among** 用於涉及兩個以上的人或物的情況。	She couldn't decide **among** the HKUST, the HKU, or the Chinese University.	她無法在香港科技大學、香港大學或中文大學之中作出選擇。
	between 用於僅涉及兩個人或物的情況。	She couldn't decide **between** the Chinese University and the Hong Kong University.	她無法在中文大學和香港大學之間作出選擇。
amount（量）和 number（數）	**amount** 用於不可數名詞。	There is a large **amount of** water in the ocean.	海洋中有大量的水。
	number 用於可數名詞。	There are a large **number** of cockroaches in the kitchen.	廚房裏有很多蟑螂。
amuse（使……開心）和 enjoy（享受）	**amuse** 表示「採取一些方法娛樂自己或別人」。	With a pencil or two and a few sheets of paper, young children can **amuse** *themselves* for hours.	借助一兩支鉛筆和幾張紙，幼兒可以使自己開心幾小時。
	enjoy 表示「玩得開心」。	I made a lot of new friends during my stay in England and really **enjoyed** *myself*.	在英國期間，我結識了很多新朋友，並且非常開心。
and（和）/ or（或者）和 nor（也不）	**and** 表示「也；此外」	To tell you the good news **and** to ask after your health are the reasons why I have come here.	告訴你好消息和問候你，是我來這裏的原因。
	or 用來介紹另一種可能性。	It can be black, white **or** grey.	它可以是黑、白或灰色。
	nor 表示「另一種可能性也是不」。	Not a building **nor** a tree was left standing.	沒有一座建築物或一棵大樹仍然存在。
and / or（和 / 或者）	這種寫法不可取，會損害一個句子，並常導致混淆或含糊不清。	錯誤寫法：First of all, would an honour system successfully cut down on the amount of stealing **and / or** cheating? 正確寫法：First of all, would an honour system reduce the incidence of stealing **or** cheating **or both**?	首先，信用制度會否減少偷竊或詐騙事件還是說兩者都會？

易混淆字詞	註釋	例句	譯文
another 和 the other（另一個）	another 是單數。意思是「同類不定量東西中的另一個」。	Another problem, of course, is finding a job.	當然，另一個問題是找工作。
	當您談論兩個人或事物時，它的意思是「指的是兩者中的第二個」。	I've got one of my shoes, but I can't find the other.	我找到一隻鞋，但沒有找到另一隻。
anxious（憂慮的）和 eager（渴望的）/ nervous（緊張的）	anxious 表示「擔心，因為您擔心可能會發生或可能會發生壞事」。	I knew it was just a minor operation, but I couldn't help feeling anxious.	我知道這只是一個小手術，但我不由自主感到焦慮。
	eager 表示「非常想要或想要做某事」。	I am eager to taste the new flavours of the ice-cream.	我渴望品嚐那雪糕的新口味。
	nervous 表示「不安，害怕某事（物）」。	I always feel nervous when I have to make a speech.	當我需要演講時，我總會感到緊張。
anybody（任何人）/ any body（具體的人）	anybody 表示「任何人，無論是誰」。	If anybody comes, please ask him to wait for me.	如果有人來的話，請他等我。
	Any body 的意思是「每個人的軀體，或每人的形態，或每一個組羣」。	A homicide was thought to have committed, but the police could not discover any body.	兇殺案被認為是發生了，但警方並沒有發現任何屍體。
anyway（無論如何）和 any way（任何方法）	anyway 是副詞，它的意思是「儘管如此，無論如何，不怎樣」。	Alfred never completes his HKDSE, but he expects to go to college anyway.	阿爾弗德從未完成香港中學文憑考試，但不管怎樣他還是希望可以上大學。
	any way 是名詞性短語，意思是「任何方法」。	Alice tries to get out of her PE exam any way she can.	愛麗斯想盡一切辦法不去參加體育科的考試。
assure（保證）/ ensure（確保）/ insure（保險）	assure 表示「自信地鼓勵某人做某事」。它意味着「承諾」。	He assured me of her safety.	他向我保證了她的安全。
	ensure 表示「使事情發生。它提供了保證」。	I will ensure that the car arrives by 6 o'clock.	我將確保汽車在 6 點鐘到達。
	insure 表示「安排在某物丟失、發生事故或某人受傷的情況下支付款項」。	My house is insured against fire.	我的房屋買了火險。
athletic（體育的）和 athletics（競技）	athletic 表示「身體強壯，擅長運動」。	I have never been athletic.	我從來不是運動型。
	athletics 表示「跑步，跳高，游泳等體育運動」。	A lot of athletics reporters write for the magazine.	許多體育記者為該雜誌撰稿。

易混淆字詞	註釋	例句	譯义
authority（權威）和 authorities（當局）	authority 是單數名詞，表示「權威」。	He is an authority on nuclear physics.	他是核物理學的權威。
	authorities 是複數名詞，表示「有權力的官員或機構」。	The authorities had refused them even their basic civil rights.	當局甚至拒絕了他們基本的公民權利。
average（一般的）和 typical（具有代表性的）	average 表示「無論如何都不是特殊或不尋常的；一般標準或水平」。	The average student takes about two hours to complete the test.	一般學生大約需要兩個小時才能完成測試。
	typical 表示「具有與特定類型相同的外觀、行為或特徵」。	John's wife is a typical teacher who cares the students.	約翰的妻子是一位關心學生的模範老師。
award（獎品）和 reward（報酬）	award 表示「因做得很好而獲得的獎品、證書或獎章」。	The award for this year's best director went to Chloé Zhao.	本年度獲得最佳導演獎是趙婷。
	reward 表示「某人給予你的東西，因為你做得很好」。	As a reward for eating all her dinner, the little girl was given an ice cream.	那小女孩得到了一杯雪糕來獎勵她吃完了整頓晚飯。
awhile（片刻）和 a while（一段時間）	awhile 是副詞，意為「短時間＝一會兒」。	Stay awhile and rest.	逗留片刻，休息一下。
	while 是名詞，通常 a while 前面與 for 或 quite 連用	I'll be staying in Paris for a while.	我會在巴黎留一段時間。
base 和 basis（基礎）	base 指「有形的基礎」。	The lamp stands on a circular base.	那盞燈坐落在圓形底座上。
	basis 指「抽象的基礎」。	Political stability provides the basis for economic development.	政治穩定為經濟發展提供了基礎。
beside（在……旁邊）和 besides（也）/ apart from / except（除……之外）	beside 表示「在某人或某物的側面或旁邊」。	Do you know the girl sitting beside Alfred?	你認識阿爾弗德旁邊的女孩子嗎？
	besides 表示「此外；也」。	Besides English, they have to study French and Japanese.	除了英語，他們還必須學習法語和日語。
	except 表示「但不是」。它與 besides 意義不同；但與 apart from 是同義詞。	She eats everything except fish.	除了魚，她甚麼都吃。
	apart from 表示「除此之外」。	Apart from the goalkeeper, who was a disaster, the team played very well.	除了守門員表現太差之外，球隊的整體表現非常出色。

易混淆字詞	註釋	例句	譯文
book 和 order / reserve（預約、預訂、預留）	book 表示「預訂飛機座位、酒店房間及酒樓桌子等」。	The train was packed and I wished I had booked a seat.	火車擠得滿滿的，我真希望自己曾預訂座位。
	order 表示「預訂某些商品」。	I'm afraid that we're out of stock but I can order one for you.	恐怕我們缺貨了，但我可以為你訂購一個。
	reserve 表示「預先安排火車、戲院和酒樓的座位等，以備在特定時間使用」。	I'd like to reserve two seats in the front row for tomorrow night's performance. (=…book two seats…)	明晚的表演，我想預訂前排兩個座位。
borrow（借入）和 lend（借出）	borrow 表示「以會退還為目的」。	May I borrow the car for the evening?	我今晚可以借用那車嗎？
	lend 表示「准予暫時擁有某物」。	Will you lend me a pencil?	你能借我一支鉛筆嗎？
but（但是）和 although（雖然）	but 是並列連詞，不可受中文語法「雖然……但是……」的影響，把兩者用在同一句中。	He failed many times, but he never lost heart.	他雖然失敗多次，但從來沒有灰心。
	although 是從屬連詞。	Although he failed many times, he never lost heart.	
capture（捕獲）和 captivate（迷惑）	capture 表示「抓住並關押作為囚犯」。	That day they captured twenty enemy soldiers.	那天他們俘虜了二十名敵軍。
	captivate 表示「通過美色來迷惑某人」。	Her big black eyes and long blond hair captivated him.	她那雙大大的黑眼睛和一頭金色長髮使他着迷。
careless（粗心大意）和 carefree（無憂無慮）	careless 表示「對事情不太注意」。	If you're careless, you're bound to make mistakes.	如果你粗心大意，那肯定會犯錯。
	carefree 表示「因為沒有後顧之憂或承擔責任而不用擔心」。	How wonderful it would be to be young and carefree again!	回到年輕無憂無慮的時候，那就太好了！
care less（關心的少）	care less 與 careless 意義不同。	I couldn't care less.	我不在乎。
cause（緣故）和 reason（理由）	cause 表示「使某事發生的原因」。	The cause of the fire is still being investigated.	火災發生原因仍在調查中。
	reason 表示「提供對某事之所以發生的解釋」。	I'm sure that they must have good reasons for wanting to live abroad.	我相信他們一定有充份理由想出國居住。

易混淆字詞	註釋	例句	譯文
certainly（的確）和 naturally（自然）/ definitely（明確）	certainly 主要用來「強調某些事情確實是真的，是真的發生了等等」。	I'm sorry if I upset you. I certainly didn't mean to.	如果是我惹你不高興，那很抱歉，我確實不是故意的。
	當你的意思是「正如任何人期望的那樣時，用 naturally」。	It was the first time the little boy had seen an elephant and naturally he was a little scared.	小男孩第一次見到大象時，自然會有點害怕。
	當你的意思是「絕對確定且毫無疑問時，用 definitely」。	If they definitely can't find a job, they should be given further training.	如果他們確實找不到工作，則應該提供進一步的培訓。
certificate（證書）和 voucher（票據）	certificate 表示「陳述有關某人某些事實的正式文件」。	Mum, where's my birth certificate?	媽媽，我的出生紙在哪裏？
	voucher 表示「一種可以代替金錢使用的票據」。	The other day I was given a gift voucher, but it was only worth ten dollars.	前幾天，我得到了一張禮券，但只值十元。
character（性格）和 characteristic（特徵）	character 表示使人與眾不同的所有品質和特徵。	A person reveals his character in every act.	人會在他的行為舉動中表現出自己的性格。
	characteristic 表示「一個顯著的標記」。	The characteristic I like best in him is his cheerfulness.	我最喜歡他開朗的特徵。
cheat 和 deceive（欺騙）	cheat 表示「不公正、不誠實或用欺詐手段從搶某人的東西」。	Antonio Chan cheated us out of our share of the money.	安東尼奧 ─ 陳騙走了我們份額的錢。
	deceive 表示「使某人相信不正確的事情」。	He deceived the teacher by lying.	他説謊欺騙了老師。
choose（選擇）和 elect（推選）。	choose 表示「決定你想要哪一個」。	Some people choose marriage partners who are totally unsuitable.	有些人選擇完全不合適的婚姻伴侶。
	elect 表示「通過投票選出（某人）」。	The committee has elected a new chairman.	那委員會選出了一位新主席。
circulate（傳閱）和 revolve round（旋轉）	circulate 表示「（新聞、故事、謠言）通過從一個人傳給另一個人而傳播」。	One of the rumours circulating at the moment is that the company is about to bankrupt.	目前流傳的謠言之一是公司即將破產。
	revolve around 表示「關於（小説、電影、故事）等」。	His latest film revolves around the difficulties of being a single parent.	他最新電影關於單親父母的困難。

易混淆字詞	註釋	例句	譯文
claim（聲稱）和 declare（宣佈）/ state（聲明）	claim 表示「要求、要求得到、聲稱」	He claimed that it was entirely his own work.	他聲稱那完全是他自己的作品。
	declare 表示「宣佈、斷言，強調正式嚴正的聲明」。	I declare myself innocent.	我聲明我是清白的。
	state 表示「陳述、聲明，即肯定認真地陳述或表明，既可指證實某事的陳述，也可用於談話」。	The witness stated under oath that she had never seen the defendant.	證人宣誓說她從未見過被告。
classic 和 classical（古典的）	classic 指「經典文學或藝術」。	We admired the classic lines of the new stadium.	我們讚賞新體育館的古典式設計。
	classical 指「（古典音樂）尤其在 1800 年以前的音樂，遵循既定風格和節奏規則」。	He prefers classical music to popular music.	他喜歡古典音樂勝過流行音樂。
clothes 和 clothing（衣服）	用 clothes 表示「穿上衣服 —— 為遮蔽一個人的身體時」。	You'd better take off those wet clothes or you'll catch a cold.	最好脫下那些濕衣服，否則會患上感冒。
	用 clothing 表示「一般衣物，是集體名詞」。	The population is in desperate need of foreign aid — especially food, medicine and clothing.	人民迫切需要外國援助，特別是食物、藥品和衣物。
collaborate 和 cooperate（合作）	collaborate 表示「與某人合作完成同一任務，特別是具有科學、藝術或工業性質的任務」。	Marcus Hung and Paul Kwan collaborated on a book on Hong Kong Law.	馬克斯 —— 洪和關保羅合作編寫了一本有關香港法律的書。
	cooperate 表示「願意幫助某人取得成就」。	Faced with the threat of a full-scale military invasion, the general had no choice but to cooperate.	面對全方位軍事入侵的威脅，那將軍別無選擇，只能合作。
collusion（勾結）和 cooperation（合作）	collusion 表示「出於錯誤目的達成的秘密協議，有暗中串通、勾結、共謀的意思」。	The two companies were accused of collusion in fixing prices.	兩家公司被控串謀定價。
	cooperation 表示「為了共同的目的努力或行動」。	The workers, in cooperation with the management, have increased output by 10 per cent.	工人與管理人員合作，使產量增加了 10%。

易混淆字詞	註釋	例句	譯文
come（來）和 go（去）	come 用於向「說話者」方向走來。	He was just about to go out when his wife came into the office in tears.	當他妻子哭着走來他的辦公室時，他正要外出。
	go 用於「向其他方向走去」。	Let's go to Shanghai for a few days.	讓我們去上海幾天。
common（共同的）和 mutual（相互之間的）	common 表示「公共、所有人共享，指共有的關係」。	This is the common desire of our two people.	這是我們兩個人的共同願望。
	mutual 表示「彼此感覺、成就、談話等，指互相依存的關係」。	There were mutual congratulations all round.	到處是大家相互祝賀的祝賀。
(in) common（共同點）和 (in) general（一般來說）	如果你與某人具有相同背景、興趣、品味等，那麼你們兩人有很多共同點（in common）。	I'm sure the marriage won't last. They've got nothing in common.	我肯定婚姻不會持久。他們沒有共同之處。
	當你說某事發生或在大多數情況下是真的時候，用 in general。	Students in general have very little money to spend on luxuries.	一般來說，學生很少有錢花在奢侈品上。
compare to 和 compare with（相比）	compare to 意思是「比喻成」，是在兩個本質不同的物體中尋找相似點。	She compared the child to a noisy monkey.	她把孩子比喻成一隻吵鬧的猴子。
	compare with 表示「比較」，是在兩個本質相似的物體中尋找不同點。	Having compared the new dictionary with the old one, she found the new one more helpful.	比較新舊字典後，她發現新字典幫助更大。
compare（比較）和 contrast（對比）	compare 表示「留意相似之處，着重異同」。	The teachers will be able to visit our schools and compare our teaching methods with their own.	老師將能夠參觀我們的學校，並將我們的教學方法與他們自己的教學方法進行比較。
	contrast 表示「對照，着重差異。對比雙方的類型、性質，或不同，或相反」。	Many programmes have comparable budgets; however, there is a tremendous contrast in staffing levels.	許多方案都有可相比的預算。但是，在職員配備層次存着巨大差別。
complement（補充物）和 compliment（恭維）	complement 表示「補充的東西對原來事物的完全，完整是相互依附的」。	A bottle of white wine is considered as a complement to having seafood in a meal.	一瓶白葡萄酒被認為是品嚐海鮮的極好配搭。
	compliment 意思是「有禮貌的話」。	Your presence to my graduation ceremony is a great compliment.	你出席我的畢業典禮，我不勝榮幸。

易混淆字詞	註釋	例句	譯文
compose（構成）和 consist（組成）/ divide（劃分為）/ separate（分開）	compose 表示「部份構成整體」，可用作被動語態。	An apple is **composed** of seeds, flesh and skin.	蘋果由種子、果肉和果皮構成。
	consist 表示「整體由部份構成」，不可用被動語態。	A week **consists** of seven days.	一星期有七天。
	divide 表示「劃分為」，指整體分為若干部份，不可用作組成。	The mother **divided** the apple into four sections.	母親把蘋果分成四個部份。
	separate 表示「分開，分離，指將把靠在一起的人或連在一起的事物分開」	Break an egg into a bowl and **separate** the white from the yolk.	將雞蛋打入碗中，分開蛋白與蛋黃。
comprehension（理解）和 understanding（了解）	comprehension 表示「理解，強調理解能力」。	Please do the reading **comprehension** exercises on page 10 of this book.	請做本書第 10 頁的閱讀理解練習。
	understanding 表示「了解，含有對他人的觀感、賞識、同情、感受等」。	There is not enough **understanding** between China and the US.	中美之間的了解不足。
comprehensive 充份的 和 comprehensible 可充份理解的	comprehensive 表示「綜合的、充份的，包括所有或幾乎所有的」。	The witness provided a **comprehensive** account of the accident.	那證人提供了意外發生時的全面情況。
	comprehensible 表示「可以完全理解」。	You often find a writer's books more **comprehensible** if you know about his life.	如果您了解作者的生平，通常會更容易理解他寫的書。
content（內容）和 contents（目錄）	content（沒有 's'）表示「在書、電影、文章、演講等表達的事實，想法或觀點」。	I didn't find the **content** of your novel interesting.	我不覺得你小說的內容有趣。
	contents（有 's'）表示「書、報告內撰寫或談論的內容」。	If you want to know which chapters to read, just look at the **contents**.	如果您想了解要閱讀的章節，只需查看其目錄即可。
continual 和 continuous / perpetual（不斷的）/ regular（經常的）	continual 表示「經常性的；重複但有短暫間歇的，用於不愉快事件」。	I'm tired of his **continual** coughing.	我對他不斷咳嗽感到厭倦。
	continuous 表示「繼續發生，不斷的；沒有停止」。	Our brain needs a **continuous** supply of blood.	我們的大腦需要持續不斷的血液供應。
	perpetual 表示「連續不間斷」。	I'm tired of their **perpetual** chat.	我已經厭倦她們無休止的閒談。
	regular 表示「習慣性的、均勻的隔一次又一次的」。	She is a **regular** customer of ours.	她是我們的常客。

易混淆字詞	註釋	例句	譯文
convince（使信服）和 persuade（説服）/ advise（勸説）	convince 表示「讓某人完全確定某事是真實的。它指以論點或證據説服」。	The lawyer failed to **convince** the jury of his client's innocence.	律師未能使陪審團相信他代表的當事人是清白的。
	persuade 表示「成功讓某人同意做某事，或相信某事是正確的」。	At last I **persuaded** him that he was wrong.	最後我説服他承認他是錯的。
	advise 表示勸、勸説。對於成不成功或不一定能成功，不可用 persuade 而要用 advise。	I **advised** him not to go, but he insisted on going.	我勸他不要去，但他堅持要去。
council（委員會）和 counsel（忠告）	council 是有權作出決定的行政機構。	The Legislative **Council** is the place where laws are enacted.	立法會是制定法律的地方。
	counsel 表示「諮詢或意見」。	A wise person will give good **counsel**.	有智慧的人會給人有益的忠告。
councillor（議員）和 counsellor（顧問）	councillor 指「委員會成員」。	Do you like to be elected as a Legislative **Councillor**?	您想當選為立法會議員嗎？
	counsellor 指「顧問」。	Mr Lee is our school **counsellor**.	李先生是我們的學校顧問。
damage（損壞）和 injure（損害）/ wound（創傷）	damage 表示「損壞了，主要指對非生物的損壞」。	The notebook was too badly **damaged** to be repaired.	那手提電腦損毀太嚴重，無法修理。
	injure 表示「損害，主要指對生物在肉體或精神方面的損壞」。	The scaffolding collapsed, killing one of the construction workers and **injuring** two passers-by.	棚架倒塌，壓死一名建築工人和壓傷兩名途人。
	wound 表示「傷口；通常指的是被槍或刀等武器傷害的人」。	Ten soldiers were killed and thirty **wounded**.	十名士兵被殺，三十人受傷。
damage（損害）和 harm（傷害）/ damages（賠償）	damage 是不可數名詞。它的意思是「造成價值損失的傷害」，用於非生命物體。	The car crashed into a tree and suffered severe **damage**.	汽車撞上了樹，受到了嚴重破壞。
	harm 表示「傷害」，但只能用於有生命的物體，可指人或動物受到的損害，妨礙健全發展，指人時，側重精神或肉體方面傷害。	Too much drinking will do you **harm**.	飲酒過多對你身體有害。
	damages（複數）表示「某人在法院裁決所判給的賠贖」。	She was awarded $300,000 in **damages** for wrongful dismissal.	她因被無理解僱而獲得 30 萬元的賠償。

易混淆字詞	註釋	例句	譯文
damp（微濕的）和 wet（用水浸着的）/ humid（濕氣重的）/ moist（濕潤的）/ soaking（濕透的）	damp 表示「略微潮濕，尤其是在寒冷和令人不愉快的情況下」。	On damp days, we have to dry the washing indoors.	在潮濕日子裏，我們必須在室內烘乾衣物。
	wet 表示「用水、裝滿水或其他液體覆蓋」。	It is dangerous to drive on wet roads.	在潮濕道路上駕駛是很危險的。
	humid 表示「溫暖而充滿水氣」。	The air in tropical forests is extremely humid.	熱帶森林中的空氣極為潮濕。
	moist 表示「濕潤讓人感到舒暢的」。	These plants prefer a warm, moist atmosphere.	這些植物更喜歡溫暖潮濕的空氣。
	soaking 表示「完全濕透」。	Her clothes were soaking and her hair was in a terrible mess.	她的衣服濕透了，頭髮亂成一團。
deal in（經營）和 deal with（與……有關）	deal in 表示「買賣」。	Her husband deals in used cars.	她丈夫經營二手車。
	deal with 表示「與書籍、文章等有關」。	The last chapter of this book deals with economic issues.	本書最後一章涉及經濟問題。
decide（決定）和 determine（決心）	decide 表示從幾個選項中選擇；沒有「正確」或「錯誤」。	We must decide on a topic before we start to write.	開始寫作之前，我們必須先確定一個主題。
	determine 表示根據客觀標準評估事物；有「對」或「錯」。	They are determined to stay there till the year is up.	他們決心在那裏等到年底。
delightful（令人高興的）和 delighted（高興的）	delightful 表示「相當正式使某人感到非常高興」。	Thank you for such a delightful evening. Marty and I thoroughly enjoyed ourselves.	謝謝你這晚的款待，瑪蒂和我都非常開心。
	delighted 表示「非常高興」。	I know that Dad will be delighted if you can come.	我知道，如果你能來，爸爸會很高興的。
demur（猶豫）和 demure（假正經的）	demur 既是名詞又是動詞。作為名詞，它的意思是「反對、猶豫或抗議」。作為動詞，它的意思是「提出異議」。	As a noun The plan has been accepted without demur. As a verb The prosecutor requested a break in the court case, but the judge demurred.	作為名詞 該計劃在沒有任何異議之下獲接受了。 作為動詞 檢察官要求休庭，但法官表示反對。
	demure 是形容詞，意思是「安靜而認真，假裝害羞」。	She looked too demure ever to do such a bold thing.	她看起來太端莊，不會做這樣大膽的事。

易混淆字詞	註釋	例句	譯文
deny (否認) 和 refuse (拒絕)	deny 表示「這不是真的」。	He has been accused of stealing a car, but he **denies it.**	他被指控偷車，但他否認了。
	refuse 表示「你不會做」。	He asked his parents to help him, but they **refused.**	他請求父母幫助，但遭他們拒絕了。
desirable (合人意的) 和 desirous (渴望的)	desirable 表示「滿意、理想的、值得擁有」。	Warm weather is **desirable** for the beach party.	溫暖的天氣適合在沙灘開派對。
	desirous 表示「強烈希望」。	I am **desirous** of visiting Canada one day.	我渴望有一天到加拿大旅行。
dessert (甜品) 和 desert (沙漠)	dessert 指「飯後甜點如蛋糕、雪糕等」。	We have ice-cream for **dessert.**	我們的甜點是雪糕。
	desert 指「大面積的乾旱土地，尤其是被沙覆蓋的土地」。	We roamed in the **desert** for three days.	我們在沙漠中遊歷了三天。
destruction 和 ruin (毀壞)	destruction 強調毀壞的過程和行為。	The army left the enemy town in complete **destruction.**	軍隊完全摧毀了敵人的城鎮。
	ruin 強調由於自然力量或時間的作用而逐漸損壞。	Gambling brought about his **ruin.**	賭博毀了他。
disinterested (公正的) 和 uninterested (不感興趣的)	disinterested 表示「公正、中立、不偏袒、不受私人動機影響的」。	To give a fair judgement, you must be entirely **disinterested.**	為了作出公正的判斷，您必須完全不偏不倚。
	uninterested 表示「沒興趣；冷漠」。不要與 disinterested 混淆。	He is totally **uninterested** in gambling.	他對賭博完全不感興趣。
distinctively (特殊地) 和 distinctly (清楚地)	distinctively 表示「具有特色」。	Tea Restaurants are **distinctively** Hong Kong food culture.	茶餐廳是香港獨特的飲食文化。
	distinctly 表示「清晰地」。	Everyone in the room could hear the speaker **distinctly.**	房間裏每個人都可清楚聽到講者的聲音。
without doubt 和 no doubt (毫無疑問)	without doubt 表示「我堅信這是正確的」。	The discovery of Penicillin was, **without doubt,** a great medical advancement in medication.	毫無疑問，盤尼西林的發明是藥物治療的重大醫學成就。
	no doubt 表示「沒有懷疑、我期望或我想」。	I have **no doubt** of his ability.	我毫不懷疑他的能力。

易混淆字詞	註釋	例句	譯文
drama 和 play（戲劇）	drama（不可數名詞）是指「一種文學或特定的戲劇」。	She has always been interested in music and **drama**.	她一直對音樂和戲劇感興趣。
	play 指「戲劇表演或舞台劇」，與音樂劇、芭蕾舞劇、歌劇等不同。	After the meal, we went to see a **play** at the City Hall.	飯後，我們去大會堂看舞台劇。
driveway（汽車小路）和 highway（公路）	driveway 指「私宅的汽車道，即是一條從大街到房屋前面的汽車小路」。	Sometimes we park our car in the **driveway** in front of our house.	有時我們將車停在門前汽車小路上。
	highway 指「公共汽車道，通常指高速公路」。	It is an offence to walk along the **highway**.	沿着高速公路步行是違法的。
earn（獲得）和 gain（獲利）/ win（贏得某物）	earn 表示「通過做有報酬的工作來賺錢或維持生計」。」	She **earns** $12,000 a month.	她每月收入 12,000 元。
	gain 表示「獲得利潤。」。	Each of the boys **gained** a prize.	每個男孩都得了獎。
	win 表示「在比賽或競賽等勝出而獲得某物」。	The team are determined to **win** the prize next year.	團隊下決心明年要贏得大獎。
earnest / in earnest 和 serious（認真）	earnest 是形容詞，用來形容某人誠摯的、認真的；鄭重其事的。份	He is a scientist who has an **earnest** attitude toward his work.	他是一位態度認真的科學家。
	in earnest 是慣用語，表示「認真、嚴肅」。	Do you think Alice said that **in earnest**, or was she joking?	您認為愛麗斯是認真的，還是在開玩笑呢？
	serious 是形容詞，用於描述完全致力於某事的人。	The **serious** students never missed a class.	認真的學生從未錯過任何一堂課。
earth 和 world / planet（地球）	earth 指「我們賴以生存的地球，太陽系行星之一」。	On the journey back to **Earth**, one of the spaceship's computers failed.	在返回地球的旅程中，太空船其中一座電腦發生故障。
	world 指「地球，也稱世界，但從人、國家、城市等角度來說」。	I have friends in different parts of the **world**.	我在世界各地都有朋友。
	planet 指「地球（以行星來比喻），但從自然環境的角度來說」。	We must all work together to protect the **planet**. (N.B.: not earth)	我們大家必須共同努力保護地球（注意：這句子要用 planet，不能用 earth）。

易混淆字詞	註釋	例句	譯文
efficient (高效率的) 和 effectual (奏效的) / effective (實際的)	efficient 表示「工作迅速而沒有浪費」。	Since the new software was installed, library services have become much more **efficient**.	自從安裝新軟件以來，圖書館服務變得更高效。
	effectual 表示「產生預期的效果」。	The Financial Secretary took **effectual** action against unemployment.	財政司對失業採取了有效行動。
	effective 表示「實際，真實」。	We need more **effective** ways of dealing with environmental pollution or the problem will get worse.	我們需要更有效的應對環境污染，否則問題將會變得更嚴重。
elder (年長的) 和 older (年齡較大的)	elder 一般只用來比較家庭成員的長幼，且只能用於前置定語。	John, her **elder** son, is still at university.	她的大兒子約翰仍在上大學。
	older 用於一般人的年齡比較，也可形容事物陳舊。	He is **older** than I by two months.	他比我大兩個月。
elderly (中年以上的) 和 aged (年邁的)	elderly 是形容詞，表示「年老的」，是較禮貌的用詞，暗示尊重。	An **elderly** man with white hair and a stick was knocked down in front of the traffic lights by a bus.	一位提着拐杖的白髮老人在交通燈前被巴士撞倒。
	aged 與 elderly 相比，表示「很老」。	Although my father is an **aged** man, he doesn't want to retire.	我父親雖然年紀很大了，但他不想退休。
endemic (地方性的) 和 epidemic (時疫大流行)	endemic 是形容詞，表示「在特定地方定期發現的疾病」。	Cholera is **endemic** in certain poor countries.	霍亂於某些貧窮國家是很流行的。
	epidemic 用作名詞，表示「時疫，流行病」。	Millions of people died in the COVID-19 **epidemic**.	數百萬人死於新冠疫病大流行。
endure 和 suffer (忍受)	endure 是動詞，指「痛苦或非常不愉快的情況」。	The people in this country have had to **endure** almost a decade of economic hardship.	這國家的人已經忍受了近十年的經濟困難。
	suffer (from / with) 指患病。	More than 160 million people **suffer** from malaria.	超過 1 億 6 千萬人患有瘧疾。

易混淆字詞	註釋	例句	譯文
ensure（確保）和 assure（保證）/ insure（保險）	ensure 表示「確定（某些事情會發生或存在）」。	We need to ensure that our prices remain competitive.	我們要確保價格可以保持競爭力。
	assure 表示「告訴某人一定會發生或肯定是真的，目的是讓他們感到不那麼擔心」。	I assure you that the report will be on your desk by tomorrow lunchtime at the latest.	我向您保證，最遲在明天午飯前，我會將報告放在你的辦公桌上。
	insure 表示「購買保險，希望在遭受生命或財產損失時可獲得賠償。	I have insured myself against accidents.	我已經購買了意外保險。
equable（穩定的）和 equitable（公平的）	equable 表示「（溫度或人的性格）沒有很大變化，甚至是有規律的」。	Under the Minimum Wage Ordinance, the workmen in Hong Kong are paid equable wages.	根據《最低工資條例》，在香港的工人可獲得穩定的工資。
	equitable 表示「公平，公正」。	The lawsuit ended with an equitable settlement.	訴訟以公平解決告終。
especial 和 particular / special（特別的、特殊的）	especial 表示「特別，例外」。	She has no especial personal ambition.	她沒有特別的個人野心。
	particular 強調在同類人或物中某人或物的獨特性。	Why did you choose that particular book?	您為甚麼偏偏選擇那本書？
	special 強調不尋常或與眾不同的性質。這種性質賦予特殊的品格和用途。	Tonight is a special occasion, and we have something very special for dinner.	今晚是一個特殊時刻，而我們的晚餐有些特別。
especially（尤其）和 specially（特地）	especially 表示「尤其，特別是」主要對前面所說的內容作進一步的解釋或說明。	There is a shortage of teachers, especially of English Language.	現在特別缺教師，尤其是英語老師。
	specially 表示（為某種目的）專門地、特地，含「不是為了別的，而是為……」之義。	I come specially to see my primary school teacher.	我特地來看我的小學老師。
essential（必不可少的）和 important（重要的）/ necessary（必須的）	essential 表示「絕對有必要」。	You can live without clothes, but food and drink are essential to life.	你沒有衣服可以生存，但是飲食對生命必不可少。
	important 表示「重要性，具有重大意義」。	For me, meat for dinner is important.	對我來說，晚餐吃肉很重要。
	necessary 表示「需要，但不一定不可缺少」。	Work is a necessary part of life.	工作是生活必須的一部份。

易混淆字詞	註釋	例句	譯文
ethical（倫理的）和 moral（道德的）	ethical 表示「道德上正確」。	What ought I to do? This is an ethical question.	我該怎麼辦？這是一個道德問題。
	moral 表示「正確的行為」。	He leads a moral life.	他過着一種循規蹈矩的生活。
ever（曾經）和 always（總是）/ never（永不）	ever 表示「從來，曾經」。	Have you ever been to Japan?	你去過日本嗎？
	always 表示「從一開始到現在；每次」。	He has always been my hero.	他一直是我的英雄。
	never 表示「在任何時候都是否定」。	I had never met his wife before yesterday.	昨天之前我從未見過他妻子。
every day（每天）和 everyday（日常的）	every day 是將形容詞和名詞結合的短語。意思是「每一天」。	I practise Taiji boxing every day.	我每天練習太極拳。
	everyday 是形容詞，意思是「每天的、普通的、日常的」。	School is an everyday event for most children.	大多數孩子每天要上學。
everyone（每個人）和 every one（每一個）/ each and every one（每一個都）	everyone 表示「所有人、大家」。	Hurry up! Everyone is waiting for you.	趕快！大家都在等你。
	every one 表示「（一組）中的每一個。可以指人或物，常跟 of 短語」。	This problem affects each and every one of us.	這個問題影響到我們每個人。
	each and every one 是法律常用術語，應該避免用於學生寫作中。	錯誤用法 It should be a lesson to each and every one of us. 正確寫法 It should be a lesson to every one of us.	這對我們每個人來說都是一個教訓。
excuse 和 forgive / pardon（原諒）	excuse 僅用於輕微的過失和違法行為不能跟雙賓語。	I hope you'll excuse my untidy handwriting. I'm trying to write this letter on a bus.	希望你能原諒我亂七八糟的字體。我是在巴士上寫這封信的。
	forgive 用於所有輕微和重大的過失和違法行為。	He was sorry that he had lied to her and asked her to forgive him.	他為撒謊感到抱歉，請求她原諒他。
	pardon 表示「（正式）原諒」。	I'm sure they will pardon the occasional mistake.	我肯定他們會諒解偶然發生的錯誤。

易混淆字詞	註釋	例句	譯文
exhausting（令人疲憊不堪的）和 exhausted（筋疲力盡的）/ exhaustive（徹底的）	exhausting 表示「造成疲勞」。	Pushing the car uphill was **exhausting.**	推車上山真累。
	exhausted 表示「極度疲勞」。	I feel really **exhausted**, I must rest.	我真的很累，我必須休息。
	exhaustive 表示「如此徹底或完整，甚至不會遺漏任何最小的細節或可能性」。	An **exhaustive** investigation finally revealed the cause of the accident.	那詳盡的調查最終揭露了意外發生的原因。
extinguish（撲滅）和 exterminate（消滅）/ extinct（已滅絕的）	extinguish 是動詞，表示「使某物停止燃燒」。	Before entering the factory, please make sure that all cigarettes have been properly **extinguished.**	進入工廠前請確保所有香煙均已熄滅。
	exterminate 是動詞，表示「消滅、消除（疾病、觀念、種族等）」。	The new chemical will **exterminate** the cockroaches.	這種新化學物質能夠殺滅蟑螂。
	extinct 是形容詞，表示「（某種動物或植物）完全不存在，因為都已經死亡或被殺死」。	Many species are becoming **extinct.**	許多物種正在滅絕。
fantasy（幻想）和（想像物）/ imagination（想像力）	fantasy 指「用想像力在腦海產生的畫面」。	He lived in a world of **fantasy.**	他生活在幻想的世界裏。
	fancy 指「想像中的東西」。	The monster is a creature of the child's **fancy.**	那怪物是孩子想像出來的生物。
	imagination 指「大腦思維能力的部份構想心理圖片的能力」。	Were the voices real or just products of his **imagination?**	那些聲音是真實的還是他想像出來的產物呢？
farther（再遠點的）和 further（更多的）。	farther 用於比較長度或物理距離。	Beijing is **farther** than Shanghai.	北京比上海更遠。
	further 表示「額外時間或數量；在更大程度上」。	I shall get **further** information.	我將獲得更多資料。
favourable（贊成的）和 favourite（特別喜愛的）	favourable 表示「合適，贊成」。	The moment is not **favourable.**	時機不適合。
	favourite 表示「最喜歡，特別喜歡」。	She is his **favourite** pupil.	她是他最喜歡的學生。
fellow（某個人）和 friend（朋友）	fellow 表示「（非正式）人」。	The new manager seems a pleasant enough sort of **fellow.**	新任經理看來是個友善的傢伙。
	friend 表示「您喜歡並喜歡與之在一起的人」。	My **friends** and I were at a swimming pool where there was a party going on.	我和我的朋友們在泳池旁舉行派對。

易混淆字詞	註釋	例句	譯義
few (幾乎沒有) / a few (很少) / 和 little (不多 / a little (一點兒) / several (幾個)	few 可和複數可數名詞一起便用，表示「幾乎沒有，含否定的意義」。	Few people die of smallpox nowadays.	如今很少有人死於天花。
	a few 表示「很少數，含肯定意思」。	I saw her just a few days ago.	我幾天前見過她。
	little 用於不可數名詞，表示「不多，含否定意義」。	My grandpa had very little money, but still lived happily.	我爺爺不富有，但過着幸福的生活。
	a little 表示「一點兒，含肯定意思」。	He is able to speak a little English.	他能説一點英語。
	several 表示「有一些但不是很多」。	Chicken will keep for several days in a refrigerator.	雞肉可在冰箱中存放幾天。
fewer 和 less (較少的) / lesser (稍少的)	fewer (few 的比較級形容詞) 可用來修飾可數名詞，指的是數。	People buy fewer cigarettes now.	現在購買香煙的人減少了。
	less (little 的比較級形容詞) 可用來修飾不可數名詞，指的是量。	He has spent less time on his work than he ought to have done.	他用在工作上的時間比該用的少。
	lesser (little 的比較級形容詞) 只用作定語形容詞，多指價值或重要性。	Of the two actresses, she is the lesser known.	在這兩位女演員中，她是不大出名的那位。
fit 和 suit (適合)	fit 指「(衣服、鞋子、戒指等的) 尺寸和大小形狀應正確」。	These trousers don't fit me anymore.	這些褲子我再也穿不下了。
	suit 指「在衣服、款式、時尚等方面的正確或適當的」。	Red and black are colours that suit me very well.	紅黑兩色非常適合我。
fluid (流體) 和 liquid (液體)	fluid 表示「可以流動的東西」。	Milk, water and oxygen are fluids.	牛奶、水和氧氣都是流體。
	liquid 表示「不是固體或氣體的物質」。	Milk and oil are liquids, but oxygen is not.	牛奶和油是液體，但氧氣不是。
force 和 power (力量)	force 表示「使用權力或力量」。	The demonstrators were made to leave the building by force.	示威者被迫離開那座建築物。
	power 表示「控制人員和事件的能力」。	We must not forget Japan's economic power.	我們一定不能忘記日本的經濟實力。

易混淆字詞	註釋	例句	譯文
forecast 和 foretell / predict（預測）	forecast 表示「預測；根據數據和資料，以定量和定性分析預告或預報」。	The principal **forecasts** that 90% of his pupils will pass the HKDSE English Languages papers.	校長預測他的學生有 90％將會通過香港中學文憑英語考試。
	foretell 表示「預測、預言」。」	Perhaps certain gifted persons can **foretell** the future.	也許某些有天賦的人可以預測未來。
	predict 表示「根據事實或自然規律推測未來的事情，具有一定的科學準確性」。	The Hong Kong Weather Observatory **predicts** rain for tomorrow.	香港天文台預測明天將會下雨。
forever 和 for ever（永遠）	forever 表示「不斷；每時每刻」。	He is **forever** asking me for more pocket money.	他永遠向我要更多零用錢。
	for ever 表示「永遠，常常」。	He promised that he would love me **for ever** and a day.	他答應他會永遠愛我。
former 和 first（前者）	former 指「剛說的兩個人或事物中的第一個」。	Jack and William came in together, the **former** had no coat.	積和威廉一起來，前者沒有穿外套。
	first 表示「先於其他所有人」。	Cinema, television and theatre, the **first** of which offers actors the most substantial reward.	電影、電視和劇院，前者給予演員的報酬最高。
formally（正式地）和 formerly（從前）	formally 表示「正式、官方」。	He refused to attend the dinner because he did not like to dress **formally**.	他拒絕參加晚宴，因為他不喜歡穿正式服裝。
	formerly 表示「在早期」。	He **formerly** worked as a worker in an oil company, but now he's the CEO of the Hong Kong Stock Exchange.	他曾在一家石油公司當過工人，但現在是香港聯合交易所的首席執行官。
in future（今後）和 in the future（在將來）	in future 表示「從現在開始要改變和做不同的事（通常在公告和警告中使用）」。	**In future** anyone arriving late for class will not be admitted.	將來任何遲到的人都不准進入課室。
	in the future 表示「在將來的某個時候，即現在以後的一段時間」。	**In the future**, when my youngest child has started school, I'd like to get a job.	將來，當我最小的孩子開始上學時，我想找一份工作。

易混淆字詞	註釋	例句	譯義
gather（聚集）和 collect（收集）/ meet（相聚）/ get together（相聚）	gather 表示「將分散的東西集中帶到一個地方」。	He soon **gathered** a crowd round him.	他很快便聚集了一羣人圍住他。
	collect 表示「作為愛好或為了學習某些東西而收集（書籍、郵票等）的樣本」。	My hobby is **collecting** stamps.	我的嗜好是集郵。
	meet 表示「與朋友、客戶等聚在一起」。	We arranged to **meet** each other again next month.	我們安排下個月再見面。
	get together 與 meet 同義。	It's a long time since I got together with Jeanne.	自從上次我和珍妮相聚以來，已過了很長的一段時間。
genuine（非偽造的）和 actual（真實的）	genuine 表示「真實的，不是假的」。	This is a **genuine** pearl.	這是一顆真正的珍珠。
	actual 表示「事實上存在」。	「After my death, give this necklace to Jeanne and tell her I missed her very much.」Those were his **actual** words.	「我死後，把這條頸鍊交給珍妮，告訴她我非常想念她。」他是這樣說的。
gently（輕輕的）和 politely（有禮貌的）	gently 表示「以不會傷害或損害任何人或物的方式」。	She held the little bird very **gently**.	她輕輕抱着那隻小鳥。
	politely 表示「以一種表現良好舉止的方式」。	The shop assistant asked me **politely** what I wanted.	售貨員禮貌地問我想要甚麼。
glad（高興的）和 happy（開心的）/ fond（喜歡的）	glad 表示「對特別的事情感到高興」。	I was **glad** to see that film.	我很高興看到那部電影。
	happy 表示「享受生活」。	We hope that you will like this school and be **happy** here.	我們希望你會喜歡這間學校，並在這裏過得開心。
	fond 表示「喜歡」。	I am **fond** of seeing films.	我喜歡看電影。
goal 和 aim（目的）/ destination（目的地）	goal 表示「目的、目標，即是你希望實現的目標」。	The company's **goal** is to double its share of the personal computer market.	該公司的目標是將其在個人電腦的市場佔有率增加一倍。
	aim 表示「目的、目標，常指具體明確的短期目標，含有全力以赴之意」。	His **aim** is to pass his HKDSE and go to university this year.	他的目標是今年他通過香港中學文憑試並能入讀大學。
	destination 表示「您要去的地方」。	We reached our **destination** just after three o'clock.	我們三點鐘後才到達目的地。

易混淆字詞	註釋	例句	譯文
gold（黃金的）和 golden（金色的）	gold 用於「描述由黃金製成或金色的東西」。	My father gave me a gold watch on my 18th birthday.	父親在我 18 歲生日時給我一個金錶。
	golden 表示「金色的」，也表示「極好的」，通常用在慣用的表述中，主要用於文學風格。	It's a golden opportunity for you to study in the UK.	這是你留學英國的絕佳機會。
good（好的）和 well（很好地）	good 是一個形容詞，意思是「質量令人滿意」。	His performance is very good and outstanding.	他的表現非常出色。
	well 是副詞，意思是「以一種正確、成功、合適等的方式」。	Alfred is getting along well at school.	阿爾弗德在學校進步很快。
gratified（高興的）和 grateful / thankful（感謝的）	gratified（'gratify' 的過去分詞）表示「高興」。	She was gratified to learn you could come.	她很高興得知你可以來。
	grateful 表示「謝謝，充滿感謝」。	We are grateful to you for your help.	我們感謝您的幫助。
	thankful 表示「感謝的、感激的」，指因為發生了好事，而感到高興和欣慰。	We should all be thankful that nobody was hurt.	我們全都該因無人受傷而感恩。
greatly（大大地）和 tremendously（極大地）/ enormously（巨大地）/ a lot（很多地）	greatly 表示「很多；數量很大」。	Living standards have greatly improved.	生活水平大大提高。
	enormously 表示「非常大」。	Living standards have improved enormously in the last couple of decades.	在過去十多年以來，生活水平得到了極大改善。
	tremendously 表示「非常、非常好」。	In the last forty years, education in China has changed tremendously.	在過去四十年，中國的教育發生了翻天覆地的變化。
	a lot 表示「大量的」。	China has improved a lot in economic development in this century.	中國在本世紀的經濟發展中取得了很大進步。
gymnastic（體操的）和 gymnastics（體操）	gymnastic（沒有 -s）是形容詞，意思是「屬於或涉及體操的」。	Her gymnastic ability was recognized at a very early age.	她的體操能力在年紀很小時就獲得認可。
	gymnastics（有 -s）是名詞，意思是「體操運動」。	I took up gymnastics when I was at school.	我在學校學習體操。

易混淆字詞	註釋	例句	譯義
hard（努力地）和 hardly / scarcely / barely（幾乎不）/ rarely（很少）	hard 表示「努力地，指付出很大的努力」。	If you work **hard**, you're bound to pass.	如果你努力溫習，你一定會及格的。
	hardly 表示「很少；幾乎沒有，含否定意義，與下面 **scarcely** 和 **barely** 同義」。	I **hardly** ever went out because of the COVID-19 epidemic.	由於新冠疫病的流行，兩年以來我幾乎沒有外出。
	scarcely 表示「幾乎不、僅僅、含否定意義」。	She spoke **scarcely** a word of English.	她連一個英文字也說不出來。
	barely 表示「幾乎沒有，本身已含否定意思，不可再用 **not**」。	He can **barely** write and read.	他幾乎不懂寫字和閱讀。
	rarely 表示「不經常，含肯定意義」。	He **rarely** comes to see me now.	他現在很少來探望我。
high 和 tall（高的）	**high** 用來描述距離地面很遠的東西（或者其頂部距離地面很遠的東西），並常暗示「大」，除表示具體意義，還可表示抽象意義。	The principal has a very **high** opinion of him.	校長對他評價很高。
	tall 表示「超過平均高度」。使用 **tall** 來描述狹窄且高於平均高度的人、動物、樹木、植物和事物。	Smoke pours out of the **tall** chimneys all day long.	煙霧整天從高大的煙囱裏傾倒出來。
hinder（阻礙）和 prevent（防止）	**hinder** 表示「阻礙、延遲、阻撓」。	Higher interest rates could **hinder** economic growth.	較高的利率可能會阻礙經濟增長。
	prevent 表示「使某人無法做某事」。	His health **prevented** him from doing any hard work.	他健康太差，無法做體力勞動的工作。
hire（租用）和 rent（租入或租出）/ hire out / let（出租）	**hire** 表示「通過付錢獲得（屬於某人的東西）的使用權；短時間的租用」。	Why buy a wedding dress when you can **hire** one?	當你可以租用婚紗時，為甚麼要買呢？
	rent 表示「租出或租入，租客需要付租金的，例如租房屋、商店、辦公室等，通常需要使用長時間的」。	I'm **renting** a small room near the university.	我正在大學附近租了一個小房間。
		Mr Hung **rents** this flat to me at $5,000 per month.	洪先生租這層樓給我，租金一個月五千元。
	hire out 表示「出租」。	He **hired out** a car to me.	他租了一輛車給我用。
	let 表示「允許某人住在你的屋內以賺取金錢」。	During the holiday season we **let** the cottage to tourists.	假期期間，我們將小屋出租給遊客。

易混淆字詞	註釋	例句	譯文
historic（有歷史意義的）和 historical（歷史上的）	historic 是形容詞，描述一件事或一項發明對未來事件產生重大影響。	The Second World War is a **historic** battlefield which involved all countries over the world.	第二次世界大戰是一個歷史性的戰場，涉及世界所有國家。
	historical 是形容詞，指的是過去發生的任何事情。	In certain Middle East countries, women are not allowed to enter the monastery for **historical** reasons.	某些中東國家基於歷史原因，婦女不准進入寺院。
household（家庭）和 housework（家務）	household 表示「所有同住的家人」。	Be quiet or you'll wake the whole **household**.	請保持安靜，否則您將喚醒整家人。
	housework 表示「保持家居清潔的所有工作」。	Some women get no help with the **housework**.	有些婦女要獨力做家務，沒有得到任何幫助。
humiliate 和 disgrace（丟臉）	humiliate 表示「使（一個人）因喪失尊嚴或自尊而感到丟臉」。	Mrs Chan felt **humiliated** by her son's bad behaviour in front of the principal of the school.	陳太因兒子在校長面前的不良行為感到羞恥。
	disgrace 表示「玷污、丟臉；指降低某人在其他人心目中的地位」。	He **disgraced** his family's name.	他玷污了家庭的名聲。
ignore（不理）和 neglect（忽視）/ forget（遺忘）	ignore 表示「不注意、不理會」。	I made a suggestion but they chose to **ignore** it.	我提出了一個建議，但他們選擇不理會。
	neglect 表示「不給予或很少注意或照顧」。	Don't **neglect** to write and say 'Thank you'.	不要忘記寫和說「多謝您」。
	forget 表示「未能實現某些東西（並受其指導）」。	Some teachers **forget** how much a student can take in during one lesson.	一些老師遺忘了一個學生在一節課中頂多能夠吸收多少知識。
ill 和 sick（生病的）	ill 是表語形容詞，通常在動詞之後使用。	His father *is* seriously **ill** in hospital.	父親在醫院病得很厲害。
	sick 既可作表語，也可以作定語，所以可以用在名詞之前。	I am being trained to look after **sick** children.	我正在接受培訓照顧生病的孩子。
illicit（非法的）和 elicit（引出）	illicit 是形容詞，意思是「非法、禁止」。	He engaged in an **illicit** love affair.	他捲入了一些不正當的愛情糾紛之中。
	elicit 是動詞，意思是「獲取，得出（事實，信息）」	The judge tried to **elicit** the truth from this defendant.	法官試圖使這名被告說出真相。

易混淆字詞	註釋	例句	譯文
illusion（錯覺）和 allusion（間接提及） / delusion（錯覺） / elusion（逃避）	illusion 表示「（看到的）不存在的或與現實不同的東西；一個虛構的想像、錯誤的印象或信念」。	Mirrors give an illusion of more space in a room.	鏡子給人一個房間更多空間的錯覺。
	allusion 表示「一個間接的提及，如典故」。	His allusion to my failure made my wife feel sorry.	他間接提到我的失敗使我妻子感到難過。
	delusion 表示「錯誤的信念或觀點」。	This old woman had the delusion that the Sale Representative tried to cheat her.	這位老婦人誤認為那個銷售員想欺騙她。
	elusion 表示「躲避、逃避」。	Not attending the meeting is an elusion of your obligation to vote.	你不參加會議是想逃避應盡的投票義務。
imaginary（虛構的）和 imaginative（有想像力的） / imaginable（可想像的）	imaginary 表示「不存在於現實生活中，而僅存在於某人的腦海中」	This new novel takes the reader on an imaginary journey into space.	這本新小說將讀者帶入了一個虛構的太空之旅。
	imaginative 表示「具有或顯示出強大的想像力」。	People tend to become less imaginative as they grow older.	人們隨着年齡增長想像力會變少。
	imaginable 表示「可以想像的」。	We had the *best* time imaginable at the party.	我們在聚會上度過了可想像的最美好時光。
immanent（存在的）和 imminent（逼近的） / eminent（傑出的）	immanent 表示「（質量）存在、固有的」。	Some people believe that God is immanent in everything.	有些人相信天主存在於萬物之中。
	imminent 表示「（即將發生的事件，尤其是危險）可能很快就會發生或發生」。	The hoisting of Typhoon number 10 is imminent.	10 號風球即將懸掛。
	eminent 表示「著名、傑出」。	He is eminent for his works in fashion design.	他以時裝設計作品著稱。
immerge（浸入）和 emerge（出現） / issue（冒出） / emanate（發出）	immerge 表示「跳入、沒入、消失」。	He immerged the film in developer.	他將膠卷浸入顯影液中。
	emerge 表示「出現（出於某種原因）」。	The whale emerged from the ocean depths.	鯨魚從海洋深處冒出來。
	issue 表示「走出、流出」。	Lava issued from the volcano.	熔岩從火山中噴發出來。
	emanate 表示「來自某個來源」。	The idea emanated from a discussion we had.	那意念出自我們的一次討論。

易混淆字詞	註釋	例句	譯文
immigrant 和 emigrant（移民）	immigrant 表示「從外國遷入的移民」。	Toronto has many **immigrants** from Hong Kong.	多倫多有許多香港移民。
	emigrant 表示「一個離開自己的國家定居在另一個國家的移民」。	Hong Kong **emigrants** scattered to many countries, such as the UK, the US, Australia, Canada and so forth.	香港移民散居於許多國家，例如英國、美國、澳洲、加拿大等如此類推。
imperial（帝國的）和 imperious（迫切的）/ imperative（絕對必要的）	imperial 表示「一個非常好或宏偉的帝國」。	The **imperial** Roman army hardly ever lost a battle.	羅馬帝國的軍隊幾乎戰無不勝。
	imperious 表示「緊迫的」。	There is an **imperious** need for food in this stricken area.	這個災區急需食物。
	imperative 表示「必不可少」。	It is **imperative** for you to be on time.	您必須準時到達。
impetuous（輕舉妄動的）和 impetus（動力）	impetuous 是形容詞，意思是「匆忙完成」。	Don't be so **impetuous**!	別那麼浮躁，不要輕舉妄動！
	impetus 是名詞，意思是「動力」。	That prize gave him the **impetus** to work harder.	那個獎項使他有了努力工作的動力。
impressive（嚴肅的）和 formidable（可怕的）	impressive 表示「莊重、動人」。	The funeral was an **impressive** ceremony.	葬禮是一個嚴肅的儀式。
	formidable 表示「令人畏懼」。	This candidate is a **formidable** opponent.	這個候選人是一個強大的對手。
impulse（衝動）和 inspiration（鼓舞）	impulse 表示「突然想做某事而沒有考慮後果的慾望」。	I cannot resist the **impulse** to write you again.	我忍不住要再次寫信給你。
	inspiration 表示「創造力的來源」。	I hope your trip will provide **inspiration** for the essay you will have to write when you get back.	我希望這次旅行會為你回來時要寫的文章提供靈感。
inapt / unapt 和 inept（不適當的）	inapt 表示「不適合、沒有才能或能力」。	He is **inapt** for public speaking.	他沒有公開演講的才能。
	unapt 表示「不適合；不太可能，沒有處置，學習不快」。	He was an **unapt** student in a famous 'Band One' secondary school, but now he has got a first degree honour.	他曾在一等中學名校跟不上學習進度，但現在他獲得了一級榮譽學位。
	inept 表示「不熟練或有效」。	He was always rather **inept** at sports.	他在運動方面總是相當無能。

易混淆字詞	註釋	例句	譯文
incident（事故）和 accident（意外）/ event（事件）/ incidence（發生）	incident 表示「發生的事情；不太重要但不是值得高興的事情；在政治上，特指引起國際爭端或戰爭的事件」。	There are several **incidents** on the frontier between China and India.	中國和印度之間的邊境地區發生了幾件事。
	accident 表示「不幸的意外事故」。	An old woman was knocked down in a car **accident** this morning.	今早一個老婦在一宗交通意外中被車撞倒了。
	event 表示「發生的事情，通常是重要的事情」。	Graduation from the University is an **event**.	大學畢業是一件大事。
	incidence 表示「某事的影響程度、範圍、負擔」。	What is the **incidence** of poverty among women?	婦女陷入貧困的機率是多少？
increase（增加）和 improve（改善）/ promote（晉升）	increase 表示「變得或使（某物）數量或程度更大」。	As their profits **increase**, the companies expand.	隨着利潤增加，公司也正在擴張。
	improve 表示「成為或使（某事）變得更好」。	We can **improve** the economic situation by working harder.	我們可以更努力工作來改善經濟狀況。
	promote 表示「晉升（某人）職位或等級」。	He was **promoted** to Manager last month.	他上個月被晉升為經理。
incredible（難以置信的）和 incredulous（表示懷疑的）/ impossible（不可能的）	incredible 表示「不可能或很難相信」。	Marcus told us an **incredible** story about his grandma, aged 95, who caught three robbers two weeks' ago.	馬克斯向我們講述了一個令人難以置信的故事，他 95 歲的外婆兩週前捉住了三名劫匪。
	incredulous 表示「懷疑；不願意或不輕易相信某事」。	He is **incredulous** of the news.	他對這個消息不以為然。
	impossible 表示「很難處理」。	Honestly, you're **impossible** at times!	老實說，有時候你很難侍候！
indiscrete（不分開的）和 indiscreet（輕率的）	indiscrete 表示「非由不同部份組成」。	Creation of the world is said to have begun with **indiscrete** chaos.	據說世界的創造是從渾沌狀態開始的。
	indiscreet 表示「不得體、不明智」。	His **indiscreet** remarks have made many enemies.	他輕率的言論使許多人成為他的敵人。
indignity 和 insult（侮辱）	indignity 表示「使人感到尊嚴受損的行為」。	The employer subjected us trouble makers—as they claimed, to all sorts of **indignities**.	那僱主待我們如他們所聲稱的滋事份子，作出冒犯我們的行為。
	insult 表示「冒犯的言語或行為」。	To call a brave man a coward is an **insult**.	把一個勇敢的人稱為懦夫是一種侮辱。

易混淆字詞	註釋	例句	譯文
industrial（工業的）和 industrious（勤懇的）	industrial 表示「屬於或與工業有關」。	China has become an **industrial** country.	中國已經成為一個工業大國。
	industrious 表示「勤奮」。	The child is intelligent and **industrious**.	這個孩子聰明勤奮。
infectious 和 contagious（疾病傳染的）	infectious 表示「通過大氣或水中攜帶的細菌傳播」。	COVID-19 is an **infectious** disease.	新冠肺炎是一種傳染病。
	contagious 表示「通過接觸傳播」。	Colds are **contagious**.	感冒具有傳染性。
infer（推斷）和 imply / insinuate / intimate（暗示）	infer 表示「根據現有證據推論」。它只是將含義讀入尚未明確說明的陳述中：在字裏行間閱讀。	Since he was a farmer, we **inferred** that he got up early.	因他是農夫，我們推斷他起得早。
	imply 表示「暗含」。它在沒有明確說明的情況下暗示某事：通常是負面的。	Are you **implying** that I am a liar?	你在暗示我說謊嗎？
	insinuate 表示「以令人不快的方式暗示」。	He **insinuated** that she was lying.	他暗示她在撒謊。
	intimate 表示「點出但不說明某事」。	Her smile **intimates** that she'll accept his invitation.	她的笑容暗示她會接受他的邀請。
inflammatory（煽動性的）和 inflammable（易燃的）	inflammatory 表示「引起憤怒，傾向使人發怒」。	The speaker's **inflammatory** remarks almost started a riot.	講者煽動性的言論幾乎引發一場騷亂。
	inflammable 表示「容易着火」。	Be careful! Petrol is highly **inflammable**.	小心！汽油是高度易燃的。
ingenious（機敏的）和 ingenuous（天真的）	ingenious 表示「聰明或熟練」。	Thomas Edison was an **ingenious** inventor.	譚馬士・愛迪生是一位聰明的發明家。
	ingenuous 表示「坦率、簡單」。	I could hardly believe him as I was not young and **ingenuous**.	由於我不年輕和天真，所以我簡直不敢相信他。
inhabit（居住於）和 occupy（佔有）/ live（居住）	inhabit 表示「（通常用被動式）住在一個地方或地區，尤其是長期或永久的」。	The island is mainly **inhabited** by sheep.	島上主要是綿羊居住。
	occupy 表示「在一段時間之內居住或使用房間、房屋或建築物」。	The flat below was **occupied** by a young American couple.	下層住在一對年輕的美國夫婦。
	live 表示「居住」。	We **live** in a small flat in Chai Wan.	我們住在柴灣一個小單位裏。

易混淆字詞	註釋	例句	譯義
insist 和 persist（堅持）/ resist（抵抗）	insist 表示「堅持說或反對；或堅持認為或要求」。	She **insists** on coming with me.	她堅持要和我一起去。
	persist 表示「儘管遇到困難或反對，仍不放棄做某事」。	I **persisted** in consulting the dictionary while reading this novel.	我堅持在讀這本小說時查字典。
	resist 表示「抵抗、抗擊」。	He tried in vain to **resist** arrest.	他試圖拒絕逮捕，但徒勞無功。
insolate（暴曬）和 insulate（絕緣）	insolate 表示「在猛烈陽光中曝曬」。	Don't **insolate** yourself at noon.	不要在中午曬太陽。
	insulate 表示「用非導電材料覆蓋以防止電流通過」。	All electric wires must be **insulated**.	所有電線都必須絕緣。
inspect 和 examine（檢查）/ investigate（調查）/ see（看）	inspect 表示「仔細檢查，尋找可能存在的錯誤」。	Someone from the Education Bureau is coming to **inspect** the school next week.	下週，教育局有人來學校檢查。
	examine 表示「仔細看，旨在斷定事實，了解本質、特點或狀況」。我們常將 examine 與健康問題結合使用。	The doctor **examined** the patient with great care.	醫生非常仔細地檢查了病人。
	investigate 表示「對某事或某人的狀況等進行調查」。	The SFC is **investigating** his company relating insider trading.	證監會正在調查他的公司關於內幕交易。
	see 表示「用眼看、造訪」。	Many clients have come to **see** our new office.	許多客戶到我們的新辦公室來。
instance / case 和 example（例子）	instance 着重於個別具體事例，不一定有代表性，強調事實，支持一般真理的例子。	Going through a stop sign is an **instance** of his recklessness.	有停車標誌而不停車是他魯莽駕駛的一個例子。
	case 表示「某種事實、事件、情形發生的事例」。	It is a case of stupidity, not **dishonesty**.	那是件愚蠢行為，而不是欺詐行為。
	example 表示「典型的某物的一部份，用來代表其餘部份的例子」。	Give an **example** of what you mean.	舉個例子說說你的意思。
instigate（教唆）和 encourage（鼓勵）	instigate 表示「慫恿，常含貶義，因其教唆的行為通常是錯誤的」。	She **instigated** the man to disobey orders.	她慫恿那男子違背命令。
	encourage 表示「給予希望、勇氣或信心，旨讓某人繼續努力做某事，含褒義」。	The father **encouraged** his son to study harder.	父親鼓勵他的兒子努力學習。

易混淆字詞	註釋	例句	譯文
instil（灌輸）和 inspire（激勵）	instil 表示「循序漸進地灌輸」。	The habit of punctuality was **instilled** into me early in my life.	年幼時我就受教育要養成守時的習慣。
	inspire 表示「激起某人的想法、感覺或目標，使他能投入」。	The speech **inspired** every listener with new courage.	那演講激起了每個聽眾新的勇氣。
intend（計劃）和 tend（傾向）	**intend** 表示「計劃做某事」。	I **intend** to arrive early and make sure that I get a seat.	我打算提早到達，並確保我有位坐下來。
	tend 表示「在大多數情況下是可能或正確的」。	At that age, girls **tend** to be more mature than boys.	在那個年齡，女孩比男孩更成熟。
intense（強烈的）和 intensive（集中的）	**intense** 表示「強烈的或非常好；極端的」。	You will face **intense** competition in applying for governmental jobs.	在申請政府工作時，您將面臨激烈的競爭。
	intensive 表示「集中；深入而徹底」。	The US government has embarked on an **intensive** study of Coronavirus disease.	美國政府已着手對新冠狀病毒疾病進行深入研究。
interior 和 internal（內部的）	**interior** 表示「在建築物、房間、車輛等內部」。	The **interior** doors are still sound but the exterior doors need replacing.	內邊門仍然完好，但外邊門需要更換。
	internal 表示「涉及特定國家／地區內發生的事情」。	Each country has the right to control its own **internal** affairs.	每個國家都有權控制自己的內政。
interpret 和 explain（解釋）	**interpret** 表示「決定某物的意圖是甚麼，強調解釋者得思考過程和對事物的理解」。	The learned judge **interprets** the legislative motive of the ordinance.	博學的法官解釋該條例的立法動機。
	explain 表示「通過描述或提供有關信息來使別人不知道或不完全理解的事物加以說明」。	A dictionary tries to **explain** the meanings of words.	字典試圖解釋字的意義。
interrupt（打斷）和 disturb（擾亂）	**interrupt** 表示「說或做些事來制止某人說話或做某事」。	I'm sorry to **interrupt** but there's an urgent phone call for you.	很抱歉打擾你，但現在有一個緊急電話找您。
	disturb 表示「使某人難以繼續他們正在做的事情」。	The noise of the traffic **disturbs** the local residents.	交通的噪音打擾了當地居民。
interruption 和 break（中斷）	**interruption** 表示「突然阻止你繼續你正在做或說的事」。	To avoid further **interruption**, we locked the office door.	為避免進一步打擾，我們鎖上了辦公室的門。
	break 表示「短暫休息時期，可以暫停而自由做他們想做的事」。	Between the first two classes there is a ten-minute **break**.	前兩節課之間有十分鐘的休息時間。

易混淆字詞	註釋	例句	譯文
intolerable 和 intolerant（不能忍耐）	intolerable 表示「難以忍受，讓人受不了，多修飾物」。	The pain from the toothache was **intolerable**.	牙痛真令人無法忍受。
	intolerant 表示「不願忍受或接受，多修飾人」。	She is narrow-minded and **intolerant**.	她心胸狹窄，不寬容，缺乏耐性。
intransigent（不妥協的）和 intractable（難處理的）	intransigent 表示「拒絕達成任何協議」。	In the commercial dispute between the two firms, both remained **intransigent**.	在這宗商業糾紛裏，雙方都毫不妥協。
	intractable 表示「難以控制或管理」。	He solved an **intractable** problem.	他解決了一個棘手問題。
introduce（介紹）和 recommend（推薦）	introduce 表示「介紹某人與他人認識」。	She **introduced** her mother to her boyfriend in the company's annual dinner party.	她在公司的年度晚宴上介紹了男朋友給她母親認識。
	recommend 表示「推薦某人或物，表示支持」。	He **recommended** me this novel.	他向我推薦了這本小說。
invaluable（非常寶貴的）和 valueless（無價值的）	invaluable 表示「價值太大，無法估計」。	Honest and faithful friends are **invaluable** assets.	誠實和忠實的朋友是無價之寶
	valueless 表示「沒有價值」。	This ring, made of glass, is **valueless**.	這枚戒指由玻璃製成，毫無價值
invent（發明）和 discover（發現）	invent 表示「創建不存在的機器，儀器，系統等」。	Who **invented** the telephone?	電話是誰發明的
	discover 表示「第一次發現某些存在的但不為人知的東西」。	It will not be long before scientists **discover** a cure for this terrible disease.	不久之後，科學家們就會發現治癒這種可怕疾病的方法。
irreversible（不能逆轉的）和 irrevocable（不可撤銷的）	irreversible 表示「無法改變或逆轉，多指行動、行為方式」。	We regret that we have done something **irreversible**.	很遺憾我們做了一些不可逆轉的事。
	irrevocable 表示「不能廢止，不得召回」。	My banker has issued an **irrevocable** documentary credit in your favour.	我的銀行已經給你開出了一張不可撤銷的跟單信用證。
irruption 和 eruption（爆發）	irruption 表示「突然和暴力侵入，在生態方面，有增加之意」。	The **irruption** of violence was the main cause of political reforms.	暴力的侵入是政治改革的主要原因。
	eruption 表示「（火山、戰爭、疾病等）爆發」。	The volcano is in a state of **eruption**.	那火山正在噴發。

易混淆字詞	註釋	例句	譯文
jealousy 和 envy（妒忌）	jealousy 表示「害怕別人奪走自己的東西；渴望得到別人擁有的東西，帶有惡意」。	In a fit of **jealousy**, he tore up his friend's drawing.	由於嫉妒心發作，他撕下了他朋友的畫。
	envy 表示「對他人的好運或成功感到不滿」。	He was filled with **envy** at my success.	他妒忌我的成功。
jewellery 和 jewel（珠寶）/ jeweller's（珠寶商）	jewellery 是不可數名詞，表示「戒指、手鐲、項鍊、手錶等的總稱」。	The stolen **jewellery** has never been recovered.	被盜珠寶從未被追回。
	jewel 是可數名詞，表示「包含一個或多個寶石的佩戴裝飾品」。	She wears a ring set with a **jewel**.	她戴着鑲有寶石的戒指。
	jeweller's 表示「出售和修理珠寶的商店」。	I took the watch to my local **jeweller's** but they said it couldn't be repaired.	我把手錶帶到當地珠寶商那裏，但他們説無法修理。
join（連接）和 integrate（使成一體）	join 表示 put together or connect。	They **joined** the two islands with a bridge.	他們用橋把兩個島連在一起。
	integrate 表示「接合或加入其他東西以形成一個整體，合而為一」。	The committee tried to **integrate** the different plans.	該委員會試圖整合不同的計劃。
journey 和 travel / tour / voyage / trip（旅行）	journey 表示「一段距離的旅行，可指陸路、水上或空中旅行」。	We made the **journey** from Florida to Toronto by car.	我們乘車從佛羅里達州到達多倫多。
	travel 表示「不同目的地的旅行，尤其是到遙遠的地方，含遊歷之意」。	**Travel** is valuable because it gives us knowledge of foreign peoples.	旅行很有價值，因它可以使我們認識不同的外國人。
	tour 表示「到訪幾個名勝古蹟的旅程，指以觀光、視察、蜜月等為目的的旅行」。	We joined a guided **tour** round Hong Kong last Sunday.	上星期日我們參加了有導遊帶領的香港觀光團。
	voyage 表示「航行，尤其是指水上或空中漫長的旅程」。	She went on a long sea **voyage** from Hong Kong to Argentina.	她乘坐長途船從香港到阿根廷。
	trip 表示「任何方式的旅程，可以是一次愉快的遊覽或短途旅行」。	The **trip** was cancelled because of the typhoon.	這次旅行因颱風取消。

易混淆字詞	註釋	例句	譯文
jovial（風趣）和 jocular（詼諧）	jovial 表示「充滿幽默感，快樂」。	He seems to be in very jovial mood this morning.	今早他心情似乎特別愉快。
	jocular 表示「愛開玩笑、引人發笑的」。	Being in a jocular mood, the speaker told several amusing stories.	講者以開玩笑的心情，講了幾個逗人的故事。
joyous（使人高興）和 joyful（充滿歡樂）	joyous 表示「充滿或引起歡樂，通常指人或物本身具有快樂的特質」。	Their 50th wedding anniversary was a joyous occasion.	他們 50 週年的結婚紀念日是一件令人高興的大事。
	joyful 表示「滿心歡喜，通常由外來因素引起」。	He was joyful to see his brother again.	再次見到弟弟，他極為高興。
judicious（明智）和 judicial（司法的）	judicious 表示「展現智慧、有判斷力的，指任何理智、深思熟慮的決定或言行」。	The doctor's decision to operate proved to be judicious.	醫生決定做手術，結果證明是明智的。
	judicial 表示「法官或法院」。	The lawyers awaited the judicial decisions.	律師們在等待司法判決。
juncture 和 junction（結合處）	juncture 表示「事情的狀態或時機」。	At this juncture, we must decide whether to advance or retreat.	在這個關頭，我們必須決定前進還是後退。
	junction 表示「事物集結的地方」。	This railway station is a busy junction for lines from all over the country.	這個火車站是來自全國各條鐵路的集合處，車務非常繁忙。
junk 和 litter（廢物）/ rubbish（垃圾）	junk 表示「舊的、無價值或無用的東西」。	The room was full of old junk that hadn't been used for years.	房間裏堆滿了多年沒用過的廢物。
	litter 表示「棄置在公共場所的物品如塑膠袋、空汽水罐、煙頭等」。	If you are caught dropping litter in the street, you are fined.	在街上亂抛垃圾將被罰款。
	rubbish 表示「毫無用處，被扔掉的廢物」。	Please throw the rubbish out.	請把垃圾扔出去。

易混淆字詞	註釋	例句	譯文
know（明白）和 realize（意識到）/ care for（知道）/ learn（知悉）	know 表示「在記憶中清楚得知某一信息」，也指「掌握事實」。	My son knows three languages.	我兒子會三種語言。
	realize 表示「理解並明白某件事」。	Do you realize that you might catch a cold in your weakened condition?	您是否意識到身體虛弱可能會患上感冒？
	care for 表示「關心、重視，指關注人或事」。	He cares only for eating.	他只知道吃。
	learn 表示「聽見、被告知。」，常指通過他人獲得信息，強調「從不知到知的變化」。	Let's help each other and learn from each other.	讓我們互相幫助，互相學習。
laborious（費力的）和 hard-working（勤奮的）	laborious 表示「需要很大努力」。	I hate this job — it is so laborious and boring.	我討厭這份工作 —— 它既費力又枯燥。
	hard-working 表示「用功」。	He is a hard-working student and deserves to do well in his examination.	他是勤奮的學生，所以他考試成績好是理所當然的。
landscape 和 scenery（景致）/ scene（景象）/ view（景物）	landscape 表示「（風景、繪畫或照片上）看到大片土地，尤其是在農村」。	Having reached the top of the hill, we sat and admired the landscape that stretched far into the distance.	到達山頂後，我們坐下來欣賞遠處延伸着的景觀。
	scenery 表示「景色，通常指鄉村的自然特徵（丘陵、山谷、田野等）考慮到它們的美麗，尤其是從特定地方看到的那些」。	The scenery surrounding the village is really beautiful.	村莊周圍的風景真的很美。
	scene 表示「當你在一個地方時看到的，尤其是一些不尋常、令人震驚的景象，側重眼前的景象」。	He arrived by helicopter to witness a scene of total chaos.	他乘直升機抵達現場，目睹一片混亂。
	view 表示「可以從某位置看到整個區域，尤指看到很遠的景物」。	From the window, there was a beautiful view of the lake.	從窗戶可以看到美麗的湖景。
lane（小巷）和 path（路徑）	lane 表示「狹窄的道路或街道」。	We rode our bikes along the little country lanes.	我們沿着鄉村小道騎單車。
	path 表示「花園或公園裏供人步行的狹長小道」。	It was so dark in the park that she kept wandering from the path.	公園裏太黑了，她一直在小路上徘徊。

易混淆字詞	註釋	例句	譯義
last（最後的人或物）和 later（後來）/ latter（後者）/ latest（最新的）/ updated（更新的）/ ultimate（最後的）	last 是代詞，意思是「最後的東西」。	He was the last off the ship.	他是最後一個下船。
	later 是比較式形容詞或副詞，意思是「較晚」。	Later this year I'm going to Canada.	今年晚些時候我打算去加拿大。
	latter 是代詞，意思是「剛才提到兩個中的第二個」。	He mentioned it in the latter part of his speech.	他演講的後半部分提到這點。
	latest 是比較式最高級形容詞或副詞，表示「設計 / 製作 / 出版等比其他任何東西都更近、更新」。	As a dress designer, I am very interested in the latest fashions.	作為一名服裝設計師，我對最新的時裝很感興趣。
	updated 表示「擁有並包括最新的知識、信息、發明等」。	This version is no good. I need an updated one.	這個版本不好。我需要更新的版本。
	ultimate 表示「最後、根本的」。	The ultimate cause of some diseases is unknown.	某些病的致病原因仍未知道。
late（晚）/ lately（近來）和 recently（最近）/ just（剛剛）	late 表示「晚、遲」。	Last night I went to bed late.	昨晚我很晚才睡。
	lately 表示「不久前一段時間，還可表示一點時間」。	Have you seen Sam lately?	你最近見過阿森嗎？
	recently 表示「不久之前已開始的時間段」。	I heard he went abroad recently.	聽說他最近出國了。
	just 表示「剛才、就在不久之前」。	My son has just left school.	我兒子剛從學校畢業。
lay / put（放）和 lie（躺）	lay（lays, laying, laid, lald）表示「放置；將某人或物置於特定位置」。	Please lay a cloth on the table.	請鋪布在桌面。
	put（put, putting, put, put）表示「把東西移到某地方，然後留在那裏」。	Put the chair near the table.	把椅子放在桌旁。
	lie（lies, lying, lay, lain），表示「躺下；在上面平放」。	The book has been lying on the table for two days.	這書已在桌面放了兩天。

易混淆字詞	註釋	例句	譯文
lazy 和 idle（懶惰的）	lazy 表示「不喜歡和迴避功課或工作，有責備之意」。	He failed in the final exam because he was too **lazy** to revise.	他期末考試不及格，因為他懶得溫習。
	idle 表示「無事可做，並無貶義」。	Because of the delay in the arrival of supplies, the work crew was **idle** for seven hours.	由於貨物延遲送到，工人閒待了七個小時。
legal（法律的）和 legitimate（合法的）	legal 表示「屬於或與法律有關的；符合法規和普通法的要求」。	She even denied the **legal** right of the people to hold such meeting.	她甚至否認人民有舉行這種集會的合法權利。
	legitimate 表示「合法、合理、符合禮儀風俗、傳統習慣或邏輯推理」。	Sickness is a **legitimate** reason for a child's being absent from school.	生病是孩子不上課的合理原因。
legible 和 readable（可讀、易辨認的）	legible 表示「可以閱讀，但沒有 readable 的意義」。	Marty's handwriting is very **legible**.	馬蒂的手寫字體非常清晰。
	readable 表示「有趣或易於閱讀」。	This is the most **readable** novel I have come across in weeks.	這是幾週來我讀過最有趣的小説。
lengthen（延長）和 prolong（拖延）/ extend（延伸）	lengthen 表示「長度變得更長，不包括寬度」。	As evening fell, the shadows **lengthened**.	黃昏時，影子變長了。
	prolong 表示「防止一種感覺、活動或生命結束」。	The question is whether doctors should **prolong** life when there is no hope of recovery.	問題是在沒有康復希望的情況下，醫生應否延長生命。
	extend 表示「做更長或更大，着重指延伸、擴大，以超過目前的範圍」。	There is a proposal to **extend** the road to the next village.	有一個提議是將這條路延伸到下一個村莊。
lessen 和 reduce（減少）	lessen 主要用於「與疼痛和感覺有關」。	I'll give you an injection to **lessen** the pain.	我會給你打支針來減輕痛楚。
	reduce 表示「在數量、價格或尺寸上製造更小的東西」。	The best solution is to **reduce** the amount of traffic entering the Central District.	最好的解決辦法是減少進入中區的交通量。
let（讓）和 leave（不要理……）	let 表示「讓、允許」。	**Let** her alone, or she'll be angry.	不要理她，否則她會發火。
	leave 表示「使繼續處於某種狀態」。	**Leave** the children alone, please.	請不要管那些孩子。

易混淆字詞	註釋	例句	譯文
lightning（閃電）和 lightening（放亮）	lightning 表示「由大氣中的放電引起的閃光」。	The hen house was struck by **lightning** last night.	雞舍昨晚被閃電擊中。
	lightening 表示「變得更亮的狀態」。	It was nearly dawn, and the sky was **lightening**.	黎明來了，天空開始放亮。
like（像⋯⋯）/ such as（例如）和 namely（就是⋯⋯）	like（連詞）表示「相似」，用於介紹兩個項目或兩人之間的相似性。	**Like** any politician, he often told half-truths.	像任何政治家一樣，他說話經常半真半假。
	such as（＋名詞）指「與」具有相同特徵或質量，用於列舉作用。	Young boys **such as** Alfred and William are very friendly.	像阿爾弗德和威廉這樣的年輕男孩非常友善。
	namely（副詞）表示「那是、就是、分別是」。	He knows six languages, **namely**, Chinese, French, English, Portuguese, Spanish and Japanese.	他懂六種語言，分別是中文、法文、英文、葡萄牙文、西班牙文和日文。
little（小到幾乎無）和 small（細小）	little 表示「體積小、數量少、程度低等；常用於數量少到幾乎沒有；也用於帶有感情色彩而含否定意思。	He has **little** knowledge of the difficulties involved.	他不大了解所涉及的困難。
	small 表示「數量或規模不大；不多」，通常用來形容某人或某物的大小，含肯定意思，不帶有感情色彩。	His parents died when he was still a **small** child.	他還是小孩時父母就去世了。
literal（文字上的）和 literary（文學上的）/ literate（有學問的）	literal 表示「字面義，是一個詞的基本或通常的含義」。	A **literal** translation is not always the closest to the original meaning.	直譯總不是最接近原文意思的。
	literary 表示「與文學、詩歌、小說和故事有關的」。	He is a **literary** professor.	他是一位文學教授。
	literate 表示「會讀會寫、受過教育的」。	He is an educated and **literate** young man.	他是一個受過教育和有文化的年輕人。
locate 和 find（找到）	locate 表示「找到的地方或位置」。	Can you **locate** your seat in the dining table?	能找到你用餐的座位嗎？
	find 表示「找回丟失、隱藏或未知的人或物」。	I can't **find** my gold watch.	我找不到我的金錶。

易混淆字詞	註釋	例句	譯文
loose（鬆開的）和 lose（遺失）	loose 是形容詞，意思是「不緊」。	Athletes prefer loose clothing for exercise.	運動員更喜歡穿寬鬆的衣服進行鍛煉。
	lose 是一個動詞，表示「找不到，具有誤入歧途、跟不上、遭受剝奪等含義。	He frequently loses his car keys.	他經常丟失汽車鑰匙。
luxury（奢侈）和 luxurious（奢侈的）/ luxuriant（繁茂的）	luxury 是不可數名詞，表示「你不需要的東西」。	Consumers are offered more and more luxury goods.	向消費者提供越來越多的奢侈品。
	luxurious 表示「非常舒服、很貴的」。	The car's soft cream leather interior was extremely luxurious.	這汽車奶油色的軟皮裝飾極度奢華。
	luxuriant 表示「生長強勁、豐富的」。	He is a man with luxuriant beard.	他是留大鬍子的男人。
machine（機械）和 engine（引擎）/ motor（電動機）	machine 表示「執行有用工作的設備，例如縫紉機、洗衣機或電腦」。	To operate this machine, simply select the type of coffee you require and press the green button.	要操作本機，只需選擇你要的咖啡類型並按下綠色按鈕。
	engine 表示「為機動車輛、火車、飛機等提供動力的裝置」。	Over eighty per cent of these cars are old, and so are their engines.	這些汽車 80% 以上是舊的，它們的發動機也一樣舊。
	motor 表示「將電能轉化為動力的機器部件」。	My video camera isn't working. Either the battery is flat or there's something wrong with the motor.	我的攝錄機壞了。不是電池沒電，就是電機有問題。
magnet（磁鐵）和 magnate（大亨）	magnet 表示「磁鐵；也可指吸引（人）的人或事物」。	The actor was the magnet that drew great audiences.	那演員磁鐵般地吸引了大批觀眾。
	magnate 表示「一個富有或有權力的人」。	He is a real estate magnate.	他是一位地產大亨。
mandatary（受托人）和 mandatory（強制性的）	mandatary 表示「被授權的人」。	The Legislative counsellor regards himself as mandatary of his constituents.	立法會議員把自己看作選民的受托人。
	mandatory 表示「必須這樣做 / 如此」。	The employers have the obligation to contribute Mandatory Provident Funds for their employees.	僱主有責任為其僱員提供強制性公積金。

易混淆字詞	註釋	例句	譯義
marriage（婚姻）和 wedding（婚禮）	marriage 表示「從法律角度考慮的男女結合關係或狀態」。	Her parents are against their **marriage**.	她父母反對他們結婚。
	wedding 表示「舉行結婚儀式的場合以及隨之而來的慶祝活動」。	Why didn't you invite me to your **wedding**?	你為甚麼不邀請我參加你們的婚禮？
material（材料）和 materialistic（物質主義的）/ matter（物質）	material 表示「製造物品的具體材料或原料」。	When building **materials** cost more, the price of houses increases.	當建材成本增加時，房價就會上漲。
	materialistic 表示「相信金錢能買到的東西比甚麼都重要」。	In today's **materialistic** society, most people think only about money.	在當今物慾橫流的社會裏，大多數人只想着錢。
	matter 表示「構成一切有形物的物質或某類物質」。	The entire universe is made up of different kinds of **matter**.	全宇宙是由不同物質組成的。
maybe 和 perhaps（或者）/ probably（也許）	maybe 表示「或者、也許；主要用於非正式語體，如口語」。	**Maybe** you should see a doctor.	也許你應該去看醫生。
	perhaps 表示「或者、也許；主要用於所有語體（正式和非正式，如書面語和口語），可能性大致對半，含有不確定因素」。	**Perhaps** this helps to explain why there are so many divorces.	也許這有助解釋為甚麼會有這麼多離婚。
	probably 表示「可能、也許，有較大可能性，有幾分根據的推測，含有主觀意願的因素」。	**Probably** she will win this time.	估計她這次可能會贏。
measure（措施）和 measurement（測量）	measure 表示「旨在產生特定效果的行動；法律或裁決」。	In my opinion, the authorities have to take even stricter **measures** to save our archaeological treasures.	在我看來，當局必須採取更嚴格的措施來保護考古文物。
	measurement 表示「某物的長度、寬度等」。	You can't buy new curtains without knowing the window **measurements**.	你不能在不知道窗戶尺寸的情況下購買新窗簾。
meat 和 flesh（肉）	meat 表示「作為食物的食用肉」。	Did you have **meat** or fish for dinner?	你晚餐吃肉還是魚？
	flesh 表示「人或動物身上的肉」。	There was hardly any **flesh** left on the starved body, just skin and bones.	餓死的人身體上幾乎沒有肉，只剩下皮膚和骨頭。

易混淆字詞	註釋	例句	譯文
mediate（調解）和 arbitrate（仲裁）	mediate 表示「充當中間人向爭論的雙方提出解決建議，但不會作出裁決」。	The United Nation is trying to mediate（in the dispute）between these two countries.	聯合國正試圖調解這兩個國家的爭端。
	arbitrate 表示「公斷，仲裁者聽取在競爭或對立的雙方意見之後，做出結論和裁決，具有權威性」	The United Nations will try to arbitrate in the international dispute.	聯合國正試圖仲裁這兩個國家的爭端。
medicine 和 chemical / drug（藥品）	medicine 表示「為預防或治癒疾病的藥品」。	What kind of medicine are you taking?	你在吃甚麼藥？
	chemical 表示「通過化學過程使用或製造的化學藥品，通常與農藥連用」。	These insects can't be killed without agricultural chemicals.	如果沒有農藥，這些昆蟲是無法殺死的。
	drug 表示「危險的藥品，如麻醉藥或毒品」。	Be careful you don't become addicted to drugs.	小心不要吸毒成癮。
medium（中間）和 average（平均）	medium 表示「不大不小，不高不矮，等等」。	The waiter was of medium height and walked with a slight limp.	那侍應生中等個子，走路時有些微跛。
	average 表示「通過將一組數量相加，然後將此總數除以該組中的數量來計算」。	The average score was about 53 out of 100.	平均分數約為 53 分（滿分 100 分）。
memory（記憶）/ recollection（回憶）和 souvenir（紀念品）/ memoirs（傳記）	memory 表示「記得某人或事，尤指很久以前的經歷」。	Although I haven't seen her for years, her face is still engraved on my memory.	我雖然多年未見她，但她的容顏依然深深印在我的腦海內。
	recollection 表示「着重經過思考才想起已遺忘的人或事」。	The old birthday cards brought many recollections of my parents.	這些昔日的生日賀卡勾起我對父母的許多回憶。
	souvenir 表示「在特定地方（尤指度假期間）購買或獲得的東西，可作為追憶」。	Each visitor received a small gift as a souvenir.	每位參觀者都會收到一份小禮物作為紀念品。
	memoirs 指「某人對其生活（某時期）的書面記錄」。	The former President's long awaited memoirs are to be published next month.	這位前總統期待已久的回憶錄將於下個月出版。

易混淆字詞	註釋	例句	譯義
menace 和 threaten（威脅）	menace 是名詞或形容詞，表示「試圖讓某人感到生命或安全極受威脅」。	<u>As a noun</u> These street gangs are a social **menace**. <u>As an adjective</u> He was convicted of **menacing** behaviour.	作為名詞 這些街頭幫派是一種社會威脅。 作為形容詞 因為犯有威脅行為的罪行，他被判刑了。
	threaten 表示「對和平、生存、安全、健康、幸福等事物的威脅」。	Nowadays world peace is **threatened**.	當今世界和平受到威脅。
mend（修理）和 amend（修改）/ emend（校訂）/ repair（修補）/ patch（補釘）	mend 表示「修理結構簡單的東西，例如屋頂、柵欄、手錶、收音機、照相機等」。	Once you've **mended** the kettle, we can have a cup of tea.	一旦你修好了水壺，我們就可以喝杯茶了。
	amend 表示「對語言通過加、刪、改等方法使其變得更好」。	He **amended** the speech by making some additions and deletions.	他通過增刪修改講稿。
	emend 表示「以找出文中錯處為目的之修改」。	He has **emended** the text of his book.	他校訂了書中的文字。
	repair 表示「使損壞結構複雜的大型物件恢復正常操作，需要一定技能」。	Old cars are easier to **repair**.	舊車更容易修理。
	patch 表示「在洞或裂縫貼上材料填補」。	The poor **patch** old clothes because they can't afford to buy new ones.	窮等人家因買不起新衣服而縫補舊衣服。
mental 和 spiritual（精神上的）/ spirituous（含酒精的）	mental 表示「影響或發生在腦中的」。	People who have had **mental** illnesses are often unwilling to talk about them.	患精神病的人不願意談論病情。
	spiritual 表示「與一個人的精神有關，而不是身體的」。	Modern society provides us with material comforts but very few **spiritual** rewards.	現代社會為我們提供了物質享受，而精神上的回報卻很少。
	spirituous 表示「含有酒精的」。	Please note that no **spirituous** beverage will be served in the reception.	請注意，招待會上不提供含酒精的飲料。

易混淆字詞	註釋	例句	譯文
migrate（移居）和 emigrate（移民）/ immigrate（移入）	migrate 表示「(鳥類或動物) 季節性遷徙，特別是尋找食物、水、溫暖的天氣等；(人們) 短期或定期移居」。	How do birds know when to **migrate** and how do they find their way back home?	鳥類如何知道何時遷徙以及如何找到回家的路呢？
	emigrate 表示「(人們) 離開自己的地區，到另一地區定居」。	If we can't earn our living here, we'll have to **emigrate**.	我們如果在這裏無法謀生，將不得不移民到別的國家去。
	immigrate 指從外地移入自己的地區。	His parents **immigrated** at the age of 20 and they've never left Hong Kong since.	他父母在二十歲時移居香港，至今他們再沒有離開過。
mimic（以模仿來取樂）和 imitate（仿效……的行為）	mimic 表示「複製 (某人或物)，尤指讓人開懷大笑」。	He **mimicked** his uncle's voice and gestures very cleverly.	他模仿叔叔的聲音和姿態，惟肖惟妙。
	imitate 表示「仿效行為，以身作則」。	You should **imitate** your father's way of helping people.	你應該效法你父親幫助他人的方式。
misplace（誤放）和 displace（移動）/ display（顯示）	misplace 表示「放錯了地方」。	I'm afraid that I've **misplaced** your letter, but I'll try hard to find it.	恐怕我把你的信放錯了地方，不過我會嘗試努力找到它。
	displace 表示「把某物 (通常是固體) 從原地永久移開」。	The flood **displaced** every structure in that section of the town.	洪水沖毀了鎮上那地區的所有建築物。
	display 表示「顯示，表現」。	Department stores **display** their goods in the windows.	百貨公司在櫥窗內陳列他們的商品。
mist 和 fog（霧）	mist 表示「空氣中的微小水滴使人難以看清遠處事物」。	As the day wore on, the early morning **mist** quickly disappeared.	一天的清晨隨着時間流逝，薄霧很快便消失了。
	fog 表示「很濃的霧」。	Her flight was held up on account of the **fog**.	她乘坐的航班因大霧而延遲起飛。
mistaken（弄錯的）和 wrong（錯誤的）	mistaken 表示「理解錯誤」。	If you thought she intended to be rude, you are **mistaken**.	你如果認為她故意無禮，那你就錯了。
	wrong 表示「不正確」。	I found several **wrong** answers in your test paper.	我發現你的試卷有幾個錯誤答案。

易混淆字詞	註釋	例句	譯文
mobile（動的）和 movable（能動的）	mobile 表示「能夠移動，對衝動和情緒作出反應，含主動意義」。	Although the player was badly injured, he was still **mobile**.	雖然這名運動員受了重傷，但他還能動。
	movable 表示「可以移動，可以重新排列，含被動意義」。	This statue is heavy but **movable**.	這尊鑄像很重，但可以移動。
moment（片刻）和 instant（即刻）/ minute（一會）	moment 表示「一段非常短暫的時間，但持續的時間可以清楚地意識到」。	I saw him for a **moment**, and then I lost sight of him in the crowd.	我看了他一眼，然後在人羣裏再也見不到他。
	instant 表示「一段非常短的時間，多用於表示迫切、瞬變、迅疾等，無法計量」。	In an **instant**, the snake vanished.	一利那間，蛇不見了。
	minute 表示「很短時間，雖短但可以計量」。	I'll be ready in a **minute**.	我馬上就準備好。
mood 和 atmosphere（氣氛）	mood 表示「情緒」，指「某人處於某種心境，例如高興、生氣等」。	The streets were full of people in a holiday **mood**.	滿街的人都充滿節日氣氛。
	atmosphere 表示「一個地方給你的總體印象」。	The hotel offers a friendly **atmosphere** and personal service.	那酒店提供了友好氛圍和人性化服務。
much 和 many（許多的）/ numerous（眾多的）	much 是形容詞，用於不可數名詞，表示「量和度」。	There isn't **much** traffic today	今天交通流量不多。
	many 是形容詞，用於複數可數名詞，也可用作代詞，表示「很多」。	<u>As adjective</u> I have **many** books. <u>As pronoun</u> **Many** of us were too tired to go further.	<u>用作形容詞</u> 我有許多書。 <u>用作代詞</u> 我們當中許多人都太累，再也走不動。
	numerous 是形容詞，表示「數量很多」。	I spoke to him about it on **numerous** occasions.	我在很多場合和他談過這件事。

易混淆字詞	註釋	例句	譯文
murder（謀殺）/ assassinate（暗殺）/ kill（殺死）和 homicide（殺人）/ manslaughter（誤殺）	murder 可以是名詞或動詞，表示「殺戮，指故意非法殺人」。	As noun The jury unanimously agreed that she has committed an offence of **murder**. As verb He **murdered** his friend in order to get the gold.	用作名詞 陪審團一致認為她犯了謀殺罪。 用作動詞 他謀殺了自己的朋友以奪取那批黃金。
	assassinate 是動詞，表示「行刺」。	John Kennedy, the famous US president, was **assassinated** in 1963.	美國著名總統約翰甘乃迪於 1963 年遇刺身亡。
	kill 是動詞表示「殺、使致死，泛指任何致死的行為或事實，不僅可指人，也可指動物、植物或其他可致命的東西」。	The COVID-19 **killed** many people in the whole world.	新冠疫病在全球造成許多人死亡。
	homicide 是名詞表示「殺人，可有意或無意」。	**Homicide** is not criminal when committed in self-defence.	自衛殺人不是刑事罪行。
	manslaughter 是名詞，表示「過失殺人，指毫無預謀地奪走人的生命」。	The careless driver responsible for the accident was charged with **manslaughter**.	導致意外那個粗心大意的司機被控誤殺。
must（必須）和 should（應該）	**must** 表示「不得不；通常指有法律或規則限制你不能自由決定」。	Candidates **must** answer all the questions in Part A and two questions in Part B.	考生必須回答 A 部分的所有問題和 B 部分的兩條問題。
	should 表示「應該；通常指有人建議你做某事但隨你自行決定時」。	Before the end of the examination, you **should** check your answers.	考試結束前，你應該檢查答案。
mutual（相互之間的）和 common（共同的）/ reciprocal（相互的）	**mutual** 表示「互相依存的關係，指一個人與另一個人有相同感覺或意見」。	I don't like her, and I think the feeling is **mutual**.	我不喜歡她，我認為她也不喜歡我。
	common 表示「共有關係，所有人共同享有」。	The married couple share a **common** property.	那對夫婦共同分享一個物業。
	reciprocal 表示「互惠的」，涉及兩人同意互相以相同方式對待對方。	The divorced couple had a **reciprocal** arrangement — each would be responsible for taking care of their children in alternate week.	那對離婚夫婦有一個互惠安排 —— 每人隔週照顧孩子。

易混淆字詞	註釋	例句	譯文
naked（裸體的）和 strip（脫衣）/ nude（裸露的）	naked 是形容詞，表示「不穿衣服的」。	The labourers constructing the road were naked to the waist.	修路工人光着上身。
	strip 是動詞，表示「從身上取下、拉動或撕下覆蓋物，例如衣服」。	The actors were told to strip to the waist.	那些男演員被告知要光着上身。
	nude 是形容詞，表示「沒穿衣服」。	The nude statue caused considerable comment.	那裸體雕像引起了相當大的反響。
narration（講述）和 narrative（故事）	narration 指「敘述、講故事」。	She interrupted his narration to say that tea was ready.	她打斷了他的敘述，說茶已經準備好了。
	narrative 指「一個故事」。	His trip through the world made an interesting narrative.	他環遊世界之旅是個有趣故事。
narrow（窄）和 shrink（縮水）	narrow 是動詞，表示「（道路、河流等）變得不那麼寬」。	Just beyond the bend, the river begins to narrow.	剛過彎道，河流開始變窄。
	shrink（尤其是布料）表示「由於被弄濕或放入水中而變小」。	After washing, the cloth shrank.	洗完後，布縮了水。
neglect（疏忽）和 negligence（大意）	neglect 可以是名詞或動詞，表示「缺乏關心和關注；指忽略工作或應負的責任」。	As noun The physician was accused of neglect of his duties. As verb Don't neglect your own health while you are studying hard.	用作名詞 那內科醫生因疏忽職守而受到指控。 用作動詞 在努力學習的同時，不要忽視自己的健康。
	negligence 表示「不注意；指人或團體疏忽工作或責任」。	Many accidents in industry are caused by negligence.	許多工業意外都是因疏忽導致的。
negligible（不重要的）和 negligent（粗心大意的）	negligible 表示「（數量）少到沒有影響」。	The cut on my finger is negligible.	我手指上的傷口並不嚴重。
	negligent 表示「粗心、未能妥善處理工作」。	The court decided that the bank was negligent of its duty.	法院裁定該銀行疏忽職守。
never（從不）和 not（沒有）/ no（決不）	never 表示「從來或將來不會」。	I never get a holiday.	我從來沒有獲得假期。
	not 表達「否定」。	I did not see him at all yesterday.	我昨天根本沒有見過他。
	no 是形容詞，意思是「不是」。	He is no financial expert.	他不是金融專家。

易混淆字詞	註釋	例句	譯文
noise（噪音）和 sound（聲音）/ voice（嗓音）	noise 表示「一種響亮的、令人不快的聲音」。	The noise of the traffic gave me a headache.	交通噪音令我頭痛。
	sound 表示「耳朵聽到或接收到的東西」。	He was woken up by the sound of broken glass.	玻璃破碎的聲音吵醒了他。
	voice 表示「說話或音樂發出的聲音」。	He has a very deep voice.	他有一把非常低沉渾厚的嗓音。
nominate（提名）和 appoint（任命）	nominate 表示「建議某人進行選舉或選擇（工作或職位）」。	We need to nominate someone to take over from Mr Wong as our Chairman.	我們需要提名一個人接替黃先生擔任主席。
	appoint 表示「給某人一份工作或職位」。	Mr Hung was appointed Executive Director and General Manager last month.	洪先生上個月被任命為執行董事兼總經理。
obeisance（鞠躬）和 obedience（服從）	obeisance 表示（尊重或敬意）「屈膝禮」。	The British made obeisance to the King.	英國人向國王鞠躬致敬。
	obedience 表示「聽話」。	Parents demand obedience from their children.	父母總要求子女聽話。
object 和 objective（目標）	object 表示「行動或事件的目的」。	The object of the game is to score as many points as possible.	遊戲目標是盡可能拿高分。
	objective 表示「你正在努力並希望在行動過程或工作結束時實現的目標」。	My objective is to improve my English as much as possible.	我的目標是將英語水平提高得越多越好。
obligation 和 duty（義務）	obligation 表示「道德義務或責任，遵照習俗、契約等必須盡的職責或義務」。	Anyone who rents a property is under an obligation to keep it clean and tidy.	任何租客都有義務保持房屋乾淨整潔。
	duty 表示「你必須做的，因為它是你職責，或者因為你認為它是對的，通常發自內心，強調自覺性」。	He felt it was his duty to report the matter to the police.	他覺得向警方報案是他的責任。
observance（遵守）和 observation（觀察）	observance 表示「遵守法律、習俗、節日等」。	Observance of laws, rules and orders is a must, as ignorance of law is no excuse.	遵守法律、規則和命令是必須的，因為不懂法律並不能作為免罪藉口。
	observation 表示「觀察或被觀察」。	The experiment requires careful observation.	那實驗需要仔細觀察。

易混淆字詞	註釋	例句	譯文
obstacle / obstruction 和 impediment（障礙物）	obstacle 表示「障礙物或必須克服的困難」。	A roadblock was set up as an obstacle to the fleeing prisoners.	已設置路障阻止逃犯。
	obstruction 表示「堵塞整個通道的東西或物體」。	A tree fallen across the road was an obstruction to our car.	橫倒路上的樹阻礙我們的車駛過。
	impediment 表示「干擾正常功能與行為的東西」。	Lack of confidence is an impediment to success.	缺乏信心是成功的障礙。
occasion（時刻） opportunity / chance（機會）	occasion 表示「事件發生的時間」。	Finally we had an occasion to talk with the principal about our plan.	最後，我們終於有機會與校長討論我們的計劃。
	opportunity 表示「有可能做某事的機會」。	Next week, I'll have an opportunity of going to London.	下星期我將有機會去倫敦。
	chance 是「機會」的非正式用語。	I never had a chance to take the IELTS examination.	我從來沒有機會參加雅思考試。
occupancy 和 occupation（佔有）	occupancy 表示「有着」。	The occupancy rate of the hotel fell to 10% last month.	該酒店的入住率上月下降至10%。
	occupation 表示「佔有，也可表示職業、工作」。	He has no definite occupation.	他沒有固定職業。
occupy（佔用）和 spare（抽出時間）	occupy 表示「佔據」。	How do you occupy your time?	你怎麼打發時間？
	spare 表示「（為他人）抽出，通常指某事所佔時間」。	Could you spare me a few minutes?	你能給我幾分鐘時間嗎？
occur 和 take place / happen（發生）	occur 為正式用語，通常表示「與計劃外的事件有關」。	Typhoon often occurs in summer.	颱風通常發生在夏季。
	take place 表示「與計劃有關的事件」。	The wedding will take place at St. Anthony church.	婚禮將在聖安多尼堂舉行。
	happen 表示「因某事而起；也與 occur 同義」。	You'd better tell them exactly what happened.	你最好告訴他們到底發生了甚麼事。
odd（奇怪的）和 odds（機會）	odd 是形容詞，意思是「奇怪的，在常規之外」。	She's an odd old woman.	她是個古怪的老婦人。
	odds 是名詞，意思是「機會，可能性」。	He is confident that the odds are in his favour.	他有信心時機對他有利。

易混淆字詞	註釋	例句	譯文
officer (軍官) 和 official (公職人員)	officer 表示「在軍隊或警察部門任職的人」。	He is a police officer.	他是一名警察。
	official (名詞) 表示「受僱於政府的文職人員」。	He is a public official who is responsible for public health.	他是一位負責公共衛生的官員。
official (官式的) 和 officious (好用權威的)	official 是形容詞，表示「正式的，與權威人士、官方或團體有關的」。	I need your official approval on the application form for travelling allowance.	我需要你在旅行津貼申請表上給予正式的批准。
	officious (表達厭惡或反對) 因為「過份殷勤；愛管閒事；過份急於發施號令或讓人遵守不重要的規則」。	His mother-in-law is so officious that he does not let her visit his house.	他的岳母非常好管閒事，他不讓她到他家來。
omission (遺漏) 和 oversight (疏忽)	omission 表示「遺漏或刪除」。	I found a number of errors and omissions through the pages.	我發現錯漏很多。
	oversight 表示「沒有注意到」。	Through oversight, I failed to date the cheque.	由於疏忽，我忘了在支票上寫日期。
oppose (反對) 和 withstand (對抗)	oppose 表示「反對、反抗」，常指「反對某種觀念或某種計劃，有時指反對人」。	They opposed the idea at once.	他們立刻反對這個主意。
	withstand 表示「不屈服」，常指「抵擋某次攻擊」。	The bridge withstood the flood.	這座橋抵擋住洪水。
oppress (壓迫) 和 suppress (鎮壓)	oppress 表示「以嚴厲和殘酷的方式管治」。	A good employer will not oppress his staff.	一個好僱主不會壓迫員工。
	suppress 表示「用武力鎮壓 (尤指一個運動、動作或狀態)」。	The police suppressed the rebellion.	警察鎮壓了叛亂。
ordnance (軍火) 和 ordinance (法例)	ordnance 表示「大砲、彈藥」。	The battle was lost and the General was killed through lack of proper ordnance.	這場戰役因缺乏彈藥和軍火而潰敗，將軍也陣亡了。
	ordinance 表示「立法會制定的法例」。	I have learnt by heart the Bills of Exchange Ordinance.	我已將票據條例牢記於心。

易混淆字詞	註釋	例句	譯文
origin（起因）和 source（來源）/ reason（原因）/ cause（原因）/ accountable（要負上責任）/ due to（因為）/ because of（因為）/ for the sake of（為了）/ on account of（因為）	origin 強調「事情的起因、根源」。	Scientists are working hard to find out the origins of life on earth.	科學家正努力尋找地球生命的起源。
	source 表示「來源」。	Do you have any other source of income apart from your job as a designer?	除了作為設計師以外，你還有其他收入來源嗎？
	reason 指導致某種結果的「原因」，說明或解釋某種結果的理由。	The reason I was absent yesterday is that I was sick.	我昨天因生病而缺席。
	cause 表示「造成某種結果的原因，主語可以是人或物」。	Do you know the cause of their sudden change of the plan?	你知道他們突然改變計劃的原因嗎？
	accountable 表示「負責任的」，其主語應該是人而不是物」。	Each person is accountable for his own behaviour.	每個人都要為自己的行為負責。
	due to 是介詞短語，表示「由於」是 attributable to 的同義詞，大致用於形容詞短語或副詞短語。	These errors are due to sheer carelessness.	這些完全是粗心大意引起的錯誤。
	because of 是介詞短語，意思是原因或理由，可用於表示「疾病、意外事故的詞語之前」。	He did not come because of illness.	他因病沒有來。
	for the sake of 表示「為了」，指「利益或目的」。	They fought for the sake of their country.	他們為國家而戰。
	on account of 是介詞短語，表示「因為」。	On account of the rise in prices, we must also charge more.	由於物價上漲，我們也必須加價。
original（本來的）和 traditional（傳統的）	original 表示「第一個存在的、原始的（通常是其他的緊隨其後）」。	The original edition contained only 170 pages.	原始版本僅有 170 頁。
	traditional 表示「在一段很長時間內被團體或社會使用的」。	The dancers were wearing traditional Thai dress.	舞蹈員身穿泰國傳統服飾。
outdoor（戶外的）和 outdoors（戶外）	outdoor（沒有 's'）是形容詞，意思是「在戶外使用、表演、生活或存在的」。	He likes outdoor sports.	他喜歡戶外運動。
	outdoors（有 's'）是副詞，意思是「不在室內或屋內」。	It is cold outdoors.	外面很冷。

易混淆字詞	註釋	例句	譯文
outline（提綱）和 summary（摘要）	outline 表示「主要觀點或事實」。	Write an outline before trying to write a composition.	作文前要先寫一個大綱。
	summary 表示「簡要說明重點」。	The speaker finished with a summary of his speech.	講者用一個撮要總結演講。
outward 和 outwards（向外）	outward（沒有 's'）既是副詞又是形容詞，意思是「朝向外面；或在外面」。	As an adverb The door opens outward, not inward. As an adjective That's only outward cheerfulness.	用作副詞 那門是向外開的，不是向內開的。 用作形容詞 那只是外表快樂而已。
	outwards（有 's'）是副詞，意思是「向外彎；或指遠離家鄉或中心區」。	Factories were spreading outwards from the downtown.	工廠從市中心向外擴展。
overcome（克服）和 conquer（征服）	overcome 表示「控制」。	We must overcome these bad habits.	我們必須改掉這些壞習慣。
	conquer 表示「征服，贏得勝利」。	They have been fighting a battle to conquer nature.	他們一直在打一場征服自然的戰鬥。
overall（總括的）和 above all（最重要的是）	overall（用作副詞）表示「一般來說」。 overall（用作形容詞）表示「包括所有一切」。	As an adverb Overall, the weather in this area is good. As an adjective We're concerned about the overall effect of these films on younger viewers.	用作副詞 總的來說，這個地區天氣很好。 用作形容詞 我們擔心這些電影對年輕觀眾產生的整體影響。
	above all 表示「最重要的是」。	His idea of a good time included the sun, the sea, jokes, laughter, and above all friendship.	他對美好時光的想法包括陽光、大海、笑話、笑聲，最重要的是友誼。
pain 和 ache（疼痛）	pain 是及物動詞，意思是「身體受傷或疾病引起的疼痛，經常跟賓語」。	My throat pains me very often.	我經常喉嚨痛。
	ache 是不及物動詞，意思是「有持續性微痛，不跟賓語」。	My tooth ached all night.	我牙痛了一夜。

易混淆字詞	註釋	例句	譯文
pair（一雙）和 couple（一對）	pair 表示「一套兩件東西」	He put on a **pair** of jeans.	他穿上了一條牛仔褲。
	couple 表示「兩個一起」	I ate a **couple** of fried eggs with ham at breakfast.	我早餐吃了火腿煎雙蛋。
pants（長褲）和 trunks（男裝運動褲）	pants 表示「覆蓋下半身和雙腿的褲子」。	Wear an old pair of **pants** when you polish the car.	將車打蠟時穿上一條舊長褲。
	trunks 表示「男性在某些運動中穿的短褲，通常指泳褲」。	He took off his pants, put on his **trunks**, and went swimming.	他脫下長褲，穿上泳褲，去游泳了。
parade（巡遊表演）和 demonstration（示威遊行）	parade 表示「慶祝性的巡遊」。	Let's go and watch the New Year **parade**.	我們去看新年巡遊吧。
	demonstration 表示「示威遊行」。	He took part in an anti-war **demonstration**.	他參加了一個反戰遊行。
partly 和 partially（部份）	partly 表示「不完全的，強調局部」。	I have only **partly** finished this book.	我只完成這本書其中一部份。
	partially 表示「沒有充份的，強調程度」。	He likes the beef **partially** cooked.	他喜歡吃半生熟牛肉。
pass（過去）/ past（過）和 spend（度過）	當 pass 與時間 結合使用時，它通常是不及物動詞。	Two weeks **passed** and there was still no reply.	兩星期過去了，仍然沒有回覆。
	past 是介詞，表示「在⋯⋯之後」。	It's half **past** six.	現在六點半鐘。
	用 spend 表示 示在某處度假期 / 一段時間（不是 pass）。	We like to **spend** our holidays near the sea.	我們喜歡在海邊度假。
passion（激情）和 emotion（情緒）	passion 表示「強烈的感覺，如愛、恨或憤怒等，指使人失去理智的」。	He has worked with **passion** on this new song.	他充滿激情地創作了這首新歌。
	emotion 表示「激動的感受，如愛、喜、恨、悲傷等」。	You need to control your **emotions**.	你需要控制自己的情緒。
pattern（模式）和 routine（日常公事）	pattern 表示「事情發生的常規方式」。	The murders all seem to follow a similar **pattern**.	這些謀殺案似乎都遵循類似的模式。
	routine 表示「每天做的事情，通常順序相同」。	His daily **routine** doesn't include exercise.	他的生活規律不包括運動。

易混淆字詞	註釋	例句	譯文
payment (支付) 和 fee (費用) / fare (車費) / price (價錢) / cost (代價) / charge (收費) / rate (價格) / value (價值) / prize (獎品)	payment 表示「為某事支付的金額」。	I had to get rid of the car because I couldn't keep up the **payments**.	我不得不賣車，因我無法再付款。
	fee 表示「支付給醫生、律師或其他專業人士的費用」。	The **fee** for one hour's consultation is $1,000.	諮詢一小時收費 1,000 元。
	fare 表示「乘坐巴士、港鐵、火車、輪船、的士等的費用」。	She spends $1,500 per month on MTR **fares**.	她每月乘搭港鐵要花 1,500 元。
	price 表示「買或賣東西的價格」。	The **price** of pork may go down next year.	明年豬肉價格可能會下降。
	cost 表示「支付的價格或其他要求的金額、成本等」。	Living **costs** are usually higher in cities than in the village.	城市的生活成本通常高於鄉村。
	charge 表示「某物的付款要求或收費」。	There is no **charge** for delivery.	送貨不收取任何費用。
	rate 表示「某人為他人工作的每小時 / 天 / 週收取的金額」。	The minimum wage **rate** is under review from time to time.	最低工資不時會被檢討。
	value 表示「真正的價值」。	The work I am doing is not of very much **value**.	我正在做的工作沒有多大價值。
	prize 表示「給予某人獎品或獎金，因為他表現比別人好」。	She gained a **prize** last year, but she failed to gain one this year.	她去年獲獎，但今年沒有。
peculiar (古怪) 和 unusual (奇異) / freak (怪誕) / particular (特殊)	peculiar 表示「奇怪、奇異的，尤指令人驚訝或不愉快的方式」。	I'm not sure about this cheese. The taste is a bit **peculiar**.	我不認識這種芝士。味道有點古怪。
	unusual 表示「罕見的、不尋常的」。	Where did you buy this cheese? The taste is very **unusual**.	你在那裏買這種芝士？味道很不尋常。
	freak 表示「荒謬的想法、怪誕的人、行為或事件」。	A storm as bad as that one is a **freak** of nature.	一場如此猛烈的風暴是大自然的一種怪現象。
	particular 表示「特殊、講究，希望一切都恰到好處，尤指個人的衣食住行等」。	My father isn't very **particular** about the food he eats.	我爸爸對吃絕不挑食。
peer (凝視) 和 glare (瞪眼)	peer 是動詞，表示「目不轉睛地看，好像看不清楚」。	She **peered** through the mist, trying to find the right path.	她隔着迷霧凝視，試圖找出路。
	glare 表示「憤怒地看，含不滿或敵對之意」。	When I came home late, my wife **glared** at me.	當我晚了回家時，妻子向我怒目而視。

易混淆字詞	註釋	例句	譯文
peer (同等級的人) 和 superior (上司)	peer 是名詞,表示「與他人具有同等功績、品質、等級的人」。	The child was disliked by his peers.	與這個孩子同齡的人都不喜歡他。
	superior 表示「佔優勢的,比另一個人或其他人更優勝或地位更高的人」。	He is the equal, if not the superior, of anyone in the club.	他在這社團裏,若算不上一個頂尖人物,也不比任何人差。
pendent (吊住的) 和 pendant (下垂物)	pendent 是形容詞,表示「懸垂的」。	The necklace was a gold band with pendent diamonds.	這條金頸鍊鑲有懸墜的鑽石。
	pendant 是名詞,表示「下垂的掛飾」。	She fastened a gold pendant on her collar.	她的衣領掛了一個金吊墜。
people 和 persons (人)	persons 是法律語用語中,複數形式「人」(person) 的稱謂。	The lift is allowed to carry 6 persons.	電梯可載六人。
	people 是集合名詞,表示「人,人們」。	I don't know any of the people in this room.	我不認識這房間內的人。
per cent (%) 和 percentage (百分比)	per cent 表示「作為百分數 (%) 的分數給出的數量或比率」。	Sixty per cent of the work has been finished.	百分之六十的工作已經完成。
	percentage 表示「某物的百分比,不與具體數字連用」。	Only a small percentage of cars failed to pass the test.	只有極少數汽車未能通過測試。
perpetrate (做壞事) 和 perpetuate (使永久)	perpetrate 表示「做壞事,犯錯、犯罪或做非常愚蠢的事情」。	If the murderer is allowed to go free, he may perpetrate more crimes.	如果讓殺人兇手逍遙法外,他可能會犯下更多罪行。
	perpetuate 表示「保留、保存、保持」。	The Run Run Shaw Foundation perpetuates the work that its founder began.	邵逸夫基金能使創始人開始的工作持續進行。
persevere / persist (堅持) 和 resist (反抗)	persevere 表示「困難中仍繼續做某事,含有褒義」。	Despite pressures from various sources, he persevered with his work.	他不理會各方壓力堅持工作。
	persist 表示「不顧反對或警告繼續做某事,含有貶義」。	He persists in his opinion.	他固守己見。
	resist 表示「抵抗,盡量不屈服」。	The boy could not resist the temptation of money and sold drugs in the school.	那男孩抵擋不住金錢誘惑,在學校裏賣毒品。

易混淆字詞	註釋	例句	譯文
personage（要人） **celebrity**（名人）和 **person**（人）	**personage** 表示「有權勢的人，他們因所做的事而聞名。他們可能是議員、公司主席、宗教人士等」。	Several famous **personages** were at the dinner last night.	昨晚有幾位重要人物出席晚宴。
	celebrity 表示「常在媒體出現的名人，如歌手、演員、音樂家等」。	Many television **celebrities** attended the opening ceremony.	許多電視名人出席開幕儀式。
	person 表示「男人、女人或孩子」。	Every **person** requires a certain amount of food.	每人都需要一定份量的食物。
personal（個人的）和 **personnel**（全體人員）	**personal**（形容詞）表示「關於或屬於個人或私人的」。	Her books deal mainly with **personal** relationships, especially marital problems.	她的書主要談及個人關係，尤指婚姻問題。
	personnel（集合名詞）表示「受僱於公司或機構組織的員工」。	She is the manager of the **Personnel** Department.	她是人事部經理。
perspicacity（聰穎）和 **perspicuity**（明晰）	**perspicacity** 表示「與人打交道的智慧和理解力及敏銳的洞察力」。	Unbelievable artistic **perspicacity** and integrity mingle with child-like humour and credulity.	令人難以置信的藝術天才和正直氣質，夾雜孩子般的幽默和輕信。
	perspicuity 表示「表達清晰，易於理解」。	There is nothing more desirable in composition than **perspicuity**.	作文最可貴的要算是表達清晰了。
peruse（細讀）和 **glance**（瀏覽）	**peruse** 表示「仔細閱讀」。	She **perused** the letter from her husband's solicitor.	她仔細閱讀了丈夫律師的來信。
	glance 表示「很快的讀或看」。	I **glanced** through the article hurriedly.	我匆匆瀏覽了這篇文章。
photograph（相片）和 **picture**（圖片）	**photograph** 表示「用照相機或手機所拍的照片」。	Have you seen Alfred's **photographs** taken in Canada?	你看到阿爾弗德在加拿大拍的照片嗎？
	picture 表示「圖畫、圖片、照片」。	The artist finished the **picture** in two days.	那畫家兩天就完成了這幅畫。

易混淆字詞	註釋	例句	譯文
plant 和 grow / raise (種植)	plant 表示「把種子放到地裏讓它生長,指下種栽苗的人的動作」。	We have **planted** some rose bushes in our garden.	我們在花園裏種了一些玫瑰。
	grow 表示「照顧種子或幼苗,指栽種和培育的全過程」。	Alice likes to **grow** flowers.	愛麗斯喜歡種花。
	raise 表示「飼養特定的農場動物或種植農作物」。	We **raise** plants, vegetables, animals etc. especially on a farm to sell as food.	我們在農場上種植物、蔬菜及飼養動物作為食物出售。
play (扮演) 和 act (表演) [動詞]	play 表示「演出,一般須説明演出地點或劇名」。	He **played** the prince in Hamlet some years ago.	幾年前他在哈雷姆特扮演王子。
	act 表示「表演,演出」。	That actress **acts** very well.	那位女演員演技很好。
play (遊戲) 和 game (遊戲) / match (比賽) [名詞]	play 表示「調劑體力和腦力的有趣遊戲或活動」。	The children are at **play**.	孩子們正在玩耍。
	game 表示「某種形式或具有特殊規則的遊戲」。	Chinese Chess is a very slow **game**.	中國象棋是一種很慢的遊戲。
	match 表示「個人、團隊或個人競爭的賽事如網球、足球、體育賽事等」。	Who won the football **match** last night?	昨晚誰贏了球賽?
pleasant / pleasing (令人愉快) 和 pleased (高興的)	pleasant 表示「含主動意義,意思是禮貌和友好。	It was **pleasant** for us to spend a quiet evening at home.	對我們來説,在家裏度過一個清靜的晚上是很愉快的。
	pleasing 表示「含主動意義,意思是給予快樂」。	The audience found the movie **pleasing**.	觀眾覺得這部電影令人愉快。
	pleased 表示「含被動意義,意思是開心,滿意」。	We would be very **pleased** if you could attend.	如果你能參加,我們將非常高興。
poetry (詩歌) 和 poem (詩文)	poetry 表示「一般的詩歌,是詩的總稱」。	She bought a Tang Dynasty **poetry** book of 300 poems.	她買了一本唐詩 300 首的詩集。
	poem 表示「具體的一首詩」。	In old days, we were asked to learn **poems** by heart.	從前我們需要背誦詩文。
police (警察部隊) 和 policeman (警察) [policewoman (女警),police officer (警官)]	(the) police 表示「警察部隊,指警察整體」。	If you get any more of these phone calls, you should report to the **police**.	如果你再接到這類電話,你應該報警。
	policeman, policewoman, police officer 泛指「一名警察或警察的個人」。	He was charged with shooting a **police officer**.	他被控向一名警察開槍。

易混淆字詞	註釋	例句	譯文
politic (精明的) 和 politics (政治) / policy (政策)	politic (沒有 's') 是形容詞，表示「明智的」。	He considered it politic to keep silence and avoid the confrontation.	他認為避免對抗最明智就是保持沉默。
	politics (有 's') 表示「指治理國家的行為，也指各個團體、公司、學校各種商業機構等內在或外在相互之間的控制或管理關係」。	The professor resigned from the University and left politics for a more peaceful life.	教授為求過更安寧的生活，已從大學辭職，也離開了辦公室政治。
	policy 表示「指導工作的計劃或行動方針」。	It's our company policy that no staff is allowed to have love affairs with colleagues.	不允許同事間發生戀情是我們公司的政策。
portion / part / proportion 和 share (部份)	portion 表示「一部份或一份的量，強調它不是整體的關係」。	The money was divided into three portions.	這筆錢被分成三份。
	part 表示「比整體少的東西，強調一部份與其他部份分開」。	Part of the fruit is rotten.	部份水果腐爛了。
	proportion 表示「比較或相對的部份或份額，強調比例角度」。	Only a small proportion of the class passed the exam.	這個班只有一小部份人考試及格。
	share 表示「份、部份，主要指分配、攤派的份額，強調接受者」。	I just want my fair share of the money.	我只想要我應得的那一份錢。
position (職位) 和 job (職業)	position 表示「職務，指就業、社會等方面的地位或等級」。	As he is knowledgeable and professional, he was promoted to the position of executive director last year.	他因知識淵博且專業，於去年升任執行董事。
	job 表示「職業，也可指已完成或必須完成的一項工作」。	She gets paid by the job. She's a clerk.	她受薪工作，是一位文員。
possess (擁有) 和 have (有)	possess 表示「擁有、佔有，包括控制和支配」。	He possesses two cars.	他擁有兩輛汽車。
	have 表示「有，指某人或物的關係，並不表示可以支配」。	To say no to your boss, you need to have great courage.	對老闆說「不」需要有很大勇氣。
possibility (可能性) 和 opportunity (機會)	possibility 表示「可發生的狀況或事情」。	What are the possibilities of rain for tonight?	今晚下雨的可能性有多大呢？
	opportunity 表示「做某事的機會」。	I regret that I had no opportunity of speaking to my grandma before she left us.	我很遺憾祖母離開我們之前我沒機會跟她說話。

易混淆字詞	註釋	例句	譯文
possible（可能的）和 feasible（可行的）	possible 表示「可能會發生或做的事，指根據情況的可能性，預計希望可能很少」。	Is there any possible solution to our existing problem?	我們現時的問題有可能的解決方案嗎？
	feasible 表示「能夠做到的，指可進行的事，預計希望很大」。	This is absolutely a feasible plan that I hope you will adopt.	這是一個絕對可行的計劃，希望你會採納。
power 和 energy（力量）	power 可指一個人的權力，意思是指他的社會、經濟或政治影響力。	The major investors have the power to make or break a company.	主要投資者有能力左右公司的成敗。
	energy 可用於談論某人的身體狀況。	The illness has left her with no energy.	那病痛讓她喪失了力氣。
powerful 和 mighty（有力的）	powerful 表示「有做重要事情的能力或權力，或表現出巨大的力量」。	He is so powerful that nobody dares to challenge him.	他太強大了，沒有人敢挑戰他。
	mighty 表示「強大，非凡」，指「具有超過他人或物的巨大力量、威力或能力」。	The pen is mightier than the gun.	筆比槍更強大有力。
practicable（可行的）和 practical（實用的）	practicable 表示「可以成功使用或採取行動（儘管尚未嘗試）」。	Is growing crops in desert practicable?	在沙漠中種植農作物可行嗎？
	practical 表示「實際的，指有效的」。	Loose-fitting clothes are practical in hot climate.	寬鬆衣服在炎熱氣候中很實用。
practise / drill（練習）和 train（訓練）	practise 表示「反覆或有規律地練習，實踐理論，掌握技巧達至精通」。	You must practise writing English.	你必須練習英語寫作。
	drill 表示「在老師或教官的指導下，反覆告訴某人某事，讓他們進行有系統的訓練」。	The teacher drills us in writing English essays.	老師訓練我們用英語作文。
	train 表示「教書育人」，強調「就某方面進行專門的訓練和培養」。	This book trains you to write more accurately.	本書訓練你作文寫得更準確。
precipitous（險峻的）和 precipitate（魯莽的）	precipitous 表示「危險陡峭」。	They looked down from the precipitous cliffs.	他們從陡峭的懸崖上往下看。
	precipitate 表示「匆忙；不加思索地行動或做事」。	Take your time, don't make a precipitate decision.	慢慢來，不要輕易作出決定。

易混淆字詞	註釋	例句	譯文
pretend（假裝）和 intend（打算）	pretend 表示「裝扮、讓人有錯誤想法」。	She hurried past, **pretending** not to see me.	她匆匆走過去，假裝沒有見到我。
	intend 表示「計劃或企圖做某事」。	As soon as the baby can be left with someone, she **intends** to go back to work.	一旦嬰孩有人照顧，她就打算再工作了。
prevent（阻止）和 deter（阻止）/ forbid（禁止）/ keep（阻止）/ protect（保護）/ prohibit（禁止）/ inhibit（抑制）	prevent 表示「阻止某人或某事發生」。	Bad weather **prevented** the plane from taking off.	惡劣天氣使飛機無法起飛。
	deter 表示「勸阻某人做某事」。	Stricter punishments would **deter** people from doing these things.	更嚴厲的懲罰會阻止人們做這些事。
	forbid 表示「不允許」。	I **forbid** you to see him again.	我禁止你再去見他。
	keep 表示「防止，但必須跟 from」。	The court **kept** him *from* leaving Hong Kong.	法庭不許他離開香港。
	protect 表示「保護某人或某物安全，也可跟 from，但不可跟 out of」。	The mother **protected** her children *from* every danger.	母親保護她的孩子免遭遇任何危險。
	prohibit 表示「在較大範圍內禁止某人做某事，有強制執行的意思，常跟含 from 的介詞短語」。	His father **prohibited** him from smoking.	他父親禁止他吸煙。
	inhibit 表示「抑制着不去做某事，常指感情或情況的制約」。	Fear of cancer **inhibited** him from learning to smoke.	對癌症的恐懼阻止了他吸煙。
prevention 和 precaution（防禦）	prevention 表示「阻止某事發生的行為」。	The police are also concerned with the **prevention** of crime.	警方也關注如何可防止罪案發生。
	precaution 表示「為避免可能的危險、損害、傷害等所採取的行動」。	I decided to take a stick with me, just as a **precaution**.	我決定隨身攜帶一根棍子，以防萬一。
previously 和 ago（以前）	previously 表示「過去某段時刻以前，常用完成式」。	I *have seen* it three years **previously**.	三年前我已見過它。
	ago 表示「現在以前，常用過去式」。	I *saw* him a year **ago**.	一年前我見過他。

易混淆字詞	註釋	例句	譯文
principle（原則）和 principal（校長）	principle 表示「原理、一般真理、規則或法律」。	The principle behind it is very simple.	它背後的原理非常簡單。
	principal 表示「大學、學院和學校的負責人」。	The principal of our school encourages us to learn English.	校長鼓勵我們學習英語。
print（發行）和 publish（公佈）（出版）	print 表示「使用機器製作書籍、報紙等」。	Due to increased demand, another six thousand copies are to be printed.	因需求增加，將再印刷六千本。
	publish 表示「製作書籍、雜誌、報紙等以向公眾出售；也可指向公眾公開某消息」。	The news was published at 11:30am this morning.	該消息於今午 11 點 30 分發佈。
problem（問題）和 question（提問）	problem 表示「需要解決或思考的問題，強調疑難或困難」。	Your instructions solved many problems for us.	您的指示為我們解決了不少問題。
	question 表示「因疑惑或不能斷定而提出要求答覆或解決的困難或問題」。	The question is really one of how to overcome these adverse situations.	問題確實是如何克服不利形勢。
proceed（前進）和 precede（處在……之前）	proceed 表示「前進，繼續進行」。	According to latest reports, negotiations are proceeding smoothly.	根據最新報導，談判進展順利。
	precede 表示「在某人或某事之前（立即）發生」。	The main film was preceded by commercial advertisements.	電影開畫前會播放商業廣告。
process（步驟）和 stage（時期）/ procedure（程序）/ procession（行列）	process 表示「為了製作或做某事而執行一系列的動作或操作過程」。	The process begins with the gathering of the coffee beans.	這個過程從收集咖啡豆開始。
	stage 表示「過程中的一個動作或操作」。	The production of a plastic rubbish bag has five stages.	生產一個塑膠垃圾袋有五個階段。
	procedure 表示「做某事的正確方式或順序，指做事的途徑或手續」。	Do you know the procedure for obtaining a new HKID card?	你知道辦領新香港身份證的程序嗎？
	procession 表示「一排人或車輛以有序、儀式性的方式向前慢慢移動」。	Last night, spectators crowded Canton Road at Tsim Sha Tsui to watch the parade procession.	昨晚觀眾擠滿尖沙咀廣東道觀看遊行隊伍。

易混淆字詞	註釋	例句	譯文
procure 和 secure（獲得）	procure 表示「通過努力獲得一些東西，尤指過程困難」。	She managed to procure a ticket for the concert.	她設法買到音樂會的門票。
	secure 表示「獲得或實現某事」，尤指得到渴望的東西，強調「有把握得到」。	The team managed to secure a place in the finals.	球隊設法在決賽中取得一席位。
produce 和 product（產品）	produce 表示「生產的東西，尤指通過成長或形成的東西，如農產品和物產等」。	He took the produce of his garden to the market every Saturday.	每個星期六他會把花園栽種的農作物帶到市場售賣。
	product 表示「農業或工業生產出來的東西；有時也可指文學或藝術作品」。	Nylon is a man-made product.	尼龍是人造產品。
profession 和 trade（職業）	profession 表示「知識性的職業」，指通過特殊訓練和學習才能獲得的工作，例如醫生、會計師、律師的工作。	He is a lawyer by profession.	他的職業是律師。
	trade 表示「與手藝、手工相關的職業，通常指需要特殊技能的工作。	He is a barber by trade.	他是一名理髮師。
profit 和 benefit（利益）	profit 表示「做生意或買賣東西時賺到的錢，尤指支付相關費用之後」。	The bank did not make a good profit last quarter.	該銀行上季度的利潤並不好。
	benefit 表示「物質或精神上的利益，指某物對社會或個人在肉體、腦力或道德等方面的益處」。	He has done it only for his own benefit.	他只是為了他本身的利益才做那事。
propaganda（宣傳）和 advertising（廣告）/ publicity（宣傳）	propaganda 表示「用於政治背景，有組織（例如由政府）地傳播某些信仰、信息或規則」。	In times of war the public will be bombarded with propaganda.	在戰爭時期，公眾會面對轟炸式的宣傳攻勢。
	advertising 表示「用於商業環境」，在電視、報紙、互聯網等製作廣告。	TV stations receive most of their money from advertising.	電視台大部份收入來自廣告。
	publicity 表示「報紙、電視、互聯網對某人的關注，並試圖將其告知公眾」。	Scandals involving prominent politicians always receive widespread publicity.	涉及著名政治家的醜聞總是受到廣泛宣傳的。

易混淆字詞	註釋	例句	譯文
proposition 和 proposal（建議）	proposition 表示「建議，提供考慮的想法或行動計劃的具體內容，含貶義，通常指不道德提議」。	He put forth a proposition so bold that I had to challenge it.	他提出了一個如此大膽的提議，我不得不對它表示異議。
	proposal 表示「提議的內容；強調直接或主動提出的正式建議或計劃」。	The Ocean Park Committee made a proposal to the HKSAR Chief Executive.	海洋公園委員會向香港特區行政長官提出一項建議。
protest（抗議）和 complain（投訴）	protest 表示「說或做某事以表明你強烈反對某事」。	The crowds were protesting against the government's purchase of nuclear weapons.	人羣抗議政府購買核武器。
	complain 表示「對某事生氣或不高興」。	She told the shop assistant that she wanted to complain about the mobile phone she had bought.	她告訴店員，她想投訴她買了的手機。
purpose（目的）和 reason（原因）	purpose 表示「希望通過做某事達到某目的」。	Their purpose in coming here is to promote Australian universities.	他們來這裏的目的是推廣澳洲的大學。
	reason 表示「促使某人做某事的理由」。	The reason why I have come here is to improve my English.	我來這裏是為了提高英語水平。
qualifications 和 qualification（資格）	qualifications（有 's'）表示「特定工作技能或經驗」。	In this job, experience counts for more than paper qualifications.	這份工作要求經驗多於文憑。
	qualification（沒有 's'）表示「學位、文憑、證書等」。	Do you have a postgraduate qualification?	你大學畢業後還有其他資歷嗎？
qualitative（性質上的）和 quantitative（數量的）	qualitative 表示「有質量的」。	There are qualitative differences between the two products.	兩種產品質量上有差異。
	quantitative 表示「關於數量，與質量無關」。	The export of rare earth is subject to quantitative limitation.	稀土出口有數量限制。

易混淆字詞	註釋	例句	譯文
quantity（數量）和 amount（數量）/ number（數目）/ lot（大量）	quantity 表示「某物的數量」。	He lost a great **quantity** of blood.	他失血過多。
	amount 表示「一定數量的東西」。	He drinks a large **amount** of Chinese tea every day.	他每天喝大量中國茶。
	number 表示「一個數或一組數目」。	A large **number** of children attended the picnic.	許多孩子參加郊遊。
	lot 表示「大數量」。	'How many do you need?' 'A **lot**.'	「你需要多少？」「很多。」
quick 和 fast（快）	quick 表示「動作的突然和短暫，強調短時間內動作要迅速和敏捷」。	He gave her a **quick** answer.	他很快答覆了她。
	fast 表示「快速移動，強調移動的人或物跨越長而迅速」的路程。	He was a **fast** reader.	他讀書速度很快。
quiet（平靜的）和 quiescent（靜止的）/ silent（寂靜的）	quiet「沒有噪音或噪音很小」。	We spent a **quiet** evening reading.	我們在一個寧靜的晚上讀書度過。
	quiescent 表示「靜止，不動的」。	The volcano is **quiescent** now.	這座火山現在是靜止的。
	silent 表示「不出聲，不說話」。	What's wrong? Why are you so **silent**?	怎麼啦？為甚麼不說話？
quite（頗）/ exactly（恰好）	quite 是副詞，意思是「完全或相當大程度上；當用 the same 時，要加 not 在前面，意思是不完全一樣」。	My hair is *not quite the same* colour as yours.	我頭髮顏色與你的不太一樣。
	exactly 是副詞，意思是「某事各方面恰到好處；可用在 the same 前面，意思是完全一樣」。	You haven't changed at all — you still look **exactly** *the same*.	你根本沒變 —— 看起來仍和以前一樣。

易混淆字詞	註釋	例句	譯義
raise (舉起) 和 rise (升起) / lift (抬起) / arise (起來) / stick (伸)	raise (raising, raised, raised) 是及物動詞,意思是「將某人或物從某處移向上較高位置」。	The strong wind raised the tiny, thin, little girl from the ground.	強風把纖瘦的小女孩從地上吹了起來。
	rise (rising, rose, risen) 是不及物動詞,意思是「指人或物向上移動到較高位置或層次」。	The river rises after the heavy rain.	大雨過後,河水上漲了。
	lift (lifting, lifted, lifted) 是及物和不及物動詞,意思是「移某物到更高位置或級別」。	Would you please help me to lift up the desk?	你能幫我抬起這書桌嗎?
	arise (arising, arose, arisen) 是不及物動詞,意思是「(尤指在困難情況下) 發生;開始形成」。	A new crisis has arisen.	新的危機出現了。
	stick (sticking, stuck, stuck) 表示「伸出、無固定方向,常與 out 配搭」。	The doctor asked me to stick my tongue *out* for his examination.	醫生叫我伸出舌頭給他檢查。
rationale (基本原理) 和 rational / reasonable (合理的)	rationale 是名詞,意思是「決策、行動方針、信念所基於的原則或原因」。	I don't see the rationale behind these decisions.	我不清楚這些決定依據的基本原理。
	rational 是形容詞,意思是「(思想或行為) 是根據理性而非情感的」。	You owed me a rational explanation — the money couldn't just disappear.	你必須給我一個合理解釋 —— 錢不能這樣就不見了。
	reasonable 是形容詞,意思是「公平、明智或實際的」。	Dividing up the work equally seems like a very reasonable decision.	平均分配工作看來是一個非常合理的決定。
recall / recollect / remember (想起) 和 remind (提醒) / memorise (背下來)	recall (正式語) 表示「追想、多指有意回想自己或他人的過去」。	I really can't recall what his wife looks like.	我實在想不起他妻子的樣貌是怎樣的。
	recollect 表示「有意的行為,想起」。	I always recollect my childhood days with pleasure.	我總會愉快地回憶我的童年時代。
	remember 表示「有意或無意的行為,記住」。	I shall always remember what she has said.	我會永遠記住她說過的話。
	remind 表示「使 (某人) 記住,指因受 (某措施、人或事) 的提醒而想起過去」。	May I remind you of what happened that day?	我可以提醒你那天發生的事嗎?
	memorize 表示「用心背下來」。	The students were asked to memorize the poem.	學生被要求背誦這首詩。

易混淆字詞	註釋	例句	譯文
recollection（回憶）和 memory（記憶）	recollection 表示「回憶、回想起來，着重經過長時間努力思考才想起已遺忘的人或事」。	This old picture has brought my recollection of my grandma who died 50 years ago.	這張舊照片讓我回憶起五十年前去世的外婆。
	memory 表示「記憶、着重記起所學到、了解或經歷事物的能力」。	Although I haven't seen her for years, her face is till engraved on my memory.	雖然多年未見，但她的容顏仍深深印在我腦海中。
recipe（食譜）和 receipt（收據）	recipe 表示「食物製作的説明，例如如何烹飪某菜式及所需食材等」。	Use butter in place of pig oil in the recipe.	這個製法要用牛油代替豬油。
	receipt 表示「收條，指已收到某物（尤指金錢）的書面證明」。	You must ask for a receipt for the deposit you have paid.	您必須索取已付定金的收據。
recover 和 retrieve / rehabilitate（恢復）	recover 表示「重新找到或獲得，一般只用於具體東西」。	The police recovered the stolen money.	警方追回了贓款。
	retrieve 表示「尋回讓它失效或惡化的東西」。	It took him a long time to retrieve his reputation.	他花了很長時間才恢復聲譽。
	rehabilitate 表示「恢復原狀，指將（某事）恢復到良好狀態」。	We must rehabilitate our economy after the coronavirus.	新冠疫情過後，我們必須恢復經濟。
redundant 和 superfluous（多餘的）	redundant 表示「不需要或沒用的，通常指説話或文字的冗贅」。	I found the lecture redundant and quite boring.	我發現那講座多餘而且很無聊。
	superfluous 表示「比你需要或想要的更多，指任何多餘的東西」。	During this difficult time, we must cut down superfluous expenditure.	在這個困難時期，我們必須削減多餘的開支。
referee 和 umpire（裁判）	referee 表示「被任命確保某些運動項目如籃球、足球、曲棍球、拳擊、擊劍等比賽按照規則進行的人」。	He was a basketball referee.	他是一名籃球裁判。
	umpire 表示「被任命確保某些運動項目如羽毛球、排球、乒乓球、網球、棒球、板球等比賽按照規則進行的人」。	He was a baseball umpire.	他是一名棒球裁判。

易混淆字詞	註釋	例句	譯文
reflective（沉思的）和 reflexive（自身的）	reflective 表示「深思熟慮」。	The judge was in a reflective mood before delivering the judgment.	法官沉思後才作出判決。
	reflexive 表示「執行行動的本身，例如反身動詞和反身代詞」。	In 'He cut himself', 'cut' is a reflexive verb and 'himself' is a reflexive pronoun.	在 'He cut himself' 這句子中，'cut' 是反身動詞，'himself' 是反身代詞。
refuge（庇護）和 refugee（難民）	refuge 表示「避難所或保護免受麻煩、危險、追擊等」。	Yesterday the Hong Kong Observatory issued the first black rainstorm signal of the year, I took refuge from the rain in a shopping arcade.	昨天天文台發出今年首個黑色暴雨信號，我到商場避雨。
	refugee 表示「難民、指被迫逃離災難危險的人，例如來自戰爭、政治迫害等」。	In Turkey, many refugees came from Syria.	在土耳其，許多難民來自敍利亞。
refuse / reject / deny（拒絕）和 decline（謝絕）/ refute（駁倒）/ contradict（反駁）	refuse 表示「（當有人希望你做或接受某事時）直截了當地說不」。	He proudly refused my help and turned away.	他驕傲地拒絕了我的幫助並轉身離開。
	reject 表示「不支持，常用於正式場合或法律文件，強調當面拒絕對方的想法、信念、建議、計劃、提議等」。	She asked her lawyer to reject his husband's divorce proposal and offer a counter proposal.	她要求她的律師拒絕丈夫的離婚提議並提出反提議。
	decline 表示「禮貌地拒絕，指以客氣的方式謝絕」。	He declined the job offer, because he had started his own business.	他謝絕了那份工作，因為他自己創業了。
	deny 表示「拒絕給予或允許」。	He was denied admission to the University.	他被拒進入這所大學。
	refute 表示「駁斥，證明是虛假或不正確的，沒有拒絕之意」。	In the court, the accused was given the opportunity to refute the accusations.	在法庭上，被告得到機會駁倒對他的指控。
	contradict 表示「反駁某事是錯誤的」。	Generally, Chinese students do not like to contradict their teachers in class.	一般來說，中國學生不喜歡在課堂上反駁老師。
regardless（不管怎樣）和 regardless of（不管）	regardless 是副詞，意思是「不管怎樣」，常用於句尾。	Get her to sign the paper, regardless!	不管怎樣，讓她在文件上簽名再說。
	regardless of 是介詞短語，表示「不管、不顧」，指「不理會某人或事；視為不重要」。	The Club welcomes all new members regardless of age.	那會所歡迎所有新會員，不分年齡。

易混淆字詞	註釋	例句	譯文
regretful（遺憾的）和 regrettable（令人遺憾的）	regretful 表示「感到懊悔、惋惜、遺憾，只能修飾人」。	The boy is regretful for being unable to join us.	那孩子為了不能加入我們而感到惋惜。
	regrettable 表示「可歎、造成遺憾，常修飾行為或事情」。	The mixup was due to a regrettable breakdown in communications.	混亂是因通訊系統中斷引起的。
reiterate（反覆說）和 repeat（重複）	reiterate 表示「第二次或多次重複說某事，是正式用語，強調某事」。	'Go away! Go away!' he reiterated.	「走開！走開！」他重重複複大叫着。
	repeat 表示「重複一次或多次說某些話或做某些行為」。	Please repeat your question.	請重複你的問題。
release（釋放）和 shed（脫去）	release 表示「釋放、允許走出來」。	He was released from the jail.	他出獄了。
	shed 表示「脫落、脫掉（衣服、皮膚、樹葉等）」。	The tree shed its leaves.	這棵樹落葉了。
remain / leave（留下）和 stay（逗留）	remain 表示「在同一地方繼續一段時間」。	I remained at the office because of the black rainstorm.	我因黑色暴雨而留在辦公室。
	leave 表示「留下來」。	She asked me to leave my phone number.	她要求我留下電話號碼。
	stay 表示「在同一地方逗留或暫住一段時間」。	We stayed in a very good hotel in Shanghai.	我們住在上海一家很好的酒店。
remise（放棄對……的權利要求）和 remiss（疏忽職守的）	remise 是動詞和法律術語，意思是「放棄索償」。	As the deceased who was single had left no will, all of his properties were remised by the Court.	因死者單身也沒有留下遺囑，法庭判令他的財產繼承權被棄置了。
	remiss 是形容詞，意思是「粗心大意」。	Sorry! It was remiss of me to forget your birthday.	對不起！忘記你的生日，我真粗心大意。
renew（更換）和 revise（修訂）	renew 表示「用同類東西更換」。	I have to renew my passport next week.	下週我要更換護照。
	revise 表示「修訂」。	This book is now being revised the second time.	本書正在進行第二次修訂。
repulse 和 repel（擊退）	repulse 表示「與攻擊你的人戰鬥並趕走他們」。	Our soldiers repulsed the enemy.	我們的士兵擊退了敵人。
	repel 表示「成功擊退攻擊」。	Troops repelled an attack to infiltrate the south of the island.	軍隊擊退了一次對該島南部的攻擊。

易混淆字詞	註釋	例句	譯義
repute 和 report（據說）	repute 表示「宣稱是，含有懷疑成份」。	He is reputed to be very wealthy.	據説他非常富有。
	report 表示「據報道，消息比較確實」。	It is reported that the prisoner is going to commit suicide.	據悉，該囚犯將會自殺。
require 和 demand / claim / prescribe（要求）	require 表示「因需要有權要求某人做某事，強調提出要求的權威性」。	The management committee requires that I present the report tomorrow morning.	管理委員會要求我明早交報告。
	demand 表示「大膽、權威地要求」。	He demanded to see the charges against him.	他要求看到對他控罪內容。
	claim 表示「根據權利提出要求，要求承認其身份、擁有或對某物享有某種權利」。	You can claim compensation from the company.	你可以向公司索賠。
	prescribe 表示「醫生需要治療病人而要求他做某事」。	The physician prescribed bed rest for the patient in hospital.	醫生要求住院病人臥床休息。
requisite 和 requirement（需要的東西）	requisite 表示「必需品」。	Food and air are requisites for life.	食物和空氣是生存必需品。
	requirement 表示「需要、要求」。	Regular exercise is a requirement for good health.	經常做運動是健康的必要條件。
resent（憤恨）和 dislike（憎恨）	resent 表示「憤怒，語氣較弱，指對他人（有關自己）的隱形感到不快，不滿或怨恨」。	He resents being called a fool.	他討厭別人稱他為蠢才。
	dislike 表示「不喜歡某人或物，可指任何程度的憎惡」。	I dislike young people smoking.	我不喜歡年輕人吸煙。
resist（忍住）和 can't stand（受不了）	resist 表示「忍住、阻止自己做自己非常想做的事情」。	I can't resist playing computer games though they have made me fail in the middle term exam.	我無法抗拒玩電腦遊戲，儘管它導致自己期中考試不及格。
	can't stand 表示「無法忍受」。	She couldn't stand his rudeness any longer and walked out of the room.	她再也受不了他的無禮，走出了房間。
resource（資源）和 source（來源）	resource 表示「資源、指可用於使任務或活動更容易的東西或解決困難的才能」。	All the teaching resources — books, notes and so on are kept in the library.	所有教學資源——書籍、筆記都放在圖書館裏。
	source 表示「來源，指某物來自的地方或可從中得到它的東西」。	Tourism is the main source of income for many countries.	旅遊業是許多國家的主要收入來源。

易混淆字詞	註釋	例句	譯文
respect（尊敬）和 admire（佩服）	respect 表示「尊重，只限於説及人或品質」。	Children should respect their teachers.	孩子該尊重他們的老師。
	admire 表示「欣賞、佩服、驚訝，以愉快和尊重的態度待人接物；有驚歎意味」。	I admire your frankness.	我很欣賞你的坦率。
respectful（尊敬的）和 respectable（應受尊敬的）/ respective（各自的）	respectful 表示「有禮、尊重他人的，尤指尊敬比你年長的人」。	The principal has warned him that unless he shows a more respectful attitude towards his teachers, he will have to leave.	校長警告他，除非他對老師的態度更尊重，否則他將會被開除。
	respectable 表示「可敬的，在外表或行為上表現出社會可接受的標準；值得尊敬」。	My father, a humble businessman, was a respectable person.	我父親是一位謙虛的商人，總是受人尊敬。
	respective 表示「各個的，意思是指分別屬於已提到的每個人或物」。	They are each recognised specialists in their respective fields.	他們都是公認為各自領域的專家。
respond 和 response / reaction（反應）	respond 是動詞，表示「回答、反應，即對某人或事作出口頭或書面答覆」。	We're still waiting for them to respond to our letter.	我們仍在等待他們回信。
	response 是名詞，表示「回應」。	I don't care what they say, as long as I get a response.	我不在乎他們説甚麼，我只要得到回應。
	reaction 表示「因應另一件事採取的行動」，強調「事件的結果」，可表示「人體對治療或藥物的反應」。	The patient's reaction to the medicine was immediate.	病人對那種藥會立刻有反應。
retire（退休）和 resign（辭職）/ depart（離開）/ surrender（放棄）	retire 表示「因到了特定年齡要離職，通常是六十五歲」。	You can withdraw your MPF only if you retire at 65.	你只有在六十五歲退休時才可以提取強積金。
	resign 表示「辭去職務」。	After just two months he resigned and went to work for a smaller company.	僅僅兩個月後，他辭職並前往一家規模較小的公司工作。
	depart 表示「離開，特別指離開某地」。	His girlfriend departed from Hong Kong for Toronto yesterday.	他女友昨天離開香港前往多倫多了。
	surrender 表示「放棄某種感覺、事物、習慣等」。	The girl surrendered her ice cream to the hungry boy.	那女孩把雪糕送了給飢餓的男孩。

易混淆字詞	註釋	例句	譯文
reversion（倒退）和 reversal（倒轉）	reversion 表示「返回」，意思是「恢復以前的狀況或習慣或以前的談話主題」。	It's a complete reversion to primitive superstition.	像未開化的人那樣迷信，完全是一種倒退。
	reversal 表示「逆轉」，指「次序、位置、性質等的反轉」。	That would be a reversal of the order of host and guest.	那將是主客顛倒了。
revert（恢復原狀）和 transform（改變）	revert 表示「回來」，強調「恢復原狀」。	He's stopped taking drugs now, but he may revert to taking them again.	他現在已經戒毒了，但可能故態復萌。
	transform 表示「徹底改變外觀、性質或性格」，強調「形式、性質或功能方面的改變」。	The elegant decoration transformed the restaurant into a starlit night club.	優雅的裝飾把餐廳變成了星光燦爛的夜總會。
rhythm（節奏）和 rhyme（押韻）	rhythm 表示「節奏、音韻，指詩歌、音樂等的規律節拍」。	The rhythm of music is often provided by the drums.	音樂的節奏感通常由鼓聲營造。
	rhyme 表示「押韻，一個字與另一個字具有相同或類似的發音」。	Rhyme occurs among *say*, *play* and *stay*.	押韻發生在 say、play 和 stay 之間。
rigorous（嚴峻的）和 vigorous（精力充沛的）	rigorous 表示「嚴酷、勞苦；認真、仔細而準確的」。	The cold weather was rigorous.	寒冷天氣是嚴酷的。
	vigorous 表示「強而有力，強壯的；使用或需要力量」。	He keeps himself vigorous by taking exercise.	他靠鍛煉使自己保持旺盛精力。
risk 和 peril / danger（危險）	risk 表示「可能遇到的危險、遭受損失或傷害等，尤指自願進行某種活動或碰運氣而冒的風險」。	Smoking can increase the risk of developing heart disease.	吸煙會增加患心臟病的風險。
	peril 表示「巨大而嚴重的危險，通常指迫近的危險或風險」。	Dealing business with the US, Chinese firms are now in grave peril.	與美國做生意的中國公司現在正處於極大危險之中。
	danger 表示「可能帶來損害或損失的任何情況，也常指如果經過事先考慮可以避免或擺脫的困境」。	The sick man's life is in danger.	那病人有生命危險。
roof（屋頂）和 ceiling（天花板）	roof 指「建築物外面頂部的覆蓋物」。	If the rain is coming in, there must be a hole in the roof.	如果下雨漏水，屋頂上一定有個洞。
	ceiling 指「建築物內部的天花板」。	Paint the ceiling before you paint the walls.	油漆牆身前先油漆天花板。

易混淆字詞	註釋	例句	譯文
row（排）和 queue（排隊）	row 表示「一行人或事物」。	Along one side of the river there was a row of cottages.	在河的一側有一排小屋。
	queue 表示「一排排的人一個個站着,等巴士、買票和輪候等」。	There was already a long queue of passengers waiting to be checked in.	檢查登機的乘客已排成很長的隊。
rotate（自轉）和 revolve（環繞轉動）	rotate 表示「圍繞自己的中心移動」。	The earth rotates once every 24 hours.	地球每二十四小時自轉一次。
	revolve 表示「(導致) 旋轉 (在中心點)」。	The earth revolves round the sun once each year.	地球每年繞太陽轉一圈。
rouse / arouse（喚起）和 incite（鼓動）/ evince（表示出）	rouse 表示「喚起,使某人變得更活躍,如克服倦意、激起熱情、喚起行動等」。	The Financial Secretary's speech failed to rouse his audience.	財政司司長的演講未能激起聽眾的興趣。
	arouse 表示「喚醒」,使某人有某種特定感覺或態度,如喚起注意、同情、引起猜疑、不快等。	Her strange behaviour aroused our suspicions.	她奇怪的行為引起了我們的懷疑。
	incite 表示「鼓勵某人產生強烈情感而引起行動或導致後果」。	It is claimed that anger was incited by the dissatisfied employees.	據稱不滿的員工激發憤怒。
	evince 表示「清楚表明你有一種感覺或品質,指表示出非眼睛所能看到得見的東西,如情感、品質等」。	He evinced little enthusiasm for the outdoor activities.	他表示對戶外活動毫不熱衷。
sack 和 bag（袋）	sack 表示「一個非常大的用紙或布製成的結實袋子」。	He's hurt his back trying to lift a sack of potatoes.	他試圖抬起一袋馬鈴薯時受了傷。
	bag 表示「由布、紙、皮革等製成的袋或包裝容器」。	When I took the two oranges out of the bag, I discovered that one of them was bad.	當我從袋裏拿出兩個橙時,我發現其中一個壞了。
sacrifice（犧牲）和 victim（犧牲者）	sacrifice 表示「(可能指為特定目的) 損失或放棄有價值的東西」。	She made a lot of sacrifice to get a degree.	為了獲得學位,她犧牲了很多。
	victim 表示「受害者,因他人犯罪、疾病、意外等受傷或死亡的人」。	He was one of the innocent victims of an arson attack.	他是縱火襲擊的無辜受害者之一。

易混淆字詞	註釋	例句	譯文
sacrosanct (不可侵犯的) 和 sacred (神聖的)	sacrosanct 表示「(指被認為太重要而不能改變) 極神聖不可侵犯的」。	I can work at 'nine, nine, six' each week, but my Sundays and Public Holidays are **sacrosanct**.	我每星期可以上班六天，「每日由早上九點至晚上九點」，但星期日和公共假期絕對不上班。
	sacred 表示「神聖的、獻給……的，指非常重要，受到極大尊重，常與 to 連用」。	This is a monument **sacred** *to* the memory of a great person.	這是為紀念一位偉人而立的碑。
salary 和 wage / honorarium / pay (工資)	salary 表示「薪金，指白領在辦公室工作的固定薪酬」。	As a junior secretary, she's on a **salary** of $260,000 a year.	作為一名初級秘書，她的年薪為二十六萬元。
	wage 表示「時薪、日薪或按件工支付工資」。	As an experienced electric worker, his **wage** is $1,800 per day.	作為一名經驗豐富的電工，他的工資是每天1,800 元。
	honorarium 表示「酬金，指沒有固定價錢的酬金」。	Professor Hung received a small **honorarium** for speaking at the conference.	洪教授因在會議上演講而獲得微薄的謝金。
	pay 是指「從工作獲得的金錢的總稱」。	The management announced a **pay** rise of $200 a month.	管理層宣佈每月加薪兩百元。
salute (敬禮) 和 welcome (歡迎)	salute 表示「敬禮，舉起右臂，正式表示尊重，是及物動詞，不能跟 to」。	Always **salute** a superior police officer.	永遠向上級警官敬禮。
	welcome 表示「迎接，當客人或朋友到達時，表明你對他們的來臨感到高興」。	A group of officials were at the airport to **welcome** the visitors.	一羣官員在機場迎接來賓。
satisfactory 和 satisfying (令人滿意的) / satisfied (滿意的)	satisfactory 表示「令人滿意，含主動意思，常以事或物作主語」。	Students are asked to leave the college if their work is not **satisfactory**.	如果學生成績未能令人滿意，他們會被開除。
	satisfying 表示「令人快樂或滿足，常以事或物作主語」。	For many people, a part-time job can be very **satisfying**.	對許多人來說，兼職工作可能會令人非常滿意。
	satisfied 表示「感到高興或滿足，含被動意思，常以人作主語」。	Despite the team's convincing 3-0 victory, the manager wasn't **satisfied**.	儘管球隊取得了令人心悅誠服的 3-0 勝利，經理人仍不滿意。
sauce (醬汁) 和 source (根源)	sauce 表示「調味品」。	This cook is an expert at making **sauces**.	這位廚師是製作醬汁的專家。
	source 表示「來源」。	The news comes from a reliable **source**.	這條消息來源可靠。

易混淆字詞	註釋	例句	譯文
saucy 和 impertinent（無禮的）	saucy 表示「莽撞、輕浮或輕率的舉止或言語」。	Her saucy remarks raised many eyebrows.	她無禮的評論使許多人產生反感。
	impertinent 表示「無禮，指粗魯而不尊重年長或更重要的人」。	Talking back to old people is impertinent.	用言語反駁長輩是沒有禮貌的。
savage（兇猛的）和 wild（野生的）	savage 表示「兇猛、殘忍的；處於原始或未開化狀態」。	The savage lion attacked the hunter.	那頭兇猛獅子襲擊了獵人。
	wild 表示「未馴服的動物，指生活在自然條件下」。	A deer is a wild animal but is not savage.	鹿是野生動物，卻不是兇猛的。
scarce 和 rare（罕見的）	scarce 表示「稀缺，常指有用但不夠、難以找到或收集的東西」。	Certain commodities have become so scarce that their prices soared.	某些商品變得如此稀缺，以至其價格飆升起來。
	rare 表示「不常見，罕見但很有價值的東西」。	Jade is a rare stone.	玉是一種稀有寶石。
seasonal（季節性的）和 seasonable（合時宜的）	seasonal 表示「依季節而變化的」。	My son gets seasonal employment at Shek O beach.	我兒子在石澳海灘得到一份季節性工作。
	seasonable 表示「一年中某時候預期的天氣情況」。	In general, typhoon is seasonable in Hong Kong from June to October.	一般來說，六月至十月是香港的風季。
see 和 look / watch（看）	see 表示「看見、看到，尤指沒有集中注意力，側重結果」。	I saw him go out.	我看到他出去了。
	look 表示「瞧，指將眼睛轉向某方向，側重動作，後面跟 at」。	She is looking at the dresses in the shop window.	她正在看櫥窗裏的裙。
	watch 表示「觀看，指注視某人或物，尤指長時間，強調過程」。	After retirement, my father watches television all day long.	我父親退休後整天看電視。
selected（挑選出來的）和 selective（選擇的）/ elective（選修的）/ optional（自由選擇的）	selected 表示「精選的」。	The factory needs a lot of selected coal.	那間工廠需要大量的精選煤。
	selective 表示「謹慎選擇人或物」。	HKU's admissions policy is very selective.	香港大學的招生政策是非常選擇性的。
	elective 表示「大學裏可自由選擇的課程」。	The first year requires you to complete five compulsory subjects and eight elective courses.	第一年你必須完成五個必修科和八個選修科。
	optional 表示「可以跟隨意願選擇做某事或擁有某東西」。	This version comes with a number of optional extras.	這版本帶有許多可自由選擇的附加功能。

易混淆字詞	註釋	例句	譯文
sensible（明智的）和 sensitive（敏感的）/ sensory（感覺的）	sensible 表示「明智、合理，指基於理性作出正確決定，並且從不以愚蠢或危險的方式行事」。	He's a sensible sort of person and has never done anything to put himself at risk.	他是一個理智的人，從沒有做過任何冒險的事。
	sensitive 表示「敏感到某物的效果而快速反應，常指容易生氣的人」。	Don't be so sensitive — he was only joking.	別那麼敏感 —— 他只是在開玩笑。
	sensory 表示「感覺的，指與感覺相關的」。	The eyes, ears and nose are sensory organs.	眼、耳和鼻是感官。
service（服役）和 servitude（苦役）	service 表示「在武裝部隊中服兵役，在某些國家是公民責任」。	Hong Kong residents are not required to perform military service.	香港居民無須服兵役。
	servitude 表示「懲罰性的強迫勞動」。	The activist was sentenced to ten years' servitude.	該活動人士被判處十年勞役。
severe / strict 和 stern（嚴厲的）	severe 表示「嚴厲的懲罰、批評、損害等」。	Driving while drunk could endanger other people's lives, so penalties are severe.	酒後駕車會危及他人生命，因此處罰十分嚴厲。
	strict 表示「必須嚴格遵守的規則或法律」。	There are strict rules as to what you can wear to school.	可以穿甚麼衣服上學是有嚴格規定的。
	stern 表示「對他人的行為非常嚴厲」。	He's much too stern with his son.	他對兒子太嚴厲了。
shade（蔭）和 shadow（影子）	shade 表示「蔭，因物體遮擋光線而造成的陰涼處」。	There was no shade anywhere.	那裏任何地方都沒有陰涼處。
	shadow 表示「陰影，指光照射在某人或物的背後時，牆壁或地上出現的影子」。	The setting sun cast long shadows down the beach.	夕陽在沙灘上投下長長的影子。
shallow 和 superficial（膚淺的）	shallow 表示「淺薄、缺乏深入或認真的思考，但不可指知識」。	In the party, they carried on a shallow conversation about clothes, shoes, and cosmetics.	晚會中他們談論衣服、鞋和化粧品的膚淺話題。
	superficial 表示「淺薄、不徹底或不深刻，可指知識」。	I never felt so keenly how superficial my knowledge was.	我從沒這樣深深感受自己的知識有多膚淺。
shameful（可恥）和 ashamed（感到羞恥）	shameful 表示「造成或帶來恥辱，用來指事物或行為」。	It's shameful the way they waste money.	他們那樣浪費金錢真可恥。
	ashamed 表示「感到羞恥或慚愧，用來指人」。	He was ashamed because he was late again.	他很慚愧，因為他又遲到了。

易混淆字詞	註釋	例句	譯文
shortly（不久）和 short（突然地）/ briefly（簡短地）	shortly 表示「很快」。	I'll be with you **shortly**.	我馬上會和你在一起了。
	short 表示「忽然」。	The driver stopped **short** when the child ran into the street.	看見孩子跑出街上，司機突然停車。
	briefly 表示「很短時間」。	She spoke very **briefly** about how she had lived during the war.	她非常簡短地談到自己在戰爭期間的生活。
sink（沉沒）和 drown（淹死）/ submerge（淹沒）	sink 表示「逐漸和緩慢下沉，指船隻和任何物體的沉沒」。	The ship had been holed in the collision and was beginning to **sink**.	這艘船在碰撞中穿了個洞，開始下沉。
	drown 表示「淹死，用於描述在水中下沉以至無法呼吸而死亡的人或動物」。	I knew that if I fell into the sea, I would **drown**.	我知道如果我掉進海裏，我就會淹死。
	submerge 表示「淹沒，指被水或其他液體覆蓋」。	I was **submerged** but soon put my head above water again.	我被淹沒了，但很快我便把頭伸上水面。
site（場所）和 sight（景象）	site 表示「位置，某物存在的地方」。	The new museum will be built on this **site**.	新博物館將在這個位置興建。
	sight 表示「看到的東西；景色；see 的名詞」。	He lost **sight** two years ago.	兩年前他失明了。
skilful（熟練的）和 talented（有才能的）	skilful 表示「嫻熟、靈巧的，指從指導和實踐中獲得的技能」。	Although he lacked Tyson's knock-out punch, he was the more **skilful** of the two boxers.	雖然他缺乏泰臣的擊倒拳，但他還是兩名拳擊手之中技術最純熟的。
	talented 表示「有才華的、指具有將某事做得特別好的才能或天賦」。	'You're lucky to have such **talented** children,' she said.	她說：「你很幸運，孩子這樣有才華」。
smell（氣味）和 flavour（味道）/ stink（臭味）/ scent（香味）	smell 表示「鼻子聞到的氣味，指嗅覺」。	**Smell** is one of the five senses.	嗅覺是五官功能之一。
	flavor 表示「舌頭體驗或品嚐到的味道，指味覺」。	She likes candy with a lemon **flavour**.	她喜歡檸檬味的糖果。
	stink 表示「惡臭，指非常難聞的氣味，是貶義詞」。	The **stink** of durian filled the refrigerator.	榴蓮的臭味充滿了冰箱。
	scent 表示「香氣，指一股甜味」。	The **scent** of flowers filled the air.	空氣中瀰漫着花香。

易混淆字詞	註釋	例句	譯文
social (社交的) 和 sociable (好交際的)	social 表示「喜歡和別人在一起，用於活動或團體」。	You must go. This is a **social** gathering.	你必須去。這是一個社交活動。
	sociable 表示「享受社交生活，常用於人」。	Being a public relations officer, you have to be **sociable**.	作為一名公關人員，你必須擅長交際。
sometime (某時候) 和 some time (某段時間) / sometimes (有時)	sometime 是副詞，表示「在某時候，但未有指定時間」。	The building was built **sometime** around 1960.	該大廈大約建於 1960 年。
	some time 是名詞詞組，表示「一段時間」。	I shall be away from **some time**.	我會離開一段時間。
	sometimes 是副詞，表示「時不時，有時」。	**Sometimes** I go out on weekday nights, but mostly I study.	平日晚上我有時會出去，但主要是為了學習。
soon (很快) 和 immediately (立即) / early (早) / recently (不久之前)	soon 表示「不久，很快，指短時間內」。	I shall **soon** be home.	我很快就會到家了。
	immediately 表示「立刻、馬上」。	I left **immediately** after I received your call.	我接到你的電話後便馬上離開。
	early 表示「在平時、規定或約定時間之前」。	We thank you for your **early** reply to our letter.	感謝你這麼早就回覆了我們的來信。
	recently 表示「不久前，用於過去，常用於一般過去式或完成式」。	She has come to see me **recently**.	她最近看過我。
specially (專門地) 和 especially (特別是)	specially 表示「不是為了別的，而是專門為了這個特殊目的」。	We've come all the way from Hong Kong **specially** to see you.	我們從香港專程來看你。
	especially 表示「對前面所說的內容或東西作進一步說明」。	There is a shortage of teachers, **especially** of science.	現在特別缺乏教師，尤其是理科教師。
spectacle (奇觀) 和 spectacles (眼鏡)	spectacle (沒有 's') 表示「引人注目或不尋常的景象」。	A big army parade is a fine **spectacle**.	大型閱兵儀式非常壯觀。
	spectacles (有 's') 表示「眼鏡」。	I can't find my **spectacles**.	我找不到眼鏡。
spectator / audience (觀眾) 和 congregation (教堂會眾)	spectator 表示「觀看體育賽事的人」。	The new stadium can hold up to 60,000 **spectators**.	新大球場可容納最多六萬名觀眾。
	audience 表示「看電影、戲劇、聽音樂會、公開演講等的人」。	At the end of the talk, members of the **audience** were invited to ask questions.	演講結束後聽眾可以提問。
	congregation 表示「參加教會崇拜的人」。	The priest stands in front of the bride and groom, facing the **congregation**.	神父站在新郎新娘之前，面向觀眾。

易混淆字詞	註釋	例句	譯文
speech 和 talk（演説）	speech 表示「向聽眾發表的正式講話」。	She made a speech in front of the whole school.	她在全校師生面前講了一次話。
	talk 表示「提供信息的講話、對話或討論，通常由講師講授」。	In 1972, I was invited to give a talk on foreign exchange trading at the Hong Kong Polytechnic.	1972 年我應邀在香港理工學院講授外匯交易。
spend 和 cost（花費）	spend 表示「花錢，指付錢購物，主語一般是人」。	I spent 8,000 dollars on this notebook.	我花了八千元買了這部手提電腦。
	cost 表示「價值多少，指價錢，主語是物」。	This notebook cost me 8,000 dollars.	這部手提電腦花了我八千元。
sport 和 sports（運動）	sport（沒有 's'）表示「各類戶內或戶外體育運動」。	I'm not very good at sport.	我不太擅長運動。
	sports（有 's'）是 sport 的複數形式，常用於名詞詞組，例如「體育中心」、「體育俱樂部」、「運動器材」、「運動損傷」等。	Tomorrow is the sports day and we'll have no class.	明天是運動會，我們不用上課。
sprain 和 strain（扭傷）	sprain 表示「（手腕或腳踝）關節扭傷」。	I stumbled and sprained my ankle.	我摔倒並扭傷了腳踝。
	strain 表示「指拉伸或拉緊引起受傷」。	My grandpa slipped and strained his ankle.	我爺爺滑倒並拉傷腳踝。
squeeze（壓）和 squash（壓扁）	squeeze 表示「用力壓住某物，尤指用手握緊它」。	She squeezed my arm and told me not to worry.	她捏住我的手臂，告訴我別擔心。
	squash 表示「壓住某物，常指用很大的力，使其變平或破裂」。	Mind you don't squash the eggs.	注意不要壓扁雞蛋。
statesman 和 politician（政治家）	statesman 表示「政治或政府領導人，尤指有智慧和頭腦冷靜的人，為褒義詞」。	It was generally agreed that Churchill, British Prime Minister during the Second War World, was a great statesman.	人們普遍同意第二次世界大戰時英國首相邱吉爾是一位偉大的政治家。
	politician 表示「政客，指出於個人利益而加入政治黨派或無黨派的人，含貶義」。	He is a skilled politician and earns many posts in government related organisations.	他是一位老練的政治家，在政府機構擔任許多職務。
stationery（文具）和 stationary（靜止的）	stationery 是名詞，表示「文具，即書寫材料如紙筆等」。	As a writer, I must spend a great deal of money on stationery.	作為一個作者，我花在文具的錢必定多。
	stationary 是形容詞，表示「在固定位置或地點靜止不動」。	The cars remained stationary for some time.	汽車停下來已一段時間了。

易混淆字詞	註釋	例句	譯文
statistic 和 statistics (統計)	statistic (沒有 's') 表示「統計數字,指一份數據顯示的事實」。	This terrible crime will soon become nothing more than a statistic in police records.	這種可怕罪行很快會變成警局統計數字中的一個記錄。
	statistics (有 's') 表示「統計學,指蒐集和使用數據作為事實的統計數字」。	Statistics show that the population has almost doubled in the last twenty years.	統計數據顯示,人口在過去二十年幾乎增加一倍。
statue (塑像) 和 stature (身材)	statue 表示「用青銅、石頭、木頭等雕刻的人、動物等」。	Nearly every city has statues of their famous men.	幾乎每個城市都有他們名人的雕像。
	stature 表示「身高,指一個人的自然身高」。	He is six feet in stature.	他身高六英尺。
steal (偷) 和 rob (搶劫)	steal 表示「偷,無權拿走屬於他人的東西」。	He stole money from his mother.	他偷了他媽媽的錢。
	rob 表示「搶劫,指以武力從一個人或地方奪取金錢或財產」。	These three men robbed the ABC Bank ten years ago, and killed a security guard.	這三個人十年前搶劫 ABC 銀行,並殺死一名保安員。
step (步伐) 和 pace (步速)	step 表示「舉步,指走路、跳舞等動作,有優美、長短、輕重之分」。	He came along the street with hurried steps.	他邁開急促步伐沿街疾走。
	pace 表示「步幅」。	He walked at a fast pace.	他步行得很快。
stimulant (興奮劑) 和 stimulus (刺激)	stimulant 表示「刺激物,是一種藥物,使頭腦或身體更活躍」。	The caffeine in coffee acts as a stimulant.	咖啡中的咖啡因是一種興奮劑。
	stimulus 表示「刺激,指引起活動、成長或更大努力的事物,但並不是藥物」。	Political stability acts as a stimulus for foreign investment.	政治穩定可以刺激外國投資。
stingy (吝嗇) 和 economical (節儉)	stingy 表示「吝嗇、不大方、小氣的」。	If you have to use money in a proper way, don't be stingy.	若錢用得恰當,就別吝嗇。
	economical 表示「不浪費、節儉、節省、經濟的」。	She has to be very economical because she hasn't much money to spend.	她沒有多少錢,必須非常節省。

易混淆字詞	註釋	例句	譯文
storey / floor（樓層）和 flat（套間）	**storey** 表示「層數；常用於描述建築物樓層的高度，下層與上層或屋頂之間的空間」。	The industrial building has ten **storeys**.	那工業大廈樓高十層。
	floor 表示「樓層；常用來談論某人居住／工作／去的地方」。	My office is on the second **floor** of this building.	我的辦公室在這棟大廈的二樓。
	flat 表示「套間，在建築物中的一套房間」。	Do you live in a house or a **flat**?	你住在房屋還是套間？
strain（緊張）和 stress（壓力）	**strain** 作為名詞，表示「緊張或過度疲勞的狀態，指體力或腦力承受重壓而感到疲累」。	It is a **strain** to work sixteen hours a day.	每天工作十六小時太緊張了。
	stress 作為名詞，表示「生活困難引起的壓力，多指感情或心理上的壓力」。	The **stress** of not knowing well of her husband before marriage was too great for her.	婚前對丈夫了解不深，這對她造成難以負荷的極大壓力。
stranger（陌生人）和 foreigner（外國人）	**stranger** 表示「生客，一個你從未見過的人」。	Young children are told not to talk to **strangers**.	告知年幼孩子別與陌生人交談。
	foreigner 表示「外來客，來自另一個國家的人」。	There are a lot of **foreigners** visiting Hong Kong.	來港的外國人很多。
subconscious（下意識的）和 unconscious（無意識的）	**subconscious** 表示「潛意識的思想或願望」。	Taichi boxing is trained to exercise at a **subconscious** level.	太極拳訓練在於融合潛意識於運動之中。
	unconscious 表示「不醒人事，指處於睡眠狀態，尤指因生病或頭部被擊中」。	After collision, the driver of the car was taken to hospital **unconscious**.	撞車後，司機昏迷不醒被送往醫院。
subtract / deduct（減去）和 detract（減損）	**subtract** 表示「減掉，扣除」。	**Subtract** four from nine is five.	九減去四，剩下五。
	deduct 表示「扣減，指從總數除去一個數量，用於數量方面」。	Because of the COVID-19, the Board of Directors has resolved to **deduct** 20% from our salaries.	由於新冠疫情，董事會議決我們減薪 20%。
	detract 表示「降低、減損」，指「去除一些價值、名譽等東西」。	His recent behaviour **detracted** from my high opinion of him.	他最近的行為使我降低對他的高度評價。

易混淆字詞	註釋	例句	譯文
successful (成功的) 和 successive (連續的) / consecutive (連續不斷的)	successful 表示「成功，勝利」。	He is very **successful** in everything.	他各方面全都非常成功。
	successive 表示「緊隨其後，強調按一定順序相接，但其中有時間上的間隔」。	They got good harvests for three **successive** leap years.	他們連續三個閏年都獲得豐收。
	consecutive 表示「接連不斷，強調不間斷，一個接一個」。	1, 2, 3 and 4 are **consecutive** numbers.	1、2、3 和 4 是連續數字。
sufferance (忍耐力) 和 suffering (苦難)	sufferance 表示「承受痛苦的能力」。	Without using anaesthesia, it is *beyond* **sufferance**.	沒有麻醉劑，它是無法忍受的。
	suffering 表示「痛苦、苦難和困難」。	The doctor quickly relieved the girl's **suffering**.	醫生很快就解除了那個女孩的痛苦。
sufficiently 和 enough (足夠地)	sufficiently 是副詞，表示「足夠，常用於書面語，須置於修飾的中心詞之前」。	The table is not **sufficiently** wide for our purpose.	這桌子不夠濶，不符合我們的要求。
	enough 是副詞，可用於動詞、形容詞和副詞之後，表示「充足、與某人需要或想要的一樣多」。	The table is not *wide* **enough** for our purpose.	這桌子不夠濶，不符合我們的要求。
suit (套裝) 和 suite (房間)	suit 表示「一套外衣，包括衫、褲或裙」。	A man's **suit** consists of a jacket and trousers.	男士的西裝由上衣和褲子組成。
	suite 表示「一組房間，尤指酒店房間」。	When my parents married, they lived in a luxury honeymoon **suite** of this hotel.	我父母結婚時，住在這酒店的豪華蜜月套房裏。
summit 和 top (頂部)	summit 表示「山頂，指山的最高點」。	They reached the **summit** at midday.	他們中午到達山頂。
	top 表示「頂部，指任何物體的最高處」。	He got to the **top** of the house.	他爬上了屋頂。
sunburn (曬傷) 和 tan (曬黑的皮膚)	sunburn 表示「在烈日下曬傷，導致皮膚變紅和起泡」。	After lying in the hot sun all day she was suffering from **sunburn**.	在烈日下躺了一整天後，她被曬傷了。
	tan 表示「曬傷皮膚的黃褐色」。	Those girls lie in the sun so as to get a good **tan**.	那些女孩躺在太陽底下以便把皮膚曬黑。

易混淆字詞	註釋	例句	譯文
sunlight / sunshine 和 sun (陽光)	sunlight 表示「太陽發出的光線」。	Outdoor **sunlight** is very good for the health.	戶外陽光對健康非常有益。
	sunshine 表示「來自太陽光的溫暖，是褒義詞，含感情色彩」。	The children are playing in the **sunshine**.	孩子在陽光下玩耍。
	sun 表示「來自太陽的光和熱，是中性詞」。	I like to sit in the **sun**.	我喜歡坐在陽光下。
supernatural (超自然的) 和 unnatural (不自然的)	**supernatural** 表示「神奇、超越自然或物理的」。	Angels and devils are **supernatural** beings.	天使和魔鬼都是超自然的生靈。
	unnatural 表示「不自然、反常的」，指「違背普通的良好行為方式」。	Have you noticed that her reaction was **unnatural**?	你注意到她的反應很不自然嗎？
supersede (取代) 和 surpass (超過)	**supersede** 表示「代替，佔領他的位置」。	Will high-speed trains **supersede** aeroplanes?	高鐵會取代飛機嗎？
	surpass 表示「勝過、優於或超過，指出類拔萃」。	She, in the age of 10, has **surpassed** her sister who was 15, in intelligence.	十歲的她，智商已經超過她十五歲的姐姐。
supplementary 和 complementary (補充的)	**supplementary** 表示「附加、額外的」。	A traffic allowance was **supplementary** to her monthly pay.	她每月除了工資之外，還有交通津貼。
	complementary 表示「互相依附，指必不可少的補充」。	The four seasons are **complementary** parts of the year.	四季構成完整的一年。
supposedly 和 presumably (假定)	**supposedly** 表示「想像、臆測、指沒有根據的假設或猜想」。	**Supposedly**, she is a rich woman.	據說，她是個富婆。
	presumably 表示「可能、也許」，指「有根據地推測被認為是真實的」。	Since he is a professor in physics, **presumably** he knew what Hawking's talking about.	既然他是物理學教授，或許他知道霍金在說甚麼。
surely 和 certainly / definitely (確實地)	**surely** 表示「毫無疑問」，常用於「對所說內容是否真實表達強烈的信念，並鼓勵聽者同意」。	**Surely** they should have arrived by now!	他們該早就到了。
	certainly 表示「無疑地，肯定地」。	Without treatment, she will almost **certainly** die.	如果不治療，她幾乎肯定會死。
	definitely 表示「明確地，指對某事完全確定的感覺」。	Please say **definitely** whether you will be coming or not.	來或不來請務必說清楚。

易混淆字詞	註釋	例句	譯義
suspicious 和 doubtful / sceptical（懷疑的）	suspicious 表示「不信任，指對行為目的或事件的真實性有所懷疑」。	I started to get suspicious when he refused to tell me where he had been.	當他拒絕告訴我他去過甚麼地方時，我開始懷疑。
	doubtful 表示「懷疑某事，需要進一步的證據來證明」。	It is doubtful if we can get a taxi in such a rush hour.	我們能否在這繁忙時間乘搭的士是很難説的。
	sceptical 表示「對某項主張或陳述的真實性或某事將會發生有懷疑」。	Before I actually started to use one, I was sceptical about the value of the camera.	我真正開始使用這照相機之前，我對它的價值抱懷疑態度。
sympathetic 和 pitying（同情的）	sympathetic 表示「感到或表示同情，指贊同某種意見或想法」。	Among the committee members, he was the only one who was sympathetic to my opinion.	在委員會成員中，他是唯一贊同我意見的人。
	pitying 表示「憐憫，對某人表示同情，通常以表明你認為自己的方式比他們更好」。	After winning the game, he shows a pitying smile on me.	贏了比賽後，他對我露出了憐憫的笑容。
tacit（心照不宣的）和 taciturn（沉默寡言的）	tacit 表示「不言而喻，心照不宣」。	The couple has a tacit agreement to help each other in their whole life.	這對夫婦有一個默契，要在他們的一生中互相幫助。
	taciturn 表示「習慣上不愛説話，看起來不友好」。	He is so taciturn that no one knows whether he likes our companion or not.	他沉默寡言，沒人知道他是否喜歡與我們結伴同行。
tale 和 story（故事）	tale 表示「虛構故事」。	When I was a little boy, my mother always told me about fairy tales.	我還是個小男孩時，媽媽總是給我講童話故事。
	story 表示「引起讀者或聽眾興趣的故事、身世等，可能是真實事件，也可能是虛構故事」。	I like reading short horror stories.	我喜歡閱讀短篇恐怖故事。
tasteful（有鑑賞力的）和 tasty（美味的）	tasteful 表示「雅致，有品味的，通常指能夠判斷哪種藝術、音樂、家具等有良好的製作水平或吸引力」。	The design of the room was very tasteful — pale colours with matching furniture.	房間的設計很有品味——淺色配搭配套家具。
	tasty 表示「食物的味道很好」。	The food was excellent and very tasty.	食物一流，非常好吃。

易混淆字詞	註釋	例句	譯文
teach 和 instruct（教授）	**teach** 表示「教導，指通過學校、大學等場所有計劃地為學生提供知識，使他們能獲得一門學問或技能」。	My husband **teaches** at an international school in Hong Kong.	我丈夫在香港的一間國際學校裏任教。
	instruct 表示「指導，指按一定方法連續或正式告訴某人做某事」。	The manager **instructed** me in the best way of doing the job by using 'production management' technique.	經理指導我「生產管理」技巧是完成這項工作的最好方法。
technique / technology 和 technical（技術）	**technique** 是名詞，意思是「技巧、技能、技術，指具體的技術或方法，尤指需要特殊訓練的」。	Thanks to these new surgical **techniques**, patients spend far shorter periods in hospital.	感謝這些新外科技術，它們大大縮短了患者在醫院的時間。
	technology 是名詞，意思是「生產工藝或技術，將科學理論和方法應用於實際項目」。	Because of modern **technology**, we have much higher standard of living.	我們的生活水平因現代科技而大大提高了。
	technical 是形容詞，意思是「專門技術的，通常指與特殊的藝術、科學、手工藝等有關」。	Hawking's books on black hole are too **technical** for me.	霍金關於黑洞的書對我來說太專業了。
teens（十幾歲的人）和 teenager（十三至十九歲的人）	**teens** 表示「十幾歲的人」。	She is still in her **teens**.	她還不到二十歲。
	teenager 表示「十三至十九歲的年輕人」。	Although he is now 80 years old, his son is a **teenager**.	雖然他現在已經八十歲了，但他兒子還是十三歲。
tell（告訴）和 say（說）	**tell** 表示「告訴、告知，只用於間接引語前加表示人的直接賓語」。	He **told** me he wasn't going.	他告訴我他不去。
	say 表示「說或告訴，可用於直接和間接引語」。	He **said** he wasn't going.	他說他不去。
temper（脾氣）和 temperament（性情）	**temper** 表示「脾氣，指心靈狀態，容易感到生氣與否」。	She is a nice girl and always keeps her **temper**.	她是一個很友善的女孩子，從不發脾氣。
	temperament 表示「氣質、本性，指左右人的思想感情或行動的特質」。	Success depends on one's **temperament**.	一個人的成功取決於氣質。
tender 和 offer（提供）	**tender** 表示「提供，贈與，指提供服務等，而並不是實物」。	I **tendered** my resignation yesterday.	我昨天遞交了辭職信。
	offer 表示「提供實物或具體的事物供選擇，讓對方接受或拒絕」。	I was **offered** a job in an IT firm, but I rejected.	一家科技公司想聘用我，但遭我拒絕了。

易混淆字詞	註釋	例句	譯文
terrible / terrify 和 terrified（恐懼）	terrible 是形容詞，表示「使人感到可怕的，指引起極大恐懼，含主動意義」。	There was a **terrible** storm last night; the thunder just made me sleepless.	昨晚有一場可怕的風暴；雷聲令我失眠。
	terrify 是動詞，表示「使恐懼，使驚嚇」。	His idea to raise a snake at home **terrifies** his mother.	他想在家裏養一條蛇，這想法使他母親感到驚嚇。
	terrified 是 terrify 的過去分詞，可用作形容詞，表示「感到恐懼，含被動意思」。	Having been locked in a dark room, the **terrified** little girl screamed.	被鎖在漆黑的房間裏，遭嚇壞的小女孩尖叫了起來。
terror 和 horror（恐怖）	terror 表示「自身感到危險而極度害怕」。	After running from the mountain fire in **terror**, I've never gone hiking.	自從沒命地逃離山火後，我再也沒有去遠足了。
	horror 表示「看到危險、醜陋或怪異東西時感到極度恐懼」。	To my **horror**, a baby was thrown from the window of the fifth floor.	一個嬰孩從五樓的窗戶被扔了出去，令我毛骨悚然。
text（原文）和 article（文章）	text 表示「原文，指關於學術主題的文章」。	The first two **texts** on the reading list are general introductions.	閱讀清單上前兩篇文章是用作一般介紹的。
	article 表示「報章雜誌上的文章」。	She told me she is writing an **article** about Bitcorn for our local newspaper.	她告訴我她正在為當地報章寫一篇比特幣的文章。
than（比）和 then（然後）	than 是用於比較的連詞，意思是「比……」。	The climate in Hong Kong is warmer **than** that in Shanghai.	香港的氣候比上海溫暖。
	then 表示「下一個，之後」。	Participants in the study first completed a demographic questionnaire, and **then** they participated in the focus group discussion.	該研究的參與者首先完成了人口調查問卷，然後參加了焦點小組討論。

易混淆字詞	註釋	例句	譯文
thought / notion / idea / conception（想法）和 belief（信念）/ opinion（意見）	thought 表示「突然想到、記住或意識到的東西，指不是單憑幻想形成的想法」。	Does anyone have any **thoughts** about where we should eat?	有人想提議我們在那裏吃飯嗎？
	notion 表示「對某事的想法、信念，指沒有徹底形成的想法」。	I have only a **notion** of what you mean.	我只明白了一點點你的意思。
	idea 表示「計劃、想法或建議，指有具體清晰的概念、了解或意圖」。	This book should give you a rough **idea** of 'production management' in banking.	這書該幫助你大致了解銀行業的「生產管理」。
	conception 表示「形成想法或計劃的過程，指完整詳細，甚至是複雜的想法」。	The plan was brilliant in its **conception** but failed because of lack of money.	該計劃構思精妙，但因缺錢而失敗。
	belief 表示「信念，指是否相信某事真實、好或壞的感覺」。	They are prepared to kill in order to defend their **beliefs**.	他們準備殺人以捍衛信仰。
	opinion 表示「意見，指思考長時間之後，對某事的看法」。	People's attitudes and **opinions** don't change overnight.	人的態度和意見不會一夜之間改變。
in time（及時）和 on time（準時）	in time 表示「及時，沒有遲到」。	Make sure you arrive **in time** to see the beginning of the film.	確保準時到達才可看到電影開畫的片頭。
	on time 表示「在正確時間內準時到達或完成工作」。	We have to rush to get to work **on time**.	我們必須趕時間準時上班。
timetable 和 schedule（時間表）	timetable 表示「上課時間或巴士、火車等到達和離開時間的車程表」。	According to my **timetable**, English composition is on every Thursday.	根據我的時間表，每星期四有英語作文堂。
	schedule 表示「必須完成事情的詳細計劃時間表」。	The manager's **schedule** next week is very busy.	經理下星期的時間日程很忙。
tiresome（煩人的）和 tiring / tired（疲倦的）	tiresome 表示「使人厭倦，不愉快的，含主動意義」。	I find these so-called jokes extremely **tiresome**.	我覺得這些所謂笑話非常令人厭煩。
	tiring 表示「使人疲乏，筋疲力盡」。	The direct flight from Hong Kong to Toronto is very **tiring**.	香港到多倫多的直飛使人感到疲乏。
	tired 表示「疲倦，累的，含被動意義」。	The lecture lasted no less than five hours and everyone was **tired**.	講座持續了五個小時，大家都感到厭倦。

易混淆字詞	註釋	例句	譯義
title / headline（標題）和 subject（主題）	title 表示「標題、題目，可指書名、戲劇名、繪畫名、音樂名等的名稱」。	I can remember the title of the book but not the author.	我記得書名，但記不起作者是誰。
	headline 表示「在報章上文章的標題，尤其指在頭版的主要報導」。	Today's newspaper headlines are all about national security.	今天的報章頭條都是關於國家安全的。
	subject 表示「主題、題目，指想要談、寫、討論的內容」。	The subject of today's lesson is 'how to use preposition'.	今天課程的主題是「如何使用介詞」。
torturous（折磨人的）和 tortuous（曲折的）	torturous 表示「是 torture 的衍生詞，意思與酷刑有關，形容痛苦，折磨人的」。	He is suffering from the latest stage of torturous cancer.	他正遭受末期癌症的折磨。
	tortuous 表示「曲折，彎曲的」。	The road to the peak of the mountain is steep and tortuous.	通往山頂的道路陡峭彎曲。
transport（運輸系統）和 transportation（運輸）/ traffic（交通）	transport 是不可數名詞，意思是「將乘客或貨物從一個地方運送到另一個地方的系統」。	Hong Kong's public transport is not a problem.	香港的公共交通運作暢順。
	transportation 表示「運輸、運送，通常指將貨物從一個地方運送到另一個地方的工序」。	Information regarding the transportation and storage of nuclear waste is difficult to obtain.	很難獲得有關核廢料運輸和儲存的信息。
	traffic 表示「交通往來，指人或車輛在道路上的往來，也適用於船、飛機等」。	Tuen Mun Road is always crowded with traffic in the morning.	屯門公路早上交通總是非常繁忙。
trait（特性）和 feature（特徵）	trait 表示「一個人的性格特質」。	His generosity and great-hearted are his most pleasing traits.	他為人慷慨和大度是他最討人喜歡的個性。
	feature 表示「特色、特徵，指吸引人注意的東西或卓越的品質」。	The main features of the resort are its climate and its scenery.	該度假村主要憑氣候和風景特色吸引人。
transmit（傳送）和 send（送發）	transmit 表示「發送電子信號、無線電或電視廣播，指把信息或信號從某人或某處傳送給另一個人或另一處」。	He has already transmitted the message to the group by WhatsApp.	他已通過 WhatsApp 將這條消息傳送給羣組了。
	send 表示「把某人或物從某處送到另一處，常指通過普通郵件、電郵或運輸等方式」。	On my birthday, don't send anything to me, please.	我生日時請不要送任何東西給我。

易混淆字詞	註釋	例句	譯文
undergo (遭受) 和 experience (經歷)	undergo 表示「遭受痛苦、困難或不愉快的事」。	My mother underwent major surgery last year.	我媽媽去年動了大手術。
	experience 表示「經歷,指體驗特定的事、情緒或身體感覺」。	In that place she experienced real fear for the first time in her life.	在那處她生平第一次體驗真正的恐懼。
underlay (置於……之下) 和 underlie (以……為基礎)	underlay (underlaying, underlaid, underlaid) 表示「將某事放在另一事之下」。	The Telecommunication Company underlaid the sea with a cable.	那電訊公司在海底鋪設了電纜。
	underlie (underlying, underlay, underlain) 表示「以 (理論、行為、學說等) 為基礎」。	His essay is badly written, but the idea underlying it is good.	他的文章寫得不好,但它背後的想法是好的。
undermine 和 weaken (使變弱)	undermine 表示「削弱,指以秘密或卑鄙手段逐漸使某人或物的力量減弱」。	She jealously tried to undermine our friendship.	她出於嫉妒試圖破壞我們的友誼。
	weaken 表示「導致或使變弱,指因某種原因或以某種方式使某人或物喪失能力或力量」。	Poor communication skills have severely weakened his department's position in the company.	溝通能力差,嚴重削弱了他部門在公司的地位。
uniform (制服) 和 dress / costume (服裝)	uniform 表示「制服,指士兵、警察、護士或其他工作人員執勤時穿的衣服,以及學生穿的校服」。	Some children hate having to wear their school uniform.	有些孩子討厭穿校服。
	dress 表示「婦女或女孩的服裝」。	All ladies have to wear evening dress for the annual dinner party.	所有女士都必須穿晚禮服參加年度晚宴。
	costume 表示「演員或表演者所穿的服裝,也指帶地方或民間色彩的服裝」。	Every year we make new costumes for the Lunar New Year night parade.	每年我們都會為農曆新年的春晚巡遊製造新服裝。
uneatable 和 inedible (不能吃的)	uneatable 表示「食品沒有做好不能吃」。	It's a common knowledge that uncooked pork is uneatable.	生豬肉是不能吃的,這是常識。
	inedible 表示「因質量差或有毒而對身體有害不能吃」。	It is an inedible mushroom.	它是一種不可食用的蘑菇。
unharmed 和 harmless (無傷害的)	unharmed 表示「無害、未受到傷害的,含被動意思」。	The four men managed to escape from the fire unharmed.	那四人成功從火裏逃脫,毫髮無損。
	harmless 表示「不會引起或不會造成任何傷害的,含主動意思」。	Dogs and cats are harmless pets.	狗和貓是不會傷人的寵物。

易混淆字詞	註釋	例句	譯文
universal 和 general（普遍的）	universal 表示「完全地，指在任何時候和地方都是正確的，強調沒有例外」。	War causes universal misery.	戰爭導致普遍的苦痛。
	general 表示「普遍地，指所有或大多數人、地點或同類事物都共同關心或感受到，但可能有例外」。	The price of food is a matter of general anxiety.	食品價格是大家關心的議題。
unknown（不出名的）和 unfamiliar（不熟悉的）/ famous（著名的）/ infamous（無恥的）/ notorious（臭名遠播的）	unknown 表示「不詳、知名度不高的，常用來描述一般人不知道的事情」。	Although the book has been printed several times, the author is unknown.	該書雖已多次印刷，但作者不詳。
	unfamiliar 表示「不熟悉的，指以前沒有見過、聽過或經歷過的東西」。	I don't like driving on unfamiliar roads.	我不喜歡在不熟悉的道路上駕駛。
	famous 是褒義詞，表示「（因某人有成就、才能或某處有重要事物）非常聞名」。	This city is famous for its temples and shrines.	這座城市以其寺廟和神社而聞名。
	infamous 表示「聲名狼藉的、以壞或邪惡而聞名的，是貶義詞」。	He is an infamous political swindler.	他是臭名昭著的政治騙子。
	notorious 表示「眾所周知、臭名遠播的，指名聲很壞，是貶義詞」。	He is notorious for dirty tricks.	他以骯髒的伎倆而臭名遠播。
usual 和 customary（通常的）/ habitual（習慣的）/ ordinary（普通的）	usual 表示「通常的，指對某事很熟悉，大多數時間或情況下都可以見到的」。	We'll meet at the usual time.	我們會按平常約定的時間見面。
	customary 表示「通常的、習慣性的，指與個人或羣體行為有關的習慣性」。	She parked her car in its customary space.	她把車停在一貫停放的地方。
	habitual 表示「習慣性的，有做某事的習慣」。	He was a surly person with a habitual scowl on his face.	他是個脾氣暴躁的人，習慣皺眉頭。
	ordinary 表示「普通的、沒有任何特別的」。	I thought it was just an ordinary parcel but then it began to move across the table.	我以為它只是一個普通包裹，但後來它開始在桌上移動。
vacant 和 empty（空的）	vacant 表示「不被任何人佔用而空着的」	The flat has been vacant for several months.	該單位已空置了數月。
	empty 表示「裏面甚麼都沒有而空着的」。	An empty mineral water bottle was placed next to the dustbin.	垃圾桶旁邊放着一個空的礦泉水瓶。

易混淆字詞	註釋	例句	譯文
vacillate 和 fluctuate（波動）	vacillate 表示「對意見等變化不定，無法在它們之間作出決定，猶疑不決」。	They vacillated between going away and staying where they were.	他們對離開還是留在原地，舉棋不定。
	fluctuate 表示「水平、標準、價格等上下波動」。	Prices fluctuate from year to year.	價錢逐年波動。
valuable（貴重的）和 worth（有……價值的）/ expensive（昂貴的）/ precious（珍貴的）	valuable 表示「有價值的，值錢的」。	Your stamp collection must be quite valuable by now.	你的郵票藏品現在一定很值錢。
	worth 表示「有……價值的、等於、值得」。	I can say this book is very good. It is worth buying.	我可以説這書非常好，值得購買。
	expensive 表示「昂貴的，指具體商品要花費很多錢」。	We really don't need such an expensive car for our executive director.	我們的執行董事確實不需要這樣昂貴的車。
	precious 表示「珍貴、很有價值的，指因得來不易而非常寶貴」。	Don't waste your time. It's very precious.	不要浪費時間，它是非常珍貴的。
valueless（沒有價值的）和 invaluable（無價的）	valueless 表示「沒有價值的，指分文不值，是貶義詞」。	This ring is made of glass. It is valueless.	這是玻璃做的戒指，它毫無價值。
	invaluable 表示「價值連城而無法估計，是褒義詞」。	Honest and faithful friends are invaluable.	忠誠的朋友是無價的。
vanish 和 disappear（消失）/ hide（隱藏）	vanish 表示「（以神秘或奇怪方式）消失」。	The thief ran into the crowd and vanished.	小偷衝進人羣消失了。
	disappear 表示「消失不見了，指突然或逐漸從視線中消失」。	Then sun disappeared slowly below the horizon.	太陽漸漸在地平線上消失了。
	hide 表示「隱藏，指防止被發現」。	His grandma hid the money under her bed.	他外婆把錢藏在床下。
variable（可變的）和 various（不同的）	variable 表示「多變，不確定的」。	In the tropics, rainfall is variable.	在熱帶地區裏，降雨量是多變的。
	various 表示「不同，許多的」。	His reasons for leaving are many and various.	他離開的原因是多種多樣的。
veracity（忠實）和 truth（真理）	veracity 表示「誠實，指對真理和實際情況的堅持」。	The veracity of her story is questionable.	她故事的真實性存疑。
	truth 表示「實情、真理，指事實、信念等被認為是真實的」。	I doubt the truth of that statement.	我懷疑這種説法的真實性。

易混淆字詞	註釋	例句	譯文
vestige（遺跡）和 trace（痕跡）	vestige 表示「遺跡，指過去之物的真實標標記、軌跡或其他證據」。	Not a **vestige** of the abbey remains.	那修道院的遺跡已不存在了。
	trace 表示「痕跡，指一個明顯標記或標誌等，表明某人或事出現或發生過」。	There are some **traces** of glacier.	有些冰川的痕跡。
virtually 和 practically（實際上）	virtually 表示「簡直、幾乎、實際上，是就程度而言」。	My book is **virtually** finished; I've only a few changes to make in the writing.	我的書幾乎寫完了；只要修改幾處地方。
	practically 表示「實質上，是就本質而言」。	Try to view your situation **practically**.	要嘗試實際地看待你的處境。
visible（可見的）和 perceptible（可以察覺的）	visible 表示「眼睛可見的事物，沒有抽象概念」。	He got a **visible** change after marriage.	婚後他有明顯的改變。
	perceptible 表示「看得到的有形事物，也可指可感覺得到的抽象概念」。	The price increase had had no **perceptible** effect on sales.	加價對銷售沒有明顯影響。
vision 和 view（見解）	vision 表示「想像力，先見，指在腦海中描繪未來的樣子」。	This romantic **vision** of a world without war is far removed from reality.	世界沒有戰爭這種浪漫主義的願景，是與現實相去甚遠的。
	view 表示「展望、看法，指思考現時存在事物的方式」。	We'd like to know your personal **view** of the situation.	我們想知道你對這形勢的個人看法。
vocabulary（詞彙）和 word（字）	vocabulary 表示「詞彙量，是集體名詞，沒有複數」。	In order to pass the English Language exam, you need to expand your English **vocabulary**.	要通過英語考試，你需要擴大英語詞彙量。
	word 表示「字、詞，是可數名詞」。	She didn't say a **word** about what has happened.	她沒有說發生過的事情。
voluntary（自願的）和 spontaneous（自發的）	voluntary 表示「心甘情願做某事，指出於自己的意志而產生的」。	He made a **voluntary** statement to the police.	他自願向警方作口供。
	spontaneous 表示「由自然感覺或沒有外力的原因產生，特別是指快速且無計劃的」。	Her remarks were **spontaneous** and obviously not planned.	她的話是脱口而出的，顯然不是預先準備好的。

易混淆字詞	註釋	例句	譯文
vote（投票）和 elect（推選）	vote 表示「投票，指通過在一張紙上做標記或舉手的方式，表明你的選擇」。	On the day of the election, they couldn't be bothered to go and **vote**.	選舉當天，他們懶得去投票。
	elect 表示「選舉某人任某職，指通過投票選出領導人或代表」。	Last year a new president of the US was **elected**.	去年美國新總統當選。
wait（等待）和 expect（期待）	wait 表示「等、等待，指留在原地，直到某人或事到來」。	I'll **wait** here until you get back.	我會在這裏等你回來。
	expect 表示「期待、盼望，預期，指相信某人或事會來」。	The train is **expected** to arrive in the next five minutes.	預計火車將在五分鐘內到達。
weather（天氣）和 climate（氣候）	weather 表示「天氣，指一特定時間內或一段時間內的風、雨、晴、雪等狀況」。	We had a nice **weather** yesterday.	昨天天氣很好。
	climate 表示「氣候，指特定地區多年來一般的天氣情況」。	I don't like the **climate** in Toronto, Canada.	我不喜歡加拿大多倫多的氣候。
whole 和 all / entire / total（全部的）	whole 表示「完全的、強調完整性，即個體的完整」。	He spent the **whole** day writing.	他花了一整天的時間寫作。
	all 表示「全數，強調整體性，即全體的數量」。	She drank **all** the wine.	她把所有酒都喝光了。
	entire 表示「一切，全部」每個部份」。	The **entire** village was flooded.	整個村莊都被淹沒了。
	total 表示「總數，指把所有東西計算在內」。	What are your **total** debts?	你的總債務是多少？
wide 和 broad（寬的）	wide 表示「濶度，指測量從一側到另一側的特定距離」。	The desk is three feet **wide**.	那書桌三英尺濶。
	broad 表示「寬的，常用來描述肩背或胸部」。	The young man has **broad** backs.	那年輕人身材很寬橫。
win（贏得）和 beat（擊敗）/ defeat（打敗）/ triumph（戰勝）	win 表示「通過努力獲得比賽或選舉的勝利」。	Who **won** the FA Cup last year?	去年誰贏了足總杯呢？
	beat 表示「擊敗，指在遊戲、比賽、選舉裏比對手表現得更好」。	We have never **beaten** your team.	我隊從未擊敗過貴隊。
	defeat 表示「打敗，贏得勝利」。	They **defeated** their enemy.	他們打敗了敵人。
	triumph 表示「戰勝，指成功打敗某人或物」。	He **triumphed** over various obstacles and achieved success.	他克服種種障礙才取得成功。

易混淆字詞	註釋	例句	譯文
wish / desire / hope 和 want（希望）	**wish** 表示「可能實現的願望，想做某事，常用來描述委婉的語氣」。	I **wish** you would come.	我希望你能來。
	desire 表示「想要一些東西，指懷着熱切心情盼望達到某目的或獲得某東西，實現的可能性較大」。	The child received whatever he **desired**.	那孩子得到任何他想要的東西。
	want 表示「渴望、希望，常用來描述語氣簡單直接」。	I don't **want** anyone meddling in my affairs.	我不希望任何人干涉我的事。
	hope 表示「希望某事發生，充滿信心認為這是可能的」。	I **hope** you will enjoy your stay here.	我希望你在這裏過得愉快。
worthwhile 和 worthy（值得）	**worthwhile** 表示「值得花費時間、金錢或精力的，常用來談及事件的重要性、趣味性、娛樂性等」。	She has a very **worthwhile** job.	她有一份非常值得做的工作。
	worthy 表示「值得，指擁有值得某人或事稱讚的特質」。	His behaviour is **worthy** of praise.	他的行為值得稱讚。

文體範例 Sample Writing of Different Text Types

★ 1 專題文章 Article

專題文章通常是為報章雜誌或互聯網讀者而寫的。所謂「專題」即不包括新聞、社論和廣告等內容。撰寫這類文章，主要作用是解釋事物、傳遞信息或知識，有些作者會試圖在情感上吸引讀者。所以，除了提供事實和數字等確實信息外，這類文章還該有趣味性，可使用隱喻、擬人法以及其他修辭手法，例如諺語、引語、俗語等達到這個目的。

專題文章一般要注意以下重點：

» 喚起讀者的情緒反應，例如喜悅、同情、憤怒、沮喪、滿足等
» 澄清新聞或深度解釋複雜的問題和意義
» 遵循良好的創意寫作技巧
» 避免直接報導新聞故事
» 首段便要吸引讀者注意
» 使用適合其主題的語氣和風格

結構 Structure

文章該包含五個要素：

1.	標題	該簡短又能吸引讀者的。它告訴讀者這篇文章關於甚麼。標題可以寫得幽默，如使用雙關語或文字遊戲。
2.	作者姓名	通常會用真姓名。
3.	首段	目的是鼓勵讀者進一步閱讀。它介紹文章的主題，還包括一些要點，這些要點會在主體內討論發展。

正文　　是文章的主要部份。在正文中，應該：

將正文內容分成段落並按邏輯順序排列

清楚闡述觀點或事情細節

每段應該有主題句

清楚解釋主題句

用例子支持想法

結尾　　總結正文中的觀點，回應正文，並回答之前可能提出的任何問題。有時，作者也會提出
最後的問題供讀者考慮，或對未來進行預測。

範文八：要求銀行轉賬表明詐騙

Requesting Bank Transfer Indicates Scam

Requesting Bank Transfer Indicates Scam

By Chan Dai Man

Last week, I received a message informing me that I had won a prize of five million Hong Kong dollars. Although I did remember entering a few vaccination lucky draws, I was still sceptical about the message. However, I decided to trust it and followed the instructions provided.

標題：吸引讀者

作者姓名

引言：帶出詐騙故事，而作者為甚麼會受騙

The sender of the message asked for my bank account information and stated that they needed a payment of three thousand dollars as an administration fee to transfer the winnings to my bank account. They instructed me to remit the money to an overseas bank account in advance.

正文段（一），騙局第一步要求銀行戶口資料。設計巧妙，看似合理

When I considered the situation, I realized that 3,000 dollars was a small amount compared to my supposed winnings. Therefore, I followed their instructions and remitted the money, eagerly awaiting a response. However, no reply was received. Later, I discovered that some of my friends had also fallen victim to the same scam. Scammers take advantage of people's trust and carelessness by sending messages like this, and it's important to remain vigilant and cautious when receiving unsolicited messages or offers.

正文段（二），說出作者心理狀態，因而墮入騙局，受騙經過和經驗的體會

If I had been more careful, I would not have fallen victim to this scam. It's important to verify the authenticity of such messages by checking with the organising company and confirming the draw results. As the saying goes, 'Better safe than sorry'.

結尾：闡述問題所在，以諺語總結經驗教訓

要求銀行轉賬表明是騙局

陳大文

上星期，我收到一條消息，告訴我獲得了五百萬港元的獎金。我確實記得參加過幾次疫苗接種抽獎活動。所以我相信這條消息，並按照信息中告訴我的去做。

信息的發送者問我銀行戶口資料，並說他們需要三千元作為行政費才能將獎金轉入我的銀行賬戶。他們要求我提前把這筆錢匯到他的海外銀行戶口。

我細想一下，三千元相比我中獎的獎金不算多，我就按照他們的指示匯了錢，急切地等待他們的答覆。但是，他們沒有回覆。後來發現我有些朋友也是受害者。這是一個騙局。騙子利用人們的信任和粗心大意，向他們發送了這樣的信息，在收到未經證實的訊息或優惠時，保持警惕和謹慎是很重要的。

如果不是我粗心大意，我就不會成為該騙局的受害者。我應該向組織機構查詢並核實抽獎結果。現在，我記起一句古老成語，「小心使得萬年船」。

範文九：互聯網對社會有益還是有害？

Is the Internet Beneficial Or Detrimental to Our Society?

Is the Internet Beneficial Or Detrimental to Our Society?	標題：說明這是一篇議論文
The development of internet technology has brought numerous benefits to our daily lives. However, it has also introduced some unwanted elements and disadvantages. This essay aims to examine both the advantages and disadvantages of using the internet.	首段：開門見山，說出互聯網有利有弊
The internet enables the interconnection of various computer networks worldwide. Its versatility allows us to use it for numerous purposes, such as searching for information, communicating with others, conducting business, making new friends, and sharing information with friends, relatives, classmates, and colleagues. Without the internet, we would not be able to study, work, conduct business, have fun, or even carry out our daily lives.	正文段（一）：描述互聯網的優點，與世界連接，用於學習、工作、經商、信息共享等

Moreover, the internet has significantly increased the efficiency and convenience of our lives. For example, we are not required to physically go to the bank to pay a bill or write a letter by hand and send it through the post. With the outbreak of the COVID-19 pandemic and consequent lockdowns, staying at home became necessary for our safety. Online shopping has been a lifesaver, enabling us to purchase essential items and even enjoy meals from outside establishments from the comfort of our homes. All of this can be accomplished with just a click of a mouse or a tap on our mobile phones. Furthermore, the internet has allowed us to continue our studies without interruption. It provides numerous websites that offer books, notes, articles, and other learning materials. Additionally, it facilitates face-to-face interaction between students and their teachers through various apps such as WhatsApp, Skype, Zoom, and more.

正文段（二）：繼續說互聯網的優點，方便又效率，在家學習、購物等

However, there is a growing concern that our society is becoming addicted to the internet, and some students may misuse it. Studies have shown that teenagers in Hong Kong spend a significant amount of time on online games and other activities. Furthermore, gaming can create an online community and virtual life that some players may become deeply addicted to. Reports of individuals neglecting their family, school, work, and even their health to the point of death have become increasingly common.

正文段（三）：描述互聯網的缺點：沉迷虛擬世界，影響健康

In conclusion, while there are both advantages and disadvantages to using the internet, it is evident that it brings numerous benefits to our society. Sharing information through the internet is easy, cost-effective, and fast. Without the internet, fields such as education, commerce, science, art, and culture would all suffer, making life more challenging and less exhilarating. However, it is crucial for people to learn how to avoid the negative effects of the internet while utilizing its advantages.

尾段：重申作者的觀點，明確說明互聯網的優點大於缺點，但作者也奉勸讀者小心使用互聯網以防止禍害發生

互聯網對社會有益還是有害？

互聯網技術的發展為日常生活帶來了無數好處。但是，它也引入了一些不好的元素和缺點。本文旨在探討使用互聯網的優點和缺點。

互聯網允許世界範圍內各種電腦網絡互相連接。它的多功能性使我們可以將其用於多種用途，例如搜索信息、與他人交流、開展業務、結交新朋友以及與朋友、親戚、同學和同事共享信息。沒有互聯網，我們將無法學習、工作、開展業務、娛樂，甚至無法開展日常生活。

此外，互聯網大大提高了生活的效率和便利性。例如，我們不需要親自去銀行支付賬單或手寫信件並通過郵局發送。隨着新冠病毒大流行的爆發和隨之而來的封鎖，為了我們的安全，必須留在家裏。在線購物一直是應急方法，使我們能夠購買必需品，甚至可以在家中舒適地享用餐廳食物。這一切都可以通過點擊鼠標或輕點手機來完成。而且，互聯網使我們能夠不受干擾地持續學習。它提供了許多關於書籍、筆記、文章和其他學習材料的網站。另外，它還通過 WhatsApp、Skype、Zoom 等各種應用程式促進學生與教師之間的面對面交流。

然而，越來越多人擔心社會正在沉迷於互聯網，一些學生可能會濫用它。研究指出，香港青少年花大量時間玩網絡遊戲和其他活動。此外，遊戲創造了一個在線社區和虛擬生活，使玩家沉溺其中。個人忽視家庭、學校、工作甚至健康以至死亡的報告越來越普遍。

總而言之，雖然使用互聯網既有優點也有缺點，但很明顯它為社會帶來了很多好處。通過互聯網共享信息簡單、經濟且快速。沒有互聯網、教育、商業、科學、藝術和文化等領域都會受到影響，使生活變得困難和毫不令人振奮。然而，學習如何利用其優勢的同時，要避免互聯網的負面影響，這對人至關重要。

✤ 2 博客 / 日記 Blog / Diary

　　博客和日記的寫法幾乎相同，兩者都是記錄日常生活的文體，通常會在博客和日記裏記錄一天曾經發生較有趣的事或感受較深的事，這些事值得和讀者分享或讓自己可以回憶或回味的。博客和日記都具有較強的個人風格和意識，包括想法、感受和意見。博客是公開的，但日記是私密的。

　　在寫法上，博客和日記都是靈活多變的，可以記事、描寫、抒情、也可以議論。記述文或議論文是最普遍的體裁。但在博客的寫法上，經常會用非正式的、對話式語言和幽默與讀者聯繫，但日記就像寫信給你信賴的朋友。

　　在語言應用方面，常用第一人稱和一般過去時，去描述事件發生的起因、經過和結果。但在描寫景物或對某事發表意見時，可用一般現在時。

結構 Structure

1. 日期 / 時間 / 條目：要依次有星期、日期和時間。日記需說明當天的天氣，但不需要時間。例如：

    （博客）：於 7 月 23 日下午 5 點發佈

    （日記）：星期日，8 月 15 日，雷雨，雷

2. 標題：給博客一個有趣的標題（日記可免寫標題）

3. 首段：介紹博客的主題或在日記中的心情

4. 正文段落：分段記錄事情的起因和經過，提供有關的詳細信息，例如你所做的某事，也可以記錄感受，例如因何事而有感受

5. 尾段：對當天發生的事作總結或展望未來

範文十：為期三天的本地遊旅行團

A Three-day Local Guided Tour

Posted by Chan Man on 12th August 20XX	日期／時間／條目

Posted by Chan Man on 12th August 20XX

日期／時間／條目

A Three-day Local Guided Tour

標題：介紹博客的主題

Today marked the first day of our local tour, and we visited a place called Tai Mei Tuk. This location is well-known for its picturesque scenery, hiking trails, and barbeque facilities.

首段：説明旅遊目的地

After enjoying a delicious buffet breakfast at the hotel, we began our journey to Tai Mei Tuk and arrived around 11 am. The bright sun and stunning view took me by surprise.

正文段落：

分段記錄第一天旅行團的具體行程，提供有關的詳細信息

Our first stop was the nearby reservoir known as Plover Cove, or Bride's Pool. As we walked, we observed people flying kites and doing exercises. The guide even led us in some gymnastics, and soon everyone was jumping up and down with joy! It was a great way to have fun and get some exercise.

每段要有層次的描述，例如用 first, at lunch time, in the afternoon, before sunset 的順序寫法

During lunchtime, we headed to a beautiful BBQ site in Tai Mei Tuk, located in the Plover Cove Country Park, which boasts many rural and leisure facilities. There's nothing quite like enjoying a hearty barbecue while taking in the spectacular view of the dam. Many people were grilling a variety of foods, including beef, chicken wings, and pork chops, which were not only delectable but also filled the air with a wonderful aroma. Soon, it was our turn to cook our own food. One member of our tour group surprised us all by eating ten sausages and more than a dozen chicken wings, despite her small and skinny stature!

注意時態的運用：用「一般過去時」描述事件發生的起因、經過和結果。但在描寫景物時，要用「一般現在時」

In the afternoon, we visited the Bride's Pool Nature Trail, which is lined with trees on both sides. Along the route, I observed many birds and insects, as well as unique geological features. We continued upstream and discovered unusual rocky potholes and the stunning Bride's Pool waterfalls. The entire experience of exploring nature in this area was thoroughly enjoyable.

As the sun began to set, we returned to the hotel by coach, feeling exhausted after a day filled with delicious BBQ and exciting excursions. What a fantastic day it was! Tomorrow, we'll have another tourist attraction planned, so stay tuned for my latest updates.

尾段：總結一天的行程，寫出作者的感受和下回伏筆

參考譯文

陳民於 20XX 年 8 月 12 日發佈

為期三天的本地遊旅行團

今天是本地遊的第一天，我們去了大美督。這個位置以其如畫的風景、遠足徑和燒烤設施聞名。

在酒店享用過美味的自助早餐後，我們開始了前往大美篤的旅程，在大約 11 點到達那裏。陽光明媚，吸引人的景致讓我驚喜。

第一站是步行到附近的水塘，叫做船灣淡水湖或新娘潭。我們經過見到有人在放風箏，有人在做運動。導遊還帶領我們做了一些體操，很快大家就高興得跳起來！這是享受樂趣和鍛煉身體的好方法。

午餐時間，我們前往大美督一個美麗的燒烤場，它位於船灣郊野公園，擁有許多鄉村和休閒設施。一邊欣賞水壩的壯麗景色，一邊享用豐盛的燒烤，再好不過了。許多人在烤各種食物，有牛肉、雞翅、豬排等，不僅美味，而且空氣中瀰漫美妙的香氣。很快輪到我們了。旅行團的一位成員儘管身材瘦小，卻吃了十根香腸和多過一打的雞翅，讓我們所有人都感到驚訝！

下午，我們參觀了新娘潭自然教育徑，兩旁綠樹成蔭。一路上，我觀察到了許多鳥類和昆蟲，以及獨特的地質特徵。我們繼續向上遊，發現了不尋常的岩石坑窪和令人驚歎的新娘潭瀑布。在這地區探索大自然的整個體驗非常愉快。

夕陽西下，我們坐旅遊車回到酒店，經過一天充滿了美味的燒烤和刺激的短途旅行後，我們感到筋疲力盡。這是多美好的一天！明天，我們計劃了另一個旅遊景點，敬請期待我的最新消息。

A Diary

Wednesday 4thAugust 20XX

Shower

日期／時間／
天氣

Today's entry in my diary serves as a reminder of a painful experience, to help me remember what to do in the future.

首段：開門
見山說明寫
這篇日記的
原因

Yesterday marked the first full rehearsal for a play I wrote and directed. Unfortunately, it ended in failure, and it was a disappointing experience for me.

正文為五
段式
交代事件的
主要內容，詳
細描述事件
的發展經過，
並且講述事
件慘痛之處
和其結果，發
表感想、無奈
的感覺並且
提出需要反
省和改進的
地方和方法

To start with, the lead actor of the play failed to show up for the rehearsal. Despite clearly notifying him of the time and location last week, he did not appear. It was expected that he would come on time, but he never showed up. It wasn't until later that I learned he had undergone an appendectomy the night before and had been hospitalized.

Without the main actor, I struggled to proceed with the rehearsal. I attempted to rehearse only the parts that did not involve him, but I was unable to find a suitable scene. In a moment of desperation, I asked the assistant director, who had memorized the script by heart, to temporarily act as the main actor. 'Luck never comes in pairs and trouble never comes singly': that assistant director accidentally tripped over a water bottle and broke his leg, making him unable to attend further rehearsals. Despite my efforts to find a replacement, no one was available, and I was left feeling helpless and desperate.

I had to halt the rehearsals due to both the absence of the main actor and equipment issues. Despite arranging for some nice background music for the play, the outdated equipment lent to us by one of our classmates' parents did not work properly. In retrospect, I should have followed our teacher's advice and purchased a new machine instead of relying on borrowed equipment.

I was extremely disappointed by the outcome of the first rehearsal, and I must learn from this experience to ensure it never happens again. Firstly, the rehearsal should be limited to a small number of actors, such as only rehearsing the parts of the two protagonists. Secondly, we should have backup actors on standby, so that if someone falls ill, someone else can take their place. Thirdly, I will remind my classmates to pay attention to safety measures before rehearsals to avoid accidents in the future. Lastly, we need to check the equipment beforehand to prevent unexpected technical issues from arising.

It's imperative that the next rehearsal goes smoothly, and I am determined to ensure that the issues we faced during the previous rehearsal do not repeat themselves.

尾段：總結教訓，展望未來

參考譯文

20XX 年 8 月 4 日星期三 　　　　　　　　　　　　　　　　　　驟雨

今天的日記是一段慘痛經歷的回憶，幫助我緊記以後該怎麼做。

昨天是我自編自導的劇本第一次全面綵排。不幸的是，它以失敗告終，這對我來說，是一次令人失望的經歷。

首先，該劇的男主角並沒有出現。上星期我明明通知了他綵排的時間和地點，我以為他會準時到，但是他並沒有出現。最後我得知他前一晚進了醫院並且進行了割盲腸手術。

沒有了男主角，我的綵排怎麼繼續呢？我於是決定只排練不涉及男主角的部份，但我找不到合適場景。於是，我請熟記劇本的副導演暫時擔任男主角，讓綵排可以繼續。「福無重至，禍不單行」：那副導演不小心踏着一個水瓶而絆倒，摔斷了腿。結果，他無法參加綵排。我需要尋找另一個合適的人來做這件事。但是沒有可用人選。你能感受到那一刻我多絕望嗎？

由於主角缺席和設備問題，我不得不停止排練。儘管為演出安排了一些悅耳的背景音樂，但一位同學的父母借給我們的陳舊設備無法正常工作。回想起來，我該聽從老師的建議，購買一台新機器，而不是依賴借來的設備。

我對第一次綵排的結果感到非常失望，我必須吸取這次經驗，以確保它不再發生。首先，綵排該限制在少數演員的範圍內，比如只排練兩個主角的部份。其次，我們要有後備人手待命，有人生病了，還要有人替補。第三，我會提醒同學在綵排前注意安全措施，以免日後發生意外。最後，我們需要事先檢查設備，以防出現意想不到的技術問題。

下次綵排一定要順利，我必定確保上次綵排遇到的問題不再重演。

★ 3 社論 Editorial

　　社論是發表在報章或專業刊物的文章，通常反映該報章主編的觀點，可以署名或不署名。社論作者以論證為基礎，試圖說服讀者用與他相同的方式思考問題，旨在影響公眾輿論，促進批判性思維，有時還會促使人們對某問題採取行動。

　　社論應該包含對問題的客觀解釋，尤其是一些複雜的問題，並從所有可能性方面進行討論。對此，首先要以引文、事實和數字作出認同或對立的觀點。良好的社論不罵人，採取積極主動的方法，通過鼓勵批判性思維來改善情況。一篇社論該以堅定而簡潔的文字，總結作者的觀點，並與首段或標題互相呼應。

社論的寫法以目的為中心

1. 解釋

　　社論經常用來解釋報紙上報導敏感或有爭議性的主題。社論也可能解釋新法規或特定團體的工作，例如環保、飲食、健康、體育等事宜。

2. 批評

　　有些社論會對一些行動、決定或情況作建設性的批評，同時為所確定的問題提供解決方案，但其目的其實是讓讀者看到和了解問題，而不是要讀者遵從作者的解決方案。

3. 說服

　　說服性的社論旨在讓讀者認同解決方案，而不是問題，從一開始，便鼓勵讀者採取具體積極的行動去處理問題。

4. 表揚

　　這種社論讚揚某些人或團體組織做得好的事，例如通過奧運會讚揚香港政府對香港運動員的資助等。

結構 Structure

社論的寫作包含四個要素：

1. 標題：要吸引讀者注意
2. 簡介：首段，可能包括一個發人深省的問題
3. 正文：應對問題原因和解決方案
4. 結論：結尾段，陳述主要觀點，包括號召性用語

範文十二：年輕的吸毒者

Young Drug Abusers

Young Drug Abusers
One Single Slip Brings an Eternal Regret

標題：用一句諺語吸引讀者的注意

Police in Hong Kong recently arrested a father and his two daughters on charges of drug trafficking, seizing heroin worth 28 million dollars. Over the past month, the police have confiscated drugs worth HK$586 million. This news has raised concerns about a potential drug crisis in our city, prompting me to wonder about the severity of the issue.

首段：提出社會問題，開始這篇具說服性質的社論

In recent years, the trend of psychotropic substance abuse among adolescents in Hong Kong has continued unabated, with drugs such as marijuana and ecstasy being illegally consumed. While these drugs may be considered recreational in other countries, they are illegal in Hong Kong. According to government statistics, nearly half of drug users in Hong Kong are teenagers, a trend that declined in the mid-1990s but began to rise again in the early 2000s.

正文段（一）：香港青少年吸毒的情況，帶出軟性毒品的普遍性

Teenagers may turn to drug use due to a variety of factors, such as curiosity, peer influence, rebellion, boredom, and even escapism. In some cases, young people may be experiencing emotional distress and find it difficult to cope with exam or work-related stress. They may be unable to resist the temptation to use stimulant psychotropic drugs as a means of coping with stress.

正文段（二）：說明青少年吸毒的原因

Drug abuse poses a clear and present danger to both our health and safety. It can increase the spread of infectious diseases such as AIDS, hepatitis B, and kidney disease. The distorted perceptions and responses to the environment that drugs create can also be detrimental to our well-being. Additionally, drug abuse can change behaviour and cause emotional harm. Moreover, it can have negative impacts on personal relationships, work or school performance, and financial stability, potentially leading to the loss of friends or even family.

正文段（三）：
描述吸毒的害處

Drug abuse is a serious threat to our city, especially to our youth. If approached with drugs, they should say 'no' and communicate their concerns to their parents, teachers, or social workers. Our government should take steps to tackle substance abuse and prevent drug smugglers from entering our borders. Parents should focus on fostering a happy and healthy family environment where their children are less likely to fall prey to drug use. Schools should also encourage students to engage in recreational activities and develop healthy hobbies, helping to promote a drug-free lifestyle.

正文段（四）：
指出年輕人、政
府、家長和學校
要採取甚麼措施
來預防吸毒

In conclusion, I would like to remind young addicts of the following proverb: 'One single slip can lead to an eternal regret'.

結尾段：以一句
諺語作為總結

參考譯文

年輕的吸毒者
失足成千古恨

香港警方以販毒罪名拘捕了一名父親和他兩個女兒，繳獲價值二千八百萬元的海洛英。僅在過去一個月內，警方就充公了價值五億八千六百萬港元的毒品。這消息引起了人們對我們城市潛在毒品危機的擔憂，促使我想知道這個問題的嚴重性。

近年來，許多青少年都吸毒，濫用精神藥物的趨勢有增無減。大麻和搖頭丸等毒品在其他國家可被視為消遣性藥物，但在香港是非法的。根據香港政府統計，近一半吸毒者為青少年，這種趨勢在 1990 年代中期下滑，但在 21 世紀初又回升。

青少年吸毒是因為好奇心、同輩影響、叛逆、無聊，甚至是逃避現實。青年人可能會遭受情緒困擾，無法承受考試或工作壓力。他們無法抗拒使用刺激精神藥物的誘惑來應對壓力。

濫用藥物對我們的健康和安全構成了明顯而現實的危險。它增加傳染病的傳播，如愛滋病、乙型肝炎、腎臟疾病等。它的認知扭曲和對環境的歪曲反應，都損害我們。它還可以改變行為並造成情緒傷害。更重要的是，它可能會導致人際關係、工作或學業以及財務穩定性出現問題，可能導致失去朋友甚至家人。

藥物濫用對我們的城市，尤其是對年青人來說，是一個非常實在的威脅。當被引誘毒品時，他們應該說「不」，並對父母、老師或社工說出他們的問題。我們的政府應該解決濫用藥物問題，並阻止邊境的毒品走私者。家長應該栽培一個幸福家庭，讓孩子不會成為毒品獵物。學校該鼓勵學生多參加康樂活動，培養健康嗜好，促進無毒品的生活方式。

總而言之，我要提醒年輕吸毒者：「一失足成千古恨」。

範文十三：網上購物

Online Shopping

Online Shopping
Convenience, Theft or Addiction

The rapid development of new technologies has led many business organizations to shift from traditional sales methods to electronic sales methods. With the spread of the COVID-19 pandemic, people have been forced to stay at home, and the trend of online shopping has further expanded. Even today, after the pandemic, online shopping continues to rise, as the pandemic has accelerated the growth of e-commerce. More people are turning to online shopping to avoid crowded stores and reduce their risk of exposure to the virus.

Online shopping offers a range of conveniences, including the ability to purchase items from the comfort of our homes at any time of day or night, without the pressure of salespeople that we might encounter in physical stores. Additionally, online shopping eliminates the need to wait in line at a cash counter, as we can complete transactions using electronic payment methods. This also allows us to easily compare the features and prices of products displayed in different stores, enabling us to choose the store that offers the best discounts. Online shops also have lower overhead costs than physical stores, which allows them to offer attractive discounts. Furthermore, if we receive defective goods, we can return them for a refund.

While online shopping offers many benefits, it can also pose problems for consumers. One potential issue is the inability to touch and check the quality of products before purchasing, which can result in the purchase of lower-quality items. Additionally, there is a risk of counterfeit products when dealing with fake online stores. Identity theft is another well-known risk of online shopping, as paying with a credit card over the internet can expose personal and bank account details to thieves. Late or non-delivery of items is also a common problem, as items can get lost in the mail, especially when purchased from another country. Worst of all, online shopping can lead to addiction, as browsing the web for attractive products can be enjoyable and easy. Unfortunately, for some people, this enjoyment can turn into a problem as they become addicted to shopping online, spending too much money or buying unnecessary items that they cannot control.

標題：試圖吸引讀者注意

首段：用新冠疫情大流行為引子，帶出要討論的問題

正文段（一）：常見的寫法，用一段來陳述網上購物的好處

正文段（二）：說出網上購物的壞處

In short, the COVID-19 pandemic has accelerated the demand for online shopping, which is no longer limited to consumer goods but has also extended to the automotive and real estate markets. However, it's important to be aware of the risks associated with online shopping. Make sure to only deal with legitimate online shops on sites you are familiar with, and only visit these shops when you need to make a purchase.

結尾段：雖然網上購物的好處多，但作者提醒讀者注意網上購物的危險性

參考譯文

網上購物

便利、盜竊或成癮

由於新科技發展迅速，商業機構已經從傳統銷售方式轉變為電子銷售方式。隨着新冠疫情的蔓延，人被迫留在家裏，網上購物的趨勢進一步擴大。即使在疫情過後的今天，網上購物仍然呈上升趨勢。隨着越來越多人轉向網購以避免擁擠的商店並降低接觸病毒的風險，這種流行病加速了電子商務的發展。

網購很方便，我們可以在白天或晚上任何時間在舒適的家中購買商品，而不必親自去商店，那裏的銷售人員會影響我們的購買動機，但這種壓力並不存在於網購。而且，在實體店，我們需要在現金櫃台排隊付費，通過網購，我們使用電子支付來完成交易。此外，網購使我們能夠比較不同商店展示的產品功能和價格，所以我們可以選擇提供最高折扣的商店。由於不用維持店鋪成本和租金，與實體店相比，網上商店能夠以誘人的折扣銷售產品。更重要的是，收到有瑕疵的貨物可以退貨和退錢。

另一方面，網購會給消費者帶來問題。例如，我們無法觸摸和檢查想買產品的質量，因此，我們可能會買到質量較差的商品。還有一種風險，就是網上商店是假的，而我們買的產品實際上是假貨。網購一個眾所周知的風險是身份盜用，通過互聯網購物並使用信用卡進行結算，可能會使買家的銀行戶口或個人詳細信息洩漏，而被竊賊利用。網購另一個問題是延遲交貨甚至不交貨，付款後沒有到貨，商品可能會在郵寄過程中丟失，尤其是從其他國家或地區購買的商品，或者交貨遲延。最壞的是，網購可能會導致購物成癮，網上購物相對容易和愉快，因為上網瀏覽尋找有吸引力的產品是很有趣的過程，但對於一些沉迷於這樣做的人來說，這可能是一個問題。他們最終會花太多錢或購買無用的東西。不幸的是，他們無法控制這種習慣。

簡而言之，新冠疫情大流行加速了網購的需求。現今，網購不僅限於消費品，還延伸到汽車和房地產。當然，我們必須注意網上買東西的風險。要確保你在熟悉的網站上與合法的在線商店打交道，並且僅在需要時才登錄在線商店。

✦ 4 電子郵件 E-mail

電子郵件簡稱電郵，是利用網絡發出的信件，無論是甚麼問題，都可以用電郵交流。電郵可分為兩類：

1. 個人電郵（非正式的）

個人電郵通常是寫給親朋戚友的，關係親密，所以可使用非正式語言，語氣應該是輕鬆的，還可以包括情緒表達。寫法可用縮略語，如 I'll（I will）和 pls（please）等。

2. 商業性或官方式電郵（正式的）

通過電郵發送商業或官方式信件時，不應使用情緒化的表達方式。寫法需正式，不能用縮略語，在商業性電郵中，通常用第一人稱複數「我們（we）發出，但在官方式電郵中，也可用第一人稱單數「我（I）」。

格式

From（發件人的電郵地址）

To（收件人的電郵地址）

Subject（主旨：寫作原因）

常見句式的例子

	電子郵件	
	個人	**商業性或官方式**
歡迎詞:	Hi ... 嗨……	Dear ... 親愛的……
	My dearest ... 我最親愛的	Dear Mr / Ms ... 親愛的……先生 / 女士
首段常 用句式	How are you? 你好嗎?	We refer to your email of today and confirm that... 關於您今天的電郵我們確認……
	I hope everything is fine. I'm writing to... 我希望一切安好,我寫這信是為了……	Thank you for your kind invitation to... 感謝您誠意的邀請……
	I'm sorry that I haven't been in touch as I've just been very busy. 很抱歉我一直很忙,所以沒有聯絡。	In reply to your email, we would like to confirm that... 我們回覆您的電郵並確認……
	Thanks for writing to me regarding... 多謝你來信關於……	Further to your email dated..., we write to inform you that... 針對您……月……日的電郵,我們寫信告訴您……
	Sorry I haven't written for ages, but I've been really busy. 很抱歉,我好久沒寫信給你了,但我真的很忙。	We apologise for not replying to your email until now as it has to take time to investigate the matter. 我們很抱歉直到現在才回覆您的電郵,因為調查此事需要一些時間。

	電子郵件	
	個人	商業性或官方式
正文常用句式	Just a short note about... 這只是一個短筆記關於……	We are delighted to tell you that... 我們很高興告訴您……
	See attached. I was shocked! 見附件。我很震驚！	We enclose the attached report for your reference, in which you will notice that... 我們隨函附上報告供您參考，您會在其中注意到……
	I can confirm that... 我可以確認……	We are pleased to confirm that... 我們很高興可以確認……
	I've looked into it and found that... 我調查了並發現……	Our investigation reveals that... 我們的調查顯示……
結尾段常用句式	Anyway, got to go now. 不管如何，現在該走了。	Are there any particular problems do you think we could help? 你有甚麼特別問題我們可以幫忙嗎？
	Drop me a line if you are free. 如有空，給我寫幾個字。	We would be more than pleased to answer any further questions you may have. 我們非常樂意回答您任何進一步的問題。
	Just give me a call if you have any questions. 如果你有任何問題，請打電話給我。	Please feel free to contact us if you have any questions. 如果您有任何問題，請隨時與我們聯繫。
	Keep in touch. 保持聯絡	We are looking forward to... 我們很期待……
結尾敬語	Speak to you soon. 等一下再和你談。	Thanks and regards 謝謝並恭祝安康
	Take care. 照顧好自己。	Give my regards to... 代我向……問好
	Love 愛你的	With best regards 最誠摯的問候
署名及稱號	son 兒子	Chan Yat Ming, Supervisor, Imports 入口部主任陳日明

Studies in Space Technology

From: mschan@gmail.com

To: tkwong@yahoo.com.hk

Subject: Studies in Space Technology

Hi TK,

You were telling me about your plan to apply for the Space Technology degree programme at Hong Kong University of Science and Technology! I remember you said you saw an advertisement from China's space agency about recruiting people from Hong Kong for their manned space programme, and it inspired you to pursue this field. You even asked me for my advice!

Wow, you got a 5** grade in both Mathematics and Physics in your HKDSE! That's amazing! With your academic achievements and your ability to handle complex and challenging subjects, I have no doubt that you'll meet the college entry requirements for the Space Technology programme. I fully support your decision to pursue this field of study.

However, if you're looking to enter and work in the space industry, it's important to have strong communication skills in English. English is used worldwide in international space projects, so it's a crucial skill to have. But don't worry, I'm sure you'll do great, and I'm here to support you every step of the way.

I'm sure you're aware that space technology is not only used for space exploration, but it also has numerous applications in our daily lives. It's remarkable how hundreds of technical innovations generated by space programs have made our lives easier and more efficient. For instance, improved home appliances, advanced farming equipment, faster communication, accurate weather forecasting, and enhanced medical instruments, among others. Did you know that the technology behind portable vacuum cleaners was first discovered for space exploration? And that the web technology that gave rise to the Internet was developed by space technologists and scientists? It's fascinating to see how space technology can impact our lives in so many ways!

電郵格式：簡單說明主旨

稱呼：直呼其名

首段：説明寫電郵的由來

正文段（一）：講述學歷要求

正文段（二）：講述語言要求

正文段（三）：介紹太空科技與日常生活的關係

By the way, did you know that most big nations have a high budget for space exploration? It stimulates the creation of numerous job vacancies for young people who are interested in space-related careers. After completing your course, I'm sure there will be many attractive job opportunities out there for you to choose from! I believe that the field of space technology has so much potential, and it's exciting to think about all the possibilities. Who knows, maybe you'll even be a part of a team that discovers something new and ground breaking in space! I'm here to support you and cheer you on every step of the way.

TK, I have to stop writing for now. But before I go, I wanted to say that I'm rooting for you and your university admission! Please keep me updated on your progress, and if you get accepted, we definitely need to celebrate! Let's go out for a meal to celebrate your achievement!

Wishing you good luck and love,

Man San

發件人：alanchan@gmail.com

收件人：tkwong@yahoo.com.hk

主旨：太空科技學科

嗨，德光：

你告訴我要申請香港科技大學的太空科技學位課程，因受到中國航天局的廣告啟發，説它正在為載人航天計劃從香港招聘人才。您還徵求我的建議。

嘩，你在香港中學文憑試的數學和物理科都考獲 5** 的成績！太棒了！憑藉你的學術成就及處理複雜並具挑戰性科目的能力，我相信你會達到太空科技課程的大學入學要求。我完全支持你從事這一研究領域的決定。

但是，如果您希望進入航天科技行業並在其中工作，那麼擁有良好英語溝通能力是非常重要的。全球的國際太空項目都使用英語，因此英語是至關重要的技能。但別擔心，我相信你會做得很好，我會在這裏支持你的每一步。

我相信你知道太空科技不僅用於太空探索，而且也應用於日常生活中。太空計劃所產生的數百項技術創新讓我們生活得更輕鬆、更高效，這一點令人矚目。例如，改進的家用電器、先進的農業設備、更快的通信、準確的天氣預報和功能增強的醫療儀器等。您是否知道便攜式真空吸塵機背後的技術，最初是因太空探索而發現的，而互聯網的網絡技術也是由太空科技專家和科學家開發的呢？看到太空科技如何以多種方式影響日常生活，真令人着迷！

順便問一下，你知道大多數大國的太空探索預算都很多嗎？它為對太空相關職業感興趣的年輕人創造了大量職位空缺。完成課程後，相信會有很多吸引人的工作機會供您選擇！相信太空技術領域擁有如此巨大的潛力，而且考慮到所有的可能性都令人興奮。誰知道呢，也許您甚至會成為發現太空新事物和突破性事物的團隊中的一員！我在這裏支持你，為你的每一步加油。

德光，我現在必須停筆了。但在我結束之前，我想説我為您加油和支持您獲得大學錄取！請讓我知道您的最新進展，如果您獲錄取，絕對需要慶祝一下！讓我們吃頓飯來慶祝你的成就吧！

德光，我現在必須停筆了。如果你獲大學錄取，請告訴我。

祝你好運，愛你的

雯珊

範文十五：體育課

Physical Education Lessons

From: chanlili@gmail.com

To: wongyy@stmarycollege.com

Subject: Physical Education Lessons

Dear Principal,

I'm writing to you on behalf of our Association to express some concerns that have been brought to our attention regarding the current Physical Education (PE) lessons at the school. Specifically, certain committee members have expressed disappointment with the lessons, as many students have reported that they fail to spark their interest in sports and physical activities. As the President of our Association, I feel it is my duty to bring this matter to your attention and reflect the opinions of these committee members.

After collecting opinions from 150 members of our Association, I have identified three main reasons for their negative attitude towards PE lessons. Firstly, many students simply dislike exercising and would prefer to take music or drama classes instead of PE. Secondly, some students feel that our PE lessons only focus on basic sports skills and do not provide meaningful opportunities to learn how to play sports. Poor planning and limited teaching time have also made it difficult for students to make progressive improvements in their physical abilities, which has led to many students seeing PE lessons as a waste of time. Additionally, students who are not good at sports often struggle to fully enjoy the lessons, preferring to do classwork in the covered playground instead. On the other hand, some more enthusiastic students find the PE lessons boring as they are too simple.

Physical education serves an important role in improving students' mental health and reducing stress levels. By engaging in physical activity, students can exercise and then relax, leading to an overall sense of happiness and comfort in their schooling. To achieve these goals, our survey suggests that healthy dance or Taichi boxing be introduced into the PE curriculum. We believe that these activities will provide students with a fun and engaging way to exercise, while also promoting mental and emotional well-being.

電郵格式：簡單説明主旨

稱呼：正式官方稱謂

首段：説明寫電郵的原因

正文段（一）：收集同學意見及詳細説明不喜歡體育課的理由

正文段（二）：解釋體育課的目的，提出改革項目，以提高同學興趣

When it comes to incorporating healthy dance into the PE curriculum, I suggest we start with 'Move for Health' introduced by the Leisure and Cultural Services Department. By offering regular healthy dance lessons, students can improve the endurance of their body muscles, allowing them to work harder for longer periods of time without feeling tired. Dancing also raises the body's heart rate, which can help to improve stamina. In addition, healthy dance encourages active participation from students who are less physically active, creating a more enjoyable experience for all students during PE lessons.

正文段（三）：改革項目之一：健康舞

Another recommendation for the PE curriculum is Taichi boxing, a traditional internal Chinese martial art practised for both its health benefits and defence training. Taichi is known for its ability to improve muscle strength, both in the lower and upper body. It is also a great way to engage students in their PE lessons, as they learn the unique fighting techniques of Taichi. Additionally, we believe that it is important for girls to learn some basic self-defence skills, and Taichi boxing can provide them with a valuable set of tools in case of need.

正文段（四）：改革項目之一：太極拳

I understand that implementing these new activities in the PE curriculum would require the school to allocate additional resources. For example, we may need to hire qualified healthy dance instructors or Taichi educators to teach in our PE classes. However, I strongly believe that the effort and investment are worth it in terms of engaging students in Physical Education.

正文段（五）：說明學校的負擔

By introducing these new activities, we can provide students with a fun and engaging way to exercise and promote their overall health and well-being. We believe that the benefits of these activities will have a positive impact on students both in and out of the classroom.

結尾段：請校長考慮

Your attention to this matter is highly appreciated.

客套的結尾語

Best regards,

結尾敬語

Lai Lai Chan

署名

President, Students' Association

稱號

發件人：chanlili@gmail.com

收件人：wongyy@yahoo.com.hk

主旨：體育課

親愛的校長：

我代表我們的協會寫信給您，表達我們對學校當前體育課程的一些擔憂。具體來說，某些委員會成員對這些課程表示失望，因為許多學生報告說這些課程未能激發他們對運動和體育活動的興趣。作為協會會長，我覺得有責任提請您注意此事並反映這些委員會成員的意見。

收集了協會 150 名會員的意見後，我找出了他們對體育課持消極態度的三個主要原因。首先，許多學生根本不喜歡運動，更願意上音樂或戲劇課而不是體育課。其次，有些學生認為我們的體育課只注重基本運動技能，並沒有提供有意義的學習運動的機會。計劃不周詳和教學時間有限，也讓學生的身體能力難以逐步提高，這導致許多學生認為體育課是浪費時間的。此外，不擅長運動的學生難以充份享受課程，更喜歡在有蓋操場上做功課。另一方面，有些比較熱心的學生覺得體育課太簡單，以至感到無聊。

體育在改善學生的心理健康和減輕壓力水平方面發揮重要作用。通過參加體育活動，學生可以鍛煉身體放鬆身心，從而在學校生活中獲得整體的幸福感和舒適感。為了實現這些目標，我們的調查建議將健康舞或太極拳引入體育課程。我們相信，這些活動將為學生提供有趣且引人入勝的鍛煉方式，同時還能促進身心健康。

將健康舞融入體育課程，我建議先從康文署推出的「跳舞強身」開始。提供定期健康舞課程，學生可以提高身體肌肉的耐力，使他們更勤力和更長時間工作而不會感到疲倦。跳舞還可以提高身體的心率，這有助提高耐力。此外，健康舞鼓勵身體不太活躍的學生積極參與，為所有學生在體育課上創造更愉快體驗。

體育課程的另一項推薦是太極拳，這是一種傳統的中國內功武術，因其有益健康和可用作防禦訓練，因此獲得推薦讓學生練習。太極拳以提高下半身和上半身肌肉力量的能力而聞名。這也是讓學生參與體育課的好方法，因為他們可以學習太極拳獨特的格鬥技巧。此外，我們認為對於女孩來說，學習基本的自衛技巧很重要，而太極拳可以為她們提供一套有價值的工具，以備不時之需。

我明白在體育課程中包含這些新活動需要學校分配額外資源。例如，我們可能需要聘請合資格的健康舞教練或太極拳老師教授體育課。然而，我堅信，就鼓勵學生參與體育課而言，付出努力和投資是值得的。

通過引入這些新活動，我們可以為學生提供有趣且引人入勝的鍛煉方式，促進他們整體的健康和福祉。我們相信，這些活動的好處將對課堂內外的學生都能產生積極影響。

非常感謝您對此事的關注。

致您最好的問候，

陳麗麗

學生會會長

★ 5 議論文 Essay

議論文是作者對某問題的分析，通過列舉事實及講道理說明是非黑白，從而表達作者的觀點、立場、態度、看法和主張。它包括「論證為主導型」和「解決問題型」兩種。

i) 論證為主導型議論文 Argument-led essay

以論證為主導的文章分兩種：單向和雙向的，單向議論文只說明自己對話題的觀點，而雙向議論文會說明話題利弊。

以論證為主導的文章應遵循以下結構：

標題　通常是用一個簡短的名詞短語來點出文章的一般主題。例如：

» The e-book is King（電子書為王）

» Will AI replace human workers in future?（未來人工智能會取代人類勞工嗎？）

首段　開門見山指出問題，提供一些背景信息並陳述你對這個問題的看法。最後，列出這篇文章的佈局。

正文　如果是單向議論文，說出觀點和原因，並提供足夠的解釋和例子來支持你的論點。

如果是雙向議論文，說出議題的優點和缺點，需要提供詳細信息，包括支持和反對論點的事實和例子。

結尾　簡單總結論點並重申觀點及提出建議。對於雙向議論文，如果想站邊，該包括一個明確陳述來支持你設定的位置。

以下是寫論證為主導型議論文的技巧：

A. 首段

首段要清楚表達主題，作者的觀點也必須在這裏表達。它是文章的引言，通常包含三個元素：

» 介紹要討論的問題
» 作者對問題的看法
» 文章正文段落的佈局

文章第一段	句型舉例	參考譯文
單向的議論文		
1. 介紹要討論的問題	Some people believe animals are their friends, but some treat animals as living meat and walking fur.	有人認為動物是他們的朋友，但也有人則將動物視為肉食和皮草。
2. 作者對問題的看法	This leads to the cruel slaughter of animals all over the world every year.	這導致全球每年都發生殘酷屠殺動物。
3. 文章正文段落的佈局	I am of the opinion that chickens, pigs, cattle, etc. are killed because they are raised for meat. For house pets and wild animals, we must treat them as our friends for the following reasons.	我認為雞、豬、牛等是因飼養是為了肉食而被屠宰。對於家庭寵物和野生動物，我們必須視它們為朋友，原因如下。
雙向議論文		
1. 介紹要討論的問題	Group study has been shown to be an effective method for students to learn successfully, but while most students have been accustomed to this way of learning, others prefer to study alone at their own pace.	集體學習已獲證實為有效的學習方法，雖然大多數學生已經習慣了這種學習方式，但有些學生寧可跟自己的步伐去學習。

文章第一段	句型舉例	參考譯文
2. 作者對問題的看法	The two approaches each have distinct advantages, and the choice depends on personal preference or external circumstances.	這兩種方法各有優勢，選擇取決於個人喜好或外部環境。
3. 文章正文段落的佈局	This essay attempts to discuss this issue from both perspectives.	本文試圖從兩個觀點來討論這個問題。

B. 正文段落

正文段落構建主要思想，它可能是兩段式或三段式寫法。每段都該包含一個想法來支持你的觀點或意見，例如：兩段式寫法是優、劣點各一段。這些段落必須互相連接，以便讀者可以遵循論點和討論的主線。

編寫正文段落時，要使用以下規則：

» 每段只表達並發展一個主要思想或立場

» 每個主要思想或立場要有它的支持點

» 決定每個主要思想或立場的順序

» 根據自己對該主題的經驗添加示例

C. 結論

你的觀點必須在結論再重複一次，也可包含沒有完全討論過、不太重要但相關的細節。總括來說，結論包含兩個元素：

» 將論點與問題聯繫起來

» 總結表明你自己的觀點或意見

結論與引言要互相呼應，但寫法不能千篇一律，要有不同的寫法，試看下面的例子，注意首段和尾段都重複一個主題，但寫法和用字都不同：

首段	When people get older, they need to retire. Different people have different ideas about whether the retirement age should be fixed. In my opinion, old people should retire at a certain age.	人老了，就該退休了。對於是否該固定退休年齡，不同人有不同看法。在我看來，老年人到了一定年齡便該退休。
尾段	All in all, I hold the view that people should retire at a certain age, as it is beneficial to both themselves and the society as a whole.	總而言之，我認為人到了一定年齡便該退休，這對自己和整個社會都有好處。

可以用以下短語開始結論：

»	In conclusion / To conclude	總結
»	In short	簡而言之
»	In general	一般來説
»	To sum up	總結
»	All in all	總而言之
»	In view of the...	鑑於……
»	From what I mentioned above, I believe that...	從我上面提到的，我相信……
»	As far as I am concerned, I firmly support the view that...	就我而言，我堅決支持以下觀點……
»	As we all agree that every coin has two sides...	我們都同意每個硬幣都有兩面……

ii) 解決問題型議論文 Problem-solution essay

解決問題型議論文的寫作或多或少與論證為主導型議論文相同，但是，解決問題型議論文是針對存在的某種現狀或者問題提出建議。

在結構方面，你應該注意以下幾點：

» 首段： 開門見山，説明現狀，確定論點，需要將問題的定義清楚寫下來，提出問題的嚴重性。

» 正文： 寫出問題的趨勢，討論可能的解決方案，該用例子和統計數據來支持論點。在寫法方面，可使用條件句和情態動詞來談論解決方案。

» 尾段： 總結論點和提出解決方法，並呼籲採取行動，更要表示對自己的解決方案有信心。

句型舉例

	句型舉例	參考譯文
首段	In recent years, the issue of … has brought to public attention.	近年來，……的問題引起了公眾關注。
	Nowadays, with the rapid development of …, there is widespread concern that…	現在，隨着……的迅速發展，人們普遍擔心……
正文	It is crucial that effective measures should be taken to reverse this trend.	必須採取有效措施扭轉這一趨勢。
	There is no easy solution to the issue of… However, steps must be immediately taken by the government to help…	沒有簡單方法可以解決……該問題。但是，政府必須立即採取措施來幫助……
尾段	In my opinion, only this way, as suggested aforesaid, can we…	在我看來，只有按照上述建議，我們才能……
	To conclude, it is necessary that the government should not only respond to the problem immediately but also explain to the public…	總而言之，政府不僅要立即回應問題，還要向公眾解釋……

範文十六：國際快餐是健康的
International Fast Food Is Healthy

International Fast Food Is Healthy

標題：表明作者
論點

The McDonald's logo has been touted as the most universally recognized symbol. Thanks to a global society, large fast food chains like KFC, Burger King, and Pizza Hut have made their way to every corner of the earth and are particularly popular among young people and children. However, some argue that these international foods are junk food and are adversely affecting families and societies. I respectfully disagree with this viewpoint. Although international fast foods may have some negative impacts on our health and society, the benefits far outweigh them.

首段：
介紹要討論的問題：快餐，提出作者的看法：健康食品文章主要論述快餐好處多過壞處

It is a well-known fact that fast foods are generally less healthy than home-cooked meals due to their use of sugar, salt, and artificial ingredients, all of which can have negative impacts on our health. However, there has been a recent trend towards healthier fast food options. For example, McDonald's now offers veggie burgers and salads on their menu, and Burger King has special menus for individuals who need to avoid certain foods for health reasons. These menus list all the ingredients, allowing people to make informed choices. The fast food landscape has changed significantly for the better, and the term 'fast food' no longer has to be synonymous with 'unhealthy food'.

正文段（一）：說明快餐並非不健康食品

In addition, fast food chains like McDonald's, KFC, and Burger King are known for their cleanliness and comfortable environment. They also maintain a high level of standardization, ensuring that customers know what to expect regardless of location. This convenience, coupled with affordable prices and fast service, makes these restaurants a popular option for individuals who need to keep up with the fast pace of doing business in places like Hong Kong. Therefore, it is reasonable to suggest that the benefits of fast food still outweigh the drawbacks.

正文段（二）：
快餐店清潔、方便、舒適、價錢便宜及快捷

Currently, the negative health reputation of fast food is somewhat questionable, as it has become more nutritious than in the past. Fast food is widely accepted and has a positive influence, as evidenced by the fact that former US President, Mr. Trump, who is known for his love of McDonald's hamburgers and potato chips, is over 70 and still very energetic. Therefore, while fast food may have some negative effects on families and society, it is not necessarily bad food. Of course, it is important to exercise caution and consume it in moderation.

尾段：
重複及表明作者自己的觀點——快餐並不是壞食品。增加細節，如特朗普總統喜愛快餐，以適度食用為結尾。

國際快餐是健康的

麥當勞商標被吹捧為最普遍認可的標誌。得益於全球一體化，肯德基、漢堡王、必勝客等大型快餐連鎖店已經遍佈全球各個角落，尤其受到年輕人和兒童的歡迎。然而，一些人認為這些國際食品是垃圾食品，對家庭和社會產生不利影響。我不同意這種觀點。儘管國際快餐可能對我們的健康和社會產生一些負面影響，但好處遠大於這些。

眾所周知，快餐由於使用糖、鹽和人工成份，通常不如住家飯菜健康，這些都會對我們的健康產生負面影響。然而，最近出現了一種更健康的快餐選擇趨勢。例如，麥當勞現在於餐單上提供素食漢堡和沙律，漢堡王為出於健康原因，為需要避免某些食物的人提供特殊餐單。這些餐單列出了所有成份，讓人作出明智選擇。快餐業的格局發生了顯著好轉，「快餐」一詞不再是「不健康食品」的代名詞。

此外，麥當勞、肯德基和漢堡王等快餐連鎖店以清潔和舒適的環境著稱。它們還保持高水平的標準化，確保客戶無論身在何處都預料會吃到甚麼。這種便利，再加上實惠價格和快速服務，使這些餐廳成為要跟隨香港快節奏經商的熱門個人選擇。因此，有理由認為快餐利大於弊。

目前，有些快餐負面的健康聲譽值得懷疑，因它比過去更有營養，而快餐被廣泛接受並產生積極影響，美國前總統特朗普先生以愛吃麥當勞漢堡飽和薯條著稱，他已經 70 多歲了，仍然精力充沛。因此，雖然快餐可能會對家庭和社會產生一些負面影響，但不一定是壞食物。當然，重要的是要小心謹慎並適度食用。

範文十七：發展人工智能在我們的社會是正面還是負面的

Has Artificial Intelligence Become a Positive Or Negative Development in Our Society?

Has Artificial Intelligence Become a Positive Or
Negative Development in Our Society?

標題：說明這是一篇雙向論證議論文

Artificial Intelligence (AI) has become an increasingly prevalent topic in recent years, with rapid advancements in technology leading to the development of more sophisticated AI systems. While there are undeniable benefits that AI can bring to society, there are also concerns about its potential negative impact. In this essay, I will examine both the beneficial and detrimental aspects of AI and argue that the benefits of AI outweigh its drawbacks.

首段：開門見山，說出互聯網有利有弊，但提出結論：好處大於壞處

One of the most significant benefits of AI is its ability to automate tasks that are repetitive, time-consuming, or dangerous for humans, leading to better decision-making, cost savings, and improved productivity. AI can also improve healthcare by analysing medical data to diagnose diseases and monitoring patients remotely. Similarly, AI-powered tools can personalise the learning experience for students and provide teachers with insights into student performance, leading to improved academic outcomes.

正文段（一）：描述人工智能的優點

However, there are also concerns about the potential negative impact of AI on society. Job displacement, ethics and privacy problems are some of the most significant concerns. Additionally, there is a potential for AI to be used for malicious purposes, such as cyber attacks or the development of autonomous weapons. Therefore, artificial intelligence may be a wolf in sheep's clothing, or even a sugar-coated poison, as a Chinese proverb says, 'Water can carry a boat but can also overturn it'.

正文段（二）：描述人工智能的缺點

Despite these concerns, the benefits of AI outweigh its drawbacks. AI has the potential to create new jobs and industries, such as in the development and maintenance of AI systems. Furthermore, the potential benefits of AI in healthcare, education, and other areas could lead to significant improvements in the quality of life for many individuals. To ensure that AI is used for the benefit of society, ethical guidelines and regulations for the development and use of AI systems are necessary. Additionally, there should be a greater investment in education and training to prepare individuals for the changing job market.

正文段（三）：說明作者的觀點：人工智能的優點必大於缺點

In conclusion, while the potential negative impact of AI is a valid concern, the benefits of AI are significant. The development and use of AI must be ethical and regulated to minimize its potential negative impact. AI has the potential to transform various aspects of society, leading to significant improvements in the quality of life for many individuals.

結尾段：重申作者的觀點，呼應首段開場白

參考譯文

發展人工智能對社會是正面還是負面

近年來，人工智能已成為日益流行的話題，技術的快速進步導致更複雜的人工智能系統的發展。雖然人工智能可以為社會帶來無可否認的好處，但也有人擔心潛在的負面影響。本文將研究人工智能有益和有害兩方面，並論證人工智能好處大於缺點。

人工智能最重要的好處之一，是它能夠自動執行對人類來說重複、耗時或危險的任務，從而作出更好決策，能節省成本並提高生產力。人工智能還可以通過分析醫療數據來診斷疾病，用遠程監控患者來改善醫療保健。同樣，人工智能工具可以為學生提供個性化學習體驗，並為教師提供對學生表現的洞察力，從而提升學業成績。

然而，也有人擔心人工智能對社會潛在的負面影響。工作流離失所、道德和隱私問題是最重要的問題。此外，人工智能有可能被用於惡意目的，例如網絡攻擊或自製武器的開發。因此，人工智能可能是披着羊皮的狼，甚至是糖衣毒藥，正如中國格言所說「水能載舟，也能覆舟」。

儘管存在這些擔憂，但人工智能的好處大於壞處。人工智能有可能創造新的就業機會和行業，例如人工智能系統的開發和維護。此外，人工智能在醫療保健、教育和其他領域的潛在好處可能會顯著改善許多人的生活質量。為確保人工智能用於造福社會，開發和使用人工智能系統的道德準則和法規是必要的。此外，應該加大對教育和培訓的投資，讓個人為不斷變化的就業市場作好準備。

總之，雖然人工智能的潛在負面影響是一個合理的擔憂，但人工智能的好處是巨大的。人工智能的開發和使用必須合乎道德並受到監管，以盡量減少其潛在的負面影響。人工智能有可能改變社會各個方面，從而顯著改善許多人的生活質素。

範文十八：共同防止網絡欺凌：當技術變得令人討厭時

Preventing Cyberbullying Together: When Technology Turns Nasty

Preventing Cyberbullying Together: When Technology Turns Nasty

In the wrong hands, technology can cause significant harm, making life meaningless at best and humiliating at worst. Cyberbullying is a prime example of how the internet can be used to threaten or humiliate another person through the use of words, photos, or videos. Cyberbullies aim to cause embarrassment, psychological humiliation, or physical harm to their victims by spreading negative, harmful, or false information about them. This form of abuse can result in significant psychological, emotional, and physical stress for children and teenagers.

According to survey statistics, 60% of parents with children aged 14 to 18 reported that their children have been bullied. Victims of cyberbullying often suffer from depression and experience high levels of anxiety. When surveyed, 81% of teenagers believed that cyberbullies engage in this behaviour because they find it funny. However, there is nothing humorous about causing someone else to experience misery. Therefore, parents, schools, and children must work together to prevent cyberbullying and promote e-safety. This essay proposes specific approaches to prevent cyberbullying from occurring.

To prevent cyberbullying, parents, schools, and the government must take action. Firstly, parents should be aware of whether their children are being bullied and advise them to ignore the bully's hurtful words and negative comments. Parents should also assist their children in reporting the bullying to the appropriate authorities, such as an online service provider, to block the cyberbullying communication. Secondly, victims should talk to their friends about the abuse and report the problem immediately to their parents and school. Thirdly, schools should establish strict rules to prohibit the distribution of cyberbullying messages and implement anti-bullying policies to discourage hostile behaviour and stop the bully in their tracks. Additionally, the government should impose sanctions to declare cyberbullying as a criminal offence.

標題：說明問題所在

引言：確定論點，將問題的定義清楚寫下來，包括：科技產生問題；網絡欺凌的定義和影響；提出問題嚴重性

正文段（一）：用統計數字說明問題的嚴重性；引出本文的提議

正文段（二）：提出解決方法，要求個人、父母、學校和政府共同努力；本段分四句順序描述；學習使用情態動詞 should 和 need 來談論解決方案

The growing prevalence of cyberbullying highlights the importance of support from individuals to stop the spread of bullying messages, awareness from parents to identify the occurrence of cyberbullying, strict rules established by schools, and laws enacted by the government. It is crucial that we stand together to prevent ourselves, our friends, and our families from becoming victims of cyberbullies.

尾段：
總結論點和解決方案；呼籲團結一起採取行動

參考譯文

共同防止網絡欺凌：當科技變得令人討厭時

在壞人手中，科技可能會造成重大傷害，使生活變得毫無意義，而在最壞的情況下會讓人感到羞辱。網絡欺凌是互聯網如何通過使用文字、照片或視頻來威脅或羞辱他人的一個典型例子。網絡欺凌旨在通過傳播有關受害者的負面、有害或虛假信息，對受害者造成尷尬、心理羞辱或身體傷害。這種形式的虐待會給兒童和青少年帶來巨大的心理、情緒和身體壓力。

據調查統計，有 14 至 18 歲孩子的父母中，有 60% 的人報告說他們的孩子曾被欺負。網絡欺凌的受害者經常患有抑鬱症並經歷高度焦慮。在接受調查時，81% 的青少年認為網絡欺凌者從事這種行為，是因為他們覺得這很有趣。然而，讓別人經歷痛苦沒有甚麼好笑的。因此，家長、學校和兒童必須共同努力，防止網絡欺凌並促進電子安全。本文提出防止網絡欺凌發生的具體方法。

為了防止網絡欺凌，家長、學校和政府必須採取行動。首先，父母該了解自己的孩子是否被欺負，並建議他們不要理會欺凌者的傷人話語和負面評論。父母還該協助孩子向有關當局（例如在線服務提供商）報告欺凌行為，以阻止網絡欺凌通信。其次，受害人該向朋友傾訴受虐情況，並立即向家長和學校報告問題。第三，學校應制定嚴格規則，禁止傳播網絡欺凌信息，並實施反欺凌政策，以阻止敵對行為，阻止欺凌行為發生。此外，政府應實施制裁，宣佈網絡欺凌為刑事犯罪。

網絡欺凌日益普遍，突顯了個人支持阻止欺凌信息傳播的重要性、家長識別網絡欺凌發生的意識、學校制定嚴格規則以及政府頒佈法律的重要性。至關重要的是，我們要團結起來，防止我們自己、朋友和家人成為網絡欺凌的受害者。

★ 6 傳單 / 海報 Leaflet / Poster

　　傳單 / 海報的寫法該突出產品或展示活動的好處 —— 將信息直接展示於讀者面前。重要的是傳單 / 海報的內容要實在，信息要簡潔和語氣要堅實。以下是四個簡單的寫作步驟：

> » 使用堅定的語氣
>
> » 撰寫引人注目的標題
>
> » 強調獨特賣點，並包括所有細節
>
> » 號召讀者採取行動

結構 Structure

1. 標題：　　　　標題要吸引讀者的注意力並展示傳單 / 海報的內容

2. 反問句：　　　通過反問句，訴諸讀者感受來引出主題。還可以讓讀者為傳單 / 海報內的某事做好準備。如宣傳活動，可以用地點和日期代替。

3. 主題陳述：　　敦促讀者必須做某事，呼籲讀者採取行動。它通常跟在反問句之前或之後，用祈使句式使陳述變得清楚、具體和直截了當。

4. 正文段落：　　這些段落提供了傳單 / 海報中大部分的重要信息，並且可能包含更具說服力的內容。段落有時會用項目符號，特別是當它們很短時。請緊記，當您製作傳單 / 海報時，你必須用讀者的角度來思考。

5. 呼籲：　　　　在傳單 / 海報的末尾要作出呼籲，敦促讀者採取行動。

6. 口號：　　　　這是一個簡短的短語，通常出現在傳單 / 海報的開頭或結尾（儘管並非所有傳單都使用它們）。一個好的口號會在讀者心中產生積極的感覺並留在他們的記憶中。

範文十九：保存「荷李活格蘭大樓」

Save 'Hollywood Grand Building'

Save 'Hollywood Grand Building'	標題
Do You Want Our Community to Be Destroyed?	反問句
Petition for Historic Preservation.	主題陳述
The Hollywood Grand Building, located in the Central District, has been home to many families for nearly 130 years since it was built in 1892. This historic and beautiful complex has undergone renovations and repairs in 1913, 1925, and 1960, and has been a residence for many lives since then. It has also been a small community, hosting a variety of shops, including a Hong Kong style grocery, a bookshop, and at one point, even a traditional Chinese doctor with his clinic. Perhaps its most famous incarnation was as a flower shop during the 1960s, with some quite famous photos of the building festooned with flowers from this period.	正文段（一） 説明建築物的歷史
In 1985, the building was acquired by a charitable organization and became a private club with two restaurants (Western and Chinese), a fitness centre, a children's playground, a swimming pool, and a small library, which was opened to the public with an entrance fee of $2,000 and a monthly fee of $100 only. Today, it has over 20,000 members.	正文段（二） 説明建築物的現在情況
The building was built in an eclectic architectural style with strong neoclassical and arts and crafts influence. Unfortunately, the owner has submitted plans to demolish it to make way for the construction of luxury apartments. This appalling decision must be stopped, and we are determined to rescue the Hollywood Grand Building. It would be a tragedy to destroy this close-knit community by building luxury apartments that are hardly affordable for ordinary people.	正文段（三） 描述建築物的價值及它要被拆卸的原因
Please sign this petition to help save this historic building from being torn down. By doing so, we will be in a better position to request our government's intervention.	呼籲
Act now to show our strength in preserving this much-loved piece of history!	口號

保存「荷李活格蘭大樓」

你想讓我們的社區被摧毀嗎？

歷史保護請願書。

位於中區的荷李活格蘭大樓自 1892 年建成以來，近 130 年來一直是許多家庭的家園。這座歷史悠久、美麗的綜合建築物在 1913 年、1925 年和 1960 年經歷了翻新和修建，一直是許多人的居所。它也是一個小型社區，擁有各種商店，包括一家港式雜貨店、書店，甚至有中醫診所。也許它最著名及最為人樂道的是 1960 年代的一家花店，它有非常著名的照片顯示了這一時期用鮮花裝飾的建築。

1985 年，該建築物被慈善機構收購，成為私人會所，設有兩間餐廳（西餐廳和中餐廳）、健身中心、兒童遊樂場、泳池和小型圖書館，並向公眾開放，入會費為 2,000 元，月費僅為 100 元。如今，它擁有超過 20,000 名會員。

該建築物採用兼收並蓄的建築風格，受強烈的新古典主義、藝術和工藝的影響。不幸的是，業主已提交拆卸它的計劃，以便為建造豪宅讓路。這個駭人聽聞的決定必須停止，我們決心拯救荷李活格蘭大樓。因要建造普通人難以負擔得起的豪宅而摧毀這個緊密聯繫的社區，將會是一場悲劇。

請簽署這份請願書，以幫助拯救這座歷史建築避免遭到拆卸。通過這樣做，我們將更能請求政府出手干預。

現在就行動起來，展示我們保護這段備受喜愛的歷史的力量！

範文二十：戲劇節

Festival of Drama

Festival of Drama	標題
Venue: *School Playground and School Theatre*	地點
Date: *Friday, 7ᵗʰ April 20XX*	日期
Students, parents, and friends, you are cordially invited to our school's first-ever 'Festival of Drama'.	主題陳述：邀請參加

The festival promises to be a fun-filled event with games and workshops for younger children, an interview with *King Sir*, and the Drama Society's production of *Romeo and Juliet*. The interview with King Sir will be held during lunchtime, and catering service will be provided by Café de Taste. A lunch coupon, including a drama play ticket, will be available for $200 per person. The drama play is free of charge, but you must obtain a ticket first.

正文段（一）：
介紹戲劇節活動

Timetable

正文段（二）：
節目時間表

Time	Event
8:30 am	Opening Speech by the School Principal
8:45 am – 12:30 pm	Games and Workshops
12:30 pm – 2:30 pm	Lunch and Interview with King Sir
3:00 pm – 5:00 pm	Drama Play: Romeo and Juliet

King Sir

正文段（三）：
介紹主角嘉賓

King Sir is an actor and pioneer of contemporary performing arts in Hong Kong. He is also a director, TV producer, programme host, and performing arts educator. He is the founder and president of the Hong Kong Federation of Drama Societies and the appointed founding dean of the School of Drama at the Hong Kong Academy for Performing Arts. King Sir has won many Drama Awards, including best director, best actor, outstanding achievement, and many others.

The interview with King Sir will include a discussion of his career history and acting techniques. He will also demonstrate how to use body language to express emotions and share his experiences and challenges as an actor or director. The interview will be held during lunchtime in our school canteen and will also be broadcast online for those who cannot attend in person.

Romeo and Juliet

正文段（四）：
介紹戲劇劇目

Romeo and Juliet is perhaps Shakespeare's most famous play, and it is certainly one of his most beloved. We are excited to present our own twist on the story – a comedy with a happy ending instead of a tragedy. The Drama Society has been preparing for several months to make this the best quality drama production ever put on in our school. We would like to express our gratitude to the parents of the main actress and actor, who generously sponsored our play, allowing us to rent expensive 19th-century costumes and sound equipment.

Please obtain your tickets from your class master teacher on a first-come, first-served basis.

呼籲

Hurry, as there are only limited tickets available.

口號

戲劇節

地點：學校操場和學校劇院

日期：星期五，20XX 年 4 月 7 日

各位同學、家長、朋友，我們誠摯邀請您參加我校首屆「戲劇節」。

這個項目有望成為一個充滿樂趣的活動，包括為年幼孩子們準備的遊戲和工作坊、景老師專訪及劇社製作的羅密歐與茱麗葉。與景老師的訪問將在午餐時間進行，餐飲由好味餐廳提供。每位 200 元可獲得一張午餐券，包括一張戲票。觀賞戲劇免費，但需先取得戲票。

時間表

時間	事件
上午 8.30	校長致開幕詞
上午 8.45 至下午 12.30	遊戲和工作坊
下午 12.30 至下午 2.30	午餐、訪問景老師
下午 3.00 至下午 5.00	戲劇：羅密歐與茱麗葉

景老師

景老師是香港當代表演藝術的演員和先驅。他還是導演、電視製作人、節目主持人和表演藝術教育家。他是香港戲劇協會的創辦人及會長，並獲委任為香港演藝學院戲劇學院創院院長。景老師曾獲得多項戲劇大獎，包括最佳導演、最佳男主角、傑出成就等多項大獎。

對景老師的採訪將包括對他的職業生涯和表演技巧的討論。他還將演示如何使用肢體語言來表達情感，並分享他作為演員或導演的經歷和挑戰。訪問將在午餐時間在我們學校食堂進行，對於無法親自參加的學生也可在網上直播觀看。

羅密歐與茱麗葉

羅密歐與茱麗葉也許是莎士比亞最著名的戲劇，當然也是他最鍾愛的戲劇之一。我們很興奮能展示對這個故事的改編創作新花樣：大團圓結局而不是悲劇收場。劇社已經準備了幾個月，以使其成為我們學校有史以來質量最好的戲劇作品。我們要感謝男女主角的父母，他們慷慨地贊助了我們的演出，讓我們租用昂貴的 19 世紀服裝和音響設備。

請以先到先得的方式向班主任老師索取門票。

快點，門票數量有限，派完即止。

★ 7 書信 Letter

　　寫信是與他人交流和表達想法和感受的方式。信件可以保存並在將來隨時閱讀。閱讀信件可以喚起對特殊人物或重要事件的回憶。信件根據其用途可分為三類：非正式、正式和半正式信函。

1. 非正式信函是私人信函，通常是寫給家人、親戚或朋友。
2. 正式信函是商務或官方公函，是寫給你不認識或從未見過的人，通常用於提供信息、表達疑慮及提出請求或投訴等。
3. 半正式信函是寫給你不太了解，但表示尊重和禮貌的人的，例如，老師、校長、上司和同事等。

格式結構 Structure

1. 上端	信紙上端包含兩個地址，即寫信人的地址及收件人的姓名和地址，它還包括寫信的日期。寫地址時，街名、姓名、月份等專有名詞要大寫。私人信函可以不寫地址。
2. 稱呼	稱呼通常以問候語「親愛的 (Dear)」一詞開頭，然後放在收件人的姓名之前，問候語及其後的姓名或稱呼需要大寫，並使用逗號結束問候語，例如：

	非正式或半正式信函	商務或官方正式信函
	朋友：Dear John,	Dear Sir,
	同事：Dear Bill,	Dear Madam,
	年長親戚：Dear Uncle Ho,	Dear Sir / Madam,
	鄰居：Dear Mr Lee,	Dear Mr Chan,
	半正式：Dear Principal,	Dear Ms Lee,

3. 正文	這僅適用於正式或半正式的信件，說明寫這封信的目的。
	非正式或半正式信函，應避免使用過於正式的結構，例如倒裝句，但可以使用縮寫和非正式標點符號。在商務或官方正式信函，就該避免使用縮寫、口語表達、俚語、笑話及非正式的標點符號等。
	首段
	首段通常是固定套語，以下是首段第一句的例子：

非正式或半正式信函

How are you?
你好嗎？

It has been a few months since I last wrote you ...
自從上次給你寫信以來已有幾個
月了……

I'm terribly sorry to take you so long to get my reply.
我非常抱歉花了這麼長時間你才得到
我的答覆。

Thanks for writing to me regarding...
感謝您寫信給我關於……

Thank you for your kind invitation to...
感謝您的盛情邀請……

I hope everything is fine. I am writing to...
我希望一切安好。我寫這信……

I have received your letter dated..., in which you...
我收到了你……日的信，其中你……

I have received your letter asking me about...
我收到了你的來信，問我關於……

You asked me to advise you about...
你讓我給你建議……

I regret that I can't accept your invitation.
我很遺憾不能接受你的邀請。

商務或官方正式信函

In response to your letter dated..., I am writing to confirm that...
回覆您……日的來信，我寫信確認……

Further to my letter of..., I write again to make certain that...
繼我……日的信函，我再次寫信以
確保……

I write to express my gratitude for your offering me help.
我寫信是為了表達我對你提供幫助的
感激之情。

We are writing with reference to your letter dated...
我們這封信是關於您……日的來信。

We are writing to ask for your assistance.
我們寫這信是為了尋求你的幫助。

We are writing to you because we are unable to...
我們寫信給您是因為我們無法……

We are writing in response to... and would like to express our views on...
我們寫這信以回應……並想表達我們
對……的看法。

You have asked me for my advice about...
關於你問我……的意見。

As requested, I write with my suggestions as follows:
根據要求，我建議如下：

We thank you for your letter dated... and are more than pleased to accept your invitation ...
我們感謝您……日的來函並非常高興
接受您的邀請……

中間段

中間段可分為幾段，視乎內容而定，例如介紹主要信息，說明寫信原因等。以下是一些中間段常用的句式：

非正式或半正式信函	商務或官方正式信函
I'll be on a trip to London from ... 由……我將前往倫敦。	We are surprised that... 我們很驚訝……
I'm now sending you my hearty greetings on your birthday. 我現在衷心祝你生日快樂。	Our records show that... 我們的記錄顯示……
These days, I'm busy with... 這些天，我忙於……	The software you sent to us was completely dissatisfactory... 你給我們的軟件完全不滿意……
I'm afraid that the company which offers you the job is... 我恐怕聘請你工作那間公司是……	Your speech at the HKU was fantastic. We would be delighted if you could accept our invitation... 你在香港大學的演講極好。我們會很高興如果你能接受我們的邀請……
Our class is going to have an outing to... and we request your sponsor... 我們班要去……郊遊，請求你贊助……	The registration procedure as mentioned in your letter is so complicated that... 你信中提到的註冊程序非常複雜，以至……

4. 結尾　　尾段

最後一段總結了意見及其主要原因，還可以表明將採取甚麼行動來處理主題，然後結尾。以下是正文段落尾段的示例：

非正式或半正式信函	商務或官方正式信函
Drop me a line if you are free. 如果有空就打電話給我。	I look forward to hearing from you without delay. 我期待立即收到您的來信。
Keep in touch! 保持聯絡！	I hope to hear from you at your earliest convenience. 希望在您方便時盡早聯繫我。

Please remember me to your family. 請代我向你家人問好。	I would appreciate your help and look forward to your prompt response. 感謝您的幫助，並期待您迅速回覆。
Have a wonderful time! 享受美好的時光！	Thank you for your assistance. 謝謝您的幫助。
I hope this information will be helpful to you. Please do let me know if I can help any further. 我希望這些信息對您有幫助。若需要進一步的幫助，請告訴我。	We are sorry that we are not in a position to help at the present moment and trust that you will understand. 很抱歉目前我們無法提供幫助，相信您會諒解。
The rest can be discussed when you come. 其餘的事情等你來的時候才討論。	Please accept our apologies for the inconvenience caused. 對於給您帶來的不便，請接受我們的歉意。
Let me know if you can make it. 如果你能做到，請告訴我。	We look forward to hearing from you soon. 我們期待您的佳音。
Take care and see you soon. 保重，很快見到你。	We hope to receive your reply shortly. 我們希望很快收到您的回覆。

5. 結束語　結束敬語寫在正文下方兩行位置，與地址一致的頁面右下角。

私人信函	正式或非正式信函	註釋
Love 愛	Yours faithfully, 您忠實的	如果您使用 Dear Sir / Madam 或 Dear Mr Lee 問候語，則應分別以 Yours faithfully 或 Yours sincerely 結束。
Your friend 你的朋友	Yours sincerely, 您真誠的	

關於結束語的 Yours，字母 Y 要大寫，但 s 之前不要加撇號，faithfully 或 sincerely 之後要有逗號。

6. 簽名　簽名指寫信人的姓名，寫在結束語下方，簽名後面不能有句號。

範文二十一：惡意破壞

Vandalism

23rd September 20XX 　　上端：寫信日期

Dear May Ling,　　　　　　　　　　　　　　稱呼：朋友常用稱呼

<u>Re: Vandalism</u>　　　　　　　　　　　　　主題：惡意破壞

I hope you've been having a good week so far. First, I want to thank you for coming to my birthday party last week. It was great to catch up with you. However, the reason for my writing today is to share a serious problem with you—vandalism.

正文段（一）：頭三句開場白，其後說明寫這信的目的

During my party, we discussed the issue of graffiti and defacement, and I mentioned that someone had sprayed graffiti on the walls of our school. Unfortunately, the situation has escalated since then. Over the past few days, the vandalism has become worse. Teachers' cars have been scratched, and litter bins in the playground have been smashed. Yesterday, the vandals broke into the school and caused extensive damage. They defaced the walls with rude and offensive language, even entering the library and throwing books on the floor. In addition, they stole expensive equipment from the laboratory and damaged electronic goods in the staff office, including computers and overhead projectors.

正文段（二）：繼續談論上次生日晚會的話題，寫出惡意破壞繼續惡化的情況

This vandalism is not only costly to clean up and maintain, but it also poses a safety risk to our students, staff, and teachers. If the vandalism continues to escalate, it could result in fires or explosions that could potentially harm individuals, and our school would be held responsible. I recently read a news report that a school was closed due to severe vandalism, and a 12-year-old was arrested in connection to the crime.

正文段（三）：害怕事情會失控

What concerns me the most is that we still do not know who is responsible for these acts, despite the principal reporting the incidents to the police. It is difficult to prevent these crimes from occurring if we do not identify the perpetrators. Some students believe that the vandalism is the result of a quest for excitement, while others think that dissatisfaction with the school's administrative and disciplinary policies is the cause. However, I hope that our own school's students are not responsible for this damage. I cannot imagine any of our students would want to cause such destruction, and I believe it is important to remind them that vandalism is a criminal act.

正文段（四）：事件可能影響深遠，又探討它的成因

I'm writing to you in the hope that perhaps you have some ideas that could help address this issue. I am concerned for the safety of our school community and hope that we can work together to prevent further vandalism.

正文尾段：發求救信息

I appreciate your taking a look at this and advising me your thoughts.

結束語

Love,

Man Ying

結束敬語
簽名

參考譯文

親愛的美玲，

關於：惡意破壞

希望您最近一週過得愉快。首先，我感謝您上週參加我的生日派對。很高興見到你。但今天寫這文章的原因，是要與您分享一個嚴重的問題 —— 惡意破壞。

在我的派對中，我們討論了塗鴉和污損的問題，我提到有人在我們學校的牆上亂塗亂畫。不幸的是，此後局勢升級。在過去的幾天裏，惡意破壞的行為變得更加嚴重。老師的車被刮花，操場的垃圾桶被砸爛。昨天，破壞者闖入學校並造成廣泛損壞。他們在牆壁塗上粗魯無禮的語言，甚至進入圖書館並將書籍扔在地上。此外，還從實驗室偷走了昂貴設備，並損壞了職員辦公室的電子產品，包括電腦和投影機。

這種故意破壞的行為不僅令清理和維護成本高昂，而且還對我們的學生、職員和教師構成安全風險。如果故意破壞行為繼續升級，可能會導致火災或爆炸，從而對個人造成潛在傷害，我們學校將要承擔責任。最近我看到一則新聞報導說，一所學校因嚴重的惡意破壞而停課，一名 12 歲的少年因涉嫌犯罪而被捕。

最讓我擔心的是，儘管校長向警方報案，但我們仍然不知道誰應對這些行為負責。如果我們不找出肇事者，就很難防止這些罪行發生。一些學生認為，惡意破壞是追求刺激的結果，另一些學生則認為，對學校的行政和紀律政策有不滿是成因。但我希望我們自己學校的學生沒需要對這種損害負責。我無法想像我們的學生會想造成這樣的破壞，我認為提醒他們破壞公物是一種犯罪行為是很重要的。

寫信給您，是希望您能想出一些主意來幫忙解決這問題。我擔心學校社區的安全，希望我們能夠共同努力，防止進一步的惡意破壞。

我感激您跟進此事並告訴我您的想法。

愛你的，

文英

20XX 年 9 月 23 日

範文二十二：英雄週

Heroes' Week

Sunlight Secondary School,   發信人地址
16 High Street,
Hong Kong

7th November 20XX   日期

Mr. Shek Kun   收信人姓名
Ken Studio (HK)   收信人地址
Level 5, Taikoo Plaza
Hong Kong

Dear Kun,   稱呼

Re: Heroes' Week   主題

I have admired your martial arts skills for a long time and have been a big fan of yours. As an old schoolmate, you have always been my favourite wizard. I'm writing to you to celebrate our school's 'Heroes' Week'. I am pleased to inform you that this letter will be published in the next issue of our school magazine.

首段：介紹寫這封信的目的

I appreciate your vast knowledge in various types of martial arts, including Chinese Kung Fu such as Tai Chi, Wing Chun, and more, as well as Western fighting styles such as Boxing and Mixed Martial Arts. Your five-movie series, "Hung Hay Kuan," has made you well-known, and your fans believe in your martial arts abilities. However, I have always seen you as more than just a Kung Fu star. Your acting skills are impressive, as demonstrated in the 2021 movie 'Father of Dirty World,' which received exceptionally positive reviews from critics who praised your versatility as an actor.

正文段（一）：描述作者對收信人的認識

In your movies, you always portray bravery, and in real life, I have seen that you possess it as well. I read a news report from Hong Kong in the late 1990s that described an incident in which you were harassed by a troublesome gang in a karaoke after helping a lady. You left the premises to avoid trouble, but the gang followed you and attacked you. You bravely fought back and defeated eight members of the gang, who were later hospitalized. I admire your courage and bravery, which is not only displayed in your movies but also in your actions.

正文段（二）：描述收信人勇猛的一面

Another quality that I admire about you is your generosity. In 2019, you received calls from the Education Bureau and the Health Department about a potential collaboration on a short martial arts film to promote Tai Chi boxing as a PE lesson at school. Even though you were on holiday with your wife to celebrate your anniversary at that time, you immediately cancelled your trip and rushed back to participate in the film. You declined any remuneration for this film and said that it was your responsibility to do so.

正文段（三）：寫信人敬佩收信人

Kun, you are not only an actor but also a premier action choreographer. You have stated that, in a fight scene, the action choreographer takes the place of the director of the film and is in full control over camera placements, camera angles, and the relationship between drama and action. This expertise led you to win the Hong Kong Film Award for Best Action Choreography in 2020. Your contributions have made Hong Kong Kung Fu movies successful and brought them to the attention of the world.

正文段（四）：收信人在電影界的成就

Finally, I would like to wish you good luck in all your future productions.

尾段

Yours Sincerely,

結束敬語

Chan Man
President, Drama Club

寫信人簽名
寫信人職位、單位

陽光中學
香港高街 16 號

20XX 年 11 月 7 日

石勤先生
勤電影工作室（香港）
香港太古廣場五樓

親愛的勤，

關於：英雄週

我仰慕您的武術已久，是您的忠實粉絲。作為老同學，您一直是我最喜歡的高手。寫信給您是為了歌頌我們學校的「英雄週」。我很高興地通知您，這封信將刊登在下期的校刊上。

我很欣賞您對各種武術的淵博知識，包括太極拳、詠春拳等中國功夫，以及拳擊和混合格鬥等西方搏擊風格。您五部電影系列片《洪熙官》讓您家傳戶曉，影迷也相信您武功了得。然而，我一直認為您不只是一個功夫明星。您的演技令人印象深刻，正如 2021 年的電影《黑社會之父》展示的那樣，該片獲得了影評人的正面高度評價，他們稱讚您是多才多藝的演員。

在您的電影裏，您總是表現出勇敢的質素，在現實生活中，我看到您同樣勇敢。九十年代後期，我在香港看到一則新聞報導，描述了一個事件，您在卡拉 OK 幫助一位女士後，被一羣麻煩的幫派騷擾。您為了避免麻煩離開了房間，但那幫人跟隨並且襲擊您。您勇敢還擊並擊敗了後來要住院的八名黑社會成員。我很佩服您的膽量和勇氣，這不僅體現在您的電影中，也體現在您的行動中。

我欽佩您的另一個品質是您的慷慨。2019 年，您接到教育局和衛生署的電話，希望合作製作一部武術短片，以在學校體育課上推廣太極拳。即使當時您正在和妻子一起度假慶祝結婚紀念日，但您還是立即取消了行程，趕回去參演。您拒絕收取這部電影的酬金，並說這是您的責任。

勤，您不僅是演員，還是一流的武術指導。您曾說過，在打鬥場面中，武術指導取代了電影導演的位置，完全控制了攝錄機的位置、攝錄機的角度及戲劇與動作之間的關係。這份專業讓您贏得 2020 年香港電影金像獎最佳武術指導。您的貢獻讓香港功夫片大獲成功，並讓它們受到世界的關注。

最後，我祝您在未來所有的作品中一切順利。

你真誠的，
陳文
戲劇社社長

<h1>範文二十三：香港污染問題</h1>

<h1>Hong Kong Pollution Problem</h1>

5/F, 62 Hill Road,
Hong Kong.
12th December 20XX

The Administration Officer,
Environmental Protection Department,
Hong Kong Government West Wing Building,
HKSAR

Dear Sir / Madam,

Re: Hong Kong Pollution Problem

I'm writing to express my concern about the growing pollution problem in Hong Kong.

Over the past decade, air quality in Hong Kong has steadily declined due to the increasing number of motor vehicles, the rise in marine vessels entering and exiting our harbour, and the use of coal and natural gas in power plants run by the two electric companies. Additionally, littering remains a problem as some people do not properly use garbage cans and recycling bins. I would like to address some of the issues and suggest possible solutions to Hong Kong's environmental pollution.

The constant haze that lingers over the harbour is a growing concern. Street-level pollution and regional smog are the biggest challenges we face. Last month, the Air Quality Health Index recorded a level of 8 or above, indicating a very high health risk. Local pollutants were identified as the main cause of this pollution. I believe the Environment Bureau should publish regular progress reports on its strategy, implementation, and achievements in reducing street-level pollution and regional smog.

Littering is a major threat to the environment and causes pollution. It is not uncommon to see people throwing fast food packaging, cigarette butts, face masks, used drink cans or bottles, and other items on the streets, in parks, and other public areas. Not only does this pollute our environment, but it also promotes the breeding of pests such as rats and cockroaches. Furthermore, the smell and toxic / chemical vapours emanating from the trash can encourage the spread of diseases, negatively affecting public health. When someone sees litter already accumulated somewhere, it gives the impression that it is the right place to discard rubbish. This reinforces the belief that Hong Kong has a culture of habitual littering.

	註解
	寫信人地址
	日期
	收信人 部門 地址
	稱呼
	主題：香港環保問題
	首段：直接指出香港環保問題
	正文段（一）：提出問題：空氣污染垃圾
	正文段（二）：煙霧的問題和解決方法
	正文段（三）：垃圾滋生的問題

Littering is a crime, but I believe our current penalties and enforcement measures do little to dissuade people from littering. I suggest increasing the littering or spitting fine from HK$3,000 to HK$6,000 and penalizing the offender to clean the street. Your department should take a more active role in enforcing the law so that violators are fined and penalized instantly. To guarantee long-term results, public education is crucial. This means raising public awareness as a top priority. You may consider introducing a reward system for those who demonstrate positive disposal behaviour so as to encourage people to dispose of litter properly.

正文段（四）：清潔香港

It is clear that we, as citizens, must take better care of our surroundings and help curb pollution by reducing energy consumption at home and properly disposing of litter. Your department should establish stricter laws and fines to tackle the issue. Only through these efforts can our city be clean and beautiful.

正文尾段：環保需要政府和市民同心

Yours faithfully,

Chan Dai Man

結束敬語 簽名

參考譯文

香港山道 62 號 5 樓
20XX 年 12 月 12 日

行政主任，
環境保護署
香港政府西翼大樓，
香港特別行政區
尊敬的先生 / 女士，

主題：香港污染問題

我寫信表達對香港污染問題日益嚴重的關注。

過去十年，由於汽車數量增加、進出本港的船隻增加，以及兩家電力公司經營的發電廠使用煤炭和天然氣，香港的空氣質量持續下降。此外，亂拋垃圾仍是一個問題，因為有些人沒有正確使用垃圾桶和回收箱。我想談談其中的一些問題，並提出解決香港環境污染的可能方案。

持續籠罩在維港上空的陰霾越來越令人擔憂。最大的挑戰是街道污染和區域霧霾。上月空氣質素健康指數錄得 8 或以上水平，顯示健康風險極高。當地污染物被確定為造成這種污染的主要原因。我認為環境局該定期發佈進度報告，介紹其在減少街道污染和區域煙霧方面的策略、實施和成果。

亂拋垃圾是對環境的主要威脅，會造成污染。人在街道、公園和其他公共場所扔掉快餐包裝、煙頭、口罩、用過的飲品罐或瓶等，不僅污染環境，還助長了老鼠、蟑螂等害蟲滋生。此外，垃圾散發的氣味和有毒 / 化學氣體會助長疾病傳播，對公眾健康產生不良影響。當人看到某處已堆積垃圾時，給人的印象是丟棄垃圾的正確地方。這強化了此信念，香港有一種習慣性亂拋垃圾的文化。

亂拋垃圾是一種犯罪行為，但我相信目前的處罰和執法措施並不能阻止人亂拋垃圾。我建議將亂拋垃圾或隨地吐痰的罰款由港幣 3,000 元提高至港幣 6,000 元，並懲罰違法者清掃街道。您的部門該在執法方面發揮更積極的作用，以便立即對違法者處以罰款和懲罰。為了保證長期效果，公眾教育是至關重要的。這意味着提高公眾認知是重中之重。您可以考慮引入獎勵制度，獎勵表現出積極處理垃圾行為的人，從而鼓勵人妥善處理垃圾。

很明顯，作為公民，我們必須在保護環境方面做得更好，並通過減少家庭能源消耗和妥善處理垃圾來幫助遏制污染。貴部門該制定更嚴格的法律和罰款來解決這問題。只有通過這些努力，我們的城市才能乾淨美麗。

你忠誠的
陳大文

★ 8 忠告 / 建議信 Letter of Advice / Suggestion

　　忠告 / 建議信都是針對某事向收信人提出忠告或建議的信件。忠告 / 建議信有可能是寫給個人，如朋友、同事等，就其遭遇到某問題提出自己的看法和觀點，來改進或解決他的煩惱，也可能是寫給某組織、部門或機構，就改進其服務提出意見或建議。忠告 / 建議信通常簡明扼要，目的明確，具有合理性和說服力。

　　忠告 / 建議信要寫得及時，所以英語時態通常用一般現在時或一般將來時。可用自己作第一人稱，語氣要真摯，所提的意見或建議要具有可行性。

結構 Structure

上端：	如果是個人信函，只需要填寫日期，但正式信件則需要有寫信人和收信人的地址。
稱呼：	如果是個人的，在收件人名字之前使用「嗨」或「親愛的」。
主題：	給出忠告 / 建議的標題
首段：	開門見山，表明你的寫作意圖，嘗試了解收件人的問題及他 / 她的感受。
正文段：	表達對收信人的關心，整體說明一下你對該問題的想法，指出對方不足之處，針對對方的困難作出回應。正文段可分幾段來寫，你在每一段只可提出一個建議。
尾段：	總結你的忠告或建議，希望意見或建議能被對方採納，並鼓勵收信人嘗試將事情處理好。
結束敬語：	如果是個人信件，可用友好結束，例如 Love（愛）、Best regards（最美好的問候）、All the best（萬事如意）等。如果是正式信函，用 Yours faithfully（你忠誠的）或 Yours sincerely（你真誠的）。
簽名：	寫信人姓名方面，私人信函只寫名字即可，但正式公函要寫上姓氏。

忠告 / 建議信常用句型

忠告 / 建議信：邀請收信人提意見

	半正式官方信函	非正式個人信函
首段：	I am writing in response to... and would like your advice on... 我寫信是為了回應⋯⋯並希望您對⋯⋯提出建議。 I would appreciate it if you could advise me what I can do. 如果你能告知我可以怎樣做，我不勝感激。	Do you have any ideas about...? 你對⋯⋯有甚麼想法嗎？ Recently, I... What should I do? 最近，我⋯⋯我該怎麼辦？
尾段：	Please write back when you have the time and let me know what you think. 有空時請回信，讓我知道您的想法。	Please drop me a line when you get the time. 有空時請給我留言。

忠告 / 建議信：給收信人提出意見

	半正式官方信函	非正式個人信函
首段：	I am sorry to hear about your current difficulties. 我很遺憾聽到你目前的困難。	I'm sorry you're having such a hard time at the moment. 我很抱歉你現在過得這樣艱難。
正文段：	You have asked me for my advice about... 關於你問我的忠告⋯⋯ In my opinion, I think it might be a good idea if you would... 在我看來，如果你會⋯⋯我認為這可能是個好主意。 This would mean that... 這將意味着⋯⋯	I think you should... 我認為你該⋯⋯ It's true that you... 沒錯，你⋯⋯ However, I think... 不過，我覺得⋯⋯

	I think you may take another option that...That would... 我想你可能會採取另一種選擇……那會……	This way, ... 這樣，……
	I feel that it would be beneficial if... 我覺得如果……會有益的。	I think it's better than... 我認為……比較好
尾段：	I hope I have been of some help. 我希望我幫得上忙。	I hope I've helped a bit. 我希望我可以提供一些幫助。
	I hope these suggestions will help you. 我希望這些建議對您有所幫助。	Don't hesitate to write again for any further help! 如需要更多幫助，別猶豫，再寫信給我！
	I hope you'll find my suggestion useful. 我希望你覺得我的建議有用。	I trust you will consider my suggestions carefully. 我相信你會仔細考慮我的建議。

忠告 / 建議信

提出建議	I would like to suggest that... 我想建議…… Here I will try to make some suggestions. 在這裏，我將嘗試提出一些建議。
接受建議	It's a great idea! 這是個好主意！ I think your idea would work really well. 我認為你的想法會很有效。 It might be worth trying. 可能值得一試。
拒絕接受 建議	I'm afraid that I might not be in a position to share with your view that... 我恐怕無法贊同你的看法…… It sounds like a good idea. However, I don't think it would work in practice. 這聽起來是個好主意。但我認為實際上行不通。 Your suggestion seems like a good idea, but it may need enhancement on ... 你的建議似乎是個好主意，但它可能需要改進……

範文二十四：請就誤導性廣告提意見

Asking for Advice on Misleading Advertisement

20th July 20XX   日期

Dear Hon Man,   稱呼

I hope you're doing well since we last spoke. I'm writing to seek your assistance with a matter that has been troubling me for some time.   首段

A few months ago, I purchased an ointment called PimpleFade online after seeing an advertisement claiming that it would eliminate my acne within a month of daily use. The ad also stated that the product was FDA-approved and made from 100% pure herbal ingredients. However, after following the instructions and using the product as directed, my acne did not improve and, in fact, became worse.   正文段（一）：介紹寫信人被廣告誤導的情況

Upon conducting some research, I discovered that PimpleFade was not listed in the FDA's approved database and contained at least two animal ingredients. I then attempted to obtain a refund by submitting an application online, but only received an acknowledgement without any information on the refund process. When I called their Customer Service Desk, I found that the telephone was merely a recorder with no live agent available to speak with. I also attempted to contact them via WhatsApp, email, and Facebook, but received no response.   正文段（二）：描述廣告與事實不符；寫信人要求退款

After several attempts, I finally received a response from them via mail, in a pre-printed computer format with no signature. They stated that my refund application had been rejected because I did not follow the instructions, despite not asking me how I used the product. To my surprise, I also discovered that the company's office address listed on the computer print-out did not exist when I visited it in person.   正文段（三）：寫信人提出她被騙錢財的經過

I would greatly appreciate your advice on this matter. Please let me know what you think and what steps I should take next.   正文段（四）：請求收信人給意見

Thank you for your time and assistance.   尾段：感謝幫忙

Best regards,   結束敬語

Wai Fun   簽名

20XX 年 7 月 20 日

親愛的漢文，

自從上次談話以來，我希望您過得很好。寫信是想就困擾我一段時間的事尋求您的幫助。

幾個月前，我在網上購買了一種名為 PimpleFade 的藥膏，因為看到一則廣告，聲稱每天用它可在一個月內消除粉刺。該廣告還表示，該產品已獲得 FDA 批准，由 100% 純草藥成份製成。然而，在遵循說明並按指示使用產品後，粉刺沒有改善，事實上，反而變得更糟。

在進行一些研究後，我發現 PimpleFade 未列入 FDA 批准的數據庫之內，並至少包含兩種動物成份。然後我試圖在網上申請退款，但只收到一封確認書，沒有任何退款程序的信息。當我打電話給他們的客戶服務台時，我發現電話只是一個錄音機，沒有可以與之交談的真人。我還嘗試通過 WhatsApp、電郵和 Facebook 聯繫他們，但沒有收到任何回覆。

經過幾次嘗試，我終於通過郵件收到回覆，郵件是預先打印好的電腦版式，沒有簽名。他們說我的退款申請被拒絕了，因為我沒有按指示去做，即是並沒有問我如何使用該產品。令我驚訝的是，當我親自到他們的辦公室時，我還發現電腦打印出來的公司辦公地址並不存在。

我將非常感謝您對此事的建議。請讓我知道您的想法及我接下來該採取的步驟。

感謝您的時間和協助。

最誠摯的問候，

惠芬

範文二十五：提供辯論意見

Providing Advice on Debate

30th August 20XX

30th August 20XX　日期

Dear Tina,　稱呼

I hope this letter can comfort you. I appreciate your reaching me out for advice on how to prepare for your upcoming debate. As promised, I'm writing to provide you with some suggestions.　首段

As the team leader responsible for giving the debate speech, it is essential to prioritize team spirit and cooperation. Each team member should be assigned specific responsibilities, such as researching necessary information, finding arguments, and gathering evidence. You should direct and guide your team members to analyse all viewpoints to prove that your team is right in opposing the debate topic, 'Fashion is becoming more highly valued in people's choice of clothes'.　正文段（一）：指出組長的責任和說明團隊精神的重要性

Since your debate topic revolves around 'fashion', it is crucial to find facts and statistics about 'stylish dressing' to support your main argument. However, it is equally important to remain objective and logical, putting aside personal views. For example, you could argue that being fashionable is unhealthy as it can lead to superficiality and neglect of more important things in life, such as friendship and being a good citizen.　正文段（二）：針對題目「時髦」，提出建議；保持客觀和避免個人主觀性意見

In preparing for the debate, it is essential to pinpoint your opponent's weaknesses accurately, find flaws in their reasoning, and rebut their arguments immediately. However, avoid attacking your opponent on a personal level, as it can give a negative impression to the judges. Instead, show that you understand their perspective.　正文段（三）：找出正方的弱點加以攻擊，但避免在個人層面上攻擊對手

What's more, writing an outline of your speech in note form, keeping it brief and well-organized, is crucial. You can include a catchy and interesting introduction to make your argument colourful, using humour and sincerity where appropriate. Predicting your opponent's arguments and preparing counter-arguments is also essential. Try to incorporate recent significant events in Hong Kong or elsewhere to support your argument.　正文段（四）：建議寫一個演講提綱

Finally, confidence is key when presenting your case. Speak clearly and concisely, emphasizing important words and varying your tone appropriately. Speak fast enough to deliver your speech within the allotted time, but slow enough to ensure your argument is not misunderstood.

I hope the above advice, drawn from my own experience, is helpful to you. Good luck with your debate!

Best regards,

Man Fai

參考譯文

20XX 年 8 月 30 日

親愛的天娜，

希望這封信能夠安慰您。您為即將參予的辯論比賽作出準備，並聯繫我尋求建議，我不勝感激。正如所承諾的，我會寫信提供一些意見給您。

作為負責辯論發言的組長，必須考慮團隊精神和合作。每個團隊成員都該獲分配特定職責，例如調查需要的信息、尋找論點和蒐集證據。你該指導和引領隊員分析所有觀點，來證明你的團隊對辯論題目「時尚在人的服裝選擇中越來越受到重視」持反對意見是正確的。

由於您的辯論主題以「時尚」為中心，因此尋找「時髦服裝」的事實和統計數據來支持主要論點至關重要。然而，同樣重要的是要保持客觀和符合邏輯，拋開個人觀點。例如，你可以爭辯說追求時尚是不健康的，因為它會導致表面性的事物而忽視生活中更重要的事物，比如友誼和做好公民的責任。

在準備辯論時，必須準確針對對手的弱點，找出他們推理中的破綻，立即駁斥他們的論點。但是，避免在個人層面上攻擊對手，因為這樣會使評委員留下負面印象。反而，您要表現出理解他們的觀點。

更重要的是，以筆記形式寫下演講大綱，要簡短而井井有條。您可以在適當時用幽默和誠懇的語氣加入動人和有趣味的引言，使論點引人入勝。預測對手論點並準備相反觀點也很重要，嘗試包含最近在香港或其他地方發生的重大事件來支持論點。

最後，用自信呈現事例是要訣。說話時要清晰簡潔，要強調影響大的詞彙，並在適當時候改變語氣。說話速度要夠快，並在規定時間內完成您的演講，但又要確保論點不被誤解。

我希望以上根據我經驗得出的建議，會對您有幫助。祝辯論順利！

最好的祝福，

文輝

★ 9 投訴信 Letter of Complaint

投訴信是寫信人對某事不滿而提出投訴的信件。從餐館或商店服務差，到產品質量惡劣，都可作為投訴對象。以書面形式提出投訴比較打電話或面對面投訴有效，因為書面讓人感覺較良好，面對面投訴可能會令人厭煩，其次，書面更能讓人認真對待所投訴的事。

寫投訴信時，通常用一般過去時，也可兼用一般現在時。在人稱方面，以第一人稱為主。信函要清楚說明原委，用詞要恰當，語氣可以不那樣客氣，但不可以無理取鬧。

寫投訴信該注意下列要點：

» 投訴信必須是正式信函

» 字眼要冷靜和鎮定，不能意氣用事，但要認真對待

» 回憶具體事件，詳細說明經過，提供適當具體的細節

» 陳述具體投訴和後果

» 附上證明文件如單據或收條等，也可引用收信人之前的來信

» 提出建議，說出希望收信人如何跟進

» 最後表示期待收信人回覆和迅速解決問題，更要繼續保持關係

結構 Structure

上端：	寫信人的地址該寫在頁面右上角，並在其下方註明日期。在左下角，該寫上收信人的姓名、職位、機構和地址。
稱呼：	正式稱呼，如果知道收信人的姓氏，則在該姓氏前面該加頭銜，例如：Dear Mr / Ms... (親愛的……先生 / 女士)。如果您不知道收信人的姓氏，用 Dear Sir / Madam (先生 / 女士閣下)。
主題：	告訴收信人投訴的主題。
首段：	說明投訴原因，要有表示遺憾之句。

正文段：	正文段提供投訴事件的詳細信息，可包含幾個段落，每個段落第一句為主題句，提出一個投訴項目或中心思想，再以支持句詳細表達理由。
尾段：	總結這封信的主要觀點，包括要求收信人做某事的聲明。
結束敬語：	該包含一個正式結束語，如信件以 Dear Sir / Madam 開頭，使用 Yours faithfully（您忠誠的）；如以 Dear Mr / Ms... 開頭，則用 Yours sincerely（您真誠的）。
簽名：	寫信人的姓名和簽名

投訴信的典型例子

首段：反映問題	I am writing to express my dissatisfaction with the events and organisation at this year's Food Festival. 我寫此信是為了表達對今年美食節活動和組織的不滿。

正文段：	主題句	支持句
第一段：投訴垃圾食品	My central complaint is that the dishes we were served fell far short of the description in the promotion leaflet. 我主要投訴的是菜餚與宣傳單張中的描述相去甚遠。	We have asked your waiters to change some of our food, but they rudely refused our request and showed an attitude of 'couldn't care less'. Also, I was shocked to see so much junk food available, especially when the theme of the festival was 'healthy eating'. From my point of view, you should have had some stalls with nutritious, healthy and home-cooked foods. I am totally opposed to this event becoming a junk food parade. 我們要求服務員給我們更換一些食物，但他們粗魯地拒絕了我們的要求，並表現出「不在乎」的態度。此外，看到這麼多垃圾食品，我很震驚，尤其是當日的主題是「健康飲食」時。在我看來，該有些有營養、健康和家常食物的攤位。我完全反對把這個活動變成垃圾食品巡禮。
第二段：投訴嘉賓並非預期的那個人	The speaker at the public talk was not the one you have advertised. 公開講者並非廣告宣稱的那個人	As a matter of fact, I have never heard of him. Your ad has specifically mentioned that 'grandpa Lee' would be the guest speaker, but it turned out that he was not in the scene. Furthermore, the cooking demonstrations were agonizingly slow and dull. 事實上，我從來沒有聽說過他。您的廣告特別提到「李爺爺」將擔任演講嘉賓，但結果他不在現場。此外，烹飪演示非常緩慢和沉悶。

I am convinced that I am not alone in saying that this year's Food Festival was nightmarish experience. Unless I receive a reasonable explanation, I shall have no choice but to boycott the festival in future.

我確信，説今年美食節是噩夢般的經歷不止我一個人。除非我得到合理的解釋，否則我將來只能杯葛這個活動。

投訴信的常用句式

首段　　I am writing 我正在寫

» in connection with my order... which arrived this morning 關於今早我收到貨的訂單……

» to complain about the quality of the (product) I bought from your website 投訴我從您網站買來的（產品）質素

» to complain about the poor service we received from your company. 投訴貴公司的劣質服務

» to draw attention to the negative attitude of... in your... department 提請注意您……部門的消極態度

正文段　» Our order dated...clearly stated that we wanted... However, you... 訂單日期……清楚表明我們想要……。然而，您……

» The goods were faulty / damaged in poor conditions. 貨物是劣質／損壞的。

» There seems to be an error in the invoice. 發票似乎有錯誤。

» There appears to be a misunderstanding between... and... ……和……之間似乎存在誤解。

» The equipment I ordered has still not been delivered, despite my phone call to you last week to say that it is needed urgently. 儘管我上星期打電話給您説急需，但我訂購的設備仍未交付。

» The goods (name) ... I received was well below the standard I expected. 我收到的貨物（名稱）……遠低於我預期的標準。

» To make matters worse, when I called your company, your staff... 更糟的是，我打電話給貴公司時，您的員工……

尾段	»	Please replace the faulty goods as soon as possible. 請盡快更換有問題的商品。
	»	We must insist on an immediate replacement. 我們要堅持立即更換。
	»	We hereby demand a full refund of the goods proceeds plus transportation cost of... 我們在此要求全額退款另加……的運輸費。
	»	Unless I receive the goods by the end of this week, I will have no alternatives but to cancel my order and claim from you any loss we may have to encounter, if any. 除非在本週末之前我收到貨物，否則我將別無選擇，只能取消訂單，就可能遇到（如果有）的任何損失向您索償。
	»	I hope that you will deal with the matter promptly as it is causing me considerable inconvenience. 希望您能及時處理這事，因這給我帶來了很大的不便。
	»	Trusting that you will take this complaint seriously, I am looking forward to your favourable reply. 相信您會認真對待此投訴，我期望令人滿意的答覆。
	»	I hope you could investigate this matter and furnish me with a favourable reply. 我希望您能調查這事並給我一個滿意的答覆。

收信人回應投訴

　　寫給投訴人的回信是收信人對投訴態度的直接反映。注意投訴人是要尊重的，無論你覺得投訴是否成立，收信人必須以同情心回應所有訴求，收信人應關注問題的發生和如何解決，而不是鬧情緒或找藉口攻擊投訴人。因此，即使你完全不同意投訴人的立場，或無法提供完全符合投訴人的期望或解決方案，你都要表現出願意了解他或她的感受和情況，才可舒緩投訴人的憤怒和失望。

結構 Structure

上端：	回信人的地址應寫在頁面的右上角，並在其下方註明回信日期。在左下角，您應該寫上投訴人的姓名、職位、機構和地址。
稱呼：	正式的稱呼。通常您會知道投訴人的姓氏，所以在該姓氏前面應加頭衛，例如：Dear Mr / Ms... (親愛的……先生 / 女士)。
主題：	覆述投訴主題，通常以 Re: 來起草。

首段：	首先需要確認收到投訴人的信件，然後重複投訴的問題，表示明白問題的所在。
正文段：	有兩種可能的回應：1「接受投訴」或 2「拒絕投訴」。若接受投訴，便要為問題道歉，更要解釋原因，提出解決方案。若拒絕投訴，則要調查問題的發生，將調查結果和拒絕責任的理由，委婉地告知投訴人，並提出怎樣可以幫助他或她解決問題。
尾段：	您應該嘗試與投訴人保持友善的關係，以留住客戶。投訴常會指出系統或程序中的弱點，從而提供改進機會。
結束敬語：	您的信該包含一個正式的結束語，如果您用 Dear Mr / Ms... 作開頭，則需用 Yours sincerely「您真誠的」來結束。
簽名：	寫信人的姓名、職位和簽名。

回應投訴信的常用句式

首段

» I am writing in response to your recent complaint regarding... 我寫信回應您最近關於⋯⋯的投訴

» We write in reply to your letter about your unpleasant experience in our restaurant a week ago. 我們寫信回覆您一星期前在我們餐廳經歷的不愉快事件。

» Thank you for your letter of (date) regarding... 感謝您（幾月幾日）關於⋯⋯的來信。

» I refer to your letter of (date) in which you... 我回覆您（幾月幾日）的來信，其中您⋯⋯

» Your letter dated... is referred. We would like to address the concerns you have raised and clarify any possible misunderstandings. 參考您幾月幾日的來信。我們想處理您提出的問題並澄清任何可能的誤解。

» I acknowledge receipt of your letter dated... Please be assured that I'll personally look into the matter and get back to you as soon as possible. 我確認收到了您（幾月幾日）的來信⋯⋯請放心，我會親自調查此事並盡快回覆您。

正文段

C.「接受
投訴」

為錯誤或過失道歉

» We were very concerned to learn about... Please accept our sincere apologies. 我們非常憂慮關於…… 請接受我們誠摯的歉意。

» Your first concern is... We must apologise for the trouble we have put you through. 您先要擔心的是…… 我們必須為給您帶來的麻煩道歉。

» We sincerely apologise for... 我們真誠地為……道歉

» Please accept our apologies for... 請接受我們對……的歉意。

» I would like to apologise for the error made by our company in... 我想在我們公司的錯誤……中道歉。

» With regard to the second issue of your complaint, we regret that the standard of our service has not met with your expectation. 關於您第二項的投訴，很遺憾我們的服務水平沒有達到您的期望。

解釋錯誤的原因或提供調查結果

» As a result of our investigation, we found that our waiters have not worked in accordance with our company policy to change your food order. 調查結果發現我們的服務員沒有按公司政策更改您的食品訂單。

» The error was caused by... 錯誤是由於……

» Apparently, the problem was the result of... 顯然，問題是……的結果。

» The reason for the mistake was... 錯誤的原因是……

» We are having a temporary problem with...We are doing everything we can to sort it out. 我們有一個短期問題……我們正盡一切努力解決它。

提議解決方法

» To show our goodwill, we would like to enclose a coupon which offers you a...% discount on your next visit to our restaurant. 為了釋出我們的善意，附上一張優惠券，讓您下次光臨我們的餐廳時可享受……% 的折扣。

» As a gratitude to our long term client, we are enclosing a...% discount coupon for your use in your next purchase of our products. 為了感謝我們的長期客戶，附上一張……% 的折扣券，供您下次購買我們的產品時使用。

» As a gesture of our regret, we are willing to... 為了表達我們的遺憾，我們願意……

» We request you to take the goods to any of our retail shop and ask for a replacement, bringing this letter as an evidence of our agreement. 我們請您將貨物帶到任何一家零售店去更換，攜帶着這封信作為我們同意的證據。

» We have dispatched the replacement by express courier. They should arrive by... 我們已將您的替換品以快遞寄出。他們該在……之前到達。

D.「拒絕
投訴」

對投訴感到遺憾

» We understand how disappointing it can be when your expectations are not met. 我們理解
期望未能滿足時您感到的失望。

» While we can understand your frustration, ... 雖然我們可理解您的沮喪，……

» We appreciate that this has caused you considerable inconvenience, but we cannot accept
any responsibility in this matter. 我們理解這給您帶來不便，但我們不承擔任何責任。

拒絕責任並說明理由

» We understand the very first issue of your complaint is that the foods you bought had been
stored beyond the expiry date. Unfortunately, we must point out that it is stated in the terms
and conditions that once foods have been consumed, they cannot be replaced or returned. 我
們理解您投訴的第一個問題是您購買的食品儲存已超過保質期。不幸的是，我們必須
指出，條款和條件中規定，一旦食物被食用，將無法更換或退貨。

» We regret to inform you that as the television you bought three years ago, the guarantee
period has expired. 我們很遺憾地通知您，因您三年前買的電視機，保養期已過了。

» I am afraid that... 我恐怕……

» Unfortunately, I must point out that... 不幸的是，我必須指出……

提出建議以幫助解決問題

» We therefore suggest that you contact... and ask them to... 我們因此建議您聯繫……並要
求他們……

» We have directed your complaint to... Please follow up with them accordingly. 我們已將您
的投訴轉至……請與他們跟進。

尾段

» We look forward to receiving your further orders, and assure you that they will be filled
promptly. 盼望收到您更多訂單，並向您保證準時供貨。

» We look forward to serving you in the future. 盼望未來能為您服務。

» We hope you will continue to visit our restaurant. 希望您繼續惠顧我們的餐廳。

» Please be assured that we will prevent this incident from happening again and will do our
best to maintain the highest quality in our services. 請放心，我們將防止這類事件再發生，
並將盡最大努力持續提供最高質素的服務。

» Thank you again for bringing the problem to our attention and bearing with us. We very
much hope you will continue to use our services in the future. 再次感謝您提點我們注意並
包容這問題。非常希望您將來繼續使用我們的服務。

» Once again, we apologise for any inconvenience caused. 對此造成的任何不便，我們再次
深表歉意。

範文二十六：有毛病的智能手機

Faulty Smartphone

---

1 Nathan Road 5/F　　　寫信人地址
Kowloon

25th May 20XX　　　日期

The General Manager　　　　　　　　　　　　收信人職位
Global Smart Phone Co. Ltd.　　　　　　　　　收信人公司
6/F Causeway Bay Plaza　　　　　　　　　　　收信人地址
Hong Kong

Dear Sir / Madam,　　　　　　　　　　　　　稱呼

Re: Faulty Global 10s Pro　　　　　　主題

I am writing to file a complaint about the unsatisfactory performance of your smartphone, the 'Global 10s Pro.' | 首段：說明投訴原因

On February 11, 20XX, I purchased a 'Global 10s Pro' smartphone from ABC Electrical Company located on Nathan Road. The invoice number for the purchase was 6746332, and the serial number was ME24876J. I have enclosed a copy of the invoice for your reference. | 正文段（一）：提供詳細信息，附上證明文件

The phone did not perform as advertised. Your advertisement explicitly states that your newly invented technology, the Smoothsound technology, provides the highest quality and ultra-clear sound that can be heard even in noisy environments. However, when I used the phone in the MTR, I could hardly hear anything. I tried to update the software as instructed in the operating manual, but this did not solve the problem. I then went to ABC Electrical Company, where the phone was purchased. They were kind enough to replace the phone with a new one, and the sound deficiency no longer occurred. | 正文段（二）：投訴項目：聲音瑕疵

However, I was not satisfied with the replacement phone as it constantly crashed when I was working on WORD documents. I went back to ABC Electrical Company for repairs, and they informed me that they had to refer the problem to your company. Regrettably, up to the time of writing, the phone has not been repaired. They told me that your company is busy preparing for the launch of the Global 11 series and has no time to deal with my matter. | 正文段（三）：投訴項目：常常死機

I am extremely disappointed with your service. I have always held Global products in high regard, but this faulty model has been a huge disappointment. I urge you to investigate this matter seriously and provide me with an early reply.

尾段

Your attention to this matter is appreciated.

結尾語

Yours faithfully,

結束敬語

Chan Chun

簽名

參考譯文

九龍彌敦道 1 號 5 樓
20XX 年 5 月 25 日

總經理
環球智能手機有限公司
香港銅鑼灣廣場 6 樓

親愛的先生 / 女士

主題：有毛病的 Global 10s Pro

我寫此信是投訴您的智能手機 **Global 10s Pro** 的性能不佳。

20XX 年 2 月 11 日，我在彌敦道的 ABC 電器公司買了一部 **Global 10s Pro** 智能手機，發票編號 6746332，序列號 ME24876J。現附上發票副本供您參考。

這款手機的性能與您的廣告所說的完全不同。廣告中明確表示，其最新發明的 Smoothsound 技術具有最高質量，可提供超清晰的聲音，即使在戶外甚至嘈雜環境中也能聽到。但我發現在港鐵使用它時幾乎聽不到任何聲音。然後我嘗試按您操作手冊中訂明的指示更新軟件。然而，這並沒有解決問題。於是我去了 ABC 電器公司，他們非常友善，換了一個新的給我。聲音的問題不再發生了。

然而，這並沒有讓我滿意，因為我在處理 WORD 文檔時，新手機總是死機。我又去了 ABC 電器公司維修。他們告訴我，他們必須將這個問題提交給貴公司，但我很遺憾，截至撰寫本文時，電話尚未修復。他們說您們公司忙於準備推出 Global 11 系列，沒時間處理我的事。

對你們的服務我感到非常失望。我一直很看好「環球」產品，但這個模型的故障令我非常失望。希望您能認真調查此事並期待您早日答覆。

感謝您對此事的關注。

您忠誠的

陳真

範文二十七：回覆客戶投訴合約

Reply to Customer's Complaint on a Contract

<table>
<tr><td></td><td>New Earth Telecom Ltd.,
101 Queen's Road Central,
Hong Kong.</td><td>回信人地址</td></tr>
<tr><td></td><td>28th September 20XX</td><td>日期</td></tr>
</table>

New Earth Telecom Ltd.,
101 Queen's Road Central,
Hong Kong.

回信人地址

28th September 20XX

日期

Mr Chan Dai Man
62 Hill Road, 2/F
Hong Kong.

投訴人姓名
投訴人地址

Dear Mr Chan,

稱呼

Re: Consumer Contract No. 123657

主題

Thank you for your letter dated September 14 regarding the attitude of our customer service officer and the problems you experienced with the slow ISP connection speed. We sincerely apologize for the inconvenience caused to you.

首段：確認收到投訴信；重複投訴信的問題；接受投訴並致歉

We are sorry to hear that our customer service officer kept you on hold for 30 minutes before answering your phone call. We understand how frustrating this must have been for you. However, we would like to inform you that during busy hours between 9.30 am – 11.00 am and 5.00 pm – 7.00 pm, callers may need to wait a bit longer. To rectify this situation, we will be introducing a voicemail service, allowing you to leave your information, and we will call back as soon as possible. We are prioritizing this issue and will notify you immediately when it is fixed.

正文段（一）：解釋遲接電話的原因，及補救方法

We are extremely sorry that you had an unpleasant experience with our customer service officer who answered your technical problem unprofessionally. We have prohibited our customer service officers from answering any technical questions from our customers to avoid misunderstandings. We will ensure that this does not happen again and take steps to ensure our staff are better trained.

正文段（二）：解釋錯誤回答技術性問題的原因及補救方法

Regarding the slow ISP connection speed, we would like to clarify that currently, the highest speed of ISP connection available in your district is only 300 Mbps. We are pleased to inform you that new fibre at a speed of 1000 Mbps will be installed into the network terminals of your area in two weeks, and the connection speed will substantially increase.

正文段（三）：
解釋網速緩慢的原因

We understand that you are paying $248 per month for 300 Mbps and wish to terminate your contract with us. However, we must remind you that under the terms of the contract, early termination will require you to pay the monthly fees for the remaining term and a $500 administration fee. As the contract will expire soon, on December 4, it may not be beneficial for you to terminate the contract.

正文段（四）：
提出合約細節

As a gesture of our regret, we would like to offer you three months of free service or $800 supermarket coupons, along with a 20% discount on the existing contract price, i.e. $198 per month after the expiration of the existing contract, provided you renew the contract for two years. Please note that your renewal contract will cover the price of 1000 Mbps instead of the existing 300 Mbps. This offer will expire on October 15, 20XX.

正文段（五）：
提出具體解決方案

We value your business and hope to continue serving you. We look forward to receiving your favourable reply on or before the expiry date of the above offer.

尾段：常見的結尾句式

Yours sincerely

結束敬語

Lee Fung Ling

簽名

Manager, Consumer Service Department

職位

新地球電訊有限公司
香港皇后大道中 101 號
二零╳╳年九月二十八日

陳大文先生
香港山道 62 號 2 樓
親愛的陳先生，

主題：客戶合約 123657

感謝您於 9 月 14 日就我們客戶主任的態度及 ISP 連接速度慢的問題來信。對於給您帶來的不便，請接受我們的歉意。

很遺憾聽到我們的客戶主任在她能夠接聽您的電話之前要您等候了 30 分鐘。我們理解這對您來說一定是非常沮喪。但我們必須承認，在上午 9.30 至 11.00 和下午 5.00 至 7.00 的繁忙時段，來電者可能需要等待較長時間。為了改善這種情況，我們即將推出語音信箱服務，只要您留言給我們，我們便會盡快回電。我們正在優先處理此問題，並會在推出後立即通知您。

此外，我們非常抱歉您與我們客戶主任的不愉快經歷，她以不專業的方式回答了您技術性的問題。事實上，為避免誤解，我們禁止客戶主任回答任何技術性問題，她犯了錯沒有將您的詢問轉交技術支援部。我們將盡一切努力確保這種情況不再發生。

現在解釋我們的情況以回應您對 ISP 連接速度緩慢的投訴。目前，您所在地區的 ISP 連接最高速度僅為 300 Mbps。我們很高興地通知您，您所在地區的網絡終端將在兩週內安裝速度為 1000 Mbps 的新光纖，連接速度將會大大提高。

我們了解到您每月為網速 300 Mbps 支付 248 元，並希望終止與我們這合同。我們必須提醒您，根據合約條款，提前終止您將要支付剩餘月份的月費和 500 元的管理費。由於合同很快到期，即 12 月 4 日，這樣做可能對您並不有利。

為了表示歉意，我們會為您提供 3 個月的免費服務或送您 800 元的超市優惠券，再加上在現有合同價格上 20% 折扣，即現有合同到期後每月只需支付 198 元，前提是您需要續約 2 年。請注意，您的續訂合同將涵蓋 1000 Mbps 光纖的價格，而不是現有的 300 Mbps。此要約有效期至 20XX 年 10 月 15 日。

我們重視您的業務，並希望繼續為您服務。我們盼望在上述要約屆滿日期或之前收到您同意的回覆。

您真誠的

李鳳玲
客戶服務部經理

⭐ 10 給編輯的信 Letter to the Editor

　　給編輯的信是半正式信件，雖然它的讀者是報章雜誌的編輯，但編輯會將它放在報章雜誌上刊登，所以實際上對象是普羅大眾。

　　一般來說，給編輯的信會就一些時事表達意見，發文者就一些報章雜誌先前發表的文章或話題作出回應，並希望讀者產生共鳴，或也希望他們發表自己的意見。雖然所有給編輯的信都是為了表達意見，但有時也想用來說服或告知讀者一些現實問題，包括讚賞、同情、哀悼、質問令人覺得冷漠、無恥或不公的事件等。

特徵

給編輯的信應該

- » 吸引讀者注意力，從而增加其發表的機會

- » 要表達清楚，在首段便要發表你的意見

- » 提供足以支持你意見的詳細信息

- » 預測讀者的觀點和潛在問題

- » 表示對該問題有透徹了解

- » 你的思維要從能吸引讀者注意力的方向出發

- » 提出問題所在和解決方案，並提供實施方法

- » 省略如 I think、in my opinion、it seems to me 類似「我的意見」的短語，因為給編輯的信已經被認定是你的意見

- » 避免謾罵、籠統的概括和不公平的指責

- » 保持禮貌和禮貌的語氣

- » 使用比較或對比、因果關係、類比、描述、定義或其他修辭方法來提高書信的效力

結構 Structure

上端：	寫信人的居住地址該寫在頁面右上角，並在其下方註明日期。在左下角，該寫上報章雜誌的名稱和地址。信件發佈在報章雜誌時，你居住的地址不會出現。
稱呼：	這是正式的稱呼：親愛的編輯 (Dear Editor)。你的來信不僅被編輯閱讀，也被公眾閱讀。因此，當這封信在報章雜誌上發表時，通常不會刊登稱呼的。
主題：	這可讓讀者了解信件的內容。例如：Global Warming is a Threat (全球變暖是一種威脅)
首段：	簡要介紹主題並明確表明你對該問題的立場及意見。
正文段：	正文段包含幾個段落。每個段落你該只提出一個觀點或中心思想，並用理據和細節支持它。建議第一句為主題句，後面的句子是支持句，是用來支持主題句的，並給出例子、事實或證據支持你的觀點，最後提出建議以幫助解決問題。
尾段：	簡短總結意見和主要原因，並利用各種修辭手法和表達方式如成語來結束。
結束敬語：	你的信該包含一個正式的結束語，即你忠實的 (Yours faithfully)。但信件發佈在報章雜誌時這敬語將不會出現。
簽名：	在信件發佈在報紙或雜誌時，你的名字將不會出現。

範文二十八：全球變暖是一種威脅

Global Warming Is a Threat

530 Sheng Wo Road, 3/F Happy Valley Hong Kong	寫信人地址
1st September 20XX	日期
The Chief Editor, The Kowloon Post 1 Hollywood Road Hong Kong	編輯報社地址
Dear Editor,	稱呼
Global Warming Is a Threat	主題
I am writing in response to Mr. Tommy Chan's letter, 'Global warming is not a real threat', which was published in your newspaper on August 20. I strongly disagree with Mr. Chan's view that global warming is not a threat and is a natural phenomenon.	首段：直接了當地表達作者的看法
The issue of global warming should not be overlooked or neglected. The average global temperature has significantly increased in the last 50 years due to climate change caused by global warming. Global warming occurs when carbon dioxide and greenhouse gases build up in the atmosphere, trapping heat and warming our planet.	正文段（一）：第 1 句為主題句。其餘是支持句，點出地球變暖的成因和不能忽視的原因
To mitigate this problem, both consumers and governments must work together. As consumers, we must reduce our carbon footprints by conserving energy as part of our daily routine. Governments worldwide should implement policies to reduce their dependence on fossil fuels and increase the use of clean energy sources like wind and solar.	正文段（二）：主題句清楚說出消費者和政府的共同責任，支持句給出例子和他們的做法
Global warming is a grave threat to our planet, and we must act now to address it. If we do not, future generations will suffer the consequences. We must not wait for a rainy day to fix the roof.	尾段：總結論點，用諺語來結束
Thank you for your attention to this urgent matter.	結尾語

Yours faithfully,

Li Lai Lai

結束敬語

簽名

參考譯文

20XX 年 9 月 1 日
跑馬地成和道 530 號三樓

總編輯

九龍報社

香港荷李活道 1 號

親愛的編輯，

全球變暖是一種威脅

我是回應陳湯美先生 8 月 20 日在你們報紙上發表的信，題為「全球變暖不是真正的威脅」。我強烈不同意陳先生的觀點，全球變暖不是威脅而是自然現象。

全球變暖問題不應被忽略或忽視。由於全球變暖引起的氣候變化，全球平均溫度在過去 50 年中顯著升高。當二氧化碳和溫室氣體在大氣中積聚、吸收熱量並使我們的星球變暖時，就會發生全球變暖。

為了緩解這個問題，消費者和政府必須共同努力。作為消費者，我們必須通過在日常生活中節約能源來減少碳足跡。世界各國政府該實施政策，減少對化石燃料的依賴，增加風能和太陽能等清潔能源的使用。

全球變暖對地球構成嚴重威脅，我們必須立即採取行動加以應對。若我們不這樣做，子孫後代將承擔後果，我們要未雨綢繆。

感謝您對這事的關注。

你忠實的

李麗麗

範文二十九：2019 冠狀病毒大流行

Covid-19 Pandemic

10 High Street, 3/F Hong Kong	寫信人地址
19th January 20XX	日期

10 High Street, 3/F

Hong Kong　　寫信人地址

19th January 20XX　　日期

The Chief Editor,　　編輯報社地址

The Kowloon Post

1 Hollywood Road

Hong Kong

Dear Editor,　　稱呼

Covid-19 Pandemic　　主題

I am writing in response to recent complaints your Post has received regarding the novel outbreak of the Covid-19 pandemic, which has been the most challenging and calamitous crisis to strike our planet in the past three years.

首段：介紹主題，帶出新冠病毒的影響是前所未有的

One complaint was that our government failed to handle the coronavirus outbreak effectively and efficiently during the first and second waves. The most compelling evidence was the sluggishness in implementing medical quarantine and border controls, as well as confusion and nonchalance over shortages in supplies. They also criticized the care home and healthcare system, citing long wait times for elderly patients outside emergency departments during the fifth wave. Finally, they complained that the government's adoption of China's 'Zero-Covid' policy had devastating effects on our economy.

正文段（一）：提出三個投訴：政府處理疫情沒有效率；護理院和醫療系統的不足；清零政策破壞經濟

I agree with them that the government failed to manage the pandemic initially. The outbreak was first reported in November 2019, and our government had plenty of time to deal with it. However, their initial responses were a dismal failure, and the worst was the attack of the Omicron variant, leading to a dramatic rise in confirmed cases.

正文段（二）：作者發表對第一個投訴的看法，同意讀者來信的觀點

Fortunately, Hong Kong eventually refined its pandemic control policy and implemented anti-Covid measures. The Hong Kong Hospital Authority set aside beds in public hospitals for Covid-19 patients and introduced new oral anti-Covid drugs. Moreover, the government bought a large number of Covid-19 vaccines and encouraged people to get vaccinated. As a result, Hong Kong did not suffer significant hardship in recent months, and the confirmed case figures have reduced substantially.

正文段（三）：作者繼續發表對第一個投訴的看法，用事實來支持作者的觀點

Regarding the complaint about the 'Zero-Covid' policy, I must respectfully disagree. The policy successfully reduced the spread of the early strains of the virus in Hong Kong when vaccines were not readily available. The Covid-19 pandemic is far more severe than the common flu virus, with a much higher infection risk. If the government had not adopted this policy, the coronavirus could have spread even more rapidly, leading to more victims and deaths. The government has introduced over 70 measures to remedy the pressing economic issues and provide relief to various sectors of the economy as well as Hong Kong residents. I am hopeful that as we continue to navigate the challenges posed by the ongoing pandemic, our economy will eventually recover and businesses will be able to bounce back.

正文段（四）：針對最後的投訴—政府控制疫情影響經濟，作者對此有不同意見

Overall, I hope the government will continue to monitor the situation and implement policies to stimulate our economy.

尾段：表明作者支持政府的防疫政策

Yours faithfully,

Chan Dai Man

結束敬語

簽名

高街 10 號三樓

20XX 年 1 月 19 日

總編輯

九龍報社

香港荷李活道 1 號

親愛的編輯，

2019 冠狀病毒大流行

我寫信是回應貴報最近收到新爆發的新冠病毒大流行的投訴，這是過去三年來襲擊地球最具挑戰性和災難性的危機。

一個投訴是政府在第一和第二波期間未能有效和高效地處理冠狀病毒的爆發。最有說服力的證據是隔離檢疫和邊境管制實施緩慢，以及對供應短缺的困惑和漠不關心。他們還批評了安老院和醫療保健系統，理由是第五波期間老年患者在急診室外等待的時間很長。最後，他們抱怨政府採取的中國「清零」政策對經濟造成了毀滅性的影響。

我同意他們的看法，即政府最初未能控制住這一流行病。疫情於 2019 年 11 月首次報告，我們的政府有足夠時間來應對。然而，他們最初的反應是慘淡的失敗，最糟糕的是奧米隆變種的攻擊，導致確診病例急劇上升。

幸運的是，香港最終完善了其病毒控制政策並實施了對抗新冠病毒的措施。香港醫院管理局對抗新冠肺炎時在公立醫院為病患者預留床位，並推出新口服抗病毒藥物。此外，政府購買了大量抗新冠病毒疫苗，並鼓勵市民接種疫苗。因此，香港近月沒有遭遇太大困難，確診個案數字亦大幅減少。

關於「清零」政策的投訴，我必須恭敬地表示不同意。當疫苗不易獲得時，該政策成功減少早期病毒株在香港的傳播。新冠病毒大流行遠比普通流感病毒嚴重，感染風險也高得多。如果政府沒有採取這項政策，冠狀病毒可能會傳播得更快，導致更多受害者和死亡個案。政府推出了超過 70 項措施，以解決緊迫的經濟問題，為經濟領域和香港居民提供紓緩壓力。我希望，隨着我們繼續應對持續流行病帶來的挑戰，我們的經濟最終會復甦，企業將能夠反彈。

總的來說，我希望政府繼續監察情況，落實刺激經濟的政策。

你忠實的

陳大文

範文三十：香港青少年體育活動

Hong Kong Youngsters' Sporting Activities

<table>
<tr><td align="right">32/F, 8 Third Street,
Hong Kong.</td><td>寫信人地址</td></tr>
<tr><td align="right">27th March 20XX</td><td>日期</td></tr>
</table>

The Chief Editor,
Daily Evening Post
4 King's Road, North Point
Hong Kong

寫信人地址

日期

編輯報社地址

Dear Editor,

稱呼

Hong Kong youngsters' sporting activities

主題

I recently read a report in your newspaper that Hong Kong's youngsters do not engage in enough exercise and have been given a D grade for their overall physical activity levels. The report's author commented that youngsters' sporting activities are influenced by a whole array of factors, including the individual, the family, schools, and the support of the government. I fully agree with his comments.

首段：介紹主題，並表明作者對主題的意見

To begin with, many youngsters are too lazy to exercise, and the prevalence of smartphones and internet applications is a major contributing factor. This sedentary lifestyle keeps them indoors and limits their movement. Additionally, participating in sporting activities can be challenging, and many young people find sweating and breathlessness unappealing. Some young people are unaware that without exercise, their muscles weaken and shrink. They also fail to understand that sports are beneficial for their minds and can help them concentrate better, resulting in better academic performance. Furthermore, they do not realize that a lack of physical activity can contribute to feelings of anxiety and depression.

正文段（一）：說出年輕人對體育活動的想法

Parents must educate their children about the benefits of sporting activities. They should encourage their children to participate in sports regularly and emphasize how sports help the body grow and develop properly. More importantly, parents must set a good example by being active in sports themselves, reinforcing the benefits of exercise and instilling sporting habits from a young age. For instance, getting outdoors and enjoying nature can be a great way to help children see the benefits of being fit and healthy. This can include visits to beaches, country parks, playgrounds, walks, bicycle tracks, and other outdoor activities as part of their daily or weekly family life.

正文段（二）：說明父母應有的態度

Schools must also play a role in helping young people engage in more physical activity. They should provide more time in the class timetable for sports and organize more team sports, such as football, basketball, volleyball, etc. Team sports provide students with opportunities to learn how to work together, enhancing social interaction and boosting confidence in social occasions. During sports, students need to make spontaneous moves, which would help them make better and prompt decisions in their future career life.

正文段（三）：說明學校的重要性

Finally, the government should encourage and inspire young people's interest in physical activities. Students like to see that the government is supporting physical activities in school. Hence, the government should provide guidelines, rules, and regulations for schools in the promotion of physical education. Furthermore, the government should organize and subsidize inter-school competitions to promote individual and team sports. Lastly, the government should provide resources and professional support to schools and PE teachers with the aim of training more young athletes for national and international sports competitions.

正文段（四）：說明政府的參與

Thank you for printing this letter in your paper. I hope that more discussions about this topic will take place, so that youngsters will understand that sporting activities are not just a matter of fun, but also lifelong lessons for a healthy and active lifestyle that are crucial for success.

尾段：總結作者的意見，希望其他人也發表意見

Yours faithfully,

Chan Dai Man

結束敬語

簽名

第三街八號三十二樓
20XX 年 3 月 27 日

總編輯
每日晚報
香港北角英皇道四號

親愛的編輯：

香港青少年體育活動

我最近在您的報紙上看到一篇報告，說香港的年輕人運動量不足，他們整體體力活動水平被評為 D 級。該報告的作者評論說，青少年的體育活動受個人、家庭、學校和政府支持等一系列因素影響，我完全同意他的意見。

首先，年輕人懶得鍛煉。智能手機和互聯網應用的普及是主要原因。這導致年輕人留在家裏，不願走動。而且，參加體育活動會上氣不接下氣及出汗，這不是很有趣的。大多數年輕人太年輕而無法意識到如果不運動，肌肉會變弱和大量流失。他們也不明白運動對大腦有好處，可以幫助他們學會集中注意力，從而在學業上取得更好成績。更重要的是，他們沒有意識到缺乏體育鍛煉會增加焦慮和抑鬱。

父母必須教育他們的孩子了解在體育活動中可以獲得的好處。他們應該鼓勵孩子定期運動，並強調運動有助於身體正常的生長和修正。更重要的是，父母必須樹立積極運動的好榜樣，從而加強積極鍛煉的好處，以及引導孩子從小養成運動習慣。例如，到戶外和郊野是讓孩子看到健康的好處的有效方法，例如常常去沙灘、郊野公園、遊樂場、散步和在單車徑上踏單車等等，作為他們日常或每星期家庭生活的一部份。

為了幫助年輕人多做運動，學校的參與是必不可少的。學校必須在上課時間表上提供更多運動時間。學校還需要組織更多團隊運動，如足球、籃球、排球等。團隊運動讓學生有機會學習與他人共事，從而提高社交互動，增強在社交場合中的自信心。在運動過程中，學生需要做出自本能的動作，這將有助他們在未來的職業生涯中作出更好更及時的決定。

最後，政府應扮演一個角色去鼓勵和激發年輕人對體育活動的興趣。學生們喜歡看到政府支持學校的體育活動。因此，政府該為學校推廣體育提供指引、規則和規例。此外，政府會組織和資助學校舉辦校際比賽，以促進個人和團隊運動。最後但是同樣重要的，是政府該為學校和體育教師提供資源和專業支持，以培養更多年輕運動員參加國內和國際體育比賽。

感謝您在您的報章刊登這封信。我希望這個話題會有更多討論，讓年輕人明白到體育不僅是有趣的活動，而且是終身課程，養成健康和積極的生活方式對成功至關重要。

你忠實的

陳大文

★ 11 邀請信 Letter of Invitation

邀請信的目的是向對方發出邀請，請對方參加或出席一些活動，例如生日聚會、主禮嘉賓、演講嘉賓、音樂、體育或健康飲食活動等。邀請函可以是正式的（商務／官方）或非正式的（朋友／熟人）。正式邀請信屬於公函類，用詞要正規，非正式邀請信則是私人信件，在詞句方面不需要多加斟酌。但是，它們的佈局結構或多或少是相同的。

結構 Structure

上端：	寫信人的地址該寫在頁面右上角，並在其下方註明日期。在左下角，該寫上收件人姓名和地址。私人邀請函可不用加寫信人地址。
稱呼：	這是正式稱呼，例如，正式邀請信：親愛的……先生／女士（Dear Mr／Ms...）；私人邀請信：親愛的（名字：如愛麗斯）（Dear Alice）
主題：	這可以讓對方了解這封邀請函的目的。
首段：	開門見山，直接說明寫信的目的，發出邀請。
正文段：	首先表明邀請對方的原因，提供有關活動的詳細信息，並介紹具體內容，希望邀請人參加的理由和任何特殊要求等。
結尾段：	希望對方接受邀請，提及回覆的最後日期。如屬正式邀請函，提供聯繫和回覆方式，並表示感謝。
結束敬語：	邀請信應該包含一個正式結束語，即你忠誠的（Yours sincerely）。
簽名：	若屬正式邀請函，寫上你的姓名、職位和組織機構名稱。

在寫正式邀請信時，該使用禮貌寫法，但當你寫非正式邀請信時，可以用直接簡單的寫法。舉例如下：

直接簡單的寫法	有禮貌的寫法
1. 發出邀請	

	直接簡單的寫法	有禮貌的寫法
首段	I am pleased to invite you... 我很高興邀請您…… I cordially invite you to... 我誠摯邀請您……	I am writing in connection with... 我正在撰寫與……有關的邀請信。
正文段	（請求） Can you...? 你是否可以…… Please could you...? 請問可以……嗎？	Could you be kind enough to accept our invitation...? 您能不能接受我們的邀請……？ I would appreciate it if you could accept our invitation. 若您接受我們邀請的話，我將不勝感激。
	（請求許可） Can I... ? 我可以嗎……？ Could I... ? 我可否……？	Is it all right if I...? 若我……可以嗎？ I wonder if I could... 我想知道我是否可以……
	（提出建議） What about... ? ……怎麼樣？ Shall we... ? 我們要不要……？	Why don't you... ? 你為甚麼不……？ Perhaps you would... 也許你會……？
結尾段	I look forward to your reply. 我期待您的回覆。 I look forward to seeing you. 我期待與你見面。	Would you please furnish us with your reply by (date) ... ? 能否請您在（日期）……之前答覆我們？ We look forward to receiving your response by telephone at (number) ... by (date) ... 我們期待在（日期）……之前收到您的電話（號碼）……答覆。 If you would attend, we could appreciate your replying us by telephone number... or by return email. 若您參加的話，我們感謝您來電回覆，電話號碼是……或回覆此電郵。

直接簡單的寫法	有禮貌的寫法

2. 接受邀請

首段	Thank you for inviting me to... 謝謝您邀請我…… We were delighted to receive your invitation to ... 我們很高興收到您的邀請……	Thank you for your kind invitation to... 感謝您的盛情邀請…… I'm more than pleased that you would invite me to... 我很高興您能邀請我……
結尾段	I appreciate your thinking of me and look forward to sharing the happy event with you. 我感謝您想起我，並期待與您分享幸福大事。	We look forward to another great evening with you. 我們期待與您共度另一個美好的夜晚。

3. 拒絕邀請

首段	Thanks for your invitation, unfortunately, I... 感謝您的邀請，不幸的是，我……	I appreciate your gracious invitation. Of course, I would like to attend ..., but regret that ... 感謝您的盛情邀請。當然，我很想參加……，但很遺憾……
結尾段	I'm sorry I am unable to assist you in this occasion. I hope I will be of help in future. 很抱歉，我無法在這種情況下幫助您。我希望我今後可以幫忙。	I trust, even without my presence, you still will have a wonderful time. Please do not hesitate to contact me again if I can offer my assistance in future. 我相信，就算我不能參加，您仍然會度過一段美好的時光。如果今後我可以提供幫助，請不要猶豫再與我聯繫。

範文三十一：高中學校一年一度運動會

High School Annual Sports Day

Tai Po Girls High School
230 Tai Po Road
New Territories

16th October 2023

寫信人地址

日期

Ms Siobhan Bernadette Haughey
Hong Kong Sports Institute
25 Yuen Wo Road,
Shatin
New Territories

收信人地址

Dear Ms Haughey,

稱呼

Re: Tai Po Girls High School Annual Sports Day

主題

On behalf of Tai Po Girls High School, it is my great pleasure to invite you to be our guest of honour at our annual Sports Day. As you may know, Tai Po Girls High School is renowned for its sporting achievements, and Sports Day is the most important event of the school year. This year, the event will be held at the Tai Po Central Sports Complex on December 25, from 10:00 am to 9:30 pm.

首段：開門見山，直接説明寫信目的，發出邀請

The Sports Day will begin with an opening speech by Ms. Chan, the President of the Hong Kong Swimming Association, at 10:00 am. The athletics competition will commence at 10:30 am, and a prize-giving ceremony will be held at 5:30 pm. Lunchboxes and soft drinks will be provided during lunchtime, and a buffet dinner reception for all guests, teachers, and parents who sponsor the event will be served at the Sports Complex Western Restaurant at 6:30 pm.

正文段（一）：邀請函是針對學校活動的，因此提供所有詳細信息非常重要，例如活動日期、時間和日程表

As a well-known athlete and Hong Kong's first Olympic swimming silver medallist, your presence as our guest of honour would encourage our student athletes greatly. We would be extremely grateful if you could agree to be our chief referee for all our swimming matches and present the medals and award certificates for these games. We sincerely hope that you will join us at the dinner reception.

正文段（二）：解釋貴賓出席的重要性以及它將如何使活動和參與者受益。

We understand how busy your daily work schedule must be, so we kindly request that you inform us of your availability by the 15th of next month. We appreciate your participation and look forward to the possibility of welcoming you to our Sports Day in December.

尾段：尊重貴賓的時間和日程安排，給予他足夠時間決定參加與否

Thank you for your kind attention to this matter.

禮貌的結語

Yours sincerely,

結束敬語

Wong Lai
Chairwoman, Sports Club

簽名

職位，組織

參考譯文

大埔女子高中學校
新界大埔道 230 號
20XX 年 10 月 16 日

何詩蓓女士
香港體育學院
新界沙田元和道 25 號

親愛的何女士，

主題：大埔女子中學一年一度運動會

我代表大埔女子中學，很榮幸邀請您作為特邀嘉賓參加我們學校一年一度的運動會。您或許知道，大埔女子中學以體育成績著稱，而運動會是每個學年最重要的活動。今年的賽事將於 12 月 25 日上午 10 時至晚上 9 時 30 分在大埔中央綜合體育館舉行。

運動會以香港游泳總會會長陳先生在 10 時的開幕致辭拉開帷幕，體育競技比賽將於上午 10 時 30 分開始，在下午 5 時 30 分將舉行頒獎儀式，午餐時段將提供午餐飯盒和飲料，並於下午 6 時 30 分在體育綜合樓西餐廳為所有賓客、老師和贊助活動的家長提供自助餐晚宴。

作為香港首位奧運游泳銀牌得主，能出席作為我們的特邀嘉賓，將為我們的學生運動員帶來很大鼓勵。若您能同意擔任泳賽的主裁判並頒發獎牌和證書，將不勝感激，更深切希望您能參加我們的晚宴。

我們了解您日常工作安排很忙，若您能在下月 15 日之前回覆能否參加是次活動，我們將不勝感激。我們真正感謝您的參與，並期待在 12 月能夠歡迎您蒞臨我們的運動會。

感謝您對此事的關注。

你忠誠的

王麗
體育社主席

範文三十二：演藝事業

Acting Profession

<table>
<tr><td></td><td>Chaiwan Girls Secondary School
Chai Wan
Hong Kong</td><td>寫信人地址</td></tr>
<tr><td></td><td>9th April 20XX</td><td>日期</td></tr>
</table>

Chaiwan Girls Secondary School
Chai Wan
Hong Kong
寫信人地址

9th April 20XX
日期

Malinda Hung Arts Studio
Kowloon Bay Industrial Building, 4/F
Kowloon
收信人地址

Dear Ms Hung,
稱呼

Re: Acting Profession Event
主題

Our school is organizing a special event, 'Acting Profession', on October 31st, 20XX. On behalf of the Drama Club, I am writing to inquire whether you would be interested in joining us and giving a talk to our students, their parents, and our guests about your experiences in the entertainment industry.
首段：開門見山，直接說明寫信目的和原因，發出邀請

Drama is a popular subject at our school, and the focus of this event is to provide our students and their parents with the opportunity to meet people working in the entertainment industry and learn more about their profession.
正文段（一）：介紹學生和家長演藝事業工作

Ms. Hung, I have long been an admirer of your work and have watched all of your performances, whether on television, in film, or on stage. My favourite role of yours was as the headmistress of four infants in 'A Lifetime Educator'. Your performance in this film was exceptional and truly touched my heart. I also enjoy the songs you have played in your films and television drama series. Furthermore, I have read all of your publications, including your autobiography and the best-seller, *Acting Life, Tears of Joy*.
正文段（二）：解釋為何選擇洪女士為是次活動的嘉賓

When I was asked to write a letter to a local actress for this special event, I immediately suggested you as our guest of honour. All committee members of the Drama Club unanimously agreed with enthusiasm and look forward to learning from you. We believe that your appearance at our school on this occasion would be of great benefit to our students, as it will give them a rare opportunity to truly understand what it is like to be a successful actress. We would be delighted if you would be willing to give us a talk, sharing your experiences and successes. Your suggestions and advice would certainly help our students in their job searches.

We understand that you are a busy person, and we would appreciate it if you could let us know by return mail whether you are prepared to accept our invitation to speak at our 'Acting Profession' event. Should you have any further questions regarding this event, please feel free to contact me at telephone 2345 9876.

Your kind attention to this matter is highly appreciated.

Yours sincerely,

Lee Wai Sum

President, Drama Club

正文段（三）：繼續說明大會對洪女士的讚賞。對學生們來說有很多好處，因為這將給他們一個難得的機會，向一位成功的女演員學習。

尾段：希望收信人接受邀請，提供如何回覆邀請的明確說明

禮貌性的結語

結束敬語

簽名

組織，職位

20XX 年 4 月 9 日

馬琳達洪藝術工作室
九龍灣工業大樓 4 樓

親愛的洪小姐

主題：演藝事業活動

我校將於 20XX 年 10 月 31 日舉辦一場名為「演藝職業」的特別活動。我有幸代表劇社寫信邀請您參加這次活動，並為我們的學生、家長以及賓客發表關於您工作的演講。

戲劇是我們學校的熱門科目。我們主題活動的重點是讓學生和父母有機會認識在娛樂事業工作的人士，多了解這個行業。

洪小姐，我一直對您的作品情有獨鍾，您每一場演出，電視、電影、舞台，我都看過。我最喜歡您的角色是在〈終身教育家〉中飾演四個孤兒的校長。您在影片中的表現非常出色，真正感動了我。我也喜歡您在所有您主演過的電影和電視劇中演唱的歌曲。此外，我是您所有出版書籍的忠實讀者，包括您的自傳和暢銷書《演藝人生，快樂的眼淚》。

當我被要求為這特殊活動「演藝事業」寫信給一位女演員時，我認為我要邀請一位真正熱愛娛樂事業的人。我立即提議您做我們的貴賓，劇社全體委員一致同意，熱情洋溢，並期待向您學習。相信您出席這個學校活動對學生來說，是非常有益的，這將給他們一個難得的機會，真正了解成為一名成功演員的感覺。如果您願意發表演講，分享您的經驗和成功，我們將非常高興，這對我們任何一個考慮將演藝作為她們職業的學生來說，將非常鼓舞人心。考慮到您在娛樂圈的知名度，您的建議和忠告肯定會對學生求職有幫助。

若您能回信告訴我會否接受「演藝事業」演講的邀請，我將不勝感激。如果您對是次活動還有任何疑問，請隨時致電 2345 9876 與我聯繫。

你真誠的

李慧心

劇社會長

柴灣女子中學

範文三十三：週年紀念大減價

Anniversary Sales

Vinton Technology Limited 505 Queen's Road Central Hong Kong	寫信人公司 地址
February 23, 20XX	日期

88 Peak Road
Hong Kong

收信人地址

Dear Ms Lau Pui Hing,

稱呼

Anniversary Sales Event from April 1 to April 15

主題

According to our records, you have been one of our gold or platinum card customers since our grand opening last year. We would like to express our gratitude for your patronage by inviting you to our 'Anniversary Sales' event, which will be held from April 1 to April 15.

首段：發出邀請對收件人表示感謝，並解釋他們被邀請參加活動的原因。

This sales event will take place during two separate time periods. The morning session is by invitation only and will be open to our valued customers like you from 9:00 am each day. You are welcome to bring along your family members or friends. A complimentary buffet breakfast will be served until 11:30 am. The afternoon session is open to the public and will begin at noon.

正文段（一）：提供關於活動的清晰細節。上午時段只對受邀嘉賓開放，下午時段則對公眾開放。

All of our products, including electronic goods such as cell phones, personal computers, digital watches, cameras, and electric appliances like televisions, refrigerators, washing machines, etc., will be marked down by 20% – 50%. In addition, we have enclosed a $100 gift coupon to use with your purchase of $1,000 or more, as well as a $200 gift coupon to use with a purchase over $2,000. If your total purchase is above $3,000, you may use both coupons, which amounts to $300 in total. Furthermore, platinum card customers will receive an additional 10% discount with a total purchase above $10,000 net.

正文段（二）：參加活動的好處。具體說明貨品價格和優惠內容

We are excited to serve you in April. For registration purposes, please bring this invitation letter with you, as it is necessary for admittance during the morning session.

正文段（三）：鼓勵收件人參加活動

Thank you for your continued patronage. We hope to see you soon.

尾段：以禮貌和尊重方式結束

Yours sincerely,

結束敬語

Wong Chun Bor

簽名

General Manager

職位

參考譯文

永頓科技有限公司
皇后大道中 505 號
20XX 年 2 月 23 日

香港山頂道 88 號

親愛的劉佩卿女士，

4 月 1 日至 4 月 15 日 —— 週年紀念大特賣

記錄顯示自去年盛大開業以來，閣下是金卡或白金卡客戶之一。感謝您的惠顧，我們邀請您參加於 4 月 1 日至 4 月 15 日舉行的「週年大銷售」。

此銷售包括兩個不同時段。上午時段僅限獲邀客戶。我們將從每天上午 9 時開始為像您這樣的尊貴客戶服務。若您和家人朋友一齊來，我們無任歡迎。免費自助早餐供應至上午 11 時 30 分。下午時段向公眾開放，將於中午開始。

我們所有庫存，包括手機、個人電腦、數碼手錶、相機等電子產品，以及電視機、冰箱、洗衣機等電器，都將降價 20% 至 50%。請接受隨函附上的 100 元禮券，可用於購買一千元或以上的商品，以及 200 元的禮券，可用於購買超過二千元的商品。換句話說，如果您購買金額超過三千元，可同時使用這兩張優惠券，總額 300 元。此外，白金卡客戶淨消費總額超過一萬元，還可再享 10% 折扣。

我們期待四月接待您。請攜帶這封邀請函以便登記，因為它是上午入場時段必須的。

感謝您一直以來的惠顧。我們希望能很快見到你。

你真誠的

王鎮波
總經理

✦ 12 看圖作文 Picture Description

　　看圖作文根據一幅或多幅圖畫寫成，內容千變萬化。在小學階段，學生只要將圖畫由上而下、由左至右，描述一次即可，而在中學階段，看圖作文可以是記敘文，將圖畫信息表達出來，例如描繪風景；也可以是說明文，根據圖畫內容、時間、過程、步驟等予以解釋；更可以是議論文，描繪圖畫現象，得出結論及提出解決問題的方法；也可將圖畫寫成故事。

　　看圖作文可分四個寫作步驟：

思考：	想像圖畫寓意，發揮創作能力，確定文章主題，如果是多幅圖畫，要了解它們之間的關係，最後選擇文體。
內容：	細化寫作提綱，根據要點，確定三大段落的內容：首段、正文段和尾段。首段揭示寓意及引出話題。正文段可分為幾段，主要是展開論述、陳述事件經過、分析論證等。尾段展示文章的結論，包括自己的觀點、看法或故事結局等。
成文：	根據提綱進行寫作。日記、週記、議論文一般採用第一人稱。
修飾：	修改文章，最後定稿。

　　以下圖片可以寫成記敘文，記載戲院人頭湧湧，全院滿座的盛況。也可以寫成議論文，討論一下現時娛樂事業的市場，比較一下在家的家庭影院與前往戲院看電影的讀者。本文作者選擇用這幅圖片寫成一個故事：

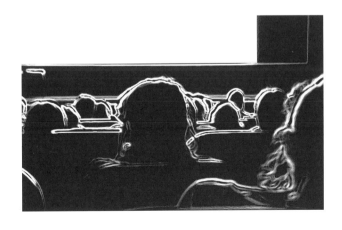

In the Cinema

The cinema in the picture appeared to be packed with people, indicating that a popular film was showing. This reminded me of an incident that happened last summer. A friend of mine had strongly recommended that I watch the movie 'An Endless Love', and even bought me a ticket. I grabbed a can of Coke and made my way into the theatre.	首段：引出話題
To my dismay, I found myself seated behind a large man with an enormous head, much like in the picture. However, unlike the calm and quiet man in the picture, the man in front of me was wearing a cap and making a ruckus. He was drinking Coke as well, but with great noise, and would occasionally let out loud burps. To make matters worse, he couldn't sit still and kept moving his head around. Every time he shifted to the right, I had to move my head to the left to get a glimpse of the screen. And whenever he moved to the left, I had to shift to the right. Unfortunately, he always managed to position himself directly in front of me, making it impossible for me to see the movie. I was getting increasingly agitated.	正文段（一）：故事開始發生。介紹故事內容與圖畫的聯繫
Finally, I had no choice but to tap him on the shoulder and politely ask, 'Excuse me, sir, would you mind lowering your head a bit so I can see the picture?' He turned towards me and replied, 'No, sir. That's not comfortable for me.' After a while, he suddenly turned back and said, 'Okay, if you give me $500.' I was shocked and infuriated. I decided to walk out without watching the movie.	正文段（二）：忍無可忍，請求讓一讓。但竟然提出無理要求
After that day, I have not been to a cinema. I prefer watching movies at home where there are no distractions or rude people.	尾段：這故事讓我不敢再到戲院看戲

參考譯文

畫面中的戲院似乎擠滿了人，說明正在放映一部受歡迎的影片。這讓我想起了去年夏天發生的一件事。我的一個朋友極力推薦我看電影〈無盡的愛〉，還給我買了票。我拿起一罐可樂便走進戲院。

令我沮喪的是，我發現自己坐在一個腦袋很大的大個子後面，就像照片中的一樣。然而，與畫面中靜靜坐着的男子不同，眼前這個男子戴着鴨舌帽，也喝着可樂，聲音很大，時不時會打出很大的嗝。更糟糕的是，他坐不住了，腦袋不停轉來轉去。每次他向右移動時，我都必須將頭向左移動才能瞥見屏幕。每當他向左移動時，我就不得不向右移動。不幸的是，他總是設法遮在我的正前方，讓我看不到電影。我越來越煩躁了。

最後，我只好拍了拍他的肩膀，客氣地問：「請問，先生，您是否可以把頭放低一點，讓我看到影片？」他轉向我，回答說：「不能，先生。這讓我不舒服。」過了一會兒，他突然回頭說：「好吧，如果你給我 500 元。」我感到震驚和憤怒。我決定不看電影就走出去了。

那天之後，我再也沒有去過電影院。我更喜歡在家裏看電影，那裏沒有干擾或粗魯的人。

範文三十五：大排檔

Dai-pai-dong

This picture depicts a type of open-air food stall known as a dai-pai-dong. In English, the term 'dai-pai-dong' literally means 'big licence stall'. Dai-pai-dong was one of Hong Kong's unique street food cultures. It was characterized by operating on the roadside or in alleys with an untidy atmosphere and a lack of air conditioning. However, its dishes, mainly Cantonese stir-fry and soy-braised, were cheap, tasty, and delicious. Dai-pai-dong was famous for its 'wok hei' meaning 'smoky flavour produced at high temperature,' which was considered its signature. Today, only a few licensed dai-pai-dongs exist in Hong Kong, as the government has been phasing them out due to concerns about hygiene and traffic congestion.

首段描述圖片所見的主要內容及解釋其歷史

The picture shows a traditional dai-pai-dong. It appears to be a licensed outdoor restaurant with permission to have extended seating on the street. The owner of the restaurant wants to keep it as an affordable, no-frills dining place for the ordinary working class. As a result, there is no fancy decor, only steel kitchen utensils such as metal pots and pans, and simple furniture such as foldable tables with white cloths, plastic stools, and so on. This signifies that it offers cheap and low-cost dining facilities to customers. The chef is stir-frying clams with salted bean and pepper, and I presume he is going to add a spoonful of soy sauce.

正文段詳細描述圖片的實際狀況

These alfresco eateries have served us and our city for decades, offering top-notch Cantonese cuisine with a distinctive flavour and character. Today, we can still find a few dai-pai-dongs, but most of them have relocated to indoor premises, particularly cooked food markets in commercial buildings. This means that the open-air feature is completely out of the picture. Nonetheless, the legacy of the dai-pai-dong continues to live on in Hong Kong's culinary culture, and it remains an important part of the city's history and heritage.

尾段說明大排檔以另一種形式存在

參考譯文

這幅圖描繪了一種露天食檔，名為大牌檔，英語字面意思是「領有執照的檔口」。大牌檔是香港獨特街頭飲食文化之一，它的特點是在路邊或小巷裏經營，氣氛不整潔，沒有空調，但它的菜色以廣東小炒和紅燒為主，價廉物美，味道可口。它以「鑊氣」聞名，即是在「高溫下產生多煙的香氣」，這被認為是它的標誌。今天，由於衛生和交通擁擠，香港只有少數有營業執照的大牌檔，因為政府一直逐步淘汰它們。

附圖顯示了一間傳統大牌檔。它似乎是一家有營業執照的外部餐廳，可允許街道外面設擴展座位。餐廳老闆希望將餐廳保持為普通工人階級負擔得起、簡單隨便的吃飯地方。所以，沒有花哨的裝飾 —— 只有鋼製廚具，如金屬鍋碗瓢盆和簡單的家具，即鋪白布的折疊桌子、塑膠櫈等。這意味着它為顧客提供廉價低成本的餐飲設施。廚師正做豉椒炒蜆，我認為他正想放上一匙的豉油。

畢竟，這些露天餐廳已為我們和我們的城市服務幾十年，提供具有獨特風味和特色的頂級粵菜。今天還能找到一些大牌檔，但大部份都搬進室內，尤其是商業大廈的熟食市場，這意味着露天特徵已完全消失了。儘管如此，大牌檔在香港飲食文化中繼續存在，並且仍然是這城市的歷史和文化遺產。

★ 13 新聞稿 Press Release

新聞稿是一篇交給媒體的聲明。要撰寫好的新聞稿，該包含引人注目的標題、強而有力的引言和內容豐富的正文。

佈局結構 Structure

序號	內容	解釋
1.	標題：	標題該引起讀者注意，可包括副標題。
2.	首段：	首段是引言，也就是新聞稿主要的發佈內容。
3.	正文段：	新聞稿的正文段該回答一些問題，例如：「這是關於甚麼？」、「它為何重要？」、「何時？」、「哪裏？」、「誰參與其中？」等。正文段還該包含有關產品或活動以及涉及其詳細信息。
4.	結尾段：	可用作解釋內容，以便讀者可以獲得更多信息，也可提供聯繫方式，讓新聞稿全面發揮作用。

範文三十六：香港電子展銷會

Hong Kong Electronics Fair

Hong Kong Electronics Fair

(to be held in December)

標題
副標題

The Hong Kong Electronics Association has announced that it will host the Hong Kong Small Electronics Fair in December this year. The fair will be held from 12 to 15 December (Saturday to Tuesday) at the Hong Kong Convention and Exhibition Centre, from 8.30 am to 10.30 pm. Tickets will be available at the door for $25 each.

首段：展銷會
時間、地點

Over 200 exhibiting companies will participate in the fair, presenting their latest releases of electronic components and digital technologies. There will be a wide selection of electronic products, from the smallest capacitor to the brightest light-emitting diode (LED) . The latest editions and features in consumer or home electronic equipment will also be displayed, including digital cameras, smartphones, personal computers, video game consoles, karaoke machines, and more. Additionally, there will be hands-on demonstrations of the latest developments in augmented reality (AR) and virtual reality (VR) devices, showcasing how they are used in entertainment and in work, such as VR game software Horizon Worlds and workplace program Horizon Workrooms. Mr. David Baszucki, Chairman of VR platform Roblox, will lead a video conference on the special topic 'Metaverse'.

正文段（一）：
概括展銷
產品

Hong Kong is a great place for people who are interested in electronics and digital technologies. Despite the ongoing trade friction between China and the United States, the Hong Kong Electronics Association is still hosting this fair and running the associated events without a hitch. It is expected that people from all over the world will come here to shop for cameras, smartphones, laptops, games consoles, peripherals, and all the latest software.

正文段（二）：
描述展銷會
的目的

Just in time for this new Electronics Fair, signature gift wrap is available with the purchase of most electronic products, including smartphones and software, for an amount over $2,000. Online retail shops also offer eligible students and faculty members special education pricing on laptops, iPads, and more. The entrance fee of $25 will be deducted for all purchases over $1,000.

正文段（三）：
購買產品
優惠

For more information, please contact the Hong Kong Electronics Association at 5F, Prosperous Mansions, Queen's Road East, Wan Chai, tel: 2678 1234, email: info@hkelecass.com.

尾段：提供聯
繫方式

參考譯文

香港電子展銷會

（在 12 月舉行）

香港電子商會宣佈將於今年 12 月舉辦香港電子展銷會。展銷會將於 12 月 11 日至 14 日（星期六至星期二）上午 8 時 30 分至晚上 10 時 30 分假香港會議展覽中心舉行。門票將在售票處出售，每張 25 元。

超過 200 間參展公司將會參加是次展銷會，並展示他們最新發佈的電子部件和數碼技術。電子產品選擇的範圍很廣，從最小的電容器到最亮的發光二極管。當然，最新版本和功能的消費或家用電子設備也將展出，包括數碼相機、智能手機、個人電腦、視頻遊戲機、卡拉 OK 機等。此外，還在現場演示擴增實境（AR）和虛擬實境（VR）設備的最新發展，展示它們如何在娛樂和工作中使用，例如虛擬實境遊戲軟件，平線世界和工作室程序。虛擬平台董事長大衛巴薩隆先生將主持關於「元宇宙」專題的視頻會議。

香港對於就電子和數碼技術感興趣的人來說是很好的地方。儘管中美貿易磨擦不斷，香港電子商會仍順利主辦是次展銷會並舉辦相關活動，預計來自世界各地的人將到這裏購買相機、智能手機、手提電腦、遊戲機、其他外圍設備和所有最新軟件等。

正好是時候到這新的電子展銷會購買電子產品，包括智能手機和軟件，購買超過 2,000 元大多數都可獲得簽名禮品包裝紙。網上零售商店還可讓符合條件的學生和教職員在手提電腦、平板電腦等享受特殊教育定價。凡購買 1,000 元以上，將可扣除 25 元的入場費。

如欲獲取更多資訊，請聯繫：香港電子協會，灣仔皇后大道東富盛大廈 5 樓，電話：2678 1234，郵箱：info@hkelecass.com

範文三十七：香港非物質文化遺產

The Intangible Cultural Heritage of Hong Kong

The Intangible Cultural Heritage of Hong Kong *The Representative List*	標題 副標題
Intangible cultural heritage comprises the non-physical aspects of a culture, such as oral traditions, performing arts, social practices, rituals, and knowledge about nature and the universe. These elements are considered an essential part of a community's identity and heritage, and are passed down from generation to generation.	首段：介紹甚麼是非物質文化遺產
The Hong Kong Government has recently announced that its Representative List of the Intangible Cultural Heritage of Hong Kong now includes 20 items. These items are categorized as follows:	正文段（一）：開門見山說出代表名單有20項
I. Performing Arts, which consists of Cantonese Opera, Quanzhen Temples Taoist Ritual Music, Hakka Unicorn Dance in Hang Hau in Sai Kung, and Nanyin (Southern Tunes) . II. Social Practices, Rituals, and Festive Events, which comprise Cheung Chau Jiao Festival, Mid-Autumn Festival–The Hang Fire Dragon Dance, Tai O Dragon Boat Water Parade, Tin Hau Festival in Hong Kong, Wong Tai Sin Belief and Customs, Yu Lan Festival of the Hong Kong Chiu Chou Community, Mid-Autumn Festival–The Pok Fu Lam Fire Dragon Dance, Sek Pun (Basin Feast) , Spring and Autumn Ancestral Worship of Clans, and the Taoist Ritual Tradition of the Zhengyi School. III. Knowledge and Practices Concerning Nature and the Universe, which includes Herbal Tea. IV. Traditional Craftsmanship, which is composed of The Arts of Old Qin Making, Technique of Making Hong Kong Cheongsam and Kwan Kwa Wedding Costume, Bamboo Building Technique, and Hong Kong-Style Milk Tea Making Technique.	正文段（二）、（三）及（四）：主題內容即是香港非物質文化遺產代表名單有四大分類
Among these, Cantonese Opera, The Tin Hau Festival, and the Hong Kong Cheongsam Making Technique were recently added to UNESCO's Representative List of the Intangible Cultural Heritage of Humanity, and were announced by the HKSAR in June 2021.	正文段（五）：最近加入名單的香港非物質文化遺產

The inclusion of Hong Kong's intangible cultural heritage in UNESCO's Representative List can promote tourism and cultural exchange, while also safeguarding these traditions for future generations. It helps to raise awareness of Hong Kong's unique cultural practices and traditions, both locally and internationally. Furthermore, it can contribute to the promotion of cultural diversity and intercultural dialogue, and to sustainable development.

尾段：解釋香港非物質文化遺產的地位、作用及貢獻，使讀者獲得更多知識

參考譯文

香港非物質文化遺產

代表名單

非物質文化遺產包括文化的非物質方面，例如口頭傳統、表演藝術、社會實踐、儀式以及關於自然和宇宙的知識。這些元素被認為是社區身份和遺產的重要組成部份，並代代相傳。

香港政府公佈香港非物質文化遺產代表名單，涵蓋共 20 個項目。以下是 20 個項目的列表：

I. 表演藝術包括粵劇，全真道堂科儀音樂，西貢坑口客家舞麒麟，南音

II. 社會實踐、儀式、節慶活動涵蓋大澳端午龍舟遊，中秋節 —— 大坑舞火龍、長洲太平清醮、香港天后誕、香港潮人盂蘭勝會、黃大仙信俗、中秋節 —— 薄扶林舞火龍、正一道教儀式傳統、宗族春秋二祭、食盆菜

III. 有關自然界和宇宙的知識和實踐包括涼茶

傳統手工藝有古琴藝術，香港中式長衫和婚禮裙褂製作技藝，搭棚技藝，港式奶茶製作技藝

其中，粵劇、天后誕和香港旗袍製作技藝，是近期被聯合國教科文組織列入非物質文化遺產代表名單的，是香港特別行政區於 2021 年 6 月公佈的。

將香港非物質文化遺產列入聯合國教科文組織的代表作名單，可促進旅遊和文化交流，同時為子孫後代保護這些傳統，有助提高本地和國際對香港獨特文化習俗和傳統的認識。此外，它還有助促進文化多樣性和文化之間的對話及可持續發展。

★ 14 提案 Proposal

在中學作文考試中，你可能要就某些問題寫提案。寫提案的目標是希望找到支持你建議的人。如果你能以清晰簡潔、引人入勝的方式提出想法或計劃，便有很大可能獲得認同、批准或支持，所以要學習如何撰寫有説服力、引人入勝的提案。

提案有多種類型的寫法，可以用報告形式、電郵 / 信函方式或用備忘錄形式等。提案是一種正式寫作文體，因此，禮貌的語言是必須的。你還該使用標題説明主題項目和用副標題劃分內容，包括引言、背景、目的、建議和結論。

佈局結構 Structure

序號	內容	解釋
1.	標題：	為您的提案命名，説出主題，主題必須簡短而準確。
2.	引言：	介紹提案的主題，引出問題所在，並簡單地寫下你的提案建議。
3.	背景：	提供背景信息，描述你對該主題的了解和看法，陳述一些事實去支持你的提案，以及你期望的結果。
4.	目的：	清楚説明你的目標，背後的基本原理。
5.	建議：	你打算提出甚麼建議，寫下你的行動計劃，以帶有序列方式表達。
6.	結論：	用一兩句話重申並總結你的建議，提供一個有説服力的結尾。

範文三十八：取締不人道動物園運動

Campaign to Ban Inhumane Zoos

這範文是一篇典型的提案報告：

PROPOSAL

Subject: Campaign to Ban Inhumane Zoos

Introduction

Zoos are popular attractions for people all over the world. However, many of these zoos keep animals in inhumane conditions, causing them to suffer. This proposal aims to raise awareness about the issue and campaign to ban inhumane zoos.

Background

While zoos do important work in animal conservation and breeding, some zoos are not keeping animals in humane conditions. Animals are taken from their natural habitats and placed in confined spaces, often alone, causing them to become bored and stressed. It is important to ensure that animals are treated humanely and in a way that respects their natural behaviour.

Objective

The objective of this proposal is to raise awareness about the suffering of animals in inhumane zoos and campaign for their closure.

Recommendation

To achieve this objective, we propose an awareness campaign that starts with educating our students. We will create leaflets with photos of animals in terrible conditions and distribute them to all our students. We will encourage them to share this information with their families and friends, and to spread the message through social media.

Conclusion

This campaign may not lead to the closure of all inhumane zoos, but it will raise awareness and change attitudes towards zoos. We believe that by educating people about the conditions these animals endure, we can bring about positive change and help to ensure that all animals are treated humanely.

提案
標題：主題

引言：引出問題，不人道的動物園

背景：提供背景信息，描述作者對動物園的了解，比如動物保育，但被放置在狹窄的空間。

目的：清楚說明提案的目標

建議：行動計劃，以帶有序列方式表達

結論：總結建議

提案

主題：取締不人道動物園運動

引言

動物園是世界各地人們的熱門旅遊景點。然而，許多這樣的動物園讓動物處於不人道環境中，導致牠們受苦。這提案旨在提高人們對禁止不人道動物園的問題和運動的認識。

背景

雖然動物園在動物保護和繁殖方面做着重要工作，但一些動物園並沒有讓動物處於人道環境中。動物從牠們的自然棲息地被帶走並安置在密閉空間內，通常是單獨的，這導致牠們感到無聊和有壓力。重要的是要確保以尊重動物自然行為的人道方式對待動物。

目的

這提案的目的是提高人們對不人道動物園中動物所受痛苦的認識，並發起關閉動物園的運動。

建議

為了實現這一目標，我們提出了從教育學生開始的一項宣傳活動。我們將製作帶有處於惡劣環境中的動物照片的傳單，並將其分發給我們所有的學生。我們將鼓勵他們與家人和朋友分享這些信息，並通過社交媒體傳播出去。

結論

這場運動可能不會導致所有不人道動物園的關閉，但它會提高人們對動物園的認識，並且改變他們的態度。我們相信，通過教育人們了解這些動物所承受的條件，可以帶來積極的變化，有助確保所有動物都得到人道對待。

範文三十九：提高戲劇社會員人數

Increase in Drama Club Membership

提案可用備忘錄方式表達，請看以下範文：

MEMORANDUM

To: The Principal; Head of Drama Department

From: President of Drama Club

Subject: Proposal to Increase Drama Club Membership

Date: 11th October 20XX

收件人：兩位收件人

發件人

主題

日期

Introduction

As you are aware, the Drama Club is currently experiencing a decline in membership. This memo aims to propose some ideas to address this issue.

引言：寫提案的原因

Background

Our last quarterly school magazine reported a significant decrease in the number of students choosing to join the extra-curricular Drama Club at our school. A survey conducted by the club found that we are not the only club to experience this decline in membership. More than 75% of students interviewed expressed no interest in becoming a member of any extra-curricular club, and half of all respondents cited a lack of spare time as the reason. Some even stated that they prefer to stay at home and play computer games.

背景：從統計數字看問題的所在

Objective

The Drama Club aims to provide students with opportunities to develop their acting and drama skills. The decrease in membership poses a threat to the survival of the club. The following recommendations aim to increase membership and promote the club.

目的：清楚説明目標和背後的基本原理

Recommendation

I propose three activities as follows:

建議：提出三種活動：會社海報；戲劇節；參觀電視台

1. Club Poster

The Drama Club should create a poster listing the benefits of extra-curricular activities, such as physical development, creativity, and stress relief. This poster should also highlight the activities organized by the club and encourage students to join. Displaying the poster on the school notice board will help to raise awareness of the club's activities and attract potential members.

2. Festival of Drama

Organizing a 'Festival of Drama' at our school would be a fun way to promote the club. The festival could include drama-based games and special events, such as interviews with well-known actors or actresses and drama plays performed by the school Drama Club. Inviting parents and friends to watch the performances would also help to raise awareness of the club and attract new members.

3. Tours to Television Stations

Arranging tours to television stations and participating in their drama productions could attract students to become members of the Drama Club. The club could establish relationships with Hong Kong-based television broadcasting companies and involve its members in the actual production of drama series. This would give students the opportunity to see behind the scenes of a drama and possibly work as extras. Emphasizing that only members of the Drama Club are eligible for these activities would encourage students to join.

Conclusion

結論：期望以上提議可增加會員人數和促進課外活動

Extracurricular activities are essential for student development, and the Drama Club provides an excellent opportunity for students to develop their acting and drama skills. By implementing these recommendations, we hope to increase membership in the club and promote the benefits of extra-curricular activities to our students.

備忘錄

致：	校長；戲劇部主管
由：	劇社會長
主題：	提案建議提高劇社會員人數的活動
日期	二零╳╳年十月十一日

引言

如您所知，劇社目前會員人數正在下降。本備忘錄旨在提出一些想法解決這個問題。

背景

我們上一季的學校雜誌報導說，選擇加入學校劇社的學生人數顯著減少。本社進行的一項調查發現，我們不是唯一一個會員人數下降的課外活動社。超過 75% 的受訪學生表示，沒有興趣成為任何課外活動社的成員，一半受訪者表示缺乏空餘時間。一些人甚至表示他們更喜歡呆在家裏玩電腦遊戲。

目的

劇社旨在為學生提供發展表演和戲劇技巧的機會。會員人數的減少對劇社的生存構成威脅。以下建議旨在增加會員人數和宣傳分會。

建議

我想發起三種活動：

1. 會社海報

劇社該製作一張海報，列出課外活動的好處，例如有助身體發育、發展創造力和緩解壓力。這張海報還該突出會社所組織的活動，並鼓勵學生參加。在學校佈告欄上展示海報，將有助提高對會社活動的認識並吸引潛在會員。

2. 戲劇節

在學校組織「戲劇節」將是宣傳會社的有趣方式。這節目可以包括以戲劇為基礎的遊戲和特別活動，例如對知名演員或女演員的採訪以及學校劇社表演的戲劇，邀請家長和朋友觀看表演，有助提高會社知名度和吸引新會員。

3. 參觀電視台

安排參觀電視台和參與其戲劇製作，可以吸引學生成為劇社成員。劇社可以與香港的電視廣播公司建立關係，並讓其成員參與電視劇的實際製作。這將使學生有機會看到戲劇幕後，並可能擔任臨時演員。強調只有劇社成員才有資格參加這些活動將鼓勵學生加入劇社。

結論

課外活動對學生的發展至關重要，劇社為學生提供發展表演和戲劇技能的絕佳機會。通過實施這些建議，希望增加劇社會員，並向學生宣傳課外活動的好處。

★ 15 報告 Report

本書介紹三類報告：

1. 對事實的分析提出某些建議
2. 記錄最近發生的事件
3. 新聞報告

第一類 —— 分析報告

這類報告是分析事實、發現結果、得出結論及作出建議。因此，撰寫這類報告涉及：分析提供或收集的信息、從分析中發現結果、根據結果得出結論而提出建議。

在寫作方面，報告是一種正式的寫作文體，因此該採用嚴肅語氣。在撰寫報告時，避免使用第一人稱代詞，即我 (I) 或我們 (we)，所以在結構上，使用「被動語態」較為穩妥，例如：用 It was found that... 比較用 We found that... 好些。

佈局結構 Structure

1. 題目： 必須準確說明主題。

2. 首段： 陳述報告的目的，可以包括背景信息、如何收集信息的詳細信息或報告中各部份的預覽。

3. 正文： 陳述事件、數據來源以及結果和發現。提供事件詳細的敘述、解釋或結果、發現的原因。信息該以清晰易讀的方式呈現。你必須為每個要點開始一個新段落，每個段落給與一個小標題。

4. 尾段： 總結：從分析中得出結論。
   推薦：面對結論中提出的結果，建議進一步的行動或研究。

5. 日期： 寫報告的日子。

範文四十：廣告推廣報告

Report on an Advertising Campaign

Report on the 'PowerShoot' Advertising Campaign	題目

Introduction

The purpose of this report is to analyse the effectiveness of using a celebrity in an MTR poster campaign for our new digital camera, 'PowerShoot'. The campaign featured celebrity actor Ronnie Fung, who was the face of the campaign, and his poster using our new 'PowerShoot' camera was displayed in MTR stations from July to December last year. Ronnie Fung was famous in Hong Kong for his role in the TV drama series 'Tai Chi Master Yeung Lo Sim', which aired in 2019.

首段：報告用來分析廣告推廣的成效

Data Collection Methods

The sales department provided sales data that was used to analyse the sales performance of the 'PowerShoot'. The data covered three periods: before, during, and after the advertising campaign. The first period covered two months before the start of the campaign (May and June), the second period covered the first three months of the campaign (July, August, and September), and the third period covered two months after the campaign (January and February).

正文段（一）：報告採用的數據收集方法

Findings

The findings indicate that 950 units and 1,200 units were sold in May and June, respectively, before the launch of the advertising campaign. However, during the campaign, sales rose dramatically in July, August, and September. The highest sales during this period were 3,000 units in September, and the lowest were 1,650 in July. Sales continued to rise after the campaign, reaching 4,500 in February but dropping back to 3,150 in March.

正文段（二）：報告指出發現結果

Data Analysis

The significant increase in sales during the advertising campaign was due to the campaign itself. Additionally, due to the lasting effects of the advertising campaign, sales remained higher even after the end of the campaign and in the beginning of the year. The highest figures in February were likely due to the Chinese New Year holidays.

正文段（三）：報告提供數據分析

Conclusion

The poster campaign featuring the well-known celebrity actor Ronnie Fung was a tremendous success. The strategy of celebrity advertising has proven to be effective for our product.

尾段：總結分析結果

Recommendation   提出建議

It is recommended that the strategy of using Ronnie Fung as our advertising campaign should continue to be used in the coming year. Furthermore, it is also suggested to hire him as the spokesperson for our new robot camera.

Date: 30th September 20XX   日期

參考譯文

「力射相機」廣告推廣報告

引言

本報告的目的，是分析港鐵海報聘用名人在數碼相機「力射」的廣告推廣中的效果。名人演員馮郎尼是這次活動的主角，他的海報和全新的「力射」相機於去年 7 月至 12 月在港鐵站張貼。馮氏憑藉 2019 年播出的電視劇集〈太極拳師楊露禪〉在香港聲名鵲起。

數據收集方法

銷售部門蒐集用於分析「力射相機」銷售業績的數據。它涵蓋三個時期 —— 廣告推廣之前期、期間和後期。第一個時期涵蓋活動開始前的兩個月（即 5 月和 6 月）；第二個時期涵蓋活動期間的頭三個月（即 7 月、8 月和 9 月）；第三個時期涵蓋活動之後的兩個月（即 1 月、2 月）。

發現結果

調查結果顯示，5 月和 6 月分別售出了 950 個和 1,200 個。那是廣告推廣活動啟動前的兩個月。然而，在推廣活動期間，7 月、8 月和 9 月的銷售額急劇上升。這一時期的最高銷量是 9 月的 3,000 個，最低的是 7 月的 1,650 個。推廣活動結束後的銷量在 2 月繼續上升至 4,500 個，但 3 月回落至 3,150 個。

數據分析

廣告推廣活動期間，銷售額急劇增長，原因在於活動本身。此外，由於廣告活動持續的影響，即使活動在今年年頭結束後，銷售額仍保持較高水平。2 月最高的數字可能受惠於農曆新年假期。

結論

名人演員馮氏的海報大獲成功。名人廣告策略已獲證實對產品有效。

推薦

建議來年繼續使用馮氏作為廣告宣傳策略。此外，還建議聘請他為我們新機器人相機的代言人。

日期：20XX 年 9 月 30 日

第二類 —— 簡明記錄

這類報告清楚陳述事實，說明事故的具體情況、起因和過程。通常用第一人稱和一般過去時來撰寫。

佈局結構 Structure

1. 題目：　　必須準確說明主題。

2. 首段：　　陳述報告的目的，包括背景信息等。

3. 正文：　　可分幾段陳述事件的由來、過程、結果等。

4. 簽名：　　報告呈遞人簽字。

5. 日期：　　寫報告的日子。

範文四十一：證人口供

Witness Statement

以下是一位途人目擊交通意外後給警察的一份口供。

Witness Statement	題目
I, Chan Dai Man, of 30 Hill Road, 20/F, Sai Ying Poon, Hong Kong, witnessed a traffic accident in Tsim Sha Tsui on 1st September 20XX at approximately 12:30 pm. While waiting in front of the Jade Restaurant for my friend, I saw the accident happen.	首段：陳述報告的目的，包括背景信息等
I observed a red car driving down Ping On Lane. It was travelling quite fast, and above the average speed for such a narrow road. I also saw a white car slowly reversing out of a parking space outside the restaurant. Suddenly, the red car rear-ended the white car.	正文段（一）：講述意外發生經過
The drivers of both cars got out, and I noticed that the driver of the red car was a young man, probably in his twenties, while the driver of the white car was a woman in her thirties. Neither of them appeared to be hurt. They discussed the incident and exchanged details. However, they did not seem to reach an agreement. At that point, my friend had arrived, and we were about to go inside the restaurant for lunch.	正文段（二）：講述司機交涉過程
The driver of the white car approached us and asked, 'Did you see the accident?' I replied that I had seen it. She then requested my contact details, in case the police needed a statement from me. I agreed and provided my name and telephone number.	正文段（三）：筆者被邀請做證人的經過
It was a sunny day, and I noticed that both cars had sustained damage. The rear left-hand side of the white car was damaged, as was the front bumper of the red car.	尾段：車輛損毀程度
Signed: Chan Dai Man	簽名
Dated: 3rd September 20XX	日期

證人口供

我陳大文,來自香港西營盤山道 30 號 20 樓,於 20XX 年 9 月 1 日下午約 12 點 30 分在尖沙咀目睹了一宗交通意外。當時我在翡翠酒樓門口等我的朋友,我看到了事故發生。

我注意到一輛紅色車從平安里向下駛來。在如此狹窄的馬路上行駛,它似乎開得太快,並且高於平均速度。我還看到一輛白色汽車從酒樓外的一個泊車位緩緩從後退車出來。突然,它被那輛紅色車追尾了。

兩個司機都下了車。紅色車的司機是個年輕男子,約二十來歲。白色車的司機是一位約三十歲的女子,他們看來沒有受傷,談及這事故並交換了細節。令我驚訝的是,他們似乎沒有達成協議。這時,我朋友已經到了,我們正要進酒樓吃午飯。

白色車的司機走近我們問道:「你看到事故了嗎?」我回答說我看到了。然後她要了我的詳細聯繫方式,以防警察需要我的口供。我同意並提供了我的姓名和電話號碼。

那是一個陽光明媚的日子。我注意到兩輛車都有破損,白色車的左後方和紅色車前面的防撞桿都損壞了。

簽名:陳大文

日期:20XX 年 9 月 3 日

第三類 —— 新聞報告

新聞報告就是對最近發生的事件如實客觀地介紹,內容必須及時、真實和有轉達性的。新聞報告是透過報章、雜誌或其他形式的媒介把新聞內容告訴羣體的文體。寫作時通常以第三人稱和一般過去時為主。

佈局結構 Structure

1. 題目: 包括標題和副標題,必須簡潔和醒目。
2. 首段: 開門見山,介紹事件。
3. 正文段: 可分為幾個段落,陳述事件由來、過程、結果等。
4. 尾段: 總結事件、影響或評語。

範文四十二：學生戰勝老師

Students Triumph over Teachers

Students Triumph over Teachers with 2-1 Victory in Football Match	題目
Last Saturday, a crowd of 2,000 students and parents gathered at the school sports playground for an exciting football match between the 'Students' and 'Teachers' teams. At halftime, the score was 1-0 in favour of the Teachers, but they failed to capitalize on their lead in the second half. The Students fought back and scored two goals, ultimately securing a 2-1 victory.	首段：介紹足球比賽，結果學生勝出
In the 12th minute of the first half, Mr. Chan Hong, an English Language teacher for Form 5, scored the first goal with an incredible pass. He dribbled past three student defenders and struck the ball powerfully past the stunned goalkeeper.	正文段（一）：上半場比賽實況
In the second half, Wong Bing Shing, a Form 6 student, successfully equalized the game in the 51st minute with an incredible header. Just two minutes later, Wong Bing Shing struck the ball beautifully past the Teachers' goalkeeper for a well-deserved hat-trick and the winning goal.	正文段（二）：下半場比賽實況
Lau Lai Fan, the teacher who organized the game, commented, 'It was a great performance by the Students' football team, especially Wong Bing Shing. There was simply nothing the Teachers' team could do to stop him. I think Bing Shing is really energetic and skilful'.	正文段（三）：主辦老師評論
The match concluded with a cocktail reception, which provided an opportunity for parents to talk to teachers and school officials about matters of interest.	尾段：家長老師聚會

參考譯文

學生在足球比賽中以 2-1 戰勝老師

上週六，2,000 名學生和家長在學校體育操場觀看了一場緊張刺激的足球比賽，學生隊對教師隊。上半場的比分是教師隊勝 1-0，但他們在下半場沒能再得分。相反，學生隊在下半場反擊入了兩球，最終以 2-1 勝出。

上半場第 12 分鐘，中五英語教師陳康妙傳率先破門。他運球越過三名學生防守球員，有力地擊球，球越過了目瞪口呆的守門員。

下半場，中六學生王炳誠在第 51 分鐘以一記不可思議的頭槌成功扳平。僅僅兩分鐘後，王炳誠漂亮地表演帽子戲法，射球越過教師隊的守門員，實現了制勝的一球。

組織比賽的劉麗芬老師説：「學生隊的表現非常出色，尤其是王炳誠。老師根本無法阻止他。我覺得炳誠真是精力充沛，技術嫻熟。」

比賽以雞尾酒會結束，家長們有機會與老師和學校行政人員討論感興趣的問題。

✦ 16 評論 Review

中學英語作文考試，你可能會被要求撰寫評論，所以，你該仔細了解需要評論的內容是甚麼，比如：

» 書籍

» 產品

» 電影

» 酒樓餐廳

» 任何活動，例如比賽等

撰寫評論必須介紹主題，評估其各種特徵並給出建議。寫作時，你該運用個人經驗和知識，結合它提供的信息和功能，說明會否推薦它。

語言特點

1. 在時態方面，使用一般過去時談論具體細節，例如：
   » The decor *was* unimpressive but the service *was* notable.（裝飾不起眼，但服務值得欣賞。）

2. 評論電影，傳統上用現在時。但談到其他人對這部電影的任何評論時，一定要使用過去時，比較以下例子：
   » The story *begins* in 1945, two months before the end of the Second World War.（故事開始於 1945 年，即第二次世界大戰結束前兩個月。）

   » The critic gave this film a better review only by comparing it to films that were worse.（評論家僅將此影片與更差的影片比較，從而給予較好的評價。）

3. 通常用第一人稱和／或第二人稱來撰寫你的評論，例如：
   » *I* ordered the restaurants signature dish.（我點了酒樓的招牌菜。）

   » *We* found the decor unimpressive.（我們發現裝飾不起眼。）

   » *You* will not be disappointed by the food.（在食物方面，你不會感到失望。）

4. 使用副詞和形容詞描述主題的不同特徵，例如：

   » The meat was cooked *just right* so it remained *tender* and *juicy*. (肉煮得恰到好處，所以它仍然柔軟多汁。)

書評

　　若書評重點是個人觀點，最好使用過去時，但若要分享你對別人的看法，最好使用現在時了。講故事時通常用一般過去時。以下是一篇書評的佈局結構：

1. 主題： 　　説出這是書評，將書名用副標題方式表達。
2. 首段： 　　分幾段，簡單介紹內容、作者和其他信息。
3. 正文段： 分幾段，介紹大綱和整個故事。
4. 尾段： 　　評價；説明會否推薦給讀者。

範文四十三：羅密歐與茱麗葉

Romeo & Juliet

Book Review
'Shakespeare: Romeo & Juliet'

'Romeo and Juliet' is a timeless classic in literature and a common text studied in schools. It is widely regarded as the greatest love story of all time, as the love between Romeo and Juliet was pure, innocent, and genuine. Despite being members of two feuding families, they fell deeply in love, and nothing else mattered. However, the tragic ending of the play saw the deaths of both lovers, ultimately uniting their feuding families.

The play was written in beautiful Shakespearean English, containing touching poetry and employing several dramatic techniques that shifted from hope to despair and from comedy to tragedy. Initially, the play was largely a comedy, but after Romeo's banishment, it became a tragedy.

The story takes place in Verona, where two feuding noble houses, the Montagues and the Capulets, were sworn enemies. As a result, the Prince of Verona intervened and issued an edict that imposed a death sentence on anyone who duelled. Romeo, a Montague, met Juliet, a Capulet, and fell in love with her. Juliet also loved him.

The pair of young lovers, with the aid of a Catholic Franciscan friar, made plans to be married in secret. However, Tybalt, Juliet's cousin, challenged Romeo to a duel, which Romeo refused to fight. Romeo's best friend took up Tybalt's challenge and died, enraging Romeo, who then killed Tybalt. Romeo was banished by the Prince of Verona for violating his edict but still consummated his secret marriage with Juliet.

While Romeo was away, the Capulets tried to marry off Juliet to a cousin of the Prince. Juliet visited the Franciscan friar for help, and he offered her a potion that would make her seem dead for forty-two hours. The friar sent a message to Romeo so that he could rescue her from her tomb in time. Unfortunately, there was a delay in sending the message, and Romeo heard that Juliet had died. Grief-stricken, Romeo decided to take poison and die by her tomb. Romeo found the Prince's cousin at Juliet's tomb and killed him before taking his own life with poison. Juliet awoke and discovered that Romeo was dead. She was so desperate that she stabbed herself with his dagger and joined him in death.

題目：書評
副標題：作者：書名

開場白：介紹這本書的內容；介紹故事大綱和說明這是一個悲劇結局的故事

正文：
介紹整個故事內容
羅密歐與茱麗葉的家族仇恨和相愛過程；悲劇成因；雙雙死去的過程；家族和解

The feuding families, Montagues and Capulets, and the Prince met at the tomb to find all three dead. The families were reconciled by their children's deaths and agreed to end their enmity with each other.

Shakespeare became the most famous playwright ever because of 'Romeo and Juliet' and many of his other works. After hundreds of years, many still pride themselves on Shakespearean English. 'Romeo and Juliet' was among Shakespeare's most popular plays during his lifetime and, along with 'Hamlet', is one of his most frequently performed plays. Today, the title characters of 'Romeo & Juliet' are regarded as archetypal young lovers.

I highly recommend this book to all secondary school students. It contains themes that still resonate with readers today, such as love, hate, revenge, and the consequences of actions. Reading 'Romeo and Juliet' will not only improve your understanding of literature but also provide a window into the past and the world of Shakespearean theatre.

尾段：
評語；推薦給中學生

參考譯文

書評

「莎士比亞：羅密歐與茱麗葉」

《羅密歐與茱麗葉》是文學中永恆的經典，也是學校裏常用的課文。它被稱為有史以來最偉大的愛情故事，因為羅密歐與茱麗葉之間的愛情純潔、天真和真誠。儘管他們是兩個在戰爭中不和的家庭的兩個成員，他們彼此相愛，其他的都不重要。然而，該劇的悲慘結局見證了兩個戀人的死亡，最終使他們不和的家庭團結起來。

這劇本是用美麗的莎士比亞英語寫成的，帶着感人的詩歌。莎士比亞運用了多種戲劇技巧，將希望轉變為絕望，從批評轉變為讚美；最引人注目的是從喜劇到悲劇的突變。一開始，這齣戲主要是一部喜劇，但在羅密歐被放逐後，它變成了悲劇。

維羅納兩個長期爭吵的貴族，蒙太古家族和凱普勒家族，是有不共戴天之仇的敵人。結果，維羅納親王進行了干預，並發佈了一項法令，對任何決鬥者判處死刑。羅密歐，一個蒙太古族人，認識了凱普勒家族的茱麗葉，並愛上了她；茱麗葉也愛他。

這對年輕戀人在天主教方濟各會修士幫助下，計劃秘密結婚。茱麗葉的堂兄提伯特向羅密歐挑戰決鬥，但羅密歐拒絕戰鬥。羅密歐最好的朋友接受了提伯特的挑戰並死去，激怒了羅密歐，他於是殺死了提伯特。羅密歐因違反了法令而被維羅納親王放逐，但促使了他的秘密完婚。

羅密歐不在時，凱普勒家族試圖將茱麗葉嫁給親王的堂弟。茱麗葉求助於方濟各會修士，他給了她一服魔藥，可以讓她假死四十二小時內復活。方濟各會修士向羅密歐送發此信息，以便他可以及時將她從墳墓中救出。不幸的是，這消息延遲送出了，羅密歐悲痛欲絕，決定服毒死在她的墳墓旁。羅密歐發現親王的堂弟在茱麗葉的墓前，於是殺死了他，然後服下毒藥。茱麗葉醒來發現羅密歐已經死了，她是如此絕望，她用他的匕首自殺了，隨他一同死去。

不和的家庭（蒙太古和凱普勒）和親王在墳墓會面，發現三個人都死了，家族因孩子的死亡和解了，並同意結束彼此的仇恨。

莎士比亞因《羅密歐與茱麗葉》和他的許多其他作品而成為有史以來最著名的劇作家。數百年後，許多人仍為莎士比亞的英語感到自豪。《羅密歐與茱麗葉》是莎士比亞生前最受歡迎的戲劇之一，和《哈姆雷特》一樣，是他上演次數最多的戲劇之一。如今，《羅密歐與茱麗葉》的主角被視為典範的年輕戀人。

我向所有中學生強烈推薦這本書。它包含的主題至今仍能引起讀者共鳴，例如愛、恨、報復和行為的後果。閱讀《羅密歐與茱麗葉》不僅可以增進您對文學的理解，還可以讓您了解莎士比亞戲劇的過去和世界。

ii) 產品評論

　　產品評論通常使用一般現在時。以下是產品評價的佈局結構：

1.	主題：	說出這是產品評論，將產品用副標題方式表達。
2.	首段：	簡單介紹產品的基本信息。
3.	正文段：	介紹產品優缺點。
4.	結尾段：	說明會否推薦給讀者。

範文四十四：「天藍」3D 電子書閱讀器 2022 版

'Sky Blue' 3D-Reader 2022 Version

Product Review

'Sky Blue' 3D-Reader 2022 Version

主題

產品名稱

Basic Information

The 'Sky Blue' is a basic, no-frills 3D-Reader primarily used for reading digital e-books. Its 2022 version boasts a much longer battery life, better readability, and the ability to use 3D printers to print pictures and diagrams. Its 21-inch crystal clear folded screen is also claimed to be the first colour-folded e-Reader with such a size on the market. The 'Sky Blue' states that there are tens of millions of e-books available free of charge.

首段：基本資料

Positive Aspects

I purchased the 'Sky Blue' for my grandmother, who is not tech-savvy and often struggles with using computers. Surprisingly, she had no problem using the 'Sky Blue'. The device can use the internet through Wi-Fi and allows users to download e-books from a computer or cell phone. The 3D printer function always makes my grandma laugh because she can print a figure to touch and play with. It also helps my son, as the e-Reader links to an English-Chinese dictionary for the meaning and definitions of difficult words, or even the translation of the entire sentence. Thus, both my grandmother and her grandson can easily understand complex texts. Additionally, the price is not expensive, at only $1,380 each.

正文段（一）：優點

Criticism

The drawbacks of the 'Sky Blue' are similar to those of most other e-Readers. First, some people still prefer reading the physical part of a paper book, as the subject matter can be glanced over quickly. Second, customers are only able to download books from a limited selection available in the 3D-Reader online shop, despite the company claiming to have tens of millions of free books. Thus, books purchased in the open market but not available in the 3D-Reader online shop cannot be read free of charge. Furthermore, the 3D-Reader with a 21-inch screen is too heavy for an elderly person to carry. Lastly, the 'Sky Blue' only has a one-year warranty.

正文段（二）：缺點

Recommendation

In short, if reading e-books is all an elderly person wants to do at home, and they also want a 3D printing feature, I would recommend the 'Sky Blue'. It has a larger screen than any other e-Reader in the market, making it easier for older people to read. However, if the user wants access to a wider range of books and a device that is more portable, other e-Readers may be a better choice.

尾段：推薦

產品評論
「天藍」3D 電子書閱讀器 2022 版

基本信息
本信息閱讀器是一款基本、簡潔的 3D 閱讀器，主要用於閱讀數碼電子書。它於 2022 年發佈的新版本聲稱可以提供更長的電池壽命和更好的可讀性。更重要的是，它使用戶能夠使用 3D 打印機打印圖片和圖表。其 21 英寸晶瑩剔透的摺叠屏幕，據稱也是市場上第一款這種尺寸的彩色摺叠電子閱讀器。「天藍」聲稱有數千萬本免費電子書。

優點
我買了一部給我的外婆，她不懂科技，經常發覺使用電腦有困難。驚奇地，她可以毫無問題地使用「天藍」。「天藍」可以通過 Wi-Fi 上網，允許用戶從電腦或手機下載電子書。其 3D 打印機功能總讓我婆婆發笑，因她可以打印一個模型來觸摸和玩耍。這對我兒子也有幫助，因為電子閱讀器鏈接到英漢詞典，可以了解艱難詞義，甚至整個句子的翻譯。因此，我外婆和她孫兒都能輕鬆理解複雜的文本。另外，價格也不貴，每部只是 1,380 元。

批評
「天藍」的缺點與大多數其他電子閱讀器的缺點相似。首先，有些人仍然喜歡閱讀紙本書，因為題材可以快速瀏覽。其次，客戶只能從 3D 閱讀器的網上商店中下載有限書籍，儘管他們聲稱擁有數千萬本免費書籍。因此，在公開市場上可以購買得到，但 3D 閱讀器的網上商店中沒有的書籍，就無法免費閱讀了。此外，21 英寸屏幕的 3D 閱讀器體型太重，一位老人家無法攜帶。最後，「天藍」只有一年的保養期。

推薦
簡而言之，如果長者只想在家看電子書，又喜歡 3D 打印功能，我推薦「天藍」，它的屏幕比市場上任何其他電子閱讀器都大。但是，如果用戶想要閱讀範圍更廣的書籍和更方便攜帶的設備，其他電子閱讀器可能是更好的選擇。

iii) 影評

影評通常使用現在時，也可用各種形容詞使評論變得有趣。正式的影評該常使用被動語態。以下是影評的佈局結構：

1.	主題：	説出這是影評，將戲名用副標題方式表達。
2.	首段：	簡單介紹電影的基本信息。
3.	正文段：	介紹電影劇情、角色、音響效果等。
4.	尾段：	説明會否推薦給讀者。

範文四十五：異形侵略戰

Battle: Los Angeles

<table>
<tr><td>

Film Review

Battle: Los Angeles

</td><td>

主題
戲名

</td></tr>
<tr><td>

'Battle: Los Angeles', also known as 'World Invasion: Battle Los Angeles', is a 2011 American military science fiction film.

</td><td>

首段：基本
資料

</td></tr>
<tr><td>

Plot

The story begins with a series of strange objects flying towards Earth from outer space. They land in the world's oceans, near 20 major coastal cities, and prove to be spacecraft containing hostile extra-terrestrials. The aliens begin attacking the citizens of the cities, and in Los Angeles, Staff Sergeant Michael Nantz and Lieutenant William Martinez lead a group of young US marines into the war zone to rescue some civilians hiding in a police station. The marines soon come face-to-face with the aliens, realizing that the extra-terrestrials have better weapons. The marines fight for their lives and try to save the trapped civilians.

</td><td>

正文段（一）：
介紹劇情

</td></tr>
<tr><td>

Cast

The film was directed by Jonathan Liebesman, with Aaron Eckhart as the main actor. The ensemble cast includes Michelle Rodriguez, Romon Rodriguez, Bridget Moynahan, Ne-Yo, and Michael Pena. Eckhart is excellent as the experienced sergeant leading the rescue team.

</td><td>

正文段（二）：
角色

</td></tr>
<tr><td>

Production and Visual Effects

This Category IIA film has a running time of 116 minutes. The director intended the film to be a realistic depiction of an alien invasion in the style of a war film, using practical visual effects and gritty fighting scenes to create a stunning but believable film. Some commented that 'this is a war movie, a documentary-style war movie—with aliens in it. '

</td><td>

正文段（三）：
製作和音響
效果

</td></tr>
<tr><td>

Recommendation

While some film critics criticized 'Battle: Los Angeles' as 'noisy, violent, ugly, and stupid', the film received award nominations for 'Favourite Movie Actor', 'Favourite Movie Actress', 'Best Film', and 'Best Special Effects', with composer Brian Tyler winning the BMI TV Music Award. Despite mixed reviews, I recommend this film to those who enjoy plenty of action and explosions.

</td><td>

尾段：
不推薦的原因
和推薦的原因

</td></tr>
</table>

影評

異形侵略戰

《異形侵略戰》又名《世界入侵：決戰洛杉磯》，是一部 2011 年的美國軍事科幻小說。

情節

故事始於一系列從外太空飛向地球的奇怪物體。他們降落在世界各大洋中，靠近 20 個主要沿海城市。這些物體被證明是載有敵對外星人的太空船。太空船內的外星人開始攻擊城市裏的居民。在洛杉磯，中士邁克爾南茲和威廉馬丁內斯中尉帶領一羣年輕的美國海軍陸戰隊員進入戰區，營救一些躲在警局裏的平民。海軍陸戰隊很快遇到外星人，對他們一無所知，但很快就意識到外星人擁有更好的武器。海軍陸戰隊必須為自己的生命而戰，拯救被困平民。

卡士

該片由 Jonathan Liebesman 執導。主要演員是 Aaron Eckhart，其他演員包括 Michelle Rodriguez、Romon Rodriguez、Bridget Moynahan、Ne-Yo 和 Michael Pena。Aaron Eckhart 飾演帶領拯救隊經驗豐富的中士，演出非常出色。

製作和視覺效果

這是 IIA 級電影，片長 116 分鐘。導演希望這部電影能以戰爭片的風格，真實描繪外星人入侵。他使用真實視覺效果和果敢的打鬥場面，旨在創作一部令人驚歎但非常可信的電影。有人評論說，這是一部「裏面有外星人」的戰爭片，紀錄片式的戰爭片。

推薦

一些影評人不推薦這部電影，批評這部電影「嘈雜、暴力、醜陋和愚蠢」。他們還嚴厲批評了電影的寫作、效果設計、攝影和剪輯。然而，換個角度來看，該片獲得了「最喜愛電影男演員」、「最喜愛電影女演員」、「最佳電影」和「最佳特殊效果」等獎項的提名。它的作曲家 Brian Tyler 獲得了 BMI 電視音樂獎。所以，我仍向那些喜歡大量動作和爆炸場面的人推薦這部電影。

★ 17 演講稿 Speech

演講為講者提供一個難得機會表達對某現象、活動或事件的意見。

講稿是事先準備好的文稿，必須開門見山表述講者的觀點，又要以生動有趣的方式切合主題抓住聽眾。講者結合敘述、描述、解釋和說服技巧，完成一篇符合邏輯的文章，並以產生讀者共鳴為目的。所以，要用修辭技巧包括說服藝術來吸引聽眾，但要注意不同場合有不同讀者，因此講稿寫法也各有不同，措辭也不一樣。總體來說，講稿主題內容必須鮮明，表達完整，有據有理，結構緊湊。

講稿一般比較嚴肅，需要知道你在和誰說話，演講目的以及你說話的時間，更要將演講內容和主要觀點按照將要提出的問題、分析、解決方案順序排列。英語語法方面，要準確運用時態，通常以一般現在時為主，可用第一人稱或第二人稱。

佈局結構 Structure

開場白： 表示榮幸能發表演講，簡單介紹自己。

舉例	譯文
Good afternoon, everyone. It's an honour to be able to talk to you all today.	大家下午好，很榮幸今天能與大家交流。
Good morning parents, teachers and fellow students. On behalf of..., I would like to welcome you all in participating today's function, ...	各位家長，老師和同學早上好，我代表……歡迎大家參加今天的……活動。

引言： 明確表達演講主題。

舉例	譯文
The motion today is ...	今天的議題是……
I would like to share with you...	我想和您們分享……

正文段： 該用例子表達主要觀點和分析問題。可分為幾段開展論述或究其原因，但始終要將它們聯繫在一起，確保每段都以流暢、合乎邏輯的方式進行。

尾段： 簡要總結主要想法，並呼籲大家以行動去做某事。

舉例	譯文
If we can do all of the above, I'm sure...	如果我們能做到以上一切，我敢肯定……
To sum up, I dare to urge you to go a step further so that we can all benefit.	總而言之，我敢於敦促您們多走一步，讓我們都能受益。

結束語： 表示感謝聽眾的聆聽和關注。

舉例	譯文
I'm looking forward to seeing you again. Thank you.	我期望再見到您們。謝謝。
I sincerely hope that you will visit our school again in the near future. Thank you.	我真誠希望您們在不久的將來再到訪我們學校。謝謝。

<h1>範例四十六：節約用水</h1>

<h2>Save Water</h2>

Good morning parents and fellow students.

開場白

I am pleased to be here to talk about the importance of saving water and why every drop must be counted. Today, I will discuss two key points: how water is wasted as a result of our slight negligence and the ways we can conserve it.

引言：明確表達主題

As we all know, Hong Kong faces a significant challenge when it comes to water supply. We have a limited number of natural lakes and rivers, inadequate groundwater sources, high population density, and extreme seasonal variations in rainfall. Unfortunately, many people in Hong Kong are not aware of the threats posed by water scarcity, as our water supply is provided by our motherland through a long-term contract.

正文段（一）：為甚麼人們不愛惜食水

This has led to apathy towards saving water resources, as many people take it for granted. Most young people are not aware that Hong Kong experienced a water crisis in 1963-64, when water was delivered only every four days for four hours each time. Since then, the government has made every effort to remind us of the importance of water conservation and encourage us not to waste this precious resource. They have highlighted that only three percent of the Earth's water is drinkable and promoted seawater flushing systems. They have also enacted laws requiring each house to build a separate plumbing network.

正文段（二）：指出缺水的重要性和政府怎樣努力勸告我們節約用水

Despite these efforts, many people in Hong Kong are either unaware of the gravity of water scarcity or too lazy to do anything about it. They are even at a loss to know how water is wasted every day. For example, washing dishes by hand wastes a significant amount of water, and soaking in a bath consumes even more. Many people in Hong Kong like to pamper themselves with a long, hot bath after a whole day's work to relax and refresh their minds. However, the truth is that the average bath uses four times the amount of freshwater needed for a shower, which means water is needlessly wasted if people opt for a bath instead of a shower. Running water while brushing teeth or shaving is also a major waste problem, and leaky taps and faucets are very common. Unfortunately, they are seldom regarded as major problems that require immediate attention, leading to leakage of hundreds of litres of water every day.

正文段（三）：介紹節約用水的方法

The examples mentioned above have illustrated how water is wasted. Here are some actions we can take to remedy these situations and help reduce water consumption. For example, we can use an automatic electric dishwasher to wash dishes. If we have to wash dishes by hand, we should not do it with water running. The scrubbing can be done without water, and water is required only to rinse off the dish soap at the end. Additionally, rinsing should be done with all the bowls and dishes together, not one at a time. We do not need water while we are brushing our teeth, so we should wet the toothbrush and turn off the tap. We should check the pipes or faucets frequently and fix them if they are worn or leaky. Taking a shower instead of a bath is also a great way to conserve water, as a shower uses only one-fifth of the amount of water required for a bath. The list is not exhaustive, but we must be aware that even slight changes in routine activities and small steps can help conserve hundreds of litres of water daily.

尾段：呼籲用行動來節約用水

So, please remember: don't waste water! Always prepare for a rainy day. Thank you.

結束語

參考譯文

各位家長和同學早上好。

我很高興能在這裏談論節約用水的重要性以及為何每滴水都必須計算在內。今天我將講一下兩件事：我們小小的疏忽導致浪費水和節約用水的方法。

眾所周知，香港在供水方面遇到重大挑戰。我們天然湖泊和河流很少，地下水源不足，人口密度高，及時降雨變化極端。不幸的是，大多數香港人並沒有意識到缺水帶來的威脅，因我們的水源由祖國根據長期合同供應的。

這導致人們對節約用水漠不關心，因為我們習慣了用水是理所當然的。大多數年輕人不知道香港在1963至64年曾經歷缺水危機，當時每4天供水一次，每次4小時。從那時起，政府盡一切努力提醒我們節約用水的重要，並鼓勵我們不要浪費這寶貴資源。他們強調地球上只有3%的水可以飲用，推廣抽海水沖廁系統，並制定了法律，要求每間屋都設單獨的自來水工程網狀系統。

儘管作出這些努力，大多數香港人仍沒意識到缺水的危險性，也懶得採取任何行動。他們甚至不知道每天是怎樣浪費水的，例如，每天用手洗碗會浪費很多水，浸浴甚至消耗更多，許多香港人工作一整天後喜歡縱容自己浸一個長的熱水浴，放鬆身心，提神醒腦，然而，事實是，浸浴使用的淡水是淋浴所需淡水量的4倍，這意味着若人們選擇浸浴而不是淋浴，水就會不必要遭浪費了。刷牙或剃鬚時任由水喉流水也是浪費。漏水的水喉和水龍頭很常見，不幸的是，它們很少被視為重大問題而需要立即關注，導致每天數百升水的洩漏。

以上提到的例子足以說明水是如何遭到浪費的。以下是我們可以採取的一些措施，可糾正這些情況並幫助減少用水量。例如，使用自動洗碗機洗碗，如果我們必須用手洗碗，不要在水流的情況下進行，擦洗可以在沒有水的情況下進行，只需在最後沖洗洗潔精時才用水。此外，所有碗碟應一齊沖洗，而不是逐個去洗。我們在刷牙時肯定不需要水的，只需弄濕牙刷並關閉水喉即可。我們應該經常檢查水管或水龍頭，如果它們損壞或漏水，立刻修理。淋浴而不是浸浴，因為淋浴僅使用浸浴所需水量的五分之一。以上例子不可能詳盡無遺，然而，我們必須意識到，日常活動的微小改變和一小步將有助每日節約數百升水。

所以，請記住：不要浪費水！未雨綢繆。謝謝。

範例四十七：乒乓球會

Table-tennis Club

Good afternoon, everyone.

As the president of the table-tennis club, it is my pleasure to talk to you today about what has happened in our club this year.

As you all know, one of our objectives is to develop table tennis talent so that our school can lead in inter-school competitions. With this aim in mind, we have identified pupils with table-tennis talent and provided them with the support to enable them to develop their skills. This year, we proved that this strategy was successful. We won four top prizes in the inter-school table-tennis championships, including the men's and women's team championships, men's singles, and women's doubles. Specifically, our school won the team championships in men's and women's team events, Albert Chan won the gold trophy for Men's Singles, and Cecilia Cheng together with Maryann Chung won the Women's Doubles. We had a successful season, and everyone should be very proud.

When the competition started, no one imagined that we would do so well. Some of our players had to sit for the HKDSE this year, so they had very little time to practise. Furthermore, our coach, Mr. Kwok, had to return to Beijing during the competition as his father passed away at that time. This was a big shock, and I thought we would have little chance of winning any prizes. Fortunately, our players were so well-trained that they knew how to utilize their own strengths to beat the opponents. Eventually, they won the games, as noted before.

The table-tennis club started ten years ago, and it was difficult to persuade students to join the club at first because we lost all of our games and played badly. In the first two years, morale was very low. That changed when Mr. Kwok arrived. He told us that it would take five to seven years for a talented table-tennis player to achieve elite status. So we began to recruit members from our primary school. Albert, Cecilia, and Maryann were all recruited at that time. In the coming year, Mr. Kwok will continue to be our coach. We plan to recruit more primary school students to join our club. We will sponsor some outstanding club members to visit mainland schools to learn advanced techniques and exchange ways to improve their skills. We also hope our members will participate in the entry level of the Hong Kong Table Tennis Association's team championship, in addition to inter-school competitions.

開場白

引言：告訴聽
眾演講主題

正文段（一）：
提及今年的體
育活動拿到好
成績

正文段（二）：
今年的比賽要
克服多種困難

正文段（三）：
講述球會的過
去和展望未來

With the success we've had this year, it would be easy to sit back and relax next season. But we won't do that! We now have a great coach and a great team, so next season our aim is to win more trophies. Finally, I would like to congratulate Albert, Cecilia, and Maryann as they have graduated from our school and have been granted admission to universities.

尾段：要求球會明年更加要努力並祝賀得獎運動員

Thank you.

結束語

參考譯文

大家下午好。

作為乒乓球會的會長，很高興今天能和大家交談，我要談談今年我們球會發生的事情。

眾所周知，我們目標之一是培養乒乓球人才，使我們學校在校際比賽中處於領先地位。本着這一目標，我們識別了具有乒乓球天賦的學生，並為他們提供支援，使他們能夠發展。今年，我們證實這戰略是成功的。我們在校際乒乓球錦標賽獲得四項頂級獎項，包括男子和女子團體冠軍、男子單打和女子雙打冠軍。更具體地說，我校在男子和女子團體項目中獲得團體冠軍，陳礎白獲得男子單打金牌，鄭史西莉亞和鍾瑪麗安一起獲得女子雙打冠軍。我們真的有了每個人都該引以為榮的賽季。

比賽剛開始時，誰也沒有想到我們會做得這麼好。這是因為我們的一些球員今年需要參加香港中學文憑試。所以，他們練習時間很少。此外，我們的教練郭先生在比賽期間因父親去世不得不返回北京，這是一個巨大的震驚，我認為我們得獎機會渺茫。幸運的是，我們的球員訓練有素，他們知道如何利用自己的優勢擊敗對手，最終如前所述他們贏了比賽。

乒乓球會十年前成立，起初很難說服學生加入，是因為我們輸掉所有比賽，而且踢得很糟糕，首兩年士氣十分低落。當郭先生來到時，情況發生了變化，他告訴我們，一個有天賦的乒乓球員要達到精英地位，需要五至七年時間，所以我們開始從小學部招募球員。礎白、史西莉亞和瑪麗安都是當時招募的。來年，郭先生將繼續擔任我們的教練，我們計劃招募更多小學生加入我們球會，我們會贊助一些優秀球員到內地學校參觀，讓他們學習先進的技術，交流提高技能的方法。我們也希望球員除了參加校際比賽外，還能參加香港乒乓球協會團體錦標賽的入門級別。

有了今年取得的佳績，下個賽季就很容易坐下來鬆懈了。但我們不會那樣做！我們現在擁有一位出色的教練和一支出色的球隊，所以下個賽季 —— 我們的目標是贏得更多獎杯。最後，我要祝賀礎白、史西莉亞和瑪麗安，他們現已從我們學校畢業，並且都被大學取錄了。

謝謝您們。

★ 18 故事 Story

寫故事最重要的是故事本身，必須交代故事發生的時間、地點與人物、情節發展、事情發生的原因和經過、最後結局或作者的感受。

在語法方面，可用第一人稱(即作者寫自己的故事)或第三人稱(客觀呈現事件來講述故事)。在整個故事中，要始終使用相同寫法，若故事開始是作者自述，那就用第一人稱寫故事；若用第三人稱敍述故事，那整個故事也切記如此。在時態方面，主要用一般過去時，偶然使用過去進行時和過去完成時。不要混合使用現在時和過去時，也不要犯一般過去時使用過去進行時的常見錯誤。故事對話要用一般現在時、現在進行時或現在完成時，對話要放在引號中，並注意標點符號的要求。

故事內容變化萬千，視乎想像力，可能是一個真實故事，發生在你或你認識的人身上；也可能是一個科幻故事，比如鬼故事或太空旅遊等；更可能是一些令人興奮或感動的事，比如捨身救人或苦學成才等。你可以選擇任何話題，沒有固定形式，這就是故事寫作的樂趣所在，最主要是創造一個引人入勝的故事！

故事佈局很重要，就算是一篇短短數十字的故事，都要有清晰的開始、發展和圓滿的結局。講述故事可用敍述或對話方式，例如，你想報導一件事可用敍述方式，但若想表明有人在講述這事，那麼用對話方式更合適。

豐富的詞彙是寫故事的必要條件，舉例如下：

詞彙作用	舉例		
用於排序動作的有用序列詞	eventually 最終	suddenly 突然	at first 起初
用形容詞來豐富你對人或物的描述	anxious 着急 suspicious 懷疑 petrified 僵化	desperate 絕望 tragic 悲劇	nervous 緊張 wild 野性
用主動動詞和過去時為故事設定場景	rushed 匆匆忙忙 stomped 踩腳 burst (into tears) 淚流滿面 coughed 咳嗽 grabbed 抓住	shuddered 發抖 carried 攜帶 turned 轉身 whispered 低聲說	hammered 捶打 threw 扔 screamed 大叫 whimpered 嗚咽着
用副詞來增加動作的強度	endlessly 無止境的 thankfully 謝天謝地	absolutely 絕對的	increasingly 日益

佈局結構 Structure

首段：	當你開始講故事時，你需要告訴讀者三個 Ws：誰 (who)、何時 (when)、何地 (where)。誰是故事中的主要人物？故事甚麼時候開始？故事從哪裏開始？除三個 Ws 外，也需要講述他們在做甚麼 (what)，為甚麼 (why) 這樣做，怎樣做法 (how)。嘗試提及一些有趣東西，這樣會吸引讀者繼續看下去。
正文段：	正文段是故事的主要部份，可分為幾段，也是故事的進展，每段都要有一件特定的事來推動事態發展。
尾段：	尾段是故事結局。若故事以第一人稱講述，則結局會是總結或經驗教訓，或作者對事件的感受或印象。

範文四十八：女英雌

A Heroine

It was a beautiful day, with the sun shining, but the weather was a little cold, with a temperature of around 20 degrees Celsius. Ho Lai San walked along the Central and Western District Promenade, enjoying the beautiful scenery. She stopped at the Viewing Platform, where the water was clear and colourful and the lawn was green and tidy. She began to think of all the things she needed to do during the Chinese New Year holidays to prepare for the upcoming HKDSE. However, what she really wanted to do now was to take pictures of the venue and see the facilities, including the pet garden and leisure angling ancillary facilities.

首段：簡單講述故事背景

Suddenly, she heard someone crying for help. When she looked around, she saw a boy in the water, waving his arms helplessly. Without a second thought, she jumped into the water and attempted to rescue the drowning boy. The water was not deep, but the boy appeared not to know how to swim. Ho Lai San had to pull him up before he sank underneath the water. Despite feeling very cold, she swam as fast as she could. By now, a crowd of people had gathered and were watching her anxiously as she struggled to raise the boy's head above the water surface, hoping that he could breathe. Eventually, someone threw a lifebuoy out, and she carried the boy to the lawn. At first, she thought he was dead, but when he coughed and his legs started to move, she knew she had saved his life.

正文段：具體描述故事發展的過程

All the people around applauded, and she became a heroine.

尾段：總結

參考譯文

那是漂亮的一天。陽光明媚，但天氣有點冷，氣溫在攝氏 20 度左右。何麗珊沿着中西區海濱長廊散步。美麗的景色映入眼簾，她在觀景台前停了下來。水很清澈，五顏六色。草坪綠油油的，乾淨整潔。她開始思考在農曆新年假期需要做的所有事情，為即將來到的香港中學文憑試準備。她現在真正想做的是拍張照片，再去看看設施，包括寵物公園、閒釣輔助設施等等。

突然，她聽到有人在呼救。她四處張望，只見水中有個男孩，正無奈地揮動着手臂。她不假思索跳入水中，想去救水中的男孩。水不深，但男孩似乎不會游泳。在他沉入水底之前，何麗珊必須把他拉上來。所以，她雖然覺得很冷，但還是拼命地游着。這時，一羣人聚集在一起，焦急地注視着她努力將男孩的頭抬出水面，希望他能呼吸。最後，有人扔了一個救生圈，她最終把男孩抱起來放到草坪上。起初，她以為他已經死了，但當他咳嗽起來，雙腿開始動起來時，她知道她救了他的命。

圍觀的人都為之鼓掌，她成了一位女英雌。

範文四十九：一個綁架故事

A Story about Kidnapping

If I hadn't answered the phone, it would have been just another ordinary day. But I did lift the receiver and learned the news that turned my life upside down.

首段：讓讀者
有興趣看下去

My mother had been taken hostage, and her kidnapper was demanding $10 million. I didn't have the money, so I told the kidnapper that, but he ignored me. Later, the kidnapper asked me to rob a bank and told me that a revolver was hidden under the carpet at the entrance of my home. Suddenly, I heard a sharp cry from my mother and understood that she was being beaten. I was in shock, but I realized that I had to move fast. I thought about reporting it to the police, but I was afraid that my mother might be hurt or even killed since the caller had warned me not to do so.

正文段（一）：
事件發生的
原因

I had no choice but to follow the advice of the kidnapper. I found the gun under the carpet and left home. I caught a taxi and asked the driver to go to the nearest bank. As I went in through the glass door, people looked at me suspiciously. Then someone noticed the revolver and screamed.

正文段（二）：
事件進展

'If you don't move, you won't get hurt,' I pointed the gun at the teller and shouted at her. 'I want ten million dollars, now. Hand it over.' I waved the gun around wildly. The teller said nervously, 'Sir, I only have $100,000 cash in the drawer. Can you wait here? I have to go to the vault inside to get it.' 'Go immediately,' I said. While I was waiting, the alarm rang. I was so scared and rushed out of the bank. A squad car was stopped at the exit, and six policemen were surrounding the door. I wanted to surrender and put my arms up, but the policemen thought I wanted to shoot, so they opened fire. I was in so much pain and fell to the ground.

正文段（三）：
事件的結局

Oh! I woke up on the floor in my own room. I had just had a nightmare.

尾段：故事的
真實性

<u>參考譯文</u>

如果我沒有接電話，那也只是普通的一天。但我確實拿起了聽筒，並且得知了那消息，讓我的生活變得亂七八糟。

我母親被扣為人質，綁架她的人要價一千萬元，我沒有錢，所以我告訴綁匪，但不被理會。綁匪後來叫我搶劫銀行，並告訴我在我家門口的地毯下藏着一把左輪手槍。突然，我聽到媽媽尖利的哭聲，明白她被打了。我震驚了，但我意識到我必須快速行動。我想我應該向警方報案，但又害怕我母親可能會受到傷害甚至死亡，因為來電者警告我不要向報警。

我別無選擇，只能聽從綁匪的建議。我在地毯下找到了槍並離開了家，我截停一輛的士，然後叫司機去最近的銀行，當我從玻璃門走進去時，人們用懷疑的眼光看着我，然後有人注意到左輪手槍並尖叫起來。

「不動就不會受傷。」我用槍指着櫃位職員對她喊道。「我現在想要一千萬元，把它交出來。」我瘋狂地揮舞着槍。櫃位職員緊張地說：「先生，我抽屜裏只有 10 萬元現金，你能在這裏等嗎？我必須入裏面的保險庫取錢來。」「馬上去，」我說。在我等待的時候，警鐘響了，我嚇壞了，便衝出銀行。一輛警車停在出口處，六名警察圍在門口，我舉起雙臂想投降，但警察以為我想開槍，於是，他們開火了，我痛得倒在地上。

噢！我睡醒在自己房間的地板上，我剛做了一個惡夢。

範文五十：地震

An Earthquake

It was a Friday afternoon, and I was at home with my two-year-old sister and 60-year-old grandma, who were in the next room. We were living on the fourth floor of an old building, and I had just finished doing my homework and wanted to rest for a while. Suddenly, an earthquake struck.

首段：故事發生的人、時間和地點

Everything in my home started to move, and I thought the shaking would end soon, but it didn't. It became more furious as things fell off my shelves. I saw the ceiling light swaying overhead and dangling. I shouted to the next room and asked my grandma to hide. 'Grandma, put on a blanket and hide under the bed immediately.' The jolts were so big that I saw the ceiling light falling down, and the picture of my parents at their wedding, which was hung on the wall, also fell off. Seeing this filled me with fear as I could feel in my bones that this earthquake would spell disaster.

正文段（一）：地震的發生

I dashed into Grandma's room and saw her sitting in the bed, trembling. It seemed that running or hiding never entered her mind. I asked her, 'Why didn't you listen to me and hide?' Another jolt hit, and the building shook severely. I immediately held her up and placed her under the bed, but my grandma said, 'Take care of your sister first!' Then, I noticed my two-year-old sister sleeping peacefully in her bed. I rushed to her and put her in my grandma's arms, so both of them were now under cover.

正文段（二）：保護祖母和小孩

Another jolt occurred, and my head was hit by some books that had fallen from the bookshelf. 'Are you okay?' Grandma asked. 'It's okay. I was just hit by a few books. I'm alright,' I answered calmly. Actually, I lied – it was quite painful, and I knew I was bleeding. I went to my grandma and hid under the bed too. The jolts continued, and eventually, the shaking stopped. I dared not come out until I heard people outside in the corridor speaking and talking. I told my grandma that the house was not safe, so we must run downstairs to the street level. She picked up my sister onto her right arm and held me with her left hand, and we walked down four flights of stairs to the street.

正文段（三）：受傷與逃跑

After we landed on the street, there were other strong shocks that were constant and remained for quite some time. I screamed out loud, 'Wa!...' I looked up and saw things hanging from the building and shaking badly. I looked at my grandma and saw that she had been hit by a plastic bottle that had fallen from the building. She was still covering my younger sister's head with her hands and body to protect her from injury. I guessed that Grandma had been badly hurt as there was a grimace on her face from the pain she must have been in. However, she did not even moan as I knew she did not want me to worry about her.

正文段（四）：祖母受傷了

I immediately brought her to the ambulance, and she was then taken to the hospital. I was worried when she was sent to have an X-Ray of her head. Later, lying in a bed in the ward, Grandma hugged me and said, 'Good grandson, don't worry about me, I'm fine!' The doctor said she had fractured her skull, but the rest of her body was unharmed. She could go back home in a couple of days. I was greatly relieved and held her hands and said, 'I should be the one to protect you and my youngest sister, but...' I was so regretful!

正文段（五）：祖母要入醫院

I had learned a great lesson about family – the importance of loving and taking care of family members. Without a doubt, our senior family members always offer their most unconditional and greatest love to us.

尾段：作者感想

那是一個星期五的下午，我在家。我兩歲的妹妹和 60 歲的婆婆在隔壁房間。我們住在一棟舊樓的四樓。我剛做完學校功課，想休息一下，突然發生了地震。

家裏的一切都開始移動了。我以為震動會很快結束，但事實並非如此。搖動變得更猛烈了，因為有東西從架上掉下來，我看到頭頂天花板懸着的吊燈在搖晃。我大叫隔壁房間的婆婆躲起來，「婆婆，立刻蓋上絨被，躲到床底下。」搖晃如此猛烈讓我看到天花板上的吊燈跌了下來，我父母掛在牆上的結婚照片也掉了下來。看到這些，我感到恐懼，因為我能從骨子裏感覺到這場地震會帶來災難。

我立刻衝入婆婆的房間，看到她坐在床上顫抖着，她似乎從未想過要逃跑或躲藏。我問她："為甚麼不聽我話躲起來？"又是一陣顛簸，建築物劇烈晃動。我立刻把她抱起來，放到床下底。但是婆婆說：「你先照顧好你妹妹！」然後，我注意到了我兩歲的妹妹——她在床上睡得很好，我衝到她身邊，把她摟在我婆婆的臂彎裏，所以他們倆現在都有蓋遮頭了。

又一次震動發生了，我的頭被從書架上掉下來的一些書籍擊中了。「你還好？」婆婆問道。「沒關係，我只是被幾本書擊中了，我沒事。」我鎮靜地回答。其實，我撒了謊——這頗痛苦，我知道正在流血。我走到婆婆身邊，也躲在床底下。震動還在繼續，最終停止了。我不敢走出來，直到聽到外面走廊裏有人在說話和談話。我告訴婆婆，屋裏不安全，所以我們必須跑到街上。她用右手抱起我妹妹，左手扶着我，我們走四層樓梯走到街上。

我們在街上後，還有其他強烈震蕩，這些震動持續不斷，並且保持了很長時間。我大聲尖叫：「哇！……」。我抬起頭，看到建築物上有懸掛的東西搖晃得很厲害。我看到婆婆，「噢，不！」她被一個從建築物上掉下來的膠樽擊中了，她仍然用手和身體遮着我妹妹的頭，以保護她不受傷害，我猜想婆婆受傷不輕，因為她的臉上表現出痛苦模樣，然而，她甚至沒有呻吟，因為我知道她不想讓我擔心。

我立即把她帶到救護車上，她隨後被送往醫院。當她的頭部要進行 X 光檢查時，我很擔心。後來，躺在病房床上的婆婆抱住我說：「乖孫，別擔心我，我很好！」醫生說她的頭骨破裂了，但身體其餘部分都沒有受傷，過幾天她就可以回家了。我鬆了口氣，拉着她的手說：「我該是保護你和我最小的妹妹的人，但是……」。我好後悔啊！

我學到了關於家庭的重要一課——愛和照顧家人的重要性。毫無疑問，我們年長的家人，總是給予我們最無條件、最偉大的愛。

附錄 Appendices

★ 一 範文字彙一覽（List of Vocabulary）

字詞	詞性	註釋
3D（three-dimension）	n	三維
abrupt	adj	突然的
abuse	n	濫用、講壞話
academic	adj	學術的
accelerate	v	增速
access	v	（記憶體）存取
accident	n	意外
accommodate	v	容納
accommodation	n	住宿
accumulate	v	積累
achieve	v	實現、做到、達到
achievement	n	成績、成就
acknowledgment	n	確認
acne	n	粉刺
acorn	n	橡子
acquire	v	獲得
act	v	表演
act	n	行為
active	adj	積極的
activity	n	活動
actually	adv	真實的

字詞	詞性	註釋
ad（= advertisement）	n	廣告
adapt	v	適應
addict	v	沉溺
addiction	n	沉溺
adequate	adj	足夠的
administration	n	行政、政府
administrative	adj	行政的
admission	n	允許入學
admittance	n	進入許可
admit	v	接受（入學）、承認
adolescent	n	少年人
adopt	v	採用
advanced	adj	先進的
advantage	n	好處
advice	n	勸告
affectionately	adv	摯愛地
affirmative	adj	正面的
afford	v	花費得起
affordable	adj	花費得起的
aforesaid	adj	上述的
agency	n	政府內的處
aid	n	幫助

字詞	詞性	註釋
AIDS	n	愛滋病
albeit	conj	儘管
alcoholism	n	酗酒
alfresco	adj	戶外的
allergic	adj	過敏性的
allocate	v	分配
alien	n	外星人
almost	adv	幾乎
alter	v	改變
alternate	adj	後補的
ambulance	n	救護車
ample	adj	充足的
analyse	v	分析
analysis	n	分析
ancillary	adj	輔助的
angle	n	角度
angling	n	釣魚
anniversary	n	週年紀念日
anti-corruption	n	反貪污
anxiety	n	焦慮、憂慮
anyway	adv	無論如何
apathy	n	莫不關心
apology	n	道歉
appalling	adj	駭人的
appealing	adj	吸引的
appear	v	出現、看來
appearance	n	出現
appendectomy	n	盲腸切除手術
applaud	v	鼓掌

字詞	詞性	註釋
appliance	n	家用電器
application	n	申請書
appoint	v	委任
appreciate	v	鑒賞
approach	v / n	處理、方法、靠近、提議
appropriate	adj	合適的
approve	v	批准
archetypal	adj	典範的
architectural	adj	建築學的
argue	v	爭論
argument	n	爭論
aroma	n	芳香
arouse	v	喚起、引起
arrest	v	拘捕
aspirations	n	抱負
assess	v	評價、評估
assessment	n	評價
assign	v	派給
associated	adj	關繫的
association	n	社團
assume	v	想像、假定
assure	v	擔保
athlete	n	運動員
athletic	adj	運動的
atmosphere	n	大氣層
attempt	v	嘗試
attention	n	留意
attitude	n	態度

字詞	詞性	註釋
attribute	v	歸因於
augment	v	擴張
authentic	adj	正宗的
authenticity	n	真實性
authoritative	adj	有權威的
autobiography	n	自傳
automatic	adj	自動的
automobile	n	汽車
automotive	adj	汽車的
autonomous	adj	自主的
available	adj	可以得到的
avoid	v	避免
await	v	等待
award	v	獎
awareness	n	認知、關注
backup	adj	後補的
balance	v	平行
ball	n	跳舞會
ban	v	禁止
banish	v	充軍
banking	n	銀行業
banquet	n	宴會
bar	n	酒吧
barbecue	n	燒烤
basketball	n	籃球
battery	n	電池
beat（beat, beaten）	v	打、勝過、打敗
beef	n	牛肉
behaviour	n	行為

字詞	詞性	註釋
believable	adj	可信的
beloved	adj	鍾愛的、深受愛戴的
beneficial	adj	有利的
besides	adv	另外
bias	n	成見
blanket	n	絨被
bleeding	adj	流血的
block	v	攔網
boast	v	誇耀，吹噓
bookshelf	n	書架
boost	v	促進
booth	n	餐廳牆邊的隔間
border	n	邊境、邊界
bored	adj	悶
boredom	n	無聊
boring	adj	無趣的
bother	v	打擾
bowl	n	碗
bravery	n	英勇
breakdown	n	崩潰
breakfast	n	早餐
breathe	v	呼吸
breeding	n	繁育
brilliantly	adv	漂亮地
broadcast	v	廣播
broaden	v	擴潤，擴大
browse	v	瀏覽
buffet	n	自助餐

字詞	詞性	註釋
bulk	n	大量
bumper	n	(汽車的) 防撞桿
burden	n	負擔
burnout	n	(過勞或緊張引致的) 筋疲力盡
burp	v	打嗝
calamitous	adj	悲慘的
caller	n	電話來客
calmly	adv	鎮定地
camerawork	n	攝影技巧
campaign	n	運動
cannabis	n	大麻
capacitor	n	電容器
captioned	adj	上述主題的
career	n	職業生涯、事業、職業
carelessness	n	粗心大意
carpet	n	地毯
cascade	n	瀑布形狀
cast	n	卡士、選派角色
categorize	v	將……分類
catalogue	n	目錄冊
catch (caught, caught)	v	抓住
catchy	adj	動人的
cater	v	供應食物
cause	v	引起
celebrate	v	慶祝
Celsius	n	攝氏

字詞	詞性	註釋
ceremony	n	儀式
challenge	n / v	挑戰
challenging	adj	有挑戰性的
champion	n	冠軍
championship	n	錦標、錦標賽
charitable	adj	慈善的
cheer	v	鼓勵
chemical	adj	化學的
choice	n	選擇
choreographer	n	設計人
circumstance	n	情況
cite	v	説到
claim	n / v	聲稱
classic	adj	古典的
clearly	adv	清楚地
click	n	按擊
clinch	v	贏取
closure	n	關閉
coach	n	教練
coal	n	煤炭
coastal	adj	沿海的
cockroach	n	蟑螂
coexist	v	同時存在
collaboration	n	合作
colleague	n	同事
colony	n	殖民地
comedy	n	喜劇
comment	v	評論

字詞	詞性	註釋
commercial	adj	商業的
commit	v	犯、承諾
committee	n	委員會
common	adj	通常的
communicate	v	傳達
community	n	社會、社區
compel	v	強迫
compelling	adj	有說服力的
competition	n	比賽
competitive	adj	競爭性的
complain	v	投訴
complainant	n	投訴者
complex	adj	複雜的
complex	n	綜合建築物
complicated	adj	複雜的
complimentary	adj	免費贈送的
component	n	部件
composer	n	作曲家
comprehensive	adj	廣泛的
comprise	v	包含
concentrate	v	集中
concern	n	擔心
concise	adj	簡明的
conduct	v	引導
conductive	adj	有傳導力的
confidence	n	自信
confined	adj	狹窄的
confiscate	v	沒收
confusion	n	混亂

字詞	詞性	註釋
congestion	n	擁擠
congratulate	v	祝賀
connection	n	連接
conserve	v	保護、保存
console	n	操縱器
constant	adj	恒久的、繼續不斷的
construction	n	結構
consume	v	消耗
consumer	n	消費者
consummate	v	完成
contemporary	adj	當代的
continually	adv	不斷地
contract	n	合同
contribute	v	貢獻，促成
convenience	n	方便
convenient	adj	便利的
cooperate	v	合作
cordially	adv	親切地
coronavirus	n	新冠病毒
corridor	n	走廊
cough	v	咳嗽
counterfeit	adj	假冒的
coupon	n	優惠券
cousin	n	堂（表）兄弟姐妹
covered	adj	有蓋的
crack	n	裂縫
craftsmanship	n	手藝
cramming	n	（為應付考試的）強化學習

字詞	詞性	註釋
crash	v	崩潰、碰撞
create	v	創造、產生
creativity	n	創造力
crime	n	犯罪
criminal	n	刑事的
crisis	n	危機
critic	n	批評者、評論家
critical	adj	挑剔的
criticise	v	批評
critics	n	批評者
crowd	n	人羣
crucial	adj	極緊要的
cry	n	喊聲
crystal	adj	晶瑩的
cuisine	n	菜餚
culinary	adj	食物的／烹飪的
cultivate	v	培養
cultural	adj	文化的
culture	n	文化
curb	v	抑制
curiosity	n	好奇心
current	adj	現在的
currently	adv	現在
curriculum	n	課程
custom	n	習俗
dagger	n	匕首
dam	n	水壩
damage	n	損毀
dangle	v	（晃來晃去地）吊着

字詞	詞性	註釋
dash	v	闖
database	n	資料庫
dazzle	v	使眼花繚亂
debate	n	辯論
decision	n	決定
declare	v	公佈
decline	n／v	下降
dedicate	v	奉獻，供奉
deduct	v	扣除
deface	v	毀傷
defacement	n	亂塗、污損
defective	adj	有瑕疵的
defence	n	防禦
defend	v	保衛
defender	n	（足球）後衛
defer	v	延期
deficiency	n	不足
delay	n	遲誤
delectable	adj	美味的
delicious	adj	美味的
delight	v	高興
deliver	v	交付、發表
demand	v	要求
demolish	v	拆卸
demonstrate	v	示範
denouement	n	收場
density	n	稠密
depict	v	描繪
depiction	n	描述

字詞	詞性	註釋	字詞	詞性	註釋
depressed	adj	抑鬱的	discount	n	折扣
depression	n	沮喪、消沉	discuss	v	討論
deputy	adj	副手的	disguise	v	偽裝
derail	v	脫軌	dishwasher	n	洗碗機
design	n	佈局、設計	dismal	adj	淒慘的
despair	n	絕望	dismay	n	沮喪
desperate	adj	絕望的	displacement	n	取代
destination	n	目的地	display	v	陳列、展示
deteriorate	v	使惡化	displeasure	n	不高興
determine	v	決意	disposal	n	處置
detrimental	adj	有害的	disrupt	v	中斷
devastating	adj	毀滅性的	dissatisfied	adj	使不滿
develop	v	發展、開發	dissuade	v	勸阻
development	n	發展	distort	v	弄歪
deviant	adj	反常的	distraction	n	干擾
device	n	器具	distress	n	苦惱
devote	v	效力	distribute	v	分發
diagnose	v	診斷	district	n	區
dialogue	n	對話	diversity	n	多樣化
digital	adj	數字的、數碼的	dockyard	n	船舶
diode	n	二極體	documentary	n	記錄片
direct	v	引導、指導	download	v	下載
director	n	導演、公司董事	downside	n	缺點
disappear	v	消失	downstairs	adv	往樓下
disappoint	v	失望	drama	n	戲劇
disappointment	n	失望	dramatic	adj	戲劇性的
disaster	n	災難	dramatically	adv	劇烈地
discard	v	拋棄	drawback	n	弊病、弊端、缺點
disciplinary	adj	紀律的	dribble	v	（足球）帶球

字詞	詞性	註釋
drown	v	浸沒
dry	adj	枯燥的
duel	n	決鬥
dwelling	n	住宅
earthquake	n	地震
eatery	n	飯館
eclectic	adj	不拘一格的
e-commerce	n	電子商務
economic	adj	經濟的
economy	n	經濟
ecstasy	n	搖頭丸
edict	n	詔書
edit	v	編輯
education	n	教育
educator	n	教育家
effect	n	效果
effectively	adv	有效地
effectiveness	n	有效性
efficient	adj	效率高的
efficiently	adv	效力高地
effort	n	盡力
electric	adj	電力的、用電的
electronic	adj	電子的
eligible	adj	合資格的
eliminate	v	剔除
elite	n	精英
emanate	v	發出
embarrassment	n	尷尬
emergency	n	急診室

字詞	詞性	註釋
emotional	adj	情緒的、感情的
emphasise	v	強調
employ	v	使用
emotion	n	情感
enact	v	製定法律
enclose	v	附上
encounter	v	遭遇
encourage	v	鼓勵
endeavour	v	盡力
ending	n	結局
endorse	v	贊同
endurance	n	耐久力
energetic	adj	精力旺盛的
enforcement	n	實施
engagement	n	約定
enhance	v	提高，增強
enmity	n	敵意
enquire	v	詢問
enrage	v	觸怒
ensemble	n	小型樂團、劇團、舞劇團
ensure	v	保證
enthusiasm	n	熱誠
enthusiastic	adj	熱情的
entire	adj	全部的
entrance	n	入口
entrust	v	委托
environment	n	環境
environmental	adj	環境的

字詞	詞性	註釋
epigram	n	警句
equipment	n	設備
escalate	v	變得嚴重、升級
escapism	n	逃避現實
especially	adv	特別是、尤其是、格外、特別
establishment	n	機構
eternal	adj	不變的
ethical	adj	道德的
evaluate	v	評價
eventually	adv	最後
evidence	n	證據
excellent	adj	出色的
excessive	adj	過多的
exchange	v	交換，交流
exciting	adj	令人興奮的
excursion	n	短途旅行
exempt	v	豁免
exhausted	adj	筋疲力盡的
exhaustive	adj	無遺漏的
exist	v	存在
existing	adj	現存的
exit	n	出口
exotic	adj	異國風情的
experience	n / v	經歷、經驗
expertise	n	專門技能
expire	v	到期
explore	v	探索
exploration	n	勘探

字詞	詞性	註釋
explosion	n	爆破
exposure	n	曝光
extra	n	臨時演員
extra-terrestrial	adj	地球外的
extend	v	擴充
extensive	adj	廣闊的
extreme	adj	極端的
extremely	adv	非常地
facilitate	v	助長
facility	n	設施
faculty	n	書院
failure	n	失敗
faithful	adj	忠實的
fake	adj	假的
fall（fell, fallen）	v	跌落
false	adj	虛假的
fanatic	n	戲迷
fantastic	adj	極好的
farmland	n	農地
fashion	n	時尚
faucet	n	水龍頭
faulty	adj	有毛病的
favourite	adj	心愛的
feature	n	形狀、特徵
feature	v	使有特色
fencing	n	劍擊、劍術
festival	n	節日
festivities	n	祝宴
festoon	v	結彩

字詞	詞性	註釋
feuding	adj	仇恨的
fibre	n	纖維
fight（fought, fought）	v	爭奪
figure	n	人物
file	v	提出（訴訟、投訴）
financial	adj	金融的
fine	n	罰款
fists	n	拳頭
fitness	n	健康
fix	v	安裝、修理
flat	adj	平坦的
flavour	n	風味
flaws	n	瑕疵、破綻
flight	n	飛機、（一段）樓梯
flu（influenza）	n	感冒
flushing	adj	抽水沖洗的
follow	v	跟隨
football	n	足球
footprint	n	覆蓋區
form	v	形成
format	n	版式
forward	v	轉交
fossil	adj	從地下採掘出的
fracture	v	破裂
freedom	n	自由
freestyle	n	自由式
frequently	adv	頻繁
friar	n	（天主教）男修士

字詞	詞性	註釋
friction	n	摩擦
frustrate	v	沮喪
frustrating	adj	沮喪的
frustration	n	挫敗
fume	n	煙氣
furious	adj	氣憤的、猛烈的
gang	n	幫派
garbage	n	垃圾
gear	n	甲冑（古代的）
generate	v	產生
generation	n	一代
generous	adj	慷慨
genuine	adj	真心誠意的
geological	adj	地質的
germ	n	病菌
gesture	n	（友好的）表示
glance	v	瀏覽、看一眼
glass	n	玻璃
glimpse	n	一瞥
glory	n	榮耀
goal	n	目標、（足球）入球
goalkeeper	n	守龍門員
govern	v	統治
governance	n	管理方法
grab	v	（匆忙地）取
graduate	v	畢業
graffiti	n	塗鴉
grain	n	穀類食物
grant	v	授予

字詞	詞性	註釋
grassland	n	草原
grateful	adj	感激的
gratitude	n	感激
gravity	n	重要性
grill	v	（在烤架上）燒烤
grimace	n	愁眉苦臉
gritty	adj	堅韌的
groom	v	修飾
guarantee	v	保證
guest	n	客人
guide	v	帶領
guideline	n	指南
gymnastics	n	體操
habit	n	習慣
habitat	n	自然環境
habitual	adj	習慣性的
hacking	n	黑客
halt	v	停止
hamburger	n	漢堡飽
handle	v	處理
happen	v	發生
harass	v	使煩擾
harbour	n	海港
haze	n	煙霧
header	n	（足球）頭槌
headmistress	n	女校長
healthcare	n	醫療保健
heartedly	adv	有心地，用心地
heighten	v	升高

字詞	詞性	註釋
hepatitis B	n	乙型肝炎
herbal	adj	草本植物的、藥草的
heritage	n	遺產
heroin	n	海洛英
heroine	n	女英雄
hide（hid, hidden）	v	隱藏
highlight	v	強調
hiking	n	遠足
hire	v	僱用
historic	adj	歷史上有意義的
hitch	n	停止
hobby	n	嗜好
homesickness	n	思鄉病
honour	n	榮幸
horizon	n	眼界
hospital	n	醫院
hospitalise	v	送入醫院
host	v	主辦
hostage	n	人質
hostile	adj	敵對的
household	n	家庭
hug	v	擁抱
humane	adj	人道的
humble	adj	謙虛的、謙遜的
humiliate	v	使蒙羞
hydrated	adj	含水的
hype	n	被廣泛宣傳的事
identify	v	識別

字詞	詞性	註釋	字詞	詞性	註釋
identity	n	身份	inductive	adj	誘導的，歸納法的
ignore	v	忽視、忽略	infant	n	幼兒、未成年人
illegal	adj	違法的	infection	n	感染
illustrate	v	說明	influence	n / v	影響
image	n	形象	influential	adj	有影響的
immediate	adj	立即的	infuriate	v	激怒
impact	n	影響	ingredient	n	成份
impair	v	損害	inherit	v	繼承
imperative	adj	絕對必要的	inhumane	adj	不人道的
implement	v	執行	initial	adj	最初的
impose	v	強加、把…強加給、加於	initiate	v	發動、引進
impress	v	使銘記、留下深刻印象	innocent	adj	天真無邪的
			innovation	n	創新
impression	n	印象	inquiry	n	詢問
improve	v	增進、提高、增強	inscribe	v	題寫、書寫
improvement	n	進步	insight	n	洞悉
inadequate	adj	不足夠的	insist	v	堅持
incarnation	n	典型	inspire	v	鼓舞
incident	n	小事件、事故	install	v	安裝
inconvenience	n	不方便	instant	adj	立即的
incorporate	v	包含	instantly	adv	立刻地、立即地
incredible	adj	不可思議的	instill	v	逐漸灌輸
indeed	adv	實際上	instruction	n	指示
independent	adj	獨立的	instructor	n	導師、教練
indicate	v	指出、指示	intangible	adj	無形的
indifferent	adj	不聞不問，莫不關心	intend	v	打算
			intense	adj	強烈的
induction	n	歸納法	interact	v	相互作用、互動
			interaction	n	互動

字詞	詞性	註釋	字詞	詞性	註釋
intercept	v	攔截、截斷	leaky	adj	漏的
intercultural	adj	跨文化的	leave (left, left)	v	離開
internal	adj	內部的	legal	adj	法律上的
international	adj	國際的	legitimate	adj	正統的
internet	n	互聯網	lesson	n	教訓、(一節) 課
intervene	v	介入，干預	level	n	層次
interview	n / v	訪問	library	n	圖書館
introduce	v	介紹	lifebuoy	n	救生圈
invasion	n	侵略	lifelong	adj	終身的
invent	v	發明	lifestyle	n	生活方式
investigate	v	調查	lifetime	n	一生
invoice	n	發票	lift	v	舉起
involve	v	涉及	limited	adj	有限的
issue	n	論點、議題、問題	linger	v	徘徊
issue	v	頒佈	literally	adv	照字義
join	v	加入	literature	n	文獻、文學作品
jolt	n	搖晃	litre	n	升
karaoke	n	卡拉 OK	locate	v	位置在於
kidnapper	n	綁架者	logic	n	邏輯
kidney	n	腎	logo	n	商標、標識
kinsman	n	男親屬	loneliness	n	孤獨
land	v	着陸	magazine	n	雜誌
landform	n	地形	maintain	v	維持
landscape	n	景致	maintenance	n	保養
laptop	n	手提電腦	malicious	adj	惡意的
lawn	n	草地	major	adj	主要的、較大的、重大的
lead	v	指揮			
league	n	聯賽	mandatory	adj	強制的
leakage	n	漏出	marijuana	n	大麻

字詞	詞性	註釋	字詞	詞性	註釋
marine	adj	海上的	motion	n	動議
marines	n	海軍陸戰隊	motive	n	動機
market	n	市場	motto	n	座右銘
marketable	adj	有銷路的	mouse	n	滑鼠
marketing	n	市場學	movie	n	電影
masque	n	化裝舞會	muscle	n	肌肉
material	n	材料	navigate	v	處理
mature	adj	成熟的	narcotics	n	麻醉藥
meaningful	adj	意義深長的	national	adj	全國性的
measure	n	法案，措施、程度	natural	adj	野生的、天然的
medallist	n	獎牌得主	nature	n	大自然
medical	adj	醫術的	nearest	adj	最近的
medication	n	藥物處理	necessities	n	必需品
member	n	會員	needlessly	adv	不必要地
membership	n	會員人數、會籍	negative	adj	否定的、負面的
mentor	n	輔導教師	negligence	n	疏忽
merely	adv	純粹、僅僅、只	neoclassical	adj	新古典主義的
merit	n	長處、優點	nervously	adv	緊張不安
message	n	消息	net	n	淨（買、入）
metropolitan	adj	大都市的	network	n	網絡、網狀系統
mindful	adj	注意……的	nevertheless	conj	儘管如此
miserable	adj	痛苦的	newly	adv	新近
misunderstanding	n	誤會	nightlife	n	夜生活
mitigate	v	緩和	nightmare	n	惡夢
moan	v	沉吟	no-frill	n	無裝飾、簡潔樸實
modal	n	獎牌	nomination	n	提名
monitor	v	監控	nonchalance	n	不關心
morale	n	士氣	non-delivery	n	不發貨
motherland	n	祖國	notable	adj	顯要的、出色的

字詞	詞性	註釋
notably	adv	值得注意地、顯著地、特別地
notify	v	通知
novel	adj	新穎的
nudge	v	（用手臂或肘）輕推（促其注意）
numerous	adj	許多的
nutrient	n	營養物
oak	n	橡樹
objective	n	目標
objective	adj	客觀的
oblige	v	迫使
obtainable	adj	得到
obvious	adj	明顯的
occasion	n	場合
offence	n	犯罪
offender	n	犯人
offer	v	提供、供給
offer	n	要約、出價
official	n	行政人員
ointment	n	藥膏
omissions	n	遺漏
ongoing	adj	進行的
open-air	adj	露天的
operation	n	（醫學）手術
opium	n	鴉片
opponent	n	對手
opportunity	n	機會
oppose	v	反對

字詞	詞性	註釋
opt	v	選擇
ordinary	adj	普通的
organisation	n	機構
organise	v	組織
ornament	n	裝飾品
overland	adj	經由陸路的
outbreak	n	爆發
outcome	n	成果
outstanding	adj	傑出的
outweigh	v	勝過
overall	adj	綜合的
over-burdened	adj	負擔過重的
overhead	adj	在頭頂上
overload	v	過重
overnight	adj	一夜功夫
overseas	adj	海外的
overturn	v	傾倒，翻轉
overwhelm	v	不知所措
pace	n	步速、節奏
packaging	n	包裝
painful	adj	痛苦的
pamper	v	縱容
pandemic	n	大流行（傳染病）
panic	adj	恐慌的
paradise	n	天堂
paramount	adj	最高的、首要的
participate	v	參加、參與
participation	n	參與
particularly	adv	特別地

字詞	詞性	註釋
pass	n	穿過
passion	n	熱情
patronage	n	惠顧
pattern	n	方式
pay	n	薪金
peer	n	同輩
peep	v	看
penalty	n	刑罰
perceive	v	了解、領悟
perceptible	adj	可以感受到的
perception	n	知覺作用
perform	v	執行
performance	n	功績，成績、性能
period	n	時期
peripheral	n	附帶設備
permit	v	允許
perpetrator	n	作惡者
personalise	v	個人化
persuade	v	說服
pet	n	寵物
petition	n	請願
phenomenon	n	現象
philosopher	n	哲學家
photo (photograph)	n	相片
physical	adj	肉體的、物質的
picturesque	adj	風景如畫的
pimple	n	暗瘡
pinpoint	v	查明、確定、針對
pioneer	n	拓荒者

字詞	詞性	註釋
pipe	n	管
placement	n	安置
plain	adj	簡單的
planet	n	行星
plastic	adj	塑膠的
plate	n	碟
platinum	n	白金
play	n	戲劇
playwright	n	劇作家
plumbing	n	自來水工程
poetry	n	詩歌
poison	n	毒藥
policy	n	政策
pollutant	n	污染物
pollution	n	污染
popular	adj	受歡迎的、流行的、熱門的
popularity	n	受歡迎，流行
population	n	人口
pork	n	豬肉
portable	adj	輕便的
portray	v	描繪
pose	v	引起、拿出
posh	adj	高檔的，一流的
positive	adj	正面的
posthumously	adj	死後的
potential	adj	潛在的
pothole	n	壼穴
potion	n	藥水，藥劑

字詞	詞性	註釋	字詞	詞性	註釋
powerfully	adv	有力地	prioritize	v	優先
practical	adj	實務的	privacy	n	私隱
practise	v	練習	probably	adv	也許
praise	n	稱讚	problem	n	問題
precious	adj	寶貴的	producer	n	出品人
predict	v	預計	production	n	演出、製作
precisely	adj	準確地	professional	adj	專業的
premiere	adj	首要的	progressive	adj	漸進的
pre-printed	adj	預印的	prohibit	v	防止
preservation	n	保存	promenade	n	海濱步行大道
preserve	v	保存	promote	v	促進、增進
president	n	會長	promotion	n	促進
press	v	催促	prompt	v	喚起
pressing	adj	迫切的	prompt	adj	迅速的
pressure	n	壓力	properly	adv	適當地
prestigious	adj	有聲譽的	property	n	地產
presume	v	認為	proponent	n	支持者
prevalence	n	盛行	propose	v	建議
prevalent	adj	盛行的	prosper	v	繁榮
previously	adv	之前的	protective	v	防護的
prey	n	獵物、被捕食的動物	protagonist	n	主人公
pride	v	得意	prove	v	證明
primarily	adv	主要地	provide	v	提供、供給
primary	adj	初步的	psychoactive	adj	影響精神行為的、對神經起顯著作用的
prince	n	王子			
principal	n	校長	psychological	adj	心理的
principle	n	原則	psychotropic	adj	治療精神病的
print-out	n	打印紙	public	adj	公眾

字詞	詞性	註釋	字詞	詞性	註釋
publication	n	出版書刊	recall	v	想起
publish	v	出版、刊登	receiver	n	聽筒
pull	v	拉	reception	n	歡迎會
punch	n / v	用拳猛擊	recharge	n	充電
punctually	adv	準時地	recognise	v	認識
purchase	n	購買	recommendation	n	推薦
pure	adj	純的	reconcile	v	和解
pursue	v	致力於	record	n / v	記錄
push	v	推	recreational	adj	消閒的
puzzle	v	困惑	recruit	v	招聘、招募
qualified	adj	合資格的	rectify	v	糾正
quarantine	n	隔離	reduce	v	減少
quarterly	adj	按季的	reduction	n	減少
quest	n	尋求	refer	v	提到
questionable	adj	可疑的	refined	adj	文雅的
quite	adv	相當	reflect	v	反映
rainfall	n	下雨	refresh	v	使恢復
raise	v	擡起、提高、養育	refrigerator	n	雪櫃
rat	n	老鼠	refuse	v	拒絕
reach	v	到達、達到	regard	v	把……看做
readability	n	可讀性	regarding	prep	關於
realise	v	明白、意識	regards	n	問候
realistic	adj	實務的	region	n	地區
reality	n	現實、迫真	regretful	adj	後悔的
rear	adj	後面的	regretfully	adv	遺憾地、惋惜地
reasonable	adj	合理的	regular	adj	有規律的
reasoning	n	推理	regularly	adv	有規律的
rebellion	n	叛逆	regulation	n	條例
rebut	v	駁回、駁斥	rehearsal	n	排練

字詞	詞性	註釋	字詞	詞性	註釋
reinforce	v	增強	respondent	n	回答者
reject	v	拒絕	response	v	感應
relationship	n	關係	responsible	adj	有責任的
relative	n	親戚	restriction	n	限制
relatively	adv	相對地	retirement	n	退休
relax	v	使（心理）放鬆、鬆弛、鬆懈	revenue	n	收入
relay	v	傳達	revere	v	推崇
release	v / n	發行、發表、發佈	reverse	v	使顛倒
relief	n	減輕	review	v	覆閱
remain	v	留下、保持	revolve	v	圍繞
remedy	v	補救、糾正	revolver	n	左輪手槍
remind	v	提醒	reward	n	報酬
remit	v	匯寄	rigorous	adj	嚴格的
remote	adj	遙遠的	ring（rang, rung）	v	響
remuneration	n	酬金	rinse	v	沖洗掉
renew	v	重訂	ritual	n	（宗教）儀式
renovate	v	修補	roam	v	漫遊
renowned	adj	有聲望的	rob	v	打劫
repeat	v	重複	robot	n	機械人
repent	v	後悔	rocky	adj	岩石構成的
replacement	n	更換	role	n	角色、作用
representative	n	代表	romance	n	愛情關係、浪漫史
reputation	n	名譽	route	n	路線
rescue	v	營救、救	routine	adj	日常的
research	n / v	研究	rub	v	揉擦、按摩
reservoir	n	水塘	ruckus	n	喧鬧
residency	n	居住	rule	n	規則
resource	n	資源	rural	adj	農村的
			rush	v	匆匆忙忙地走、沖

字詞	詞性	註釋
sales	n	減價
sanction	n	懲罰
satisfaction	n	滿意
sausage	n	香腸
save	v	拯救
savvy	adj	有經驗的
saying	n	諺語
scale	n	尺度
scam	n	詐騙
scammer	n	騙子
scarcity	n	稀罕
scared	adj	嚇壞的
scene	n	場景
scenery	n	景色
sceptical	adj	持懷疑態度的
schedule	n	時間表
score	n	比數
score	v	得分
scratch	v	劃花
scream	v	尖聲叫喊
script	n	稿件
scrub	v	擦淨
scrumptious	adj	一流的
sculptures	n	雕刻品
search	v	尋找
seasonable	adj	合時的
sector	n	區域
sedentary	adj	慣於久坐不動的

字詞	詞性	註釋
seeming	adj	表面的
seize	v	捕獲
seldom	adv	很少
self-realization	n	自我實現
self-betterment	n	自我完善
self-improvement	n	自我改善
self-understanding	n	自知之明
separate	adj	隔離的，分開的
sergeant	n	沙展、中士
serial	adj	一系列的
seriously	adv	認真地
serve	v	侍候
session	n	一場、一段時間
several	adj	幾個的，幾次的
severe	adj	嚴重的
severely	adv	劇烈地
shake（shook shaken）	n / v	搖動
share	v	分享
sharp	adj	尖聲的
shaving	n	剃鬚
shift	v	變換
shock	n / v	震蕩 / 震驚
shoot（shot, shot）	v	發射
shortage	n	缺乏
shout	v	大聲講
shower	n	淋浴
shrink	v	收縮
sigh	v	歎氣

字詞	詞性	註釋
sight	n	視線
signature	n	簽名
significance	n	意義
significant	adj	重要的
signify	v	表達
simple	adj	簡單的
simply	adv	簡單地
sincerely	adv	真摯地
singly	adv	單獨地
site	n	場所
situation	n	情況、形勢
skilful	adj	熟練的
skinny	adj	瘦削的
skyscraper	n	高樓大廈，摩天大廈
slight	adj	輕微的
slip	n / v	滑、溜
sluggishness	n	呆滯
smartphone	n	智能手機、智能電話
smash	v	打碎
smirk	v	傻笑、假笑
smog	n	煙霧
smokey	adj	多煙的
smoothly	adv	流暢地
smuggler	n	走私客
social	adj	社會上的、社交的
society	n	社會
software	n	軟件

字詞	詞性	註釋
solely	adv	只有、僅有地
solution	n	解決
sophisticated	adj	精緻的
sound	adj	健全的
source	n	源頭
space	n	太空、空間
spacecraft	n	太空船
spacious	adj	寬敞的
spare	v	抽出
special	adj	特別的
specific	adj	特殊的
specifically	adv	具體地
spectacular	adj	壯觀的
speed	n	速度
spell	v	招致
spirit	n	精神
spit	v	隨地吐痰
spokesperson	n	代言人
sponsor	v	贊助、資助
spontaneous	adj	自發的
spray	v	噴
spread	v	散佈、傳播
squad	n	小隊
stab	v	刺
stall	n	攤檔
stamina	n	體力
standard	n	水準
standardized	adj	使標準化
standby	v	支援

字詞	詞性	註釋
standpoint	n	立場
starkly	adv	赤裸裸地，明顯地
state	v	説明
statistics	n	統計學
stature	n	身材
status	n	身份
steady	adj	平穩的
stimulant	adj	使興奮的
stimulate	v	刺激、促進
stipulate	v	訂明
straightforward	adj	坦率的、直接的
strategy	n	策略、戰略
strains	n	菌株
strength	n	長處
stress	n	壓力
stressed	adj	緊張的
stressful	adj	壓力大的
strict	adj	嚴厲的
stricter	adj	更嚴格的
strike（struck, struck）	v	攻擊、撞擊
struggle	v	掙扎
stun	v	使發愕
stunning	adj	令人震驚的
stupid	adj	愚蠢的
style	n	風格
stylish	adj	時髦
submit	v	提交
subsidize	v	給……津貼

字詞	詞性	註釋
substance	n	物質
sustainable	adj	可持續的
substantially	adv	大幅地、大量地
success	n	成功
successful	adj	成功的
suddenly	adv	突然
suitable	adj	適合的
sunny	adj	晴天
superficiality	n	表面的事物
supplies	n	生活用品
support	v	養活
surprise	n	驚奇
surrender	v	投降
surround	v	圍住
surrounding	n	環境
survey	n	調查
survival	n	生存
suspiciously	adv	懷疑地
sustainable	adj	可持續的
sway	v	搖擺
sweat	v	出汗
swerve	v	突然轉彎
swindler	n	騙子
switch	v	轉變
symbol	n	記號
system	n	體系，制度
table-tennis	n	乒乓球
tackle	v	應付
talent	n	人才

字詞	詞性	註釋
tap	n	水喉
tap	v	輕敲
task	v	派給工作
taxation	n	稅制
technical	adj	技術性的
technique	n	技能
technology	n	科技、技術
temporarily	adv	暫時地
temptation	n	誘惑
terminal	n	終端機
terminate	v	終止
termination	n	結束
terrible	adj	可怕的
territory	n	地區
theft	n	盜竊
thoroughly	adv	徹底地
threat	n	威嚇、威脅
tomb	n	墳墓
tone	n	語氣
topic	n	題目
totally	adv	完全地
touching	adj	令人感動的
tourism	n	旅遊業
toxic	adj	有毒的
trace	v	追蹤、跟着……去
traditional	adj	傳統的
traffic（trafficked, trafficking）	v	在……上交易
tragedy	n	悲劇
tragic	adj	悲劇的

字詞	詞性	註釋
trail	n	路徑
translation	n	譯文
trap	v	設陷阱
trash	n	廢料
travel	v	旅行
traveller	n	旅客
treat	v	對待
trembling	adj	發抖的
trend	n	趨勢
trophy	n	獎杯、獎座、獎盃
troublesome	adj	麻煩的
triumph	v / n	獲勝 / 勝利
tsunami	n	海嘯
trust	n	信任
tune	v	收聽
turn	v	改變
twist	n	新花樣
typical	adj	典型的
ugly	adj	醜陋的
ultimately	adv	最後的、最終
unappealing	adj	沒有吸引力的
unconditional	adj	無條件的
uncritical	adj	不加批判的
undeniable	adj	不可否認的
undergo	v	經歷
underneath	prep	在……下面
undoubtedly	adv	無疑
unfortunately	adv	不幸地
unimaginable	adj	難以想像的

字詞	詞性	註釋
unique	adj	唯一的，獨特的、獨有的
universally	adv	全面地
universe	n	宇宙
unpleasant	adj	可厭的
unpredictable	adj	不可預測的
unprofessionally	adv	不專業地
unsatisfactory	adj	不能令人滿意的
unsolicited	adj	自發的
unstable	adj	不穩定的
upstream	n	上游
utilise	v	利用
vaccinated	v	給……接種疫苗
vaccine	n	疫苗
vacuum	n	真空
vaguely	adv	含糊的
valour	n	勇猛
value	v	重視、有價
vandal	n	破壞者
vandalism	n	惡意破壞
vapour	n	氣
variant	n	變種
variation	n	變化
various	adj	各種各樣的
vary	v	改變
vast	adj	廣大的
vault	n	保險庫
venue	n	場地地點
verify	v	核實

字詞	詞性	註釋
versatility	n	多才多藝
version	n	版本
versus	prep	與……相對
victim	n	犧牲者
victory	n	勝利
vigilant	adj	警覺的
violent	adj	暴力的
view	n	風景
violate	v	違反
violator	n	違規者
virtual	adj	虛擬的
virtually	adj	虛擬地
virus	n	毒素
vision	n	視野
visual	adj	視覺的
volleyball	n	排球
vow	v	起誓
vulnerable	adj	易受傷的
wand	n	魔杖
warmly	adv	熱心地
warn	v	警告
warranty	n	保用期
waterfall	n	瀑布
weapon	n	武器
wear (wore, worn)	v	磨損
website (web)	n	網址，網絡
wedding	n	婚禮
whisper	v	細聲說
widely	adv	廣泛地

字詞	詞性	註釋
windsurfing	n	風帆
winnings	n	獎金
witness	v	目睹
witness	n	證人
wizard	n	術士
wonderful	adj	令人驚奇的
workplace	n	工作場所
workshop	n	工作坊
worldwide	adj	世界性的
worry	v	擔心
wrap	n	包裝紙

字詞	詞性	註釋
X-ray	n	X 光（射線）
yield	v	產生
zone	n	地帶

★ 二 範文短語一覽〔List of Stock Phrases〕

短語	註釋	短語	註釋
…could hardly… (= …could barely…)	不能	around the world	環遊世界
100% (= per cent)	百分之百	arts and crafts	藝術與手工品
a bit	一點點	as a result	因此，結果
a good few	好幾個	as soon as	立刻
a lot	相當，許多	as well as	同……一樣
a crowd of	一羣	at a loss	茫然
a number of	一些	at first	首先
a real mess	一團糟	at one point	在某一時間
a variety of	各種各樣	at that moment	那一刻
a wealth of	豐富的	at the age of	在……歲，在……的年齡
a wide range of	範圍廣泛的	background music	背景音樂
academic achievements	學術成果	based on	基於
according to	根據	be able to	能夠
action choreographer	武術指導	be burnt-out	使筋疲力盡
action (motion) film	動作片	be considered as	被認為是
administration fee	行政費用	be content with	滿意
advertising campaign	廣告	be known as	為……所知
after a while	過了一會兒	be limited to	只限於
all means	一切手段	be lost in the post	寄失
all over the world	世界各地的	best seller	暢銷書
allotted time	規定時間	body language	身體語言
amounting to	總計	bounce back	反彈
apart from that	除此之外	box office	票房

短語	註釋	短語	註釋
break one's leg	（某人）跌斷腳	consumer goods	消費品
breakthrough	突破	contact details	聯繫方式
bronze medal	銅牌	contract diseases	感染疾病
brushing teeth	刷牙	contrast with	與……對照
burnt out	心力交瘁	cope with	應付
by hand	用手	cordially	誠懇地
by heart	熟記	couple with	配合
by means of	藉；通過	crystal clear	清楚透徹
by the way	順便提一下	cultural exposure	文化接觸面
car parking space	泊車位	cyber attack	網絡攻擊
carbon emission	碳排放	daily life	日常生活
career life	職業生涯	data collection	數據收集
catch a coach	趕上長途汽車	deviant behaviour	越軌行為
cater for	迎合	digital camera	數碼相機
catering service	餐飲服務	digital watch	數碼手錶
cell phone (mobile phone / smartphone)	手機	dine-in	堂食
children playground	孩子遊樂場	dish soap	洗潔精
cigarette butt	煙頭	division of labour	分工
clean energy	潔淨能源	do exercises	做運動
close tie with	緊密聯繫	drama series	劇集
close-knit	緊密連接的	drinking water	飲用水
cocktail reception	雞尾酒會	drug abuse	吸毒
communication skills	溝通技巧	due to	因為
compare to	比較	earn a fortune	賺大錢
computer network	電腦網絡	eat out	出街吃飯
confirmed cases	確診病例	economic strength	經濟強項
consists of	包括	end up	結果
		energy consumption	能源消耗

短語	註釋	短語	註釋
entrance fee	入場費	for instance（= for example）	例如，舉例
escape responsibility	逃避責任	for your reference	供您參考
excuse me	對不起	foreign exchange reserve	外匯儲備
exhibiting companies	參展公司	free education system	免費教育制度
experimental test tubes	實驗試管	free of charge	免費
express our gratitude	我們表示感謝	fun-filled	充滿樂趣的
extra-curricular	課外	garbage can	垃圾桶
face-to-face	面對面	get healthier	變得更健康
fail to	未能	get out of	出來
fall in love	愛上，愛戀	get used to	習慣了
fast food chain	快餐連鎖店	gift coupon	禮券
feel free	隨時	go abroad	出國
feel like	感覺像	golden medal	金牌
fight for one's life	為自己的生命而戰	good at	擅長
financial assistance scheme	財政資助計劃	good citizen	好市民
financial institution	金融機構	good for	有利於
financial means	財富	grand opening	開幕
financial services	金融服務業	grief-stricken	悲痛欲絕
financially capable	有經濟能力	ground breaking	開創性的
first of all	首先	groundwater	地下水
first-come, first-served	先到先得	grow（somebody）up	養（某人）長大
first-ever	前所未有的	hand over	交出
fitness centre	健身中心	hands-on	親自動手
fly kites	放風箏	hard drive	硬盤
focus on	專注於	hardly agree more	非常同意
follow up	跟進	have a meal	吃飯
for a while	一陣子	have to（= have got to）	必須，不得不

短語	註釋
highest discount	最高折扣
hilly to mountainous	山多的（小山丘到大山）
house signature	招牌菜
identity theft	身份盜竊
in (somebody's) mind	在（某人）腦海中
in a nutshell (= in short)	簡而言之
in accordance with	根據
in addition to	在此之上
in advance	預先
in case of need	在需要的情況下
in comparison with	比較，和……比較
in fact	事實上
in my bones	在骨子裏
in my opinion	我的意見是
in my view	在我看來
in one's track	在……的軌道上
in order to	為了
in other words	換句話說
in pairs	一雙
in relation to	關於
in response to	回應
in retrospect	回顧
in secret	秘密
in shock	震驚
in terms of	在……方面
in terms of	按照
in the early 1970s	在 1970 年代初期
in the lead	領先

短語	註釋
in the style of	在……風格中
in the wrong hands	在壞人手中
in time	及時
in touch	聯絡
in turn	反過來
in worse cases	在更壞的情況下
instead of	代替
internet application	互聯網應用
inter-school	校際
involve in	參與
it's our turn	輪到我們
job research	工作尋找
jolt hit	顛簸
junk food	垃圾食品
lack of	缺乏
language proficiency	語言能力
last but not least	最後但並非最不重要
lasting effects	持久效果
lead to (leading to)	導致
lean protein	瘦肉（蛋白質）
leisure facility	悠閒設施
level up	墊平
light-emitting	發光
litter buns	垃圾桶
little chance	機會渺茫
little more than	比……多一點
live agent	真人
live out	活出

短語	註釋
live up to	不負眾望
local tour	本地旅行團
long term	長期
long term contract	長期合約
look down upon	鄙視
look for	尋找
luxury apartments	豪華住宅
main character / actor	主角
main course	主菜
mainland China	中國大陸
make a mistake	犯錯
make sure	確信，確保
martial art	武術
martial arts master	武術大師
master teacher	班主任
medicine clinic	診所
mental disease	精神病
mental health	心理健康
monthly fee	月費
mouth-watering	流口水（令人垂涎）
native speaker	講母語的人
natural gas	天然氣
negative attitude	負面態度
newly written	新寫的
news report	新聞報導
noble house	貴族
no-frills	沒有多餘裝飾的
not only...but also...	不僅……而且……

短語	註釋
nothing else	沒有其他的
of course	當然
on another tour	另一處旅遊
on behalf of	代表
on hold	等候接聽，暫停
on the contrary	相反
on the other hand	另一方面
one-digit	單位數
online shopping	網上購物
open fire	開火
open market	公開市場
open up	拓潤
open-minded	豁達
operating manual	操作手冊
opinion survey	意見調查
opt for	選擇
overhead cost	項目開支
overhead projector	高架投影機
overlook...on three sides	俯瞰……三面
parental care	父母關懷照顧
pass along	傳遞
passed away	去世了
pay respect	尊重，崇拜
performance-related pay	報酬與表現掛鈎
performing art	表演藝術
personal computer	個人電腦
personal growth and development	個人成長和發展

短語	註釋	短語	註釋
personal qualities	個人質素	result in	導致
personal view	個人觀點	retail shop	零售商店
physical store	實體店	return mail	郵寄回覆
play a role	扮演一個角色	reward system	獎勵系統
poor quality	低劣質量	right away	馬上
potato chips	薯條	rude words	粗話
premature sex	過早的性行為	rule of thumb	經驗法則
prepare for (something)	為（某事）做準備	run into	碰到
primary school	小學	running time	運行時間、執行時間
private sector	私營部門	running water	（開了水喉）流水
programme host	節目主持人	rush out	沖出
progress report	進度報告	safety measures	安全措施
proud of	引以為傲	sales performance	銷售成績
provided that	只要……就……倘若	sales representative	售貨員
provident fund	公積金	saving water	節約用水
public area	公共地方	school board	學校告示板
public debt	公共債務	seawater	海水
public sector	公共部門	secondary school	中學
put aside	擱置	seem dead	好像死了
rather than	而不是	seems to be	似乎是
reach sb. out	聯繫某人	set aside	挑出
rear-end	追尾	setting description	場景描述
recycling bin	回收站	share sth. with sb.	與某人分享某事
refresh rate	刷新率	shopping mall	大型購物商場
refund of money	退款	show up	出現
regardless of	不管、不論	silver medal	銀牌
report to the police	報警	similar to	類似
rest assured	放心	slow down	減慢

短語	註釋	短語	註釋
social skills	社交技能	team sports	團隊競技
social workers	社工	tech savvy	科技精通
solve one's problem	解決某人的難題	technical problem	技術問題
solve the problem	解決問題	technical support	技術支援
some sorts of	某種	tertiary education	高等教育
spare time	空閒時間	the lack of	缺乏
spark interest	激發興趣	the spread of	傳播
spell disaster	是災難的表現	theme park	主題公園
squad car	警車	thousands of	成千上萬
square kilometre	平方公里（千米）	to my surprise	我意料之外
stick with	堅持	top-notch	一流的
stock market	股票市場	touch my heart	感動我
street level	街道層面、街道水平	tour guide	導遊
strength and weakness	強項、弱點	tourist attraction	旅遊景點
stuffed duck education	填鴨式教育	trade war	貿易戰爭
suffer from	遭受	trip over	絆倒
supermarket coupon	超市禮券	tuition fee	學費
swimming final	游泳決賽	turn out	結果是
swimming pool	游泳池	turn up	出現
sworn enemies	死敵	ultra-clear sound	超清晰的聲音
take advantage of	利用	under consideration	在考慮中
take care of (somebody)	照顧（某人）	under cover	在掩護下
take for granted	把……看作理所當然	update the software	更新軟件
take part	參與	upside down	顛倒過來
take somebody's breath away	使某人感到驚喜	veggie burger	蔬菜漢堡
		video conference	視頻會議
take something to heart	記在心上	voicemail	語音信箱
take up	承擔	wake up	醒來
team leader	隊長	wander off	離羣走散

短語	註釋
waste up	浪費
water consumption	用水
water shortage	缺水
water supply	供水
water surface	水面
well deserved	應得的
well organised	井井有條

短語	註釋
well respected	備受推崇
well-being	幸福、安康
well-known	知名的
well-trained	訓練有素
well-versed	精通
with a population of	人口為
worry about	擔心

★ 三 寫作必記句型〔Sentence Pattern〕

i) 句子種類

Simple Sentence (簡單句)	主謂語 [1] 結構 (Subject + Verb + Object)	This picture **depicts a type of open-air food stall.**
Compound Sentence (複合句)	有並列連詞: FANBOYS[2] 的句子	I suggest increasing the littering or spitting fine from HK\$1,500 to HK\$3,000 **and** penalising the offender to clean the street.
Complex Sentence (複雜句)	有從句的句子	At this time, a typical picture, **which created a feeling of respect and love of God,** was full of religious symbols.
Compound-Complex Sentence (複合 - 複雜句)	結合 '複合句' 和 '複雜句' 的句子	I thought about reporting it to the police, **but** I was afraid **that** my mother might be hurt or even killed **since** the caller had warned me not to do so.

ii) 句型類別

類型	短語或句型	舉例
句子開頭	以 'to infinitive (to 不定式)' 開頭	**To prevent cyberbullying,** parents, schools, and the government must take action.
	以 gerund (動名詞) 開頭	**Predicting** your opponent's arguments and preparing counter-arguments is also essential.
	以過去分詞短語開頭	**Having collected opinions** from one hundred and fifty members of our Association, I found that there are three main reasons for their negative attitude towards PE lessons.
	用 as 為句首開頭	**As** you all know, one of our objectives is to develop talent in table-tennis so that our school would be in the lead in Inter-school competitions.

---

1   主謂語 = Subject + Predicate. 這句子為最簡單的 SVO 結構

2   FANBOYS: for, and, nor, but, or, yet, so

類型	短語或句型	舉例
	用 by 為句首開頭	**By** taking action, we can help ensure a healthier, more sustainable future for generations to come.
	用 with + 名詞短語……為句子開頭	**With your academic achievements and your ability to handle complex and challenging subjects**, I have no doubt that you'll meet the college entry requirements for the Space Technology programme.
	用 without + 名詞短語……為句子開頭	**Without the main actor**, I struggled to proceed with the rehearsal.
	用 despite（儘管）短語從句開頭，表示讓步內容	**Despite** arranging for some nice background music for the play, the outdated equipment lent to us by one of our classmates' parents did not work properly.
It 分裂句型	強調句結構：It + is / was + 過去分詞 + that / who / how 從句	**It was** later **proved that** your method was indeed effective, and finally promoted our English learning to a higher level.
	陳述重要性的強調句型：It + is / was + crucial / important /... + that 從句	**It is crucial that** we stand together to prevent ourselves, our friends, and our families from becoming victims of cyberbullies.
	It + is / was + not until + 被強調部分 + that 從句	**It wasn't until** later **that** I learned he had undergone an appendectomy the night before and had been hospitalized.
	強調一般事實或狀況：It + is / was + well-known fact + that 從句	**It is a well-known fact that** fast foods are generally less healthy than home-cooked meals due to their use of sugar, salt, and artificial ingredients, all of which can have negative impacts on our health.
This 句型	This + verb (third person singular) + that 從句結構	**This reinforces** the belief that Hong Kong has a culture of habitual littering.
	介紹文章的內容：This essay + verb...	**This essay aims** to examine both the advantages and disadvantages of using the internet.

類型	短語或句型	舉例
There 存 在句型	There + be + ... 有	While **there are** both advantages and disadvantages to using the internet, it is evident that it brings numerous benefits to our society.
	There + be + not +... 沒有	**There aren't** many places in Hong Kong where you can find this style of Thai food prepared to such high quality.
	There + be + 名詞短語 + that ... 提出使人擔憂的事實	**There is a growing concern that** our society is becoming addicted to the internet, and some students may misuse it.
	There is no doubt that... 提出 無可爭議的論點	**There is no doubt that** *going to study in a foreign country* can be a frustrating and sometimes painful experience.
主動語態 句型	主語 + 動詞 + ……	**Romeo and Juliet is** perhaps Shakespeare's most famous play.
被動語態 句型	主語 + 助動詞 + 過去分詞	Your English standard **must have been improved** a lot.
	主語 + be + to 是強調句型	**I'm** the one **to blame**[3].
	用被動語法，並不需要知道 當事人是誰	English **is used** worldwide in international space projects, so it's a crucial skill to have.
比較句型	形容詞比較式有兩種寫法： + er 和 more	This makes them feel **happier** and **more comfortable** in schooling.
	less... than...（比……更少）	It is widely known that fast foods tend to be **less healthy than** home-cooked meals.
	... more + 副詞 + 形容詞 ...	Fashion is becoming **more highly valued** in people's choice of clothes.
	the + 最高級 + 名詞 + of...	**The highest speed** of ISP connection in your district is only 300 Mbps.
	far + 比較級 + than	I'm afraid that I could barely agree with them as the Covid-19 pandemic **is far severer than** the common flu virus.

3　也可說 I'm the one to be blamed. 但通常用 I'm the one to blame. 兩者沒有分別。

類型	短語或句型	舉例
	形容詞比較式最高級有兩種寫法：most 和 +est	Our senior family members always offer their **most unconditional** and **greatest** love to us.
	just as + 形容詞 + as 強調特定情況 / 事物 / 事件	Your well-being is **just as important** to me **as** it is to you.
表示「數量」的句型	be + 過去分詞 + as one of the	He **was named** by Time **as one of the** 100 most influential people of the 20th century.
	with + 名詞 + of 結構	It has an area of 1,104 square kilometres, but **with a population of** more than 7.5 million people.
	在正式官方信函，％應寫成 per cent	The ad also stated that PimpleFade is approved by FDA as an OTC product and made of **100 per cent** pure herbal ingredients.
	「每 4 天一次，每次 4 小時」的寫法	Most young people are not aware that Hong Kong had experienced a water crisis in 1963-64 when water was delivered only **every 4 days for 4 hours each time**.
從句句型	so + adjective + that	The Pineapple Oil was **so tender and juicy that** it was the best I've found.
	... +where 引導的定語從句	There aren't many places in Hong Kong **where you can find this style of Thai food prepared to such high quality**.
	... +what 引導的賓語從句	I feel very grateful for **what you have done**.
	when + ... 陳述事實或問題	**When** someone sees litter already accumulated somewhere, it gives the impression that it is the right place to discard rubbish.
	... + that 引導的時間狀語從句	I'm very sorry **that I can't come back home**.
	... + which 引導的定語從句	Fast foods use lots of sugar, salt and artificial ingredients, all of **which** have a negative impact on our health.
	while + ... 陳述事實或問題	**While** these drugs may be considered recreational in other countries, they are illegal in Hong Kong.
	who（沒有逗號的）關係從句	People **who go abroad for study** open themselves up to experiences.

類型	短語或句型	舉例
	... + how 引導的定語從句	There will be hands-on demonstrations of the latest developments in augmented reality (AR) and virtual reality (VR) devices, showcasing **how** they are used in entertainment and in work.
	Whether 引導的賓語從句	Before making a decision, it's important to assess our financial capabilities, family goals, and most importantly, **whether** our children's talents can be effectively developed in Hong Kong.
	(...... +) 名詞 + 同位語從句 + ...	**Another thing** I admire about you **is your generosity.**
	目的狀語從句（so that）句型	You must put aside your personal views and remain objective **so that** your argument keeps logical.
倒裝句型	now 為引導詞	**Now** comes the crunch. (= Now the crunch comes.)
	to 不定式作賓語	**To support our family**, you have to work very hard. (= You have to work very hard to support our family.)
	in order to 用來表達某議題的必要性	**In order to support our family**, you have to work very hard. (= You have to work very hard in order to support our family.)
	Not only 引起的倒裝句；遞進關係	**Not only** *does* this pollute our environment, **but** it **also** promotes the breeding of pests such as rats and cockroaches.
	be 為引導詞	Ms Hung, I have long been a fanatic of your work, and have watched every one of your performances, **be it on television,** in a film or on the stage.
	Only + can + 主語 + be 為加強語氣	**Only** through these efforts **can** *our city* **be** clean and beautiful.
	nothing 引起的倒裝句	There was simply **nothing** the teachers could do to stop him. (= There was simply that the teachers could do nothing to stop him.)

類型	短語或句型	舉例
非謂語動詞句型	「謂 make + 某人 / 某物 + 過去分詞」結構：make... + sb. / sth. + past participle	This **made** Hong Kong **become** marketable in the world.
	... + enough + to do sth.（足夠做某事）	The restaurant is spacious **enough to fit** in hundred of guests.
	be + 過去分詞 + as 結構	Hong Kong **is known as** one of the world's most significant financial and commercial centres.
	... is considered as... 提出一般觀念	Hong Kong **is considered as** a wonderful unique destination for travellers.
	「such + a / an + 形容詞」形容（這樣……的）	You have been studying in **such a good school.**
	remember + gerund（verb + ing）；動詞前 + do 為加強語調	I **did** remember participating in quite a number of vaccination lucky draws.
	主語 + 動作動詞 +…… 結構	**This article attempts** to discuss the factors that attribute to this phenomenon and the drawbacks of studying abroad.
	... including...（包括）	It became a small community as it had hosted a variety of shops, **including** a Hong Kong style grocery, a bookshop and, at one point, even a traditional Chinese doctor with his clinic.
	... how（疑問詞）+ to do sth.	What's more, he will show us **how to** use body language to express ourselves and the experience and problems he encountered as an actor or director of a drama play.
	... 形容詞 + enough + to do sth...（足夠……做某事）	You must talk **fast enough** to have the time **to deliver** your speech but **slow enough** to have your argument **to be understood.**
	... too + 形容詞 + to...	Most young people are **too young to** be aware that without exercise, their muscles weaken and lose bulk.
	... such + a / an + 形容詞 + 名詞……	It seemed to be travelling quite fast and above the average speed in **such a narrow road.**

類型	短語或句型	舉例
否定句式	... hardly... more... （再沒有⋯⋯比⋯⋯更⋯⋯）	I could **hardly** agree **more** with this restaurant.
	I don't think（我認為⋯⋯不）	**I don't think** you are unable to understand it.
	nothing beats ...（沒有甚麼比⋯⋯）	After all, **nothing beats** a hearty barbecue followed by a spectacular view of the dam.
	否定詞（could hardly）= could not	I could **hardly** find a suitable scene for that.
	... have no alternative but to...	I **had no alternative but to** push him slightly and politely.
插入語句型	動名詞短語的插入	The swindlers sent the same message to them, **taking advantage of people's trust and carelessness.**
	關係從句的插入	What's more, by interacting with people from different backgrounds, overseas students can exercise and improve their social skills and language proficiency, **an experience which is of great value to their careers later in life.**
	過去分詞的插入	The Hollywood Grand Building, **located in the Central District,** has been home to many families for nearly 130 years since it was built in 1892.
	形容詞的插入	They remain there day after day, **bored and stressed.**
感歎句句型	What + a / an + 名詞短語	**What a** fantastic day!
	how + 動名詞 / 形容詞 + ⋯⋯	We understand **how frustrating** this must have been for you.
		We understand **how busy** you must be in your daily work schedule.
祈使句句型	沒有主語的簡單句	**Act** now to show our strength in preserving this much-loved piece of history!
	動詞 + infinitive 的句子	**Remember** *to have* more sleep and do some exercise.
	動詞 + that 從句	**Show** *that* you understand their perspective.

類型	短語或句型	舉例
情態動詞句型	... would like to take this opportunity... (……想利用這機會去……)	I **would like to take this opportunity** to thank them for teaching me in the past 6 years.
	主語 + should provide sb. with sth. 結構	A critical review of the literature **should provide** the reader **with** a good general picture of the major questions and issues in the field under consideration.
	should have + 過去分詞（原本應該）	I **should have referred** to the organisation and verified the results of the lucky draw.
修飾句型	用兩個逗號來「修飾」主語代詞	It is clear that we**, as citizens,** must take better care of our surroundings and help curb pollution by reducing energy consumption at home.
虛擬語氣形式	If 對過去的虛擬；would have not（便不會）	**If I had not been careless,** I would not have fallen prey to that scam.
	If + 省略句 + 主句（如果 / 一旦）	**If** approached with drugs, they should say "no" and communicate their concerns to their parents, teachers, or social workers.
	should 對將來的虛擬	**Should you have any further questions regarding this event,** please feel free to contact me at telephone 2345 9876.
問題形式	強調內容的變化	**How could** my rehearsal continue without the main character?
	交際語句	**Do you mind** sitting a little bit lower downward?
	反問句句型	They have a wonderful time watching the animals, but **have they ever noticed that the animals might actually be suffering?**
結論句型	下最終結論	**Eventually** they won the games as noted before.
		To sum up, I would remind young drug abusers of the following old saying, "One single slip brings an eternal regret".
	引用至理名言	**I would like to remind** young addicts of the following proverb: "One single slip can lead to an eternal regret".

★ 四 寫作百搭公式（Writing Pattern）

公式	學習目標	範文內容參考
actually	用來強調真實性	**Actually**, I told a lie.
additionally	補充先前所説的內容	**Additionally**, online shopping allows us to compare the features and price of the products displayed by different online shops.
although	比對對照	**Although** it is difficult to ignore a bully, parents should advise their children to ignore it.
apart from that	補充説明	**Apart from that**, our coach, Mr Kwok had to return to Peking during the competition as his father passed away at that time.
as	as + 過去分詞 + by...	I was the one to be blamed as I insisted to use the free-of-charge machine, instead of buying a new one **as advised by my schoolmates**.
	因為（= because）	The teaching methods are different **as** they will find that communication in Western countries is starkly open and straightforward.
	as，意思是「作為」	I have never thought of you only **as** a Kung Fu star, but I do think you really know how to act.
	... consider sb. / sth. as...	It would be very encouraging to anyone of our students who **considers acting as** her career.
as a result	帶出結論	**As a result**, it stimulates the creation of numerous vacancies for young men and women who want to devote in space-related career.
	點出原因與結果	**As a result of** his hard work and support from the family, Edgar was able to gain exposure to large competitions, earning quite a lot of athletic trophies at a very young age.
as for	針對特定主題	**As for** food, you will easily find dishes to satisfy and delight your palate.

公式	學習目標	範文內容參考
as well as	as well as 與 and 同義	Along the way, I could see many birds and insects, **as well as** unique landforms.
because of	説明原因	Today only a few licensed dai-pai-dong exist in Hong Kong as the government has been phasing them out **because of** concerns for hygiene and traffic congestion.
besides	補充説明	**Besides,** they do not realise that lack of physical activity can add to feelings of anxiety and depression.
but	轉換立場	This trend dropped in the mid-1990s, **but** reappeared in the beginning of the 21st century.
	表達不同情況	Hong Kong is a small **but** an international city.
despite the fact that…	despite the fact + 從句（儘管事實如此）	**Despite the fact that** Hong Kong has ample educational opportunities for young people, parents are more prevalent to choose their children to complete their schooling overseas.
do	do + 行動動詞：強調語氣	But I **did** lift the receiver and learnt the news that turned my life upside down.
due to	述説理由	**Due to** the elimination of maintenance cost and rental cost, online shops are able to sell products with attractive discounts in comparison with physical stores.
enable	… would + enable sb. to do sth.（……會讓某人做某事）	Studying abroad **would enable young people to avoid** the local high-pressure environment.
especially	用來強調特定事物	**Especially,** our senior family members always offer their most unconditional and greatest love to us.
for example	舉例論證	The rehearsal should be in small play, **for example,** for the parts played by two main characters only.
for…	以 for 作開頭，説明自己的主張	**For** a restaurant serving Thai cuisine of excellent quality, it was worth the money.
from this	陳述有明確目標	**From this** I would follow up with a more specific question.

公式	學習目標	範文內容參考
however	承接轉折；提出客觀事實	During the campaign, **however**, sales rose dramatically in July, August, and September.
I am of the view / opinion	表達意見	However, **I am of the view** that the situation has improved, and our government is now on the right track.
		I am of the opinion that studying abroad has its good and bad points.
I believe that	委婉地表達意見	So, **I believe that,** after you have completed the course, there would be lots of attractive job opportunities in the market for you to choose.
in spite of	與 despite 相同，of 是介詞，後面要接名詞或動名詞	**In spite of** becoming famous and of getting a high social position, Edgar remained humble.
moreover	補充先前所說的內容	**Moreover**, in physical stores, we need to stand in queues in cash counters to pay for the products.
nevertheless	承接轉折；提出某項事實	**Nevertheless,** I truly believe that these efforts are worth making in arousing students' interest in Physical Education.
not only… but also…	平列句，意思是'不僅……而且也……'	Edgar's victory in Tokyo Olympics 2020 **not only** ended Hong Kong's 20-year-wait for a gold medal, **but also** marked our city's first Olympic glory in fencing history.
obviously	明確指出事實	**Obviously,** there is nothing funny about making someone else miserable.
on behalf of	代表某人或某團體	**On behalf of** Tai Po High School, I have great pleasure to invite you as guest of honour to our school's annual Sports Day.
on the one hand…, on the other hand…	說明兩方面的觀點	**On the one hand,** we can highlight the activities we arrange, letting them know why drama is both enjoyable and beneficial to students, and **on the other hand**, we know how our members feel about our club so that we can find ways for improvement.

公式	學習目標	範文內容參考
owing to	述說理由	**Owing to** poor planning coupled with limited teaching time, students have been unable to make progressive improvement in their physical abilities, and thus consider PE lessons quite a waste of time.
rather	作出選擇	They **would rather** take music or drama classes.
regarding	針對特定主題的想法	**Regarding** healthy dance, I think we start with "Move for Health" introduced by the Leisure and Cultural Services Department.
sequence	用於順序，前後內容分點論述	After …Then … Of course …Later… Firstly…Secondly…Finally… First of all…Next…Lastly… To begin with…Moreover…What's more… Last but not the least… Since then…Subsequently
specifically	「更具體地說」強調特定事物	**Specifically**, our school won the team championships in men's and women's team events, Albert Chan won the gold trophy for Men's Single and Cecilia Cheng together with Maryann Chung won the Women's doubles.
such as	舉例	Nowadays, hundreds of technical innovations generated by space programmes make our life easier and more efficient, **such as** better home appliances, advanced farming equipment, faster communications, accurate weather forecasting, improved medical instruments, and so on.
thus	thus + 動名詞……（所以就會……）	They also do not understand that sports are good for their mind and help them learn to concentrate, **thus resulting** in doing better academically.
too	too + 形容詞	Critics argue that Hong Kong's education system is **too rigid** and it's **too competitive and stressful**.

公式	學習目標	範文內容參考
What's more	補充說明，有強調作用，可用來替代常用的 More importantly	**What's more**, by interacting with people from different backgrounds, overseas students can exercise and improve their social skills and language proficiency, an experience which is of great value to their careers later in life.
wish	情感交際常用詞	I would like to **wish** you good luck in all your future productions.
with regard to	針對特定主題的想法	**With regard to** the food, they are scrumptious and of the highest quality.

★ 五 自我測試答案（Self Test Answers）

1. 5W1H（Who, What, Where, When, Which, How）。

   （參閱本書第 14 頁）

2. 這個段落討論了多個話題，混淆不清。

   （參閱本書第 32 頁：怎樣寫段落。）

3. 缺少了「主題句」，例如：My favourite season is summer.

   （參閱本書第 33-34 頁：主題句。）

4. a

   解析：

   » 答案 a 的開場白最能吸引讀者讀下去。

   （參閱本書第 35 頁：怎樣寫首段。）

5. 應改為 On arriving in Hong Kong, he was met at the airport by his friend.

   解析：

» 介詞開頭的分詞短語，如果在句子開頭，必須與句子主語有關

» 介詞短語 on arriving in Hong Kong 指的是 he 而不是 his friend 抵達香港

» 所以，正確的英語寫法要以 he 作為主語，而不是 his friend

» 要符合這語法規則，這個句子要用被動語態來寫，即是 he was met at the airport by his friend 而不是 his friend met him at the airport。

（參閱本書第 48 頁，錯位修飾語。）

6. 應 改 為 She couldn't decide among the University of Hong Kong, the Chinese University of Hong Kong or the Hong Kong University of Science and Technology.

解析：

» between 只能用於兩個事物之間，而 among 可以用於許多其他事物之中

（參閱本書第 55 頁：選詞 among 和 between）

7. 應改為 An anonymous person sent the letter.

解析：

» 好文章該選擇具有精確含義的單詞，所以用 anonymous person 來替代 who did not provide his or her name 較為完善。

（參閱本書第 48 頁，簡潔原則）

8. C, A, B

（參閱本書 219 頁範文二十九）

9. Without student's union, we would have more time for after-school activities.

解析：

» Without + 名詞為句首開頭，having 是中式英語，應該省去

» 介詞 with 的用法錯誤，with 有伴隨的意思，所以這句不能用，只可以用 for。

（參閱本書附錄第 318 頁：句子開頭類型）

10. 應改為 2021 was also the best and worst year for many people.

　　解析：

　　　» 如果一個句子中用 and 連接兩個形容詞，這兩個形容詞要用同一形式，叫做平行結構原則。

　　　» best 是最高級別 (superlative) 的形容詞，而 worse 只是比較級別 (comparative) 的形容詞，所以要將 worse 改為最高級別的 worst

（參閱本書第 49 頁：平行結構原則）

　　　» a lot of 為冗餘字眼，用 many 較為簡潔

（參閱本書第 48 頁：簡潔原則）